Tumo was shinnying up the bell tower in undulating rolls of quivering fat. A growling, maddened humanoid slug.

The pulpy flesh of a thigh bulged a foot inside the third level grating. Gonji bounded over the boards and plunged the Sagami eight inches deep, ripping an arm's-length gouge across his vision. The giant bellowed in infantile anguish and squeezed the tower with all its might, as masonry crumbled and stone caved inward, spidery cracks shooting up the walls.

Gonji scurried up the curling stairwell, passed the hideous, bloody face. His heart beat at battle tempo. A section of wall caved in below him, and a great, bleeding arm reached in, slapping about. Gonji pulled back mightily, grunting with pain, and fired.

Gonji's cloth-yard arrow penetrated Tumo's cheek—just below the left eye, the head emerging through splintered bone at the eye socket.

Tumo's mouth gaped open as he fell, shaking the tower's foundation at the street below. Gonji roared in triumph at the arch, watching the screaming beast whirl about in the darkened square like a sunstroked scorpion. It tore the shaft from its ruined eye and bowled over in its pain, scattering horses and men.

With any luck, Gonji thought, the arrow had struck the brain. Death would follow. . . .

# MORE FANTASTIC READING FROM ZEBRA!

**GONJI #1: DEATHWIND OF VEDUN**            (1006, $3.25)
by T. C. Rypel
Cast out from his Japanese homeland, Gonji journeys across barbaric
Europe in quest of Vedun, the distant city in the loftiest peaks of the
Alps. Brandishing his swords with fury and skill, he is determined to
conquer his hardships and fulfill his destiny!

**GONJI #2: SAMURAI STEEL**            (1072, $3.25)
by T. C. Rypel
His journey to Vedun is ended, but Gonji's most treacherous battle
ever is about to begin. The invincible King Klann has occupied Vedun
with his hordes of murderous soldiers—and plotted the samurai's
destruction!

**GONJI #3: SAMURAI COMBAT**            (1191, $3.50)
by T. C. Rypel
King Klann and the malevolent sorcerer Mord have vanquished the
city of Vedun and lay in wait to snare the legendary warrior Gonji. But
Gonji dares not waiver—for to falter would seal the destruction of
Vedun with the crushing fury of SAMURAI COMBAT!

**SURVIVORS**            (1071, $3.25)
by John Nahmlos
It would take more than courage and skill, more than ammo and guns,
for Colonel Jack Dawson to survive the advancing nuclear war. It was
the ultimate test—protecting his loved ones, defending his country,
and rebuilding a civilization out of the ashes of war-ravaged America!

**THE SWORD OF HACHIMAN**            (1104, $3.50)
by Lynn Guest
Destiny returned the powerful sword of Hachiman to mighty Samurai
warrior Yoshitsune so he could avenge his father's brutal death. Only
he was unaware his most perilous enemy would be his own flesh and
blood!

**#3**

# GONJI

## SAMURAI COMBAT

## BY T. C. RYPEL

**ZEBRA BOOKS**
**KENSINGTON PUBLISHING CORP.**

ZEBRA BOOKS

are published by

KENSINGTON PUBLISHING CORP.
475 Park Avenue South
New York, N.Y. 10016

*This book is for*

MARTY SWIATKOWSKI....*scholar, wit and confidant*
JOE RUTT..............*critic, guide and kindred spirit*
GARY DUMM..........*purveyor of* rei *and* wa
 *And, oh yes . . .*
DAVE BUEHNER......*who skated in late*

*Such friends have I.*

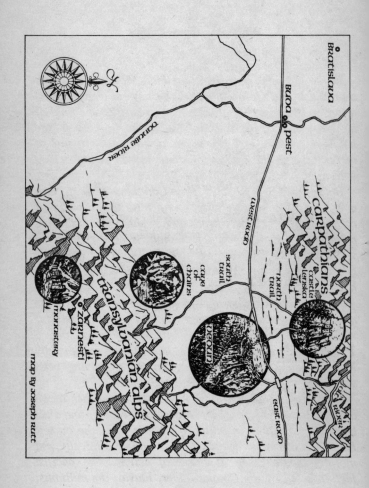

Bratislava

Buda pest

Danube River

west River

Carpathians

Castle Lepska

south trail

north trail

Cave of Charms

Neorin

east River

Transylvanian Alps

monastery

Zarnesti

map by Joseph Kurt

# What Has Gone Before

In the sixteenth century Carpathian Mountains, a lone samurai named Gonji Sabataké journeys in endless quest after the legendary Deathwind, the Beast with the Soul of a Man. Staving off assaults by primal horrors in the haunted territory, he joins for a time a company of mercenaries in the employ of a mysterious nomadic king who dubs himself Klann the Invincible.

Bolting the 3rd Royalist Free Company after a clash over their dishonorable duty, Gonji returns to a scene of carnage he helped perpetrate and is charged by a dying priest to convey a message to Simon Sardonis, whom he will find in the city of Vedun. Attacked by a wyvern, a ghastly winged dragon, Gonji is put to flight and commits himself to the beast's eventual destruction.

Bringing the body of a boy beaten to death by mercenaries in Klann's hire, the samurai enters the ancient walled city of Vedun, a citadel perched on a Transylvanian plateau-aerie. He finds the city occupied by Klann's army, the castle of Baron Rorka having been successfully breached in a single night.

Gonji finds that the dead boy was the brother of an important council member, Michael Benedetto, and thus becomes embroiled in political intrigue from the outset. He comes to side with the citizens, who are ethically and morally divided over a course of action. The pacifist faction is led by the Council Elder, Flavio; the militants, by the volatile guildsman Phlegor and the prophetess Tralayn.

*As enmity between Gonji and Klann's forces, human and inhuman, increases, so dawns his affection for the city and some of its inhabitants; notably, the blacksmith Garth Gundersen and one of his sons, Wilfred, who is consumed by the desire to rescue his beloved Genya from the invaded castle. A lovely deaf-mute girl named Helena becomes enamored of Gonji; and Gonji, in turn, of Michael's wife, Lydia.*

*Through a series of wild adventures and curious circumstances, the half-breed oriental (his mother having been a ship-wrecked Norsewoman) rises to a position of influence—a tenuous one, weakened by distrust and bigotry. In a fit of pique, obeying the dictates of his moody disposition and the cry of an empty purse, he hires on as a spy for Klann with Captain Julian Kel'Tekeli, whom he has come to hate, their personalities clashing severely. But ever the seeker after noble duty, he also contrives to become Flavio's personal bodyguard. His love of control, attention, and military game-playing thus satisfied, and characteristically mistaking serendipity for fate, he sees himself committed (in his compromising, half-Western fashion) by the* bushido *code to following the situation through to a conflict he feels inevitable. And the key to his Deathwind quest—and the now linked mystery of Simon Sardonis—seems to be withheld from him by certain fearful city leaders.*

*As* Deathwind of Vedun *closes, Gonji manipulates himself into the city delegation to the castle banquet being held by the legendary King Klann the Invincible, who has suddenly decided to break with his reclusive tradition.*

*At the castle banquet the city delegation discovers Klann to be quite a different man from the threatening myth-figure that precedes him: he appears cheerful and hospitable, exuding an air of concern for his subjects. He promises to redress the grievances brought to his attention by the city. His court sorcerer, Mord, though, proves*

8

*quite as foul as his legend and evinces a profound hatred for the city and its Christian mode of worship. And in almost comic counterpoint to the young smith's agonized concern, Wilfred's beloved Genya displays a pluckish self-confidence that has her in a position of influence in the castle.*

*Gonji is lured by Julian into an exhibition of swordsmanship designed to compare their distinctive fencing styles, culminating in a duel weighted in favor of the European blade. Gonji is defeated, shamed in his own mind despite a brilliant showing. Their enmity is further fueled.*

*While the castle revelry plays itself out, a traitor from Vedun meets in secret with Mord to plan the city's destruction. And a most disquieting revelation comes to light; Garth Gundersen, the gentle smith, is a former general of Klann, a matter he has withheld even from his closest friends.*

*Back in the city the militants demand action against the brutalizing occupation force, and Tralayn and the revolutionary artist-poet Alain Paille attempt to fire Gonji with a sense of destiny that will see him lead a militia against the invaders. Garth reveals the details of his former association with Klann and reads from an ancient parchment the story of Klann's enchanted origin: The wandering king was born septets, all endangered at birth, and combined by his royal parents' court wizard into one healthy child carrying seven distinct personages, each of whom would emerge in turn upon the death of another. Klann's obsession is to return to the island kingdom of his birth and repossess the throne wrested from his father in a sorcerous coup.*

*Meanwhile, Mord takes a magical hand toward inspiring the internecine conflict he desires: His enchantment ruins much of Vedun's harvest, causing violent repercussions that intensify the city's burden under*

9

*the aggressive invading army. Misunderstandings and the sorcerer's foul meddling polarize Klann and the city as tensions increase.*

*Gonji rises to leadership over the militia that trains in the ancient catacomb system beneath the city, but as his star rises, so do his troubles multiply. Skills and tactics must be taught to a largely nonmilitary populace; weapons and armor are difficult to obtain; while he makes many new friendships, he also has his detractors; the continued presence of Klann's bullying troops and Mord's intimidating monsters casts a pall over the combat readiness; Gonji's frustrated attraction to Lydia and ill-timed deflowering of Helena further complicate relationships; the occupying army builds in strength; Julian's suspicions grow.*

*And through it all the traitor watches and records.*

*Anticipating her own foretold death, Tralayn reveals to Gonji that the Deathwind he seeks may be the same Simon Sardonis for whom he bears a message, and the enigmatic Simon is a* werewolf *who lives a vengeful, self-pitying and egocentric life on the fringe of the territory, protected by those he now refuses to help. The possible self-mockery of his long quest casts Gonji in a gloomy frame of mind.*

*While the militia makes a successful practice foray against an occupied village in the marches, Klann comes to Vedun in an eleventh-hour appeal for peaceful coexistence. He is poisoned by Mord, who accuses Tralayn of the crime, and the next Klann personage arises phoenix-like from the corpse of the murdered one. This Klann is a harsh, vindictive man who will brook no resistance. Tralayn is summarily tried and executed by a kangaroo court at the castle after first prophesying that a Deliverer will come to the aid of the city, one who will shake the invaders' courage by his very sight. Flavio is hanged in the city square. An abortive rebellion ensues, fomented by the guild leader Phlegor. Many citizens are slaughtered, and*

10

*the city's rebellious spirit is dampened.*

*As the mistimed revolt spreads, Gonji and some of his close friends become embarrassingly drunk. His double-dealing on behalf of the city has become known to Julian, and the unconscious samurai must be spirited away by the militia.*

*Awakening to the news of his disgrace, Gonji attempts ritual suicide but is prevented by his friends, who find the practice horrifying. Angered by his inability to find satisfaction for his loss of face in the midst of this cultural conflict, he decides to leave them to make what they will of their situation.*

*In the catacombs Gonji and his accompanying band discover that Baron Rorka and the last of his knights have been savaged by a colossal carnivorous worm from the bowels of the earth. They destroy the monster in a ferocious battle that costs many lives, then begin to piece together the evidence that a traitor in their midst works for Mord and that quite possibly Mord is playing both sides against each other toward a mutual destruction for his own insidious ends.*

*Outraged at being manipulated and having all their laborious plans compromised, Gonji tells the militia that Klann must be approached with their suspicions and that, failing to convince him, they must now prepare for the worst—the dreaded clash that Mord is orchestrating. Taking with him a quiver of arrows impregnated with the potent venom of the worm-thing, Gonji rides to the lair of Simon Sardonis, where he will confront the legendary figure who so cynically rejects the hero's mantle.*

*So ends* Samurai Steel.

I sought them far and found them,
  The sure, the straight, the brave,
The hearts I lost my own to,
  The souls I could not save.
They braced their belts about them,
  They crossed in ships the sea,
They sought and found six feet of ground,
  And there they died for me.

> —A. E. Housman, *Epitaph on*
> *an Army of Mercenaries*

# Part I

## Lupus in Fabula

## Chapter One

At the Hour of the Monkey, Mord determined that Gonji must die.

The sorcerer had gained a grudging respect for the samurai. By his sword skill, cleverness, and steely nerve, and now with the proof of his training of the militia—witnessed in the extermination of the worm—he was turning the game to his favor. His continued presence might confound Mord's purpose, might compromise the plotting of the Grand Scheme. What might his next devious move be?

The militiamen had destroyed the worm as had been expected, but not at the anticipated blood-cost; not out of desperation but out of determined fury and confident might-of-arms. They had learned well. And they had not followed the worm's destruction with a precipitate rebellion stemming from their fear of the catacombs' discovery. Instead they had fired the castle tunnel.

What did they suspect? What would they do now?

The traitor's word might come too late. Mord had to know what the wily samurai was doing and he must eliminate the oriental's threat, even as he had done with Baron Rorka and his potential for enlisting Church forces.

The sorcerer stood in the dungeon chamber before his articles of magick and arcane gramarye and performed the ritual. At its culmination he ingested the scrapings of Gonji's blood he had obtained after the samurai's duel with Julian. Then he reclined on the stone altar so that he might depart his body, stretch out with his astral being at the end of the long mystical silver cord, *find* the unwitting fool wherever his barbarian blood pulsed.

As always, the blood search rewarded him: The oriental rode through the valley on a southerly course.

But something else could be felt—the pulsing of the great key, that mystery object that had baffled Mord, troubled him with its conflicting emanations for weeks. As the oriental rode on, the supernatural radiations grew stronger. Could he be riding toward a meeting with the elusive being that exerted its enigmatic presence in the territory?

Mord's unsavory mind smiled. For the longer he followed, the more certain he became.

Abruptly the wyvern was awakened from its demon sleep atop Mord's tower high above Castle Lenska. Screeching in response to its master's call, it flapped from its perch on thirty-foot wings and careened about the castle twice, eagerly accepting the controlling mind of Mord. Mord's eyes of baleful ebon supplanted the flying beast's red orbs as it pushed off with a tremendous gush of wind toward the south.

Toward the lone rider who thundered through the sylvan valley.

*Flavio swings from a gibbet, and Tralayn's been dragged off in shackles—how does that sit with your self-pitying—Iyé.* No, that was no good . . .

*You ignore the plight of these people who are dying for you—*

Gonji cursed and shook his head as the gray roncin clumped through the enshrouding forest. His jaw set with grim determination, swords jiggling in his sash with the bouncing motion of his ride, the samurai pondered glumly: Exactly how did one speak to a legend that walked hand-in-hand with death?

16

Gonji had long since left the southern valley's main trail, angling off along the path he had ridden scant days before with Tralayn, the path which led to that sinister cave concealed at the base of the northern foothills of the Carpathians' lower curve. The steed snorted as it stumbled over snaring vine and eruptions of scrub and bramble.

The samurai felt uncertain of his mount; she failed to respond to his subtle pressures on bridle and flanks as the goodly Tora would have. But Tora had not been found in the catacombs after the battle with the venomous slithering beast, and the thought that his prize stallion might have become a meal for the loathsome monster inflamed him with a shapeless, futile anger. He would have to bring such disruptive emotion under control for the meeting to come, if come it must.

And his roiling feelings were not his only enemies this night: the long day had exacted a toll; his whole body ached and sagged. The drinking bout and purging emetic had left his insides twisted. His belly churned with nausea. The brief, feverish sleep during the night of abortive rebellion in Vedun had done little to replenish his strength, and the day's battle with the worm-thing from the underworld returned its impressions with fresh pains of half-remembered bruises and abrasions, cuts and lumps.

Yet nothing so disturbed his harmony as the poignant memory of his failed duty on behalf of Flavio and the city.

Cursing the despairing voice within that bade him surrender in the name of graceful failure, he rode on.

Clenching his jaw, Gonji warded off the pine boughs that sought his face along the path, brushing and scraping at him and his mount, now and then twining about his mighty longbow so that he would be forced to halt and disentangle it. The forest seemed to grasp at him, hold

17

him back from his purpose. But at whose behest?

The roncin picked her footing in the cloying darkness. The path twisted through the lush, rich-smelling blackness of the forest, the horse's hooves thudding over the spongy pad of pine needles and fecund earth, the verdant scents intoxicating.

The night lay deep, heavy clouds mantling the treetops. Animals and insects ceased their trilling and chirruping as the man-beast clump crashed through their sanctum, only to take it up again, beratingly, at their backs as they rode on. Goatsuckers warbled their plaintive cry, and a judgmental owl hooted from the high limbs of a great oak that demarked a fork in the path. The air was cool but damp as sea spray.

Or was it his own fear-sweat that chilled Gonji's skin wherever his kimono brushed it?

He growled low in his throat and spat out a gnat. The forest shroud thinned a bit, pilfering a few lonely rays of gray moonlight. Ahead the trees grew more sparse, disdaining to negotiate a knoll in the immediate distance, overgrown with dwarf pine and furze, creeping vines and wild berry bushes.

Gonji paused to see the dance of silver light at the head of the knoll. And what might lie over the rise? Elven carousal in a private midnight amphitheater? Or was it a grim drama the creatures of the wood awaited, lacking only the arrival of the human participant?

(*further on you will meet our brothers*)

Gonji licked his dry lips and bared his teeth at the fanciful notion born of his wrath, almost wishing it were true as he spurred the roncin into a canter and clumped up the knoll, his left hand resting on the Sagami's hilt.

*Why does Mord let you live?*

Cresting the slope, he peered down into a moonlit delve, a gurgling brook meandering along its nadir. An open wound in the forest. For an instant as he sat aboard the

18

steed, squaring his shoulders against an unbidden feeling of aloneness and vulnerability, he imagined that his faulty sense of direction had betrayed him: He could not recall having passed this way with Tralayn.

But it abated at once when he caught sight of the ominous rise of the foothills before him. The sleek-faced escarpment he sought was scarcely a kilometer distant.

And now—a new awareness: The forest whispers had receded; he had penetrated into a sphere of paralysis, for although he could sense the shapes of staring things all about him, not a living thing moved save for the trees, nor did any sound come to him but the murmur of the brook and the slow, heavy soughing of the wind at his face, ruffling his clothes and hair. A deep note of warning, as of a watchdog's growl.

A misshapen frustration, topped by a many-headed anger, rose up in snarling defiance within him. He set his jaw against the press of the wind, his face an inscrutable Eastern mask; but the Western half—the tameless, emotional Western child part of him—jabbed the roncin's flanks, harder than necessary, directing it down into the delve.

Gonji eased down off the shuddering horse, allowed it to drink from the brook as he paced the bank from side to side like a predator spoiling for a fight. Weary and eager to drink though it was, the animal repeatedly paused in its slaking to cast about with rolling eyes, nostrils quivering in the wind, ears flicking to snatch at sounds beyond Gonji's range. The samurai watched it closely, keeping near lest it flee to leave him alone on foot.

Then the moon tore a hole in the scudding cloud sea and emerged in silvery glare. Gonji peered up to see the soft white ring that dimmed its edge. A portent of more rain. Leaden wisps skimmed over the moon's surface, obscuring it again, making its shape indistinct. It was bloated, bulbous. Almost full . . .

*Full?*

A sudden screaming chill along the ramparts of sanity.

*Iyé.* No. Not full. Not for two—three days yet. The last full moon had nearly seen him dead. This one must find him very much alive. Oh, very yes. There was much that must be done before he could pass with honor into the land of the dead.

The roncin nickered, trembling and stamping. Gonji spoke to it reassuringly and caught up the reins, calming it as it stamped back against his gentle pressure. He brought her under control and leapt astride, riding out a brief spate of anxious bucking.

The wind gusted through them again, swirling about, buffeting them as if shaking a fist against their continuing. Gonji experienced a momentary unbidden vision of the monstrous beasts of the nether world he had encountered in his time, few so terrifying as those he had seen in Transylvania; of the strangling white clutch of the Weeping Sisters, those foul blood-lusting things which had tried to feast on his unwilling person; and of their prophecy that he would die in this land. Hollow threat of the evil Deceiver or oracle of certain doom?

But then came the fortifying thought of the fulfillment of his destiny, so close at hand, if deadly in promise; and of his hatred for the fulsome Enchanter, who had toyed with him, had so casually regarded his prowess and his courage. And lastly he thought of the lamented dead, and of the fighting hearts of the men and women of Vedun . . .

*Karma* . . .

With a grunt he kicked the steed across the brook and up the delve's far side.

The trees soon parted. Before him lay the broad glade that fronted the concealed cave. The Cave of Chains. Frosted lances of moonlight slanted through the treetops to dance over the tall, still grass. Cool and quiet it was, the pines and larches that rimmed it as implacable as a court of inquisition. The forest at Gonji's back seemed to his heightened sensibilities to recede of its own accord, abandoning him, having offered its fair warning.

The roncin's snorting was the only sound, the wind having died away now. The animal's pounding hooves clumped forward three strides into the glade and came to a confused halt. She tossed and whinnied fretfully so that Gonji drew on the reins to steady her, but the more he tried, the more recalcitrant the horse became, tossing her head and curvetting, then clattering a full circle before he yanked her, shivering, to the fore once again.

(*Deathwind*) Stop it. That means nothing now.

(*He is here*) He's a *man,* that's all. And by all the spirits of my ancestors, I aim to learn what he's about . . .

The samurai whispered in calming tones to the steed and dismounted, lashing her tightly to a stump at the eastern end of the glade. On an impulse, he removed the longbow and quiver of poisoned arrows, looking about him circumspectly all the while. These he brought with him as he strode lightly across the grassy clearing.

Halfway to the boulder-strewn base of the hill and the cave entrance covered by tangled overgrowth, Gonji was seized by a sudden conviction of the alienness of his presence in that place. The same skin-prickling sensation he had experienced on the day he and Tralayn had entered the secret cave. At the center of the glade he lay down the bow and quiver and began pacing laterally before the cave entrance, adjusting his swords and striving to control his breathing and pulse.

He would have called it caution and not fear, and he would have been at least partly justified. For the cave emanated so palpable an aura of menace that Gonji dared not enter. So he made his stand, came to terms with the longtime focus of his destiny, there in that dread moon-limned clearing. A low rumble of thunder in the mountains both preceded and emboldened his voice:

"Hail to you, storied cave dweller! I am Sabataké Gonji-noh-Sadowara, and I would have a word with you."

The ringing mock greeting, spoken in Simon Sardonis' native French, lingered in the chill air. Gonji stood motionless, facing the cave entrance, hand lightly fisting sword hilt. When his call was not answered he released his captive breath and began to pace laterally again, more confidently now, the spell of the glade broken by the new assurance in his presence, the fresh reminder of his conviction of destiny in fulfillment. His face was the impassive mask of an aggrieved master awaiting the accountability of an underling. There was no sound but the thin wisp of the wind in the trees and the anxious snorting of the horse.

"The time has come for an accounting, *monsieur*. I think we both know whereof I speak."

A light rippling chill teased at Gonji's skin to hear the bold sound of his own words. He paused in his pacing and squinted at the play of moonbeams over the cave entrance.

He stiffened. There had been motion, but not from the cave. Something in the corner of his eye, something moving along the treeline at the western side of the glade. When he focused his eyes on that spot, it was gone.

He expelled his breath in a long choppy exhalation and began to rotate slowly clockwise, scanning the forest. When he caught a glimpse of the thing that caused the tethered steed to whinny and buck, he froze.

A gleam of eyes. Baleful, pale eyeslits that regarded him coldly a moment, then disappeared in the brush.

By the horse's tossing Gonji marked the presence's continued clockwise motion for a long moment. Then the mare's bulging eyes cast about her in all directions, confused and terrified. A cloud bank swallowed the moon.

*I am samurai, and my swords are with me.* He swallowed hard, affecting a battlefield scowl, and the burden of fear plummeted through him to vanish into the earth.

"I grow *weary* of this coy game," he growled in High German, now facing the eastern end of the clearing. "Declare yourself, if you be a man, and let us speak of Vedun."

The heraldic dash of wind at his back turned his blood to searing frost, matting his clothes to his sweating back, raking his hair and topknot. He shouldered about, grasping the *katana's* hilt with both hands, to face the terrible sight of Simon Sardonis. The man of mystery. Cold-blooded killer of the giant Ben-Draba and of untold others in Klann's employ. He of whom Tralayn had spoken her awful tale.

The tethered steed whinnied and stamped as the tall figure began to circle languidly in her direction, scowling at her instinctive panic.

Approaching Gonji at a lazy pace, the man spoke.

"Calm yourself." His voice came soft but commanding, the language a recognizable French dialect, a coarse rasp in its undertone. "What do you want here? Who told you of this place?"

*Calm yourself.* The cavalier accusation failed to penetrate at once, for Gonji's mind had exploded in flaming pinwheels of disjointed thought. In his anxious state, no coherent words would come, so he merely kept his silence and permitted instinct to move him. The glade seemed transformed, timeless. Overlays of impression unfolded to the samurai's wary consciousness. First, the soldier's assessment: Sardonis wore a short sword thrust through his wide belt, much in the manner of Gonji's own swords. No other armament was apparent. The man was alone. He strode with an air of confidence and command. His face, though, bore the occasional twitch of barely

23

contained curiosity or unease. And when he began to move laterally again once he had approached to within about forty feet of Gonji, his movement betrayed a definite limp; he was favoring his right side. The bowshot he had taken in the buttock had left its agonizing reminder.

Next Gonji took in the man's overall appearance. Under the broad belt he wore a light-colored tunic, slashed and blood-stained on the left sleeve, a thick wrap bulging beneath the ragged tear. His narrow-cut breeches and well-worn walking boots were of so similar a dark hue in moon-bathed night as to look of a piece. He was hatless, his coarse golden hair lying back stiffly, darker now than Gonji remembered, its blackened ends stirring like the ruff on a dog's back.

Finally came the insistent impression he had experienced upon entering the concealed cave with Tralayn: Gonji was an alien here, an intruder. Unwanted. Out of place. And his alienness contained less a cultural association than a metaphysical.

Gonji eased his hands off the Sagami's hilt and stood regally straight, turning slowly to keep Sardonis in the center of his vision. The longbow and quiver of envenomed arrows lay a rod away. Small comfort against the chilling memory of the speed of this man of legend: Fleeting glimpses of the event at the city's square returned to Gonji. The killing of Ben-Draba . . . the lightning escape on foot . . . the scramble up a sheer fifteen-foot wall . . . the Night of Chains . . . the full moon . . .

*He is a man. Still a man. He—*

"Well, *monsieur?*" came the grating voice again. "Has your bold blustering been so easily retired by—"

"Speak German," Gonji shot, "or Spanish—anything but French. I care as little for your native language as I do for your hermit's self-pity." Gonji felt the momentary singe of the harsh words, and then it passed. He was

24

beyond regret now. Beyond diplomacy. Beyond fear.

Sardonis' hair began to bristle like a hedgehog's. The strange man's swept-back eyes became a gleaming silver line, curving angrily. To Gonji's mind, so similar to his own. Yet different; the difference being less one of race than of . . . species.

"You've already crossed over a boundary from which few men have ever returned," Simon asserted coldly. "Once again—who sent you here? And what were you told?"

Sardonis had spoken in German now, and Gonji replied in kind.

"Tralayn," he replied softly.

"So," Simon said smugly, relaxing somewhat, "the holy woman is true to her word. Sanctimonious—"

"She's dead," Gonji shouted, "or likely so by now. Dragged off in shackles to Castle Lenska. Or is this old news to you? Were you there watching from your godlike vantage, the way you've watched all our puny mortal strugglings from the beginning?"

Simon grew rigid again, a slight coloration creeping into the paleness of his cheeks. *Caution, Gonji-san . . .*

But when Simon spoke in reply, it was in a tentative voice, his eyes for the first time falling from the samurai. "No, I—I didn't know," he acknowledged, his voice dwindling to a verbal introspection. "So that's why it wouldn't let me . . ."

Gonji was emboldened by the turn, the icy barrier of apprehension melting, his anger and frustration and sense of futility surfacing: "*Hai,* Tralayn—dead, Mark Benedetto—dead, Flavio—dead—" At this disclosure Simon's angular, predatory eyes became a silver line of menace, snapped up to lock into Gonji's own again. "*Dead,*" Gonji repeated, "swinging in the square from his beloved cross, that holy symbol under which you'd call yourself his brother. And it needn't have happened," he accused, pointing a finger at Simon for a second but almost at once lowering both his hand and his voice, for with the words had come a fresh flooding of guilt-ridden recrimination. And he continued in a near whisper:

"The priest, Father Dobret . . . dead . . . but I suppose you already know that."

Simon quaked with an inner fury at the words. "*Ja,*" he replied with a tremulous breath, "I've been there."

Gonji experienced a rash of gooseflesh. Could the strange man have learned of Gonji's own participation in the outrage at Holy Word Monastery?

Simon's trembling subsided, and he glared at Gonji.

"What did Tralayn tell you . . . of me?"

"Enough," Gonji replied evenly, gauging the reaction. Then: "*Everything.* Enough to know that you shirk your responsibility, your duty. You resist your destiny, *Señor* Thing-of-Legend—*Herr* Grejkill—*shi-kaze* . . . *Death-wind!*"

Gonji's pulse raced, and he began to pace as he spoke, circling about Simon imperiously, their roles subtly reversed now as the man of folklore and legend cast his eyes groundward again and flushed with a look that resembled shame. Or guilt. Or self-loathing.

Simon swallowed with noticeable difficulty. "She broke her vow."

"What is a vow," Gonji proposed, ambling with hands behind his back, "when measured against the lives of men?" A poignant stab: *You speak in tarnished truths, Gonji-san. Does not bushido itself demand— Iyé, I must maintain the upper hand. He must be made to see. These people—they matter.* "She broke a vow for the higher value of saving the city and the people she loved. She knew that your great power might be—"

Simon hissed him to silence with a flash of gleaming white teeth, abruptly hostile once again. "Leave this place," he shouted. "Go away from here. All I ever asked

26

of men was that they leave me alone. Alone with this accursed burden I bear like some scourge out of Hell. My every crossing with men has brought death and destruction. Now you come to me, an infidel, blaring like a herald of Death that all those I could call friend are dead. Leave me now!"

Simon turned his back to him, shoulders bunching with tension. But Gonji continued pacing around him, sweating palms rubbing over his kimono as he picked over his words like a man traversing a thicket of deadly thorns.

*"Ah, so desu ka?* Is that the truth?" Gonji probed. "You care for people only after they're dead, so that you can play godling with your aroused sense of vengeance? Why don't you try doing something for the *living* now and again?"

Simon whirled and transfixed him with the silver darts of his eyes as the pale moon burst through the cloud cover. A searching wind whirled into the glade.

"Infidel," Simon intoned venomously, "you have no idea what you're saying. If you've been told what you claim, then you must know what you ask is impossible. You could never understand my lot. And I don't like you. You .. or your idiotic methods—what in God's name was your plan last night? What kind of rebellion plan was *that?* You attack *my* sense of responsibility?"

His words stung Gonji deeply. Rampant visions swelled: The vulgar drunken spectacle he'd made of himself; his failed duty; his shame and embarrassment at being forbidden even the saving stroke of *seppuku.*

He strove to lay at rest the mocking voices, to come to terms with painful honesty.

*"Hai* . . . you're quite right," Gonji replied with a thin, tight smile. "I, too, have failed in my duty toward these people, but if I can I'm going to salvage what's left of their way of life. When I came into their service it was unbidden, owing them nothing, at least at first.

27

*You*—you—they've been protecting your secret, harboring you, sheltering you, some of them, for a year now. Abiding all the while your anti-social contempt. Now they're dying in the streets by sword and pistol and sorcery, crying out for assistance, and what do you do? Nothing but lash out on your own, strike down Klann's troops as it pleases you by cover of night, only to have citizens beaten and shot for your crimes—*ja, crimes*—"

Simon's scalding eyes followed him. "Mind your tongue, barbarian—" The ensorceled hermit began to circle warily again, such that they now described orbits around each other. The roncin mare shrilled and bucked as Simon neared her tether.

Gonji's own anger rose again. "An old Polish farmer once told me of a proverb spoken in these territories. Something about the filthiest bird being the one who befouls his own nest. From my vantage you're a pretty filthy bird these days—"

"Have a care, heathen *swine.*"

"*Hai,* call me 'heathen' as well you might. But if it's insults you crave, then call me *fool* for having sought you out these many long years. Ten—miserable—karma-laden years as a worthless *ronin,* wandering this backward continent in search of the legendary Deathwind—him who would guide me to my destiny!" Gonji snorted and spat noisily behind him. "That's for the trail I've ridden. If your wish is to insult me, then laugh at the way the gods mock my every effort."

"That's your problem."

"Ha! Mine and that of the people of Vedun, now that their lives have become entwined with mine," Gonji sneered. "How easy for you to cast aside the troubles of the world you move in, with a simple swipe of your legendary aloofness. And you're wrong, Sir Hermit—there *are* those who still care about you. Tralayn saw to that with her constant insistence to them that a

28

powerful Deliverer would be coming to their aid. Despite all my efforts on their behalf, with all the scratching and clawing and dishonorable compromise of principle I've had to bear just to win some measure of respect, they still wait for *you*."

Contempt filled the glade as they stalked each other cautiously, the wind a vortex that sledded around the clearing. Simon seemed about to respond, but Gonji grimaced and cut him short. "You think you have just reason to be bitter because your fellow man has made you an outcast? I could teach you a thing or two about loneliness, *Señor* Beast-with-the-Soul-of-a-Man—or is it the other way around? You think you're the only man who ever felt starved for the approval, the companionship, the affection of his fellows? Do you know what it's like to be a half-breed, to have no life of meaning on any continent? Those people are going to die back there in Vedun, and their deaths will be owing much to you, you and your misdirected vengeance—"

The samurai broke eye contact with him, turned his head away, his breath coming in strained pulls now. "To so lose control like this goes against all my noble training, and I would as lief die by my own hand in this spot than bare my true feelings, but I can do nothing right now but show you my revulsion for you . . ."

Simon stopped pacing and stared at him, his hard gaze transforming for a moment into a curious mix of sympathy and uncertainty. But Gonji saw nothing of it.

The tall man looked down at the bow and quiver at his feet. "Why don't you pick up your things . . . and go now."

The sheathed *katana's* hilt was squeezed in a grip that might have throttled a man as Gonji spat a choked curse and regained his harmony after a struggle. Again he met the mystery man's eyes, and now his own eyes of black marble flashed with implied threat.

29

*Do what you've come to do, by whatever means . . .*

"How can you worship as you claim?" Gonji queried. "You make a shrine of your self-pity and worship there."

Simon's eyebrows arched in quiet petulance. "You've said what you've come to say. Now go—"

"Aren't followers of Iasu supposed to band together for their common good, for the struggle against the evil things in the world? Even the civilians in Vedun have abandoned their hand-wringing for—"

"The things of which you speak are quite complex," Simon responded hotly. "I doubt that you're qualified to discuss them."

"So?" Gonji affected a coy archness. "I believe I'm educated enough in your worship to make such comment. But no matter . . ." He considered something, nodded resolutely. "If you refuse to help, maybe I'll go back to Vedun and tell everyone what kind of a . . . *thing* they harbored."

Dangerous territory. Simon began ambling toward him unsteadily, mayhem in his eyes of flaming iron.

"I can remedy that right now, infidel," he grated. "I can tear your wagging tongue from your throat."

Gonji stopped and steeled himself, returning Sardonis' wilting gaze. "Ah, intimidation—the bully's stock in trade. You think you can frighten me the way you frighten other men?" *Wisdom.* Although the bold words had caused Simon to halt and study him closely, Gonji changed the subject without transition: "*Will* you help these people?"

"*Nein.*"

"Will you help them for protecting your secret all this time, for suffering because of your vendetta?"

"They care nothing for me; I care nothing for them. They hate me as do all other men."

"*Nonsense!*" Gonji roared. "You hate *yourself*, what you are, but you can't deal with it like a man so you

30

punish others for your guilt. *Will you help* undo the trouble you've made for them?''

"What's happened has happened—I'm not to blame. What about *your* meddling, slope-head?''

The samurai bridled at the insult. *"I'm* trying the best I know how, using whatever power I can claim to help. *You're* sitting imperiously in a cave and slithering out at night to satisfy your bloodlust. Christian! Is this what your faith means to you? The prophetess spoke of you as the Wrath of God. I look at you and what do I see—a symbol of impotence. Even the priest Dobret told me to tell you to help—" Simon froze, taken aback by the statement. *"Hai,"* Gonji continued, "it was he who became my last link in the journey which led to you. He said that I should enlist your power against the evil that's descended here, and that you should avoid personal vengeance.'' His voice trembled slightly in delivering the half-lie. But conviction rushed back fast; the priest couldn't have known what would become of this business, and surely he would have urged assistance.

Simon emitted a small gasp. "By the Christ and all the saints—I swear that Tralayn's restive spirit has infused itself in you. Don't you under*stand*—any of you—that what you ask of me is utter madness? *Leave me be!* Leave me alone with my shameful curse before it destroys you all!''

Deadlocked, stubbornly determined each in his way, they stood not ten feet apart, expressions set like treasure-vault doors.

Gonji knew he was defeated, his blustering performance failing him, his appeals to reason muddled and ineffectual, his last-ditch effort at trenchant emotional probing unable to penetrate this enigmatic being's lifetime conditioning of self-centered defense. He sighed at length and voiced something that had been nagging him.

*"All-recht.* I've wasted enough of my time on you. But

31

something bothers me—"

"I've nothing more to say to you," Simon stated flatly, turning his back to him and starting for the cave. "Take your gutless animal and ride off."

Gonji raised his voice, a sarcastic quality seeping in. "I know that the chains in the cave are broken, and the full moon is scant nights off. Yet you stay. *What are you planning to do on the Night of Chains?*"

Simon halted, his shoulders bunching with tension, the hair at his neck bristling eerily in the moonlight. "What I plan," he said haltingly, "is no concern of yours, infidel." He stepped toward the cave again, more deliberately now, the limp marring the smoothness of his gait.

Gonji's wrath seethed within him like a riptide to be so dismissed. "So?" he cried. "Then you'll continue to skulk around like some kind of a night-fiend, kill whom you please, and slink back to your cave, *neh?* That's very gallant of you. Meanwhile, others will be sworded for your crimes. My, what a hero! And then on that night—on the full moon—you'll give the beast his head—" His voice rose in irate pitch, crashing through the bleak space between them until Simon turned, an ugly grimace on his countenance. "—and there'll be kills a-plenty. You dung-eating *bastard!*"

*Might as well finish it . . .*

Gonji's eyes narrowed. "These people don't need *monsters* to help them. They need *men.*"

The air filled with ozone as a terrible arc of lightning shattered the sky above the hills, and a hot blast of wind buffeted Gonji's face just ahead of the man's charge.

*"I'm not a monster, you yellow devil!"*

And suddenly the samurai was falling back, sword drawn, against the other's vicious attack. Simon's short blade lashed at him with propeller fury, a crude, emotion-charged power behind the wide strokes.

32

Despairing, uncertain, Gonji gave ground, slipping and deflecting the mighty blows with deft two-handed parries. Simon's rudimentary berserker style, all cursing and animal strength, repeatedly offered openings by which Gonji might leave him unlimbed; or so it seemed—the return speed of his sword arm was remarkable.

Yet Gonji found his head filled with conflicting thoughts, the enemies of the *ken-jutsu* fencer. He could not empty his mind, relax, and allow instinct free rein. He had lost. Failed in his intent in coming here. And the mocking thought that he had forged no alternative to failure recurred, stayed his thews. For he had not come here to kill this man, the supposed object of his time-honored quest.

But neither had he come to this place to die . . .

Wicked blue sparks showered the battleground as the blades sang off each other, and Gonji pressed an attack of his own aimed at breaking the tall man's frenzied resolve. Somehow he had to bring this senseless engagement to an unfatal end. He must disarm Simon, wound him if necessary.

But first and foremost he must remain alive himself. A sensation of bone-deep weariness responded to his calls for renewed strength and second wind.

Gonji leapt back a pace, whirling the Sagami in a flashing figure-eight of deadly steel, flicking the *katana* from one hand to the other with an effortless grace intended to distract, to divert, to intimidate his opponent with the masterful skill the motions bespoke.

Still Simon advanced. Slashing, growling, his unschooled but effective technique losing nothing of its surging, predatory energy. His eyes of chipped silver bored into Gonji's.

The samurai tried a new tack: He stood his ground, the Sagami at middle guard before him, and attempted to address Simon's whirling blows with small efficient

33

parries alone. But the passive stance failed him; Simon's brutish power tore through each parry in such a way that Gonji was forced to fall back bodily or be struck by the barely deflected strokes. He could hear the fierce whinnying of the roncin at his back now. Made out the pounding thumps of her hoof-falls and knew his danger of being trampled.

With a spinning high parry, he twisted Simon's broadsword over his head and spun around the tall man, passing his opened ribs without riposting. Now Simon's back was to the mare as he half-turned to reengage. She cried out in fear of his demonic presence.

"There!" Gonji shouted, dropping the Sagami into earth-pointed rear guard. "I could have opened your bowels. Stop this now."

Simon snarled. "Not so easily done as you think, infidel." He charged again. A deep lunge that Gonji turned aside, flicking his blade arrogantly at the other's chin.

"Again!" the samurai stormed. "Stop this madness and we'll—"

A rapid feint and vicious cutover that Gonji barely evaded. He could taste the tang of steel as it sizzled past his eyes. His stomach rolled and leapt to his throat. *Now* thought fled and impulse reigned.

They were at last united in purpose: One of them would die.

A bone-rattling clash of arcing swords, followed by another. Gonji caught Simon's next hard sally on his shrieking blade and turned it, but the powerful blow defeated his parry and slapped him solidly on the left arm with the broadsword's flat forte.

The sharp sting galvanized him. The samurai shot forward and twisted his *katana* with a whiplike snap, cutting open his opponent's shoulder.

Simon growled and contorted with shock and pain,

Gonji drawing back a step and holding his blade steady before him. The beast-man looked slowly from the wound to Gonji, and on his face there dawned the sudden terrible resolve of the wounded animal. His lower jaw thrust forward in a display of primitive anger. A devil's-breath wind lapped the clearing again, then—

What followed came in fragmented sensory impressions to Gonji: Simon—the wind—silver-gray eyes looking past him, washing over with a new focus—bristling hair and lobeless ears flattening like a cowed dog's . . .

Simon dropped the sword and launched into Gonji like a bighorn ram. The samurai saw a fleeting glimpse of the frenzied gray mare, stayed his descending *katana*. Then Simon's head butted his midsection and he went down hard on his back, losing the Sagami's grip, breath *whoofing* out of him, knees jerking up reflexively, coruscating lights filling the black sky above him.

And he felt, more than saw, the great dark shape that soared overhead, *skreeing* in premature triumph. The treetops bent stiffly into the sucking draw of the wind, and the wyvern flapped upward on supernatural wing-strength, looped across the face of the waxing moon for the return dive.

"Get out of here, idiot! Get into the trees!" Simon was howling in French. But Gonji couldn't move, couldn't breathe. Simon's life-saving tackle had knocked the wind from his diaphragm. He could only lie, paralyzed, listening to the screams of the roncin in its death throes, the sizzle of burning horse flesh. The skirring of thirty-foot batwings . . .

"Come on—crawl—*do something!*"

Gonji sucked hard for breath, but little came. He saw Simon dart across his limited field-of-view and heard him begin calling out to the flying dragon, words of challenge and insult. Then the memory of the creature's ruinous saliva and excrement pushed him into a desperate scramble over the pine-scented earth. He found the Sagami and dragged it with him toward the tree line.

Behind him, Simon dared the wyvern's strafe. The monstrous familiar of Mord took up the challenge, knifed down at the poised mystery man, flaming saliva roiling in its throat glands.

Simon held his ground, cursing the beast. Then when he could wait no longer, he began to dart from side to side into the center of the glade, against the creature's flight path, closing the ground between them rapidly. The wyvern's head coiled back; unused to dealing with a prey that chose to advance against it, it jetted two quick darts of crackling saliva that splashed the glade, searing the grasses but missing the bold adventurer.

In one motion Simon cocked and threw his broad-sword, just as the creature passed above him, not a rod above the ground.

It squalled and twisted its sinuous neck as the blade glanced off a taloned hind leg. Serpent eyes of solid black—Mord's eyes—riveted Simon with spears of demon-hate. Blatting a clump of corrosive excrement that landed twenty yards from the scrambling Gonji, the monster undulated its leathery wings, twisted into a tight arc for a return engagement with its new tormentor.

Gonji reached the trees, panting, on his knees, rubbing his aching abdomen. He drew breath in hungry gulps, grimacing at the reeking stench of the beast's waste that burned the grasses in a spreading circle nearby. He saw Simon race toward the center of the glade after his downed sword.

The wyvern bore down on him.

"*Iyé,*" he whispered. "Run, you fool! Run like the wind!"

Feeling desperate and helpless, he watched Simon slide on the ground, retrieve the useless steel, then launch into a mad zig-zag sprint toward the nearer, eastern side of the

36

glade as the wyvern arched its long neck and began to spit rapid darts of lethal yellow fluid.

The samurai's heart froze when it seemed the man had been struck. But the jet had passed him by, and with that amazing sprinting speed Gonji had seen from him once before, Simon gained the trees.

But the forest was sparse to the east. And the wyvern's night vision was keen.

Gonji remembered the bow and quiver, ran after them, his breath regulating. Grabbing up the weapons, he lashed the quiver to his back and ran toward the sound of the monster's flight. In the trees: the chilling hiss of its fulsome armament.

Gonji paused to listen an instant, staring overhead, cautious both for the beast itself and the crackle of its foul excreta. With startling suddenness the wyvern barrel-rolled over his concealed position. Gooseflesh flared over his body as he broke from the trees and into a smaller clearing; anything to avoid its direct flight path.

He nocked one of the shafts impregnated with worm's venom. "Simon," he called. "Are you hurt?"

No response.

The wyvern cried out keeningly and in a flash was nearly over him again, blotting out the gibbous moon with its tenebrous bulk.

It spotted him. Too late. It was already past when its bowels erupted in an errant dropping that melted the upper branches of a shielding pine, running down its trunk in unnatural putrefaction.

Gonji scowled. Sighting and pulling with desperate speed, he launched the poison-tipped shaft. He missed, the creature's ponderous bulk already covered by the eastern pinepeaks.

*"Choléra,"* he swore, slapping his thigh in frustration. He rubbed his sore abdomen, fought back a mild nausea. Drew another arrow and began to run deeper into the

intermittent bower, his sashed swords scraping through the brush.

"Simon," he spat in a growling whisper. Still no answer. He could hear the wyvern's wind-rush low over the treetops, but its position was lost to him.

A brook trickled through a delve on his left, the trees thinning more now. Thoughts whirling, heart racing, Gonji sprinted along the bank where a stand of oaks lent partial cover, though the farther bank lay bare to the raining death from the skies. At the eastern end of the brook the enormous trunk of a fallen oak, split by lightning, bridged the delve at head height.

*"Skreeee!"*

Gonji leapt about, saw Mord's shining black eyes in the antlered head that careened down with a vengeance. The jaws gaped as it sailed in, slowing to aim, neck poised. It hawked a hissing stream of saliva. Gonji was on the move, cutting, jigging, gurgling with the frantic effort, a cloth-yard shaft nocked on the run.

The wyvern slowed to a flapping hover, short yapping barks aimed at the samurai as it poised its bowels to blat their filth.

Gonji pulled hard and fired as he ran—

The beast cried out in shock, the war arrow needling a wing. The same wing Gonji had penetrated once before. It flapped hard, gaining altitude, the shaft falling free. But now . . . a new sensation to the sorcerer's familiar: the worm-thing's potent venom. Spreading, irritating, even with the arrow loosed.

The wyvern began to shriek and flap at an ungainly stroke, battling the numbness in the wing. It circled erratically, squawking its fear and wrath.

It turned, favoring the injured wing, to reengage the hated samurai, who reloaded and awaited it in the delve.

"You," came the shout from the forest.

Gonji half-turned. "Simon?"

38

"Hit it again. Challenge it. Bring that bastard *lower.*"

Gonji could ponder his meaning but briefly as the flying demon roared down on the delve, a hundred yards off, already spewing rapid-fire jets of burning saliva. The distance closed, the scorching saliva darts blazing nearer with a tracer-effect in the bubbling stream.

Breath held in check, Gonji pulled, arced the bow downward in the time-tested Zen manner, becoming one with his bow, one with his purpose. He gritted his teeth—

A seething splash between his feet in the brook—his face a mask of open terror and revulsion. He fired.

The creature's shriek exploded in his ears as he flung away the bow and dove like a gymnast to roll under the oaks. Arrows spilled about him from the quiver. He looked up quickly as the cold rush of reeking wind pelted at him.

The beast had dropped down, hit the water with its raking hind claws, slogging through the stream at an awkward run. Wings flapping madly, its beaked jaw twisted downward toward its underbelly, where Gonji's thirteen-fist armor-piercer arrow had sunk to half the length of its stole. Splashing through the moon-glinted water like a downed seagull, the wyvern cried to the skies in panic to feel the swift spread of the earth elemental's deadly venom.

Approaching the blockading tree bridge, the stamping horror increased the length of its stride, unfurling its rodent-furred wings for the great push it would need to again become airborne. It launched upward, hindclaws still gouging mud and water, lofting over the fallen oak.

As it passed the massive trunk, Simon Sardonis broke from concealment in the forest and bounded up the oaken bridge and onto its back with an eye-popping leap.

Gonji shouted in wild glee to see the bold maneuver. Laughing with battle frenzy, the samurai scooped up his arrows and dashed down to the brook. He grabbed up the bow again to sprint after the nightmare struggle. For an instant he lost sight of the fray, cursing in frustration. Then he passed under the oak and picked up speed along the bank, the forest again yielding up snatches of the battle to his fevered vision.

Simon straddled the wyvern's serpentine neck as it labored to gain height. He struck repeatedly with his blade, slashing it open so that inky fluid sprayed in the wind. It shrilled in pain. When it coiled about to spit or snap at him with its razor-sharp, chitinous beak, he would cling close and stab at an eye or at its soft throat glands, which bulged behind its lower jaw.

They floated ponderously through the groping branches, only the creature's frenzied wing-lashes keeping them aloft. It craned its head sharply and hissed at Simon. Its barbed tail whipped forward wickedly but could not reach him.

There came a fierce snap as the man's steel struck full force against the familiar's beak, splintering it. Squalling in pain, it lost its concentration, and its left wing tore through an ensnaring pine, skewing the beast and its unwanted rider groundward.

Tearing over the rugged terrain fifty yards behind, Gonji howled in bloodlust to see the object of his hatred and shame brought to earth. Sweat poured into his burning eyes as he pounded to catch up.

The beast ripped out of a pine thicket and into another small clearing beyond. Still Simon clung fast, climbing to its antlers now, slashing with the aroused fury of a starved mountain cat.

The wyvern leapt and bounded about the glade, the trees imprisoning it with its turnabout prey. Blatted clumps of searing excrement splattered the ground.

The monster shrieked its terror into the wind.

Gonji nocked another arrow and guided his bow, sighting on the savagely wounded beast. But at this distance he might hit Simon while the thing scrabbled about. He had to engage it head on.

He ran nearer, awaited its turn. The unearthly cries of the demon-spawned beast electrified the night. And now it turned at last. Saw him. Remembered. Gonji could see the recognition in its eyes, the ophidian eyes of Mord that supplanted the monster's own.

And it bore down on him, energized by its hellish hatred of the human that had brought it such pain.

"Damn you, Mord!" Gonji cried, sighting along the shaft. "Damn you to the foulest chamber of Hell . . ."

It lumbered near, spraying its burning saliva in a semicircle, unable to direct the stream of yellow death. Simon dropped off its back, and Gonji fired—

*"Arrryeeeee—!"*

The wyvern spun down with a heavy thump. Its great hind legs had gone totally numb. Black ichor spewed from between its snapping, curved jaws. Still it lived, though it bled from a hundred places. It pushed up on its wings and crawled toward Gonji.

*Choléra,* the thought harped. *What if it can't die?* What if—? Gonji reloaded, sneered, pulled . . .

*"Sado-war-aaaaa!"* Roaring his clan's mighty battle cry, he unleashed another arrow. It chunkered into an eye, sank six fists deep into its brain.

Its final cry choked off, the wyvern was stilled.

Gonji dropped his bow and drew the Sagami. Running up to the fallen beast in a crouch, he circled it once warily, heart pounding. He stopped when he had returned to its gargoyle's head. Gasped in a shuddering breath.

He mopped the sweat from his eyes and assessed the girth of the sinewy neck: too thick. His gaze falling on the left outcrop of its strange antlers, he raised the *katana* high in a huge arcing strike, lopping the antler off cleanly. Bobbing his head curtly, he returned the Sagami to its scabbard.

41

In that instant he wondered at the meaning of what he had seen just before the final arrow had struck the creature's brain: Mord's evil obsidian eyes had departed, leaving the creature's own volcanic red orbs to lance down at its attacker.

But then Simon had moved up beside him, panting heavily from his valiant exertion. He was bloody and slashed, and in spots his clothes had been burned through, the skin beneath raw and blistered. But in his eyes Gonji could see the twinkle of triumph.

The samurai turned and bowed to him. "Shall we begin again?" Gonji advanced. "Simon Sardonis, I presume?"

Simon's eyes narrowed, softened to a warm liquid gray. He nodded and extended his hand, which Gonji took firmly. Gonji smiled, and Simon's lips became a fine line, unreadable. A moment later they sank to their knees, exhausted, each man dealing with the aftermath of the event in his own way.

In respectful silence.


Still quaking, Mord lay on the stone slab, the minutes parading by in mockery of his helpless confusion. Frustration, loathing, and unwonted terror alternated across the arid climate of his bleak soul.

It had almost dragged him under. The wretched wyvern had resisted his efforts at departure as it twitched in its death struggle, clinging to him against the loneliness of the death experience like a frightened child to its mother's skirts. And it had nearly pulled Mord's consciousness into the gathering darkness.

But no . . . No, that was impossible. He had been a fool to fear. Had not the Dark Master promised him immortality? He could not die. His fears were unfounded.

He collected his senses and laughed, finally, a throaty cackle that echoed in the dank dungeon chamber. Echoed hollowly as Mord recalled the intrepid attack of the meddling pair. That despicable, arrogant oriental. And the other. The powerful stranger, he of the superhuman abilities who had once dared to invade the castle fastness itself. He who was doubtless the legendary Deathwind whose name was whispered in the mountains and the conclaves of secret plotting. Toward him Mord felt a gnawing fear and perplexity. He sensed the contentious spirit trapped within the human frame, that shape of evil that cried out to its dark brothers in a nameless voice that pleaded for freedom. What allegiance could it possibly owe these cross-worshippers?

The simple resolve formed: Both must die. Quickly, without fail.

The agonizing memory of the worm-venom welled up, infuriating him. How *dare* they employ his own effects against him! Puny mortals! But now they will know . . .

They'll piece it all together, reason that Mord works at cross purposes to both the city *and* Klann. He hadn't counted on their destroying both the worm and the wyvern. Now they'd be inspired by their accomplishments—which could work in favor of the Grand Scheme, if Klann could be moved to swift military retaliation against their future efforts.

But most vitally he must prevent the king from meeting with any citizens who might broach their suspicions of Mord's treachery. Must prevent Klann from receiving any messages.

Soon. In three nights—the full moon, the faith rite, and a new imputation of power that would render him omnipotent. He would bleed the faithful of their life forces when they pledged him their belief on that night of nights, and he would additionally provide for the vital mana he would need by claiming the human sacrificial victims the effete king had denied him. Then the Plan would be complete, and the Dark Master glorified.

And the sorcerer's centuries-old desire for vengeance

would be satisfied.

He removed the golden mask, moved to the dingy silver mirror on the moss-and-slime-streaked wall. Gazed at what the ancient priests had done. Trembling, he smiled to think of what was now within his grasp.

When he had presently pondered the problem of the mysterious stranger, he gave thought to the ambitious invocation he had never dared consider before. Would there be power enough on that night? Almost unthinkable, yet . . .

*Seductive.* In that way only the challenging powers of evil can be. Yes, he was ready for it. Ready to call up a fragment of Hell itself.

But only—*only* after his powers had been revitalized in the full-moon faith rite.

## Chapter Two

*"Traitor . . ."*

The word hissed out of Simon like the escape of some vile thing, and Gonji was relieved that the dark mood it provoked in his outré companion was not directed at him.

The samurai was overwhelmed by the strangeness of his surroundings. He had awakened at mid-morning in the concealed cave after a fitful sleep that left him aching and unrested. Simon had long since roused himself and prepared a meal of broth and rabbit meat—cooked over a fire beneath a natural chimney in the rock that acted as a flue—plus a coarse dried bread and a rather bland Hungarian wine with which they washed it all down.

They spoke as they ate, Gonji filling in Simon on the

details of the Vedun situation. The cave-dweller revealed by stages a compelling curiosity about gaps he hadn't been able to fill via his own clandestine investigations and actions. This apparent reversal of his declared disinterest he covered with alternating shifts between petulance and stoic blankness that Gonji read easily and found amusing despite the sense of danger in the man's presence.

Simon was clearly at a disadvantage in social circumstances, his unease obvious. As a social outcast in his own right, Gonji entered into an easy empathy with him. Yet he carried it only to a point; Simon's bizarre existence and the tale of his enchanted birthing and curse engendered in Gonji a shameful feeling of superiority on a human plane. Yet he intuited that the feeling was mutual: Simon seemed to take a perverse delight in Gonji's infidel status among European peoples.

It was just possible, the thought occurred to Gonji, that he alone among all men might penetrate the barrier of Simon's shame and enlist his powerful assistance.

Gonji sat sipping wine, cross-legged, listening to the ringing echo of the single word "traitor" the other had just spoken, gratified that Simon, too, held treachery insufferable.

The samurai glanced about him at the effects of a hermetic existence: the sagging cot and crude table and stool; the oil-stained lamps on the walls; the bundled clothing; two stacks of books and scrolls of Scripture, poetry, philosophy, art, and science—the collected accumulation of current knowledge; in a wall niche, the tiny figures carven of wood, which drew his eye repeatedly; and the broken chains, the heavy manacles he had failed to notice on his first visit to the cave with Tralayn, covered with clothing in a clumsy effort at disguising the embarrassment of an accursed life.

Gonji watched Simon as the latter moved about with animal grace despite his six-and-a-half-foot stature.

Watched the rippling of the sinew under his skin at every slight movement. The bristling of his coarse two-toned hair. The flash of his swept-back silver eyes, eyes that reminded one of tales of the little people who dwelt in forest fastnesses no man could delve. The menacing dagger-point his hair formed above and between those eyes. The occasional twitch of a gently pointed, lobeless ear in response to sounds Gonji couldn't hear. The hands, long and wiry, the nails blackened at their centers. Now and again when they were opened, Gonji could discern the white cross that blazoned, scar-like, in the palm of the left. His upper body was covered with burns inflicted by the foul blood of the wyvern, scars of assorted shapes and sizes, and Gonji winced to scan the two most recent: one on the upper left arm, the other—dealt him by Gonji—slashing the right shoulder. Both were sewn shut with ugly, ragged catgut sutures.

Gonji felt a pang of sympathy when struck by the forlorn image of a warrior extracting missiles from his own body, excruciatingly closing his own wounds.

Simon Sardonis spoke, cleaving the spell of Gonji's thoughts.

"So Rorka and his knights are dead," he said. "What will you do now that this traitor has undermined your planning?"

"As I said," Gonji replied calmly, "we believe Mord works behind Klann's back. Probably against him as well as the city. He seems moon-maddened with a lust for power and a hatred for Vedun. If he resists reporting what he's learned to Klann, then we may yet attack them with a measure of surprise."

Simon snorted, tearing off a chunk of bread and dipping it into his broth. "Utter folly," he scoffed, "to plan an attack against a force of superior power that may well know all your plans—"

"We would seem to have little choice," Gonji

46

countered. "Mord is determined to destroy the city. Tralayn has assured us of that all along."

"You ought to be wary of what *she* tells you," Simon observed with a trace of bitterness.

Gonji ignored it. "Anyway, whatever his ultimate intent, Klann has allowed enough outrages that our *casus belli* are sundry and sound. The city must fight back." Gonji pounded a fist on his knee for emphasis but at once changed his tack when he realized that he was allowing emotion to interfere with clear-headed thinking again. "Of course," he continued sedately, "There are also sound reasons for favoring an avoidance of fighting. Garth will try to speak with Klann about Mord's treachery, *if* he can gain an audience."

"Difficult words to frame," Simon reminded, "without telling the king of your *own* planning against him."

Gonji nodded. "Quite true," he said glumly.

"Garth . . ." Simon began pensively. "Who would have thought he'd have ridden with this mongrel army?"

*"Hai,"* Gonji agreed, "and I think there's more he can tell us. If I can I'll learn from him what else he hides."

Simon grunted. "Tell me what happened the night you rode out with the thirty—the madness in the city—the martial law that night."

"Ah," Gonji said, smiling. And he proceeded to relate the tale of Klann's seven lives, the legend told by Garth's ancient parchment, and of the king's murder and apparent resurrection as a new personage on that night. Simon absorbed the tale eagerly, with a more consuming interest than he had shown in anything Gonji had had to say before. At the story's conclusion the mysterious warrior's brow furrowed, a faraway glimmer drawing his eyes beyond the simple reality of the cave.

"So . . . that is why I couldn't— An enchanted king, a being who cannot die, whose sibling kin reside within him . . ." Simon chuckled harshly, less a laugh than a gurgle

47

of ironic triumph. *"Oui,"* he continued in French, "that is why—if this is true then he'll be a different man now from the one I saw—"

"So sorry," Gonji cut in, frowning, "but you're losing me. Speak German, *dozo*—did you say *you* saw Klann? When?"

Simon smiled, the first time Gonji had seen him do so, the angles of his face taking on a feral set.

"I've been inside the castle."

*"Ah, so desu ka?"* Gonji intoned in surprise. "You've been in there and gotten out again? Why in hell didn't you kill Klann or Mord, if you're so foolish—"

"That was my objective," Simon interrupted impatiently, "after I'd seen what they did at the monastery. Only I—I couldn't go through with it. I found Klann's chamber, killed his guards, and then I had him. I *had* him—there—as close to me as you are. But I couldn't finish it. I didn't know why then, but now it's clear. The reason I felt that strange empathy with him . . . and the other feeling . . . that precognition that killing him would be futile, that my anger would be misdirected. By then Mord must have sensed my presence. He began calling out to the—the thing—the beast in me. And it to him. And then the whole castle was awake, and even by moving in shadow I couldn't escape all of them. So I was forced to flee, leaving my good wishes with the bailey guards. I took this, though—"

He absently stroked the savage wound stitched together on his arm like great red jagged teeth. Gonji stared at him, spellbound at the man's valor and capabilities. And Simon went on in a maundering fashion, his voice lapping the stillness like wind-swept waves.

"So that's the reason for the purpure circles on the Klann crest . . . one for each dead brother. And the reason I felt the empathy. Misdirected anger . . . Mord . . . so it's Mord, then . . ." His eyes abruptly became sharp silver lances, meeting Gonji's squarely. "There is a thing of evil here . . . like few I've felt anywhere. There be signs of ill omen. That's the reason I've stayed in the territory. Holy Word Monastery . . ."

He gently touched the burns he'd taken in the fight with the wyvern. The ointment he'd spread on them gleamed dully in the firelight. Gonji could smell its pungent tang. The samurai's abdomen ached in reminder of the other's tackling blow that had saved him from the searing strafe of the wyvern. Neither man spoke for a moment. Then Simon rose and took the jar of ointment from a carven niche in the rock.

"When were you at the monastery?" Simon asked suddenly. "And what exactly did Father Dobret tell you?"

Gonji was stung. He sat in the lotus position with arms folded at his chest. Sweat coursed in chilly traces down his ribs, but he met Simon's gaze levelly.

"After the wyvern had done its . . . abomination. I spoke with your priest friend. He told me to tell you to help, not to seek personal vengeance."

Simon swallowed hard, nodded with resignation, kept applying the clear ointment. "Even I dare not ignore the signs of the evil epoch that is upon us. Perhaps even *Grimmolech* is about, my nemesis." His voice ground at the name as if a millwheel churned at it in his throat. "I've felt no such power of evil since— Could it be that Mord knows where I might find the Monster?" His eyes became argent wings that lofted him back through the past moon. "Do you recall the *Silence*—that awful, total moment of lifeless silence that seized the world on that first night of the city's occupation?"

Gonji remembered the palpable fear of the experience, the fleeting vision of the ghostly faces in Garth Gundersen's home that night. Nodded reverently.

"I knew then," Simon went, "that a thing of evil had

descended . . . I'll give you this: I'll stay and help you kill Mord, once I've had the chance to wring some answers from him. That much I'll do against this onslaught of evil."

Gonji's face, his entire posture where he sat, took on an adamantine cast. "Not enough," he judged, shaking his head gravely. "You must be willing to help should we make war on Klann's minions. You *must* help these suffering people."

"Your words are laced with stupid bravado. It'll never work. It's sheer suicide to take these ill-trained citizens against a veteran army."

"Who are you to judge? What do you know of our training?"

"I've watched. I was even with you during the entire cavalry exercise in the rain that night—"

"Then you're a poor judge of military matters. They were quite sharp that night, despite all their discomforts. And that was but a fraction of the active militia. Did you also miss the display of group-mindedness in their presentation of—"

Simon grunted. "Engagement with phantom enemies is rather different from the real thing." He rose and returned the ointment to its niche.

"Then you don't know of the attack on Zarnesti, when they freed the village from a whole company of mercenaries. They took it without a single casualty. I was quite proud of them that night." Gonji's eyes narrowed and he added softly: "Most of them."

Sardonis refilled his wine cup and sat on the cot, resting his chin on a fist. "So what will you do next?"

Gonji smiled thinly. "I have a plan involving—" The smile faded. "Why should I tell you if you refuse to help?"

Simon raised his head indignantly. "I *said* I'll stay to help eliminate Mord."

50

"Will you aid the militia, if it comes to war? Many must die, I fear—" The other was shaking his head, and Gonji's voice became earnest, intense, full of painful frustration. "Feel you no sympathy for the little ones, *Monsieur* Christian? The children whose lives may be destroyed in this madness?"

Simon cast the hard-packed earth a flickering glance, inhaled deeply. *"Oui* . . . I do—for the little ones. But not for what they become when they grow older—hateful, craven worshipers of the unblemished, of the *normal*. Stoning and burning every unfortunate soul, turning their backs on every plea for mercy from out of the darkness . . ."

Gonji bowed his head in sympathetic understanding. But his eyes shone with expectation.

"There's one other thing," Simon advised. "Whatever is done must be done *after* the full moon, two nights hence."

The samurai stared at him a moment, selecting his words carefully. "What will you do . . . on that night?" He indicated the broken chains behind the overhanging cloak.

Simon averted his eyes. "I'll have to be far away . . . or perhaps at the castle."

*"Iyé,"* Gonji disagreed at once, "we must act in concert or not at all."

"It was only a thought. Only an idle, boorish thought. In any case I would likely die there, and I have no wish to die before I've achieved my purpose." He paused. "And I'll not allow the Beast to vent its bloodlust."

Gonji considered the dread portent of the man's words. "How many do you think you've killed—in Klann's command, I mean?"

Stung by the naked morbidity of the question, Simon became uncomfortable. His lips trembled as he spoke. "His . . . roster is probably dotted by deserters by now. A dozen? A score?" He shrugged impatiently. "I haven't kept count. What sane man keeps a tally of those who've died by his hand? I quit trying to take on more than two at once a few days ago, though. I'm not the greatest swordsman, and some of these rogues can fight." He patted the raw scowl that was the arm wound. Then he glared at Gonji. "Why do you report to that captain?"

Gonji jolted to attention. "You mean Kel'Tekeli?"

Simon nodded in grave assent, and Gonji explained the double-dealing game he played as a counter-agent.

"I suspected as much," the man of legend told him when he had finished. "You're damned fortunate, though. Once I thought to kill you when I saw you with him—the night I dealt with that child-murdering commander."

Gonji held his gaze. "You might have found that difficult."

Simon laughed harshly. "I admire your fearlessness in badgering me. I've seen little of that. Unless, perhaps, from the boy . . . Mark. Strange, what one finds comfort in. I've already spoken more to you in the past hour than I have in the past several moons. It helps to drown the vicious Thing's whisperings . . ." He reddened, his voice trailing off, the shame of its mention swelling in him again.

"Even a leper should not be so ashamed of his lot as you are of yours."

"Not the same," Simon replied grimly. "It may be that—only Klann would truly understand."

Gonji was anxious to dispel his ill humor. He rose noisily and stretched. "I've been here before, you know," he said cheerfully.

"I know your scent."

Gonji blinked. Then the creeping apprehension assailed him again, the concern that Simon might know of his involvement in the monastery outrage via some similar inhuman power. *Iyé—no,* his reason told him. I'd have known by now, given his temperament. So it must remain a secret for the nonce, at least.

"You ask nothing of my quest," the samurai said, "though I've said it involves you. Are you the Deathwind I've sought all these years?"

*"Nein,"* Simon retorted sharply, "stop calling me that. It means nothing to me, nor does your quest." But Gonji realized that his disappointment must have shown, for Simon appended: "I wish only to be a man, not a legend."

For a time they spoke nothing of consequence, finishing the remains of the food and keeping to their private thoughts. Gonji felt his strength returning, grateful, for he knew he might need every iota in the ominous days to come. Outside it began to rain, the droplets rustling through the vine creepers at the cave entrance like a rodent horde. Yet there was comfort in the sound, solace in its very normality, its cleansing of the earth's wounds. Gonji had begun composing a *waka* to the rain as he relaxed, when the vague unease he had been feeling blossomed into an agonizing remembrance.

*"Choléra,"* he breathed, reaching down and sliding the Sagami from its scabbard.

From the stool where he sat skimming through a scroll, Simon looked up with wary curiosity.

Gonji dropped to his knees in the dirt, the gracefully curved *katana* held before him like an injured child.

"You've scarred my soul with your wild man's anger."

The magnificent blade, a masterpiece of Japanese swordmaking skill, bore a fierce nick halfway along its forte.

"It's a sword," Simon reminded.

"It's my *soul!*" Gonji shouted, but at once he regained composure, sighing heavily. "It's a rare European swordsmith indeed who can heal this." He shook his head morosely.

"You're a knight in Japan?" Simon asked with mild interest.

"A samurai," Gonji answered, and for a time they spoke of the Land of the Gods, and of Gonji's quest, and his longing for the ethereal shades of home. At length Gonji's attention was again drawn to the tiny figures carven of wood that reposed in a gouged wall niche.

"May I examine them?" Gonji asked. "They remind me of the *haniwa* of my homeland. Clay statuettes in the tombs of ancient warriors."

Simon seemed about to object, but he looked away in apparent acquiescence.

The samurai took down each in turn. They were delicate figures of a fragile beauty and charm that were all the more disarming in view of who it was that created them. There were figures of Rorka knights; one of the dead boy, Mark; others of Flavio and of Tralayn; and most surprising of all, there was a marvelous likeness in soft pine of Gonji himself, replete with sashed swords.

He looked to Simon in wonder, but the man was again regarding the scroll with evident discomfiture.

"I am honored," Gonji declared, great sincerity in his tone.

Simon shrugged. "One does what one must to remain sane in the long lonely hours."

"May I buy this one?"

The man fixed him with a hard gaze fraught with the self-consciousness of one who fears he's being ridiculed. "Take it," he said with a dismissive wave.

Gonji bowed and placed the figurine inside his kimono. He sat on the cot across from his companion and leaned forward. "What does it feel like, having such a thing living inside one?"

The effort at control showed on Simon's face as he answered. "Constant . . . exercise of the will. A conscious suppression, concentration, to keep it in its foul curling place."

A tingle of foreboding stirred inside, yet Gonji pressed on in unquenchable curiosity. "Does it have a name?"

Simon replied nothing, but he smiled stiffly and with a tense smugness that seemed so filled with emotion that Gonji dared ask no more of it.

"Your pain is evident," he said, "and I honor your noble effort at stoicism. But why do you so resist fellowship? Good friends can so often serve as a rampart against anguish."

"Ramparts shatter under assault, and friends die too easily."

*"Ah, so desu*—the inescapable fact of death hounds you. So sorry, but it is an immature attitude to allow the certainty of death to affect the way one lives his life. That is an incongruous fear among many Christians that has always puzzled me. Still, I myself have often lamented at how soon friends have betrayed my trust by dying on me—" He chuckled humorlessly. "But that's never stopped me from seeking after kindred spirits to share my strange karma."

Simon sighed and leaned back on the stool, tossed the scroll on the oaken table. "The parasite feels as I feel, knows what I know. Why should I grant it the comfort of a friend?"

Gonji thought for a space, then shook his head, for deep in his heart he could not bring himself to understand. He stood and took up his *daisho,* sashing the swords so that their hilts bristled from his waist.

He moved toward the cave exit but paused and turned to Simon. "Is it with you now?"

"Of course."

"What does it say?"

A bleak shadow crossed the man's visage, moving, threatening. "That I should tear out your heathen heart." A flash of white teeth. A slow-spreading grin.

Gonji's brow creased. The spell of the man's presence

was dashed. "You punish yourself to punish the Beast, Herr Grejkill. It's probably just as well, then, that you choose to live as a hermit. If friends are such a burden, imagine your difficulty if you had chosen to take a wife."

By Simon's sudden tensing, the glow that colored his cheeks, Gonji knew the words had borne even more of a malicious sting than he had intended. *Discretion* . . . He eased out into the rain to clear the air and permit Simon private space.

The tranquility of the rain-dappled forest sank into Gonji as he sulked under a dripping eave of granite. Bluejays *arked* in their tree lofts and starlings gathered to drink from a misty pool, fluttering away when the spray suddenly grew to a hard drizzle. Gonji moved out from under the eave and turned his face up to the rain.

*Loneliness among companions is the most dreadful sort of loneliness. Hai, that is so . . .*

He sensed Simon's presence behind him.

"Don't ever expect to understand my suffering," came the words in a tone that pleaded for the very understanding they denied. Gonji turned slowly. The pearl-gray luster in Simon's eyes surprised him, an uncommon sentimentality softening their predatory sheen.

"I've learned to confide in no one," Simon went on. "All who have known the truth of my condition in the past would see me dead . . ." He waxed wistful. "Sometimes I've gone to the city out of hopeless desperation, by night. Sat beneath a window and listened to a mother sing soothingly to a child frightened of the dark. I imagine I am that child. And then I—I—I say too much." He broke off in a strangled voice, turning away.

Gonji swallowed. "I'm afraid I spoke too soon before, *gomen nasai*—I am sorry. You see . . . I, too, have been called a monster in these territories. So I do understand, at least in part."

Simon spoke without looking at him. "How can an

56

infidel come to love a Christian people?''

Gonji sputtered."It doesn't matter *how*. The fact is that I do care for many here, and I wish to help them. There are other things, as well . . . debts to repay . . . failed duties to atone for. And a final duty still to be done.''

He looked to his sash, grasped the hilt of his *wakizashi,* the short sword used in *seppuku,* the ritual suicide. Then he broached the forbidden subject again:

"Simon . . . why *not* the Beast, Simon? Why can't the Beast be used after the full moon in the defense of the city? Is it true that you control—''

*"Nein!* I've told you, insolent fool! None may see what it does to me. I'll not suffer that pain for any man—''

"Damn you!'' Gonji fumed. "Don't you think all other men know pain? Don't you think Vedun has known suffering? With more to suffer?''

Simon glared at him. "You've heard women describe the anguish of childbirth? Imagine, then, the pain of childbirth racking one's entire body, yet without the joy of bringing forth life. My pain gives birthing to death.''

Gonji sighed with annoyance. "Where in hell will you go to be so far from warm-blooded creatures on the full moon?''

He pointed to the encircling Carpathians. "Up there. There are places I know, far above the snow line, which should seal me off from the world of men. And the animals will know their peril and abandon their shelters for safer ones on that night. Then I can bear my cross alone . . . in silence.''

Gonji stared at him, his brain itching, and he thought: All that this man's God allowed to befall him was no worse than what he had done to himself.

Simon strode back inside the cave, and Gonji followed.

"When we're back in the city we could have Garth fashion shackles for you in some well-fortified—''

"Out—of—the—*question!''* Simon roared, his back to him.

The samurai blinked at the finality of the outburst. His expression sagged with defeat. He shuffled over to his unstrung bow, stuffed the string into an inner kimono pocket where it would remain dry.

"We'd best strike out for Vedun. There is no more time to lose," Gonji decided. "At a good pace we can make it by nightfall, if our legs don't give out first."

"You go ahead," Simon said bleakly. "I'll join you in three days when my . . . time has passed."

"So sorry," Gonji countered firmly, "but if you are to help, then your presence is required at once." He saw Simson about to object and raised his voice in intensity and pitch. "There is no time to lose in planning immediate actions. How will you know our circumstances or tactical decisions if you're not with us to help form them? Three days from now we could all be dead."

Gonji stretched out with his will, defiant of their tenuous relationship, of the man's tight tether. It would be his way or no way.

Simon ran a white-knuckled hand through his coarse hair, matting it down. After a moment's indecision he retrieved his sword, which he strapped about his waist, and a threadbare traveling cloak. On second thought he went to a chest in a back corner of the cave and plucked out a short hooded mantelet. This he tossed at Gonji. The samurai bowed gratefully and smiled, a smile that Simon didn't return. They donned the cloaks and stepped through the short entrance tunnel and out into the soft rain, Gonji carrying his unstrung longbow and quiver.

"Mayhap we will cross the path of some brigands with horses," Gonji said as they began to trudge across the green misted glade. "Horses that they would be only too willing to lend us."

"It would do me no good," Simon responded wanly. "No animal will bear me."

"Well, there are steeds trained for battle and the hunt

58

that have learned to keep their instincts in check, *neh?*"
Gonji said in an effort at optimism. "We'll find you a fine
destrier that—"

"Forget it, *monsieur*. My own legs have borne us thus
far."

"But with that limp—"

"The limp is abating," Simon assured mordantly.
"And it will pass, as all my wounds do." He bent and
picked up a long straight stick, which he proceeded to use
for a walking staff.

Gonji blew an exasperated breath. "Well, surely you've
ridden a horse before."

Simon moved ahead rapidly, answering not a word but
steering them east along the brook until they came to the
place where they had slain the wyvern. Gonji was struck
wide-eyed, gasping to see its state. Already it had taken on
the aspect of a thing long dead, overgrown with moss and
slime, its entire bulk slumping, collapsing, sinking back
into the earth that could not contain it when it lived its
ghastly life. Leathery flesh petrified and shriveled like
bark, antlers spindling the air above its crushed jackal's
head, it resembled nothing so much as a downed tree of a
curious species. Days from now, passing travelers might
regard it as a momentary diversion, a freakish arboreal
hybrid, shrugging off its origin in casual bewilderment
while giving short shrift to local tales of the flying dragon
that had ravaged the countryside.

Gonji stared for a long while, scowling, leaning on his
longbow, at last shaking his head in disappointment, the
specter of illusion laughing at his mind's sudden discomfort with its definition of reality.

When he turned Simon was already far along the brook,
wending northward at a vigorous pace.

The hours passed in aching silence and weariness of
foot.

## Chapter Three

*"Kommen Sie—schnell!"*

Curses and grumbling snapped out below amid the rain rustle as Wilf wiped his eyes and peered back down the path. The peevish snorting of horses and the splashing clump of many hooves rolled up toward the old Roman road. A mile to the west, soldiers would be posted at the main southern trail into the valley. But there were none here at the summit of the twisting bramble path a half mile outside the city's western gate.

"Take it easy, Gundersen," Vlad Dobroczy complained as he lashed the barebacked steeds up the treacherous slope. The last ten surviving horses from the caverns were urged upward to the road. Among them was Gonji's prize Spanish chestnut, Tora.

"That's right," Nick Nagy agreed. "What's your rush?"

"Shut up, you crusty old buzzard," Stefan Berenyi snapped from the darkness. He broke from the deep brush, riding with the reins in his right hand. His left was heavily bound to protect the healing wound of the severed little finger.

Nagy hissed at him, turning his mount.

"Shhh, all of you." Jiri Szabo's urgent plea came through the rain.

A horse fell in the mud at the side of the path, whinnying fiercely. Tadeusz leapt to the ground at the rear of the party and spoke comfortingly to the startled animal.

Two horses broke up onto the road, prancing freely, their reins dangling. Wilf guided them back, cursing, one hand gripping two tethers. He wore Spine-cleaver under the sash that bound his waist. The others were similarly armed, but there were no bows among them. They could ill afford a scene if they were stopped and questioned. Their only long-range armament was the pistol Dobroczy had belted beneath his heavy cloak in defiance of Wilf's order.

They nearly had the skittish horses in hand on the road when the clatter of a wagon and the pounding of hoofbeats sounded through the rain-dappled forest behind them. The curve of the Roman road hid the approaching band from view.

Jiri went pale in the dim light. "What do we do, Wilf?" he breathed.

*"Ja,* now what?" Vlad added. "This was *your* stupid idea, junior Japper."

*"Stehen Sie!"* Wilf commanded. "You know the plan. Move the horses nice and easy. Show no fear or worry. Answer what they ask, if it's soldiers. That's all. Now let's move."

They led the horses at a walk toward Vedun, Berenyi singing a silly drinking song at the rear but peering back furtively now and again. They all strained to listen at their unguarded backs. The wind changed direction, grew stronger. The rain became a slapping wet hand from the south. Their eyes burned in the stinging cold, and a rash of itching spread through their number.

Behind them the wagon rattle and hoofbeats closed fast. Now voices could be heard. Gruff voices, calling out to them.

Wilf halted them with a heavy exhalation, gazing down onto the muddy track.

"Turn easily. Show no surprise."

Under his cloak, Dobroczy cocked the loaded and spannered wheel-lock piece.

"Whoa, there!" a voice ordered. Three of Klann's

61

mercenaries cantered up to them, leaving the wagon and its driver stopped behind. Two brigands unbuttoned their jacks, revealing belted pistols. "What are you up to? Get down off your horses."

Wilf waved for them to remain mounted and walked his black gelding toward the three, smiling wearily. The leader, a hollow-eyed man with pocked cheeks and sallow skin, reined in and faced him. The other two rode past to confront the rest of the party. Wilf's mount snorted, its muzzle a hand's width from the other steed. The bandit placed a fist on his hip, sweeping back the flap of his jack. The silver filigreed pistol grip glowered at Wilf.

"Horses," Wilf said, pointing a lazy thumb over his shoulder. "Lost during that crazy fighting two nights ago in the city. We've been chasing them all day. Now we're—"

"Hey, Karel—" One of the others called from behind Wilf, guiding in among the shuffling horses and pointing at Tora. "I know this stallion. It's that crazy Mongol's."

Alarmed, the brigand nearest Vlad Dobroczy drew his pistol. The farmer's reaction was instantaneous. His cloak tore open in an eruption of flame and smoke, and the soldier's face imploded in a slick black fracture.

The confrontation became a jostling chaos, as if flames had belched from the soaking ground beneath their feet. Horses shrieked and reared, broke in all directions. Wilf caught a fleeting glimpse of the silver filigreed wheel-lock in the leader's hand and kicked his gelding hard in the flanks, drawing Spine-cleaver in the same motion. His horse whinnied and leapt at its opposite number, which shrank before the flailing hooves and then itself tossed and bucked so that the mercenary leader squeezed off a poor shot.

The brigand swayed sideways and lost his hat and the smoking pistol. Righted himself and clawed at his sword hilt.

Too late. Wilf swept past, slashing him backward off the neighing steed.

The third soldier, who bore no firearm, bared his teeth and growled in desperation, swung his mount from side to side, naked blade cutting at wet air. He spied an opening and charged for it. His flight would carry him past Jiri.

Jiri slipped his sword out of its back harness and raised it high over his head. His eyes shone like beacons in a tempest to see the mercenary charge him astride the snorting warhorse. His own mount stamped backward uncertainly under Jiri's flagging guidance. The enemy bore down to engage him.

They slashed as one, a shower of golden sparks igniting the darkness as their swords clashed. Jiri's eyes clamped shut at the impact, and he withdrew from contact even as they met. But the brigand's following blow split the jaw of Szabo's horse, and the screaming steed lurched over, spilling Jiri in the mud and slamming down next to him to kick and flail in its agony. Jiri scrabbled away on hands and knees in the mire, panting but unhurt, as hooves splattered all around him.

Tadeusz intercepted the mercenary in his flight, engaging him with sparking steel. As he drew alongside, the young *bushi* missed parrying a desperate lunge that sprang out of the gloom. His mouth gaped upward at the sky like the jaws of a moon-baying wolf, blood gouting in his throat and strangling him as the soldier's swordpoint snapped off clean in his breastbone.

By now Nagy and Berenyi had run the mercenary down. Old Nikolai roared to hear Tadeusz's mortal cry. The swing of his powerful sword arm sliced open the brigand's capote and jerkin, cutting into his spine. The man fell into the muck, stunned and gasping, paralyzed.

Nagy rode a few paces off and dismounted. His younger partner, Berenyi, bounded down from the saddle, wild-eyed and vengeful, hurling imprecations at the downed enemy. He darted forward, feinting unnecessarily once with his broadsword before lunging deeply and stabbing the fallen man through the chest, withdrawing his sword with some difficulty.

Wilf's gelding jolted and kicked under him through it all, biting at other horses stamping near, its natural enjoyment of a fray aroused. The young smith tossed the reins from side to side, assessing the fight.

"Damn you, Hawk!" he swore. Vlad Dobroczy stared down with eyes like an owl's above his great nose, pistol still smoking from the tattered hole in his cloak. He seemed dazed by the shattered face that glared up in grisly ruin.

But now Wilf saw that the lone survivor aboard the wagon had wheeled his team and was lashing them back west. If he could recognize any of them and reach the outposted sentries at the southern valley road . . .

*"Hyah!"*

Wilf stormed after the jouncing wagon, traces held in his left hand, the gleaming steel of his *katana* trailing behind him in his extended right arm. He reached out with his will to restrain the fleeing dray, mentally cleaving the distance even as the gelding's hooves pounded onward through the rain and the puddling ruts in the ancient road. The heavens opened wider and shed their anger in slanting waves that obscured his vision.

The dray disappeared around a black bend like a skittering ground hog. Wilf's nape hairs prickled, a chill coursing his spine. Beyond that bend a whole company of mercenaries might lie in wait. Or a replacement column of Llorm regulars. He was one man with one sword that had been his for a mere handful of days. The knowledge of its use had been burned into him during the life of the waxing moon. And the teacher of those nascent skills—Gonji— was not with him now. Yet his spirit was his own, and its yearnings were his master.

He rode on harder and gained the bend in a minute that aged him by days.

Half the distance had dissolved between Wilf and the surging wagon when something remarkable happened. Wilf saw a tall figure leap from the brush at the side of the road and out before the wagon team. The man raised his staff before him, and the draft horses neighed and swerved, slipping off the wet stones to tumble into the ditch at the right.

The dray overturned with a crash and the driver's high-pitched scream.

Wilf pulled to a halt, the gelding stumbling but righting itself quickly. He held the curvetting steed and peered over its snorting muzzle. His unknown ally had descended on the fallen driver. There was a sudden movement behind the spinning wheel of the upset wagon. One horse broke from its harness and galloped off; its partner's legs could be seen, twitching spasmodically on the ground.

Who in hell could that be?

Wiping his eyes on a sleeve, Wilf pushed his mount toward the wreck, Spine-cleaver cocked warily along his right side.

Another figure joined the first, giving him pause. This one was smaller and hooded by a mantelet. Carrying a longbow. But even through the haze Wilf recognized him almost at once.

"Gonji," he breathed, breaking into a trot.

The young Gundersen reached them quickly. Gonji ignored his relieved greeting but Wilf was of no mind to take notice, for his astonishment at the sight of the samurai's companion caused him to gape like a speared fish.

This was Wilf's first glimpse of Simon Sardonis, who looked like no man meant to walk among other men. He gazed with ambivalence at the eyes, the ears, the long pale hands—curling now, and alive with sinew, the spiky

65

bristling of the doglike hair even in the matting rain.

Wilf tore his eyes away, gulping down the hot constriction in his throat. He returned Spine-cleaver to its scabbard. Rubbed at the nervous tic in his right eye. There was a tension in the air that undid Wilf's sense of relief at Gonji's return.

Simon poked at something in the wreckage with his staff. Within the hood of the mantelet, Gonji's eyes narrowed. He stood with folded arms and stared.

In the wreckage, something moaned like a tortured calf with nothing left of life but the final agony.

Gonji shot Wilf a look and beckoned to him. Wilf could see the driver, dead, several feet off in the scrub. The unearthly moaning sound came again, and he dismounted, his breathing tight, gooseflesh flaring his skin.

He reached the end of the overturned wagon and peered down. The ribs were caved in on the side that faced the sky, the burlap torn and askew. And when Wilf's eyes focused on what moved inside, his hand shot to his mouth in shock, muffling his unseemly outcry.

*"Jesu—Maria—"*

It crawled out of the blanket that had shrouded it with an ungainly dragging motion, its groans now reduced to a strange liquid trilling that fluttered from its partial mouth.

The half-man. Severed and sealed vertically along his middle. One-armed, one-legged, half-headed; the body-length wound coated with a pallid substance resembling tallow, leaking now in spots, oozing dark blood.

Its life-source unknowable, the pathetic creature was all that remained of the combative craft-guild leader, Phlegor.

A flash of steel, as Gonji yanked the Sagami free and raised it high overhead.

Wincing at the sound, Wilf turned his head and stifled a spate of gagging.

\* \* \*

66

Jiri Szabo wiped himself as best he could, rubbing his mud-streaked face on a soaked shirt sleeve. He retrieved his downed blade and gathered his horse's reins, all the while watching Wilfred's mad ride of pursuit.

"God, I hope he catches it," the young athlete said. "Maybe we should go after him, to help."

His words dispelled Vlad's fascination with the corpse of the man he had shot. The eagle-beaked farmer looked toward his departing rival.

"Forget it. He'll never catch them," he replied grimly. He belted his spent pistol and swiveled his mount to view their situation. "Better help me collect the horses, Jiri. There'll be more trouble than we can handle here soon."

Szabo turned to remount, stopped when he saw the twisted body of Tadeusz.

"Shouldn't we . . . pick him up?"

"*Igen,*" Hawk agreed curtly, "you do it." He moved off after the scattered horses.

Grimacing at the grisly sight of his dead friend, Jiri cast about for assistance. There seemed to be none forthcoming. He swallowed back his grief and brought up Tadeusz's mare, began to roll the militiaman's body in a blanket.

"All he ever worried about," he mumbled to himself, "was whether he could go through with killing a man in battle." He shook his head sadly, knowing all the while that the ironic eulogy had drifted up from the well of self-doubt in his own soul.


Rubbing the back of his neck for a restless moment, Nikolai Nagy studied the troubled young hostler. Stefan had acquitted himself well; his deed had been a valorous one for a man still pained by a fresh war wound.

But Berenyi exhibited a new injury now. An internal one whose scar, Nagy knew, marked every man differently. He gave Berenyi space for as long as he thought wise, watching him glance from the corpse of the man he'd dispatched to the blood-stained sword in his good hand and back again. His lips moved silently, and he licked them repeatedly as if their dryness defied the rain.

His first battlefield kill. No smirk, no jest from the jocular Berenyi now.

Nagy's impatience finally got the best of him.

"Old man's still got what it takes, eh?" He cuffed Berenyi's shoulder playfully, breaking the morbid spell.

"Hah," Berenyi sputtered out of the corner of his mouth. "*I* had to finish him, old man." His voice quavered.

Nagy bobbed his head.

"Let's get this place squared away, young pup."


His brief talk with Simon finished, Gonji climbed aboard the gelding behind Wilf, and they started back toward the squad of militiamen. He was fatigued from the long walk. Cold and numbed inside.

*What monstrous things are yet in store—?*

"That man—" Wilf said over his shoulder. "He's . . . Simon Sardonis, *nicht wahr?*"

Gonji nodded. *"Hai."*

"The one who beat Ben-Draba to death at the square?"

"The same."

"Is he . . . also *the one?*"

"What do you mean?"

"The one you've sought—the Deathwind."

Gonji pondered the question as they jounced along. Finally shook his head.

"I don't know, Wilf. It doesn't seem to matter. Why do you ask?"

"It's just that he's . . ."

*"Hai,"* Gonji filled in, "a strange one, *all-recht*. Tralayn would have us believe that he's your Deliverer. *One* man," he appended for no reason in particular.

68

"Well, I don't doubt her," Wilf said seriously, mopping the rain that slanted into his face. "Having seen him, I'd believe just about anything."

Gonji cocked an eyebrow, his memories spinning with the details of Simon's sorcerous origin, told by Tralayn. The tale of what he would become in two nights.

*Werewolf* . . .

"One shouldn't be too gullible, my friend," Gonji cautioned. "On the other hand . . . the world never ceases to surprise one. Expect nothing, accept what happens."

Like a reviving agent, Gonji's words seemed to awaken Wilf from a paralysis. He began to tremble.

"Some things you *don't* accept." Wilf's words came thick with emotion. "Like a loved one—"

"You have no choice, Wilfred."

*"Ja!* I do—that *thing* back there that used to be Phlegor—it came from the castle, didn't it?"

*"Hai,* I suppose—"

"What the hell is happening at the castle by now? How many more people are like that? Gonji, I've *got to get inside Castle Lenska—now!"*

"Quiet," Gonji commanded softly. "Now think: What good could you accomplish going off half-cocked and trying to rescue Genya from an entire castle garrison? Have you forgotten the giant?"

"I don't care about—"

"Shh! How would we even get inside right now with Klann's force on the alert against insurgent action?" Gonji thought of something, his face clouding. "Did you have the tunnel to the castle collapsed as I ordered?"

Wilf sighed. *"Ja,* they did it, though I tried to make them leave it clear in case . . ."

"Listen, Wilfred, your need is no more important than that of everyone else. We are either united in this effort or we are fodder for the invaders. If you compromise our unity of purpose, then you're as expendable as Phlegor."

"Sure," Wilf replied bitterly, "then you'd turn me in to the soldiers like you did Phlegor."

Gonji was stung by the young smith's reminder of how he had set Julian to watching Phlegor as a diversion. But he saw Wilf's shoulders bunch as he added in a near whisper:

"I'm . . . sorry, Gonji. I didn't mean—"

"What I *meant* was that Mord would love to have another subject to ply his evil magick on."

Wilf nodded glumly. "What did he do to him?"

Gonji shook his head. "It would be well to keep the news of his fate from the others, *neh?* Simon stayed back to bury him."

"What happened to your horses?" Wilf asked.

"Mine met with an accident, and he didn't have one. Did you find Tora for me?"

*"Hai,"* Wilf responded, bright-eyed and smiling. "He's with the others we were trying to bring up when those rogues stopped us."

They rounded the bend and could see in the murky distance the place where the brief action had occurred. There was no movement there now.

"They're gone," Wilf said in mild surprise.

"That's good. Your shooting may bring more soldiers." Gonji leaned over Wilf's shoulder and scanned the road ahead. Seeing nothing threatening, he continued: "Quickly now, tell me what's happened since yesterday."

Wilf recounted the busy hours: the surreptitious movement of armament and supplies from the now unsalutary catacombs; the securing of the city by Klann's troops; the beefing up of the city garrison; the restriction of movement to and from the city—Klann's paranoia ran rampant now, as well it might; the systematic search throughout the city for Gonji (which amused the samurai no end; Julian's discomfiture was a balm to his anguished spirit); and the surrender of the location of a weapons

70

cache in the foothills by the now penitent and cooperative craft guildsmen.

Gonji received the news of the unblocking of the catacombs access tunnels with enthusiasm. The catacombs were yet of strategic usefulness. The southern valley tunnel had been unblocked to permit Gonji to journey to Simon's cave. It had been reshaped to admit one horse and rider at a time. In addition, the northern foothill tunnel and the passage to the vestibule chamber that led up into the city had now been opened to allow humans through; however, creatures of unnatural size from Mord's mystic arsenal would find it difficult to pass the formidable spiked redoubts constructed at the tunnel adits.

"That's good," Gonji agreed. "I should have thought of it. Whose idea was it?"

"Michael's."

"Mmm. Encouraging to see that he's in a military state of mind. We'll need that. How is his leg?"

"Better, but he'll limp, there's no doubt. Lydia's with child," Wilf added matter-of-factly, forgetting it almost at once.

Gonji was stung, the reality of their marriage and its stumbling block to his desires was abruptly driven home with the unrelenting finality of a death sentence. He smiled crookedly, had to backtrack swiftly to catch up with Wilf's train of thought.

"—polearms were dismantled and hafts were brought up separately from the weapon heads."

"Eh? Oh—good idea. Very clever."

"*Ja,* that was Roric's. Then the armor, and the big weapons, and the really dangerous materiel—pistols, shot, powder, bows—those were a problem until . . ." Wilf shook his head, wincing at some indelicacy.

"Well?" Gonji pressed.

"God forgive us. Poor Master Flavio would have—"

Wilf peered back over his shoulder, knowing the pain of the memory he had evoked. "Sorry, Gonji."

The samurai stared at the racing, rain-stippled ground, making no reply.

"But anyway," Wilf continued, "there were many dead after the craftsmen's rebellion. The chapel—the city—filled with coffins until the funerals. A lot of those coffins . . . don't contain bodies . . ."

Gonji's face brightened. He chuckled dryly. "And whose ghoulish idea was *that?*"

Wilf snorted. "Your braying chum Paille's."

"Hah! I might've known."

"Gonji—" Wilf grew deadly serious. "Have you given any more thought to the traitor? To whom it might be?"

Gonji was slow to respond. *"Hai."*

"You don't think it's my father, do you?"

The odd question surprised him. *"Iyé*—why do you ask?"

"Oh, nothing. I've just . . . overheard talk. Well, not *talk,* exactly, but . . . you know, the way people *look* at someone they don't trust. And Papa sure hasn't done much to inspire trust lately, what with all these secrets of his. He hasn't made a move to appeal to Klann for peace and to tell him about Mord's treachery, what we suspect, you know. He wants to take my head off when I bring it up. He's become unapproachable."

Gonji thought awhile before answering. "I wouldn't worry about it, Wilf," he said, scratching an itch beside his sore belly. "Words of caution against Mord are going to be hard to form without tipping the militia's hand. And I certainly don't suspect your father of being traitorous. No spy would behave as mysteriously as he has.

*"Nein . . ."* His gaze lofted to a distant vision. "I don't think it's anyone in the council. Only the council members knew that there was no hope of Rorka raising outside assistance. So eliminating him was a futile action. It must

72

be someone in the rank and file, I suppose, who reports to Mord. But who?'' His fists balled up on his thighs.

"Do you have a plan now?'' Wilf asked. "Do you know what we'll be doing next?''

"*Hai,* sort of a plan,'' Gonji allowed, exhaling wearily. "I doubt that it will be very popular among your countrymen.''

They reached the area where the fight had transpired. Quiet now, but for the falling rain. Dark bloodstreaks whirled and eddied in puddles under soft moonglow. Drag marks and myriad hoofprints filled in rapidly with water.

"Who did you leave in charge?''

Wilf blinked, embarrassed. "I—Nagy, I guess.''

"Come on,'' Gonji said. "If they were smart, they took the horses back down into the valley.''

They cut a virgin path through tangled congeries of shedding larches that left them soaking by the time they reached the valley floor. Turning eastward for about a hundred yards, they found the party of four with the shuddering horses in tow, awaiting Wilf's return with short-tempered uncertainty.

"Gonji!'' several voices whispered in relief. Happy wet faces glowed aboard prancing steeds. Only Vlad seemed sullen and unimpressed.

"I see they're delighted to see *me* back,'' Wilf said sarcastically.

Gonji snickered. "How do you like the mantle of leadership?'' They could make out the swathed body lashed to Tadeusz's saddle. "Who's that?'' Gonji asked. Wilf told him who it must be, and he nodded grimly, but then the others were shushing them and waving them near.

"Helmets,'' Nick Nagy grated harshly when they had closed the distance. "Across the ravine to the south. Jiri saw them.''

"Klann's troops?'' Gonji inquired.

"I don't think so. The helms were sort of . . . spired.''

73

Jiri described a pointed effect in the air above his sallet.

Gonji mounted a dead mercenary's horse and, waving off accompaniment, trotted to the ravine some small distance to the south, swords at the ready.

The trees parted at the northern end, and the samurai immediately espied the mounted party at the farther end. Turks. Three of them. An armed military scouting party. This was the northernmost incursion by Turks Gonji had seen in his considerable time in the territory. They were growing bolder, their fears of the haunted Carpathians melting in the heat of acquisitive passion. With the instinct of vultures, they had sniffed out Vedun's harrowing situation and now lay back in wait.

The locals would call this a bad omen at the very least, and Gonji decided to minimize the import of the sighting.

They saw him and halted at once in their low chatter. Eyes and armament gleaming, they held their steeds steady. Gonji made no effort at concealment, his posture as stony and imposing as the mountains behind him. He had left his longbow with Wilf, but he had not come to fight. Looking back over his shoulder and hissing as if in command, he swept his long sword out of its sheath and pointed it at the Turks. Instantly, they wheeled their mounts and clumped off into the forest.

*Rapacious bastards.*

A peculiar feeling seized Gonji. He suddenly found himself wishing for one last swoop by the dead wyvern. One strafe at their departing backsides.

He shook his head to reclaim his senses. Turning and trotting back to the others, he acknowledged the awesome scale of the dark powers marshaled against the ancient city on the Carpathian plateau. Experienced a fatalistic portent of doom. Cursed the karma that had befallen Vedun, his loyalty to the city aroused.

When he returned he found Wilf and Vlad embroiled in an argument over the farmer's having brought a forbidden pistol along, instigating the deadly incident.

"They recognized his horse," Dobroczy kept repeating, indicating Tora, who now turned his head in docile approval of Gonji's presence.

"And we might have convinced them otherwise,"Wilf argued. "Now we can't get these horses up tonight whether—"

"I like staying alive," Vlad snarled.

"Shut up, idiots!" Gonji railed. They all snapped to attention. He seemed different now. Sterner.

"You're in more trouble than you realize, and there's no time for your petty quarreling." He strutted the horse before them, eyes like marbled lava.

"Now I'll give you your orders, and there'll be no more . . . squabbling."

## Chapter Four

The vestibule chamber that led to the catacombs smelled of huddled bodies, pungent moss and earth. Dirty yellow light lapped the stifling air in the cavern from torches ignited in wall cressets. Hats were removed and jerkins pulled open among the men. Sweat glistened on foreheads, and eyes glittered with anxiety.

Coughs erupted in the thick smoky air. Voices muttered like the gurgling cross-currents of intersecting brooks. In several languages it was rumored that the mighty man of valor had returned. The tall man with the supernormal powers. He who had battered the huge Field Commander Ben-Draba, broken the warrior's neck before whole companies of his men in broad daylight, leapt the fifteen-foot curtain wall that girdled Vedun despite the arrow that had found its mark in his flesh.

Simon, they said his name was. Simon, the Beast-Man.

The well-known accented voice came in German, speaking words that muffled them, mesmerized them:

"So it's come to this—*fight or die.*"

The samurai stood on a table near their center. He was dressed in only his breeches and sleeveless tunic. His *daisho* were sashed at his waist, their hilts in that ominous near-horizontal angle. Arms crossed over his chest, topknot bristling, he looked down at them imperiously.

An overseer. An accuser.

Some among the massed citizens glared back to hear his tone.

"Fight or die," he reiterated. "Or perhaps there's another way. One that nonetheless involves fighting . . . and dying."

His gaze lofted over their heads as he turned slowly on the table. Stopping when his glance fell on the iron door that leaned against the rock wall, he peered into the gloom of the catacomb. Knew that his posted guards would be on watch within. Faithful *bushi* who stood on duty at the tunnel exits. He had told them what to expect.

He rolled his vision back again over the audience, arranged in a semicircle around the table. No one dared sit too near the vestibule doorway, the portal through which Baron Rorka had so recently fallen in unnatural death.

Long faces and hollow eyes looked up to meet his stolid gaze. They were all here. All those he had called for. Those Gonji trusted most—and the least. Few had known that he would be presiding over the conclave. For now whatever secrecy and surprise he could muster would be necessary.

Front and center sat Michael and Lydia Benedetto. The young heir apparent to Council Elder Flavio's position cradled a crutch at his side. Flanking them were Garth

Gundersen and his three sons on the one side; Milorad and Anna Vargo on the other. On Gonji's left Roric Amsgard sat, an arm around the shoulders of his oldest son. Near them were Jiri Szabo and his betrothed, Greta. On the opposite side were Aldo Monetto, the lithe axe-wielder, and his ever-present companion, the dour archer Karl Gerhard. Deeper in the crowd were the sullen faces of Vlad Dobroczy, heading up a small contingent of farmers; and Paolo Sauvini, accompanied by his master, the blind wagoner, Ignace Obradek. Paolo seemed uncomfortable this night, withdrawn. It was rare indeed when the swarthy, ambitious Neapolitan eschewed the front ranks. Behind him Gonji could make out the hateful black eyes of Boris Kamarovsky, and Gonji wondered what those eyes would register to see the state of his late boss, the ill-fated Phlegor. Berenyi and Nagy sat at either hand of Nick's wife, Magda. Nary an insult between them for the moment. The bald pate of Anton, last surviving Rorka Gray knight, reflected the lambent torchlight from where he sat near one wall, at the end of a bench on which the entire Eddings family was ensconced, the faces of the men like facets of the same gem: father Stuart, brooding son William, brother John. John's petite fair-haired wife, Sarah, seemed dwarfed and frightened by it all. All on that side of the cavern appeared comically tugged as if by invisible strings, their ears cocked toward the cold, red-veined wall, where Alain Paille leaned with hands behind his back. Vedun's quirky genius, the city's most versatile translator, snapped out impatient interpretations in any language needed.

"What do you mean, *sensei?*" Monetto queried tentatively. "About . . . another way?"

Supportive murmurs.

"I mean that it is like this," Gonji clarified. "We can foster no more hope of surprise, and time has failed us as an ally. There will be no more training. Every one among you must trust to what he has learned in the training so far. All Garth's efforts at seeing Klann have been rebuffed, so sorry. Even I had great hope for such a meeting. For Garth was supposed to make it clear to Klann that we suspect Mord of treacherous and evil designs against both Vedun *and* his liege lord Klann.'' Gasps of surprise at the disclosure. ''And that is not the worst. The fact is that there is a traitor in our midst who has compromised all our secret endeavors, revealed our plans to the sorcerer.

''You see, my friends, we tread now on the backs of turtles. Never knowing when the ground will shift under our feet. We cannot tell how much of our preparation is known to Klann. Only that Mord knows, and that he can use that knowledge against us whenever he wishes. Add to this burden the fact that the baron and his knights are dead—all save the worthy Anton—and with them died all hope of allied intervention on our behalf. No army will come in rescue of you. You must do what you must as an army unto yourselves. *We* must do what we must. I am committed to your cause unto death. Many of you know the burden I carry, the stain of failed duty. My evil karma. Now I must die in this place to make amends. And a man committed to acceptance of death can accomplish much . . .''

Many eyes tilted groundward before his level gaze. No one doubted his sincerity. Thus fortified by their tacit understanding, Gonji continued:

''But those are the things which weigh against us, and I have not accounted the factors in our favor. We shall yet have unexpected help in our cause—''

''The Wallachians and Moldavians,'' a man in the rear shouted, standing and raising a clenched fist. ''They'll come to our aid!''

''Quiet now!'' Michael shouted, pushing free of Lydia's helping hand and leaning on the crutch. ''Gonji has the floor.''

He moved up to the table and turned to face the gathering.

"It's all right," Gonji objected. "Let him speak."

"Ruman unity will see the territory freed of invaders," the man added.

Gonji shook his head morosely. *"Iyé,* the Ruman independence movement is still too disorganized, too concerned with internal problems. No effective leader has arisen who can command the loyalty of all the provinces. There is simply not enough time. This place has gone rotten for you. It crawls with greed and evil on every hand."

"So what can we do?" Vlad Dobroczy fairly pleaded.

Gonji knew that he could delay the issue no longer. He clasped his hands behind his back and sighed as he paced around the table top.

"Evacuation," he rasped in High German, the word echoing in half a dozen translations amid head-shaking and confused hand waving.

"But—but I thought—" Aldo Monetto stammered. "You said that we'd have to abandon that idea after—" He weakly indicated the portal leading to the huge training chamber wherein lay the torched carcass of the great worm.

*"Hai,"* Gonji agreed, "that's true. We can no longer risk hiding the non-combatants down here for the duration. Not with the filthy sorcerer's knowledge of the place."

"So *what* then?"

"I mean that *everyone* must evacuate." A hushing bled off their breaths as they stared, disbelieving what they had heard. "My friends, you must leave Vedun behind until it can be cleansed."

"That's lunacy!" someone cried.

"Leave our homes? Everything we've worked for all these years?"

79

"Flavio's work of a lifetime?" Lydia spoke in unwonted dismay.

"For a time only, perhaps," Gonji answered gently.

"Never!"

"We'll not be driven from our homes!"

"What will we *do?*"

Gonji scowled. "Is this the only world you can conceive? The only one you've ever planned for? A life of oppression and stoic acceptance of death without raising a hand in your defense? You'll do what you must, take up new lives elsewhere until you can return to Vedun."

"It's madness. All of it."

"How would we even escape? Klann will stop any mass movement of—"

"That's only part of it," Gonji snapped. "This isn't to be a stampede of rabbits. The non-militant will be moved swiftly through the catacombs under heavy armed escort of married militiamen and brought out into the valley or the northern hills. Those tunnels are fortified but unblocked. Meanwhile, up above, the bulk of the fighting men will be locking horns with Klann's occupation troops, securing the city, and then defending against the reinforcements from the castle garrison, along with . . . whatever Mord raises against us. Once they're engaged and thus preoccupied, we rush every wagon in the city—fortified as best they can be—rush them out the west gate under the rest of the family men. They'll pick up the innocents along the way, load them into the wagons, and fly for safety in Austria. A good day's ride ought to bring you into Hapsburg territory, where Klann will be loath to follow. In any case," he sighed resolutely, "his command should be . . . considerably diminished by then. There'll be no one *to* follow."

"Ridiculous—" came the derisive cries once the translators had finished. Some stood as if to leave but were urged back into their seats by faithful *bushi*.

"What about the conscripts at the castle?" asked a farmer whose daughter had been taken as a servant.

"I was coming to that," Gonji responded, strolling again. "You see we're going to . . . take it back again . . ."

The simple confidence in the bold statement tore gasps from the onlookers. Gonji smiled thinly as he went on.

"Wilfred and I will lead a raiding party that will wrest Castle Lenska from the thieving bastards who've soiled it by their presence. We'll free the hostages and the castle servantry so that they may join you until it's fit to return and restore Vedun. To fortify it against future incursions."

"You keep speaking as if Vedun were a fortress, a military stronghold—" Milorad began.

"And so it is," Gonji shot back, eyes gleaming. "So it must be, my diplomatic friend. There is no way to think now—*fight or die.*"

"How will you mount enough men to attack Castle Lenska?" Roric thought aloud, shaking his head.

"It's not the manpower, Roric, it's the method," Gonji replied. "You know that. Maybe we'll turn some of Mord's deceptive tricks against him. You see, I say this all with utmost confidence because I want the traitor to tell Mord I'm coming for him. I want him to know that."

He smiled calmly, eyes half-lidded as if he envisioned an oracle of certain victory. Softly, he continued: "You see, I know Mord's power wanes. He grows weaker with each passing hour. His monsters die by the hands of puny men. Has any among you seen the wyvern trail its filth across your skies today? I thought not. I myself participated in his demise . . ."

A tremor of excitement and jostling. Whispers of awe.

Gonji spoke with quiet arrogance, wishing Mord to know it all, if indeed the traitor would be able to get word to him. It would be necessary for Mord to be enraged, his thinking

81

unhinged, his plans out of focus as he concentrated all his hatred on Gonji.

But was the traitor among them now? Among those he most trusted and most *dis*trusted?

*Hai.* The traitor was there. Somewhere. Pulsing with fear and wrath . . .

Wilf had stood as Gonji had mentioned his name. The young smith also now leaned against the table with arms folded.

"Can any of you doubt that we'll accomplish what Gonji says?" Wilf contributed with a forced pride that caused the samurai to stifle a smile. How well Gonji appreciated the company of the valiant and loyal *bushi* of Vedun.

His father cast his eyes groundward to hear Wilf's swaggering, while both his brothers seemed embarrassed.

"Oh—Aldo," Gonji said in sudden remembrance to the bearded biller Monetto, "don't forget to mount that party of worthies today to begin reopening the tunnel to the castle dungeons."

Monetto nodded, as he had been instructed to do.

It was a ruse. On reflection, any person who had seen the effective blocking of the tunnel in question—the supporting timbers fired, tons of earth and rock jamming the collapsed tunnel for an unguessable depth—would have known the impossibility of what Gonji asked. The samurai had taken Aldo into his confidence in this additional minor effort at keeping Mord off balance, should their plans be conveyed to him.

Madness must be met with madness, their plans sown with red herrings and apparent illogic.

"Garth," a man called out from behind the burly smith, "why does Klann refuse to see you now?"

"*Da*—were you not his trusted general once?"

Affirmations and questions echoed in reiteration. Garth seemed stung by the implications, whose innuendo defamed both his present and his past.

82

"I *tried,*" he retorted sharply, "and that is that." His ears reddened.

Lorenz rose at his side, the Executor of the Exchequer espying the accusers along his nose with courtly indignance.

"Who raises doubts regarding my father's integrity?" Lorenz bridled. "He rode to the castle and was rebuffed at the drawbridge. Captain Kel'Tekeli refused to see him unless he wished to speak of Gonji's whereabouts. Inasmuch as he possessed neither the knowledge nor the willingness the captain sought, he abandoned that tack. He next tried his old comrade Captain Sianno, who unfortunately hasn't been seen in the city since the revolt of the idiots—"

Here there was grumbling at the aspersion cast on the late Phlegor, his fate still unkown to them. A few craftsmen leapt to their feet.

"Watch it, Gundersen. Phlegor's a good man, and he has friends here."

Lorenz ignored them. "Now what would you have my father do? You all know me. I'm a rational man, will you all grant me that?" He kept talking without pausing to assess the muttering. "I believe that the militants are now right in saying that there's no recourse but a violent one. We must fight." With the single brandish of a fist, Lorenz relaxed, smoothed the creases from his well-cut doublet, and sat back down. There were shouts of assent among the groans.

Ignace Obradek cackled shrilly and slapped his thigh.

Gonji peered at Lorenz a moment, not liking the depersonalization in his phrase "the militants," which in a single cleverly inflected swoop both ignored Gonji's singular importance and voiced Lorenz's undying contempt for the very fighting men he had spoken in support of. And the off-handed remark directed at Phlegor and the craftsmen reminded Gonji of his own guilt over having set Julian to watching them in order to deflect suspicions of the real militia's effort.

"We'll have no more in-fighting," Gonji declared. "No

83

more bickering among factions within the city. We are one, or we are nothing. As for what the craftsmen did . . . They did what they felt they must at the time, believing Klann to be dead. It was a sound military principle, if ill-timed and undermanned. Now, I'm afraid, we must proceed in the belief that what Garth has told you is true—that Klann possesses more than one life." His voice had dwindled to a near whisper, but now he raised it to a sonorous command tone. "But his troops are quite mortal! We've all seen that. And we are united against them. The craftsmen have laid their weapons cache in the hills at the disposal of the militia, for which we thank them. And Phlegor—" Gonji's gloom permeated the chamber, though none knew the man's terrible fate save Wilf. "—if we never see Phlegor again, he should be thought of as a heroic defender of his city. Along with Master Flavio and Tralayn and all those others who have fallen."

A brief silence followed, punctuated by nervous coughing. Then Roric broke the spell.

"This business of the wagons, Gonji," the provisioner advanced, "are you sure there are enough of them to carry all the innocents away?"

Gonji turned his palms up. "They'll have to do, Roric."

Stefan Berenyi brightened suddenly. "Jacob Neriah's back in town with his caravan! Just back from the east yesterday. He must have twenty sturdy wagons and a dozen drays."

"That's right," Nick Nagy agreed.

"Are the draft horses nearby?" Gonji asked.

Both hostlers agreed readily.

"Sure," Berenyi said, "in the livery. Not all are at the Provender, though. Some few had to be sent over to the caravanserai at Wojcik's Haven. But there are teams for every wagon."

"Hmm." Gonji grew pensive. "There'll be tremendous pressure on you hostlers. You'll have to hitch the teams with all good speed when the time has come. Can you do it quickly and quietly enough?''

Nagy was scratching his tousled gray hair and frowning. They looked at each other across Nagy's wife and shrugged.

"You boys can do whatever you have to do," Magda said encouragingly, patting them both.

*"Igen,* sure," Nick grumbled. *"You* don't have to do any of the work!''

"She might as well, for all the work you do," Berenyi sneered.

"Hey, watch it, you little shit!"

They began snapping at each other in Hungarian, chuckles erupting all about them. Some of the tension leaked from the chamber, and Gonji let it run its course for a few seconds before clapping his hands sharply.

*Gentils,''* Michael Benedetto urged. "Shall we keep to the point? And do speak German, if you will.''

*"Hai, domo,''* Gonji agreed, smiling at the laughter.

Berenyi rubbed the back of his neck. "Well, there's no quick and quiet way to hitch wagon teams, you know.'' He shook his head. "No way to avoid attention.''

"Does it *have* to be this way?'' a voice pleaded from the audience.

*"Ja,* that's settled,'' Wilf called out impatiently. His left hand worked at the hilt of Spine-cleaver. Strom snorted from where he sat, slumped between his knees, eyes scanning the cavern floor. Lorenz curled his lip in distaste at his younger brother's posturing of leadership.

Gonji nodded gravely. "How's the hand, Stefan?''

Berenyi held up the left hand, still partially wrapped around the missing little finger. He grinned. "Doesn't seem to bother my work, but my *ken-jutsu* suffers a little. If I get behind, I'll just have to make Nagy work harder.''

Some good-natured laughter as Nagy reached across his wife with a gnarly hand as if to throttle his partner.

Gonji tugged at his chin thoughtfully. "We're going to have to create a diversion for you . . . or perhaps use the

85

wagons for some logical purpose so that their appointment for travel won't look suspicious . . ."

"I can't believe you're all really considering this," Boris Kamarovsky declared. "Leave your homes to . . ."

Some heads turned toward the craft guild party, anxious faces betraying their agreement with the wood craftsman's concern. Normally Boris would have sat with his best friend, Strom Gundersen. But Strom's seating with his father and the rest of the military council—particularly the indomitable oriental—had driven Boris to a rear bench with the rest of the alienated guildsmen. Boris's speech failed him and his eyes grew large and sheepish to see the adamant resolve of the council members.

"So how do we go about this?" the Gray knight Anton growled.

Gonji nodded curtly. "Ah—the rest of the plan. From this moment on, everyone in this room will proceed with the constant accompaniment of at least one other person here. Every one among us will keep watch over his partners. So sorry," he apologized to see the expressions his implication aroused, "but we have a traitor in our midst, and we must observe what security we can still muster. As moon-maddened as it may sound."

William Eddings rose, jaw working as if he would blare an imprecation that wouldn't come. He glared hotly at Gonji, tears brimming his eyes, but his family spoke to him softly and eased him back into his seat.

Gonji had gone on, paying it no heed: "There must be no fraternizing with Klann's troops, either Llorm or mercenary, beyond what discourse you must have with them in the pursuit of commerce. Spread the word in that matter, as it will be strictly enforced and violations will be investigated by me personally. I do have my suspicions as to the means by which the coward snivels intelligence to Mord—"

As he spoke Gonji's thoughts coruscated with anger, frustration, and a sense of futility over efforts at security. In

86

truth, he had no salient idea how the traitor plied the foul deed. It could have been accomplished in any one of a thousand ways: via notes, gestures, personal audiences with the sorcerer despite all attempts at vigilance, perhaps even by means of some mystical communication whose inscrutability might make Mord quiver with glee over their fumbling efforts.

He cursed to himself, his jaw tightening with the effort at self-control, and went on.

"Remember that I have my own operatives, and they're aware of the signs I'm watching for.

"So we work in pairs or groups of three. Teams will be given lists of citizens they will approach with our alert plan. Each team will cover one small sector of the city and report back to the council when their sector has been completed. You will tell them to prepare at once for the evacuation of Vedun. They make take only what they can carry; space will be at a premium on the wagons and on horseback. The riding steeds go to the militiamen, whose needs are first priority. Tell them all to be ready to evacuate on *the night following the full moon.*"

He paused dramatically to allow the timing to sink in.

"But," he continued, "they must prepare now. There will be no time for delays when the signal is given."

"What is the signal?" Jiri Szabo asked.

*"Shi-kaze—deathwind!"*

The entire gathering seemed to suck in a breath.

"When messengers come bearing the word *'shi-kaze,'* they must move the innocents at once through the chapel and down here, where they will be escorted out to wait the wagons."

"Such a clatter, they'll make!"

*"Ja,* how will we disguise our purpose?"

Michael held up a restraining hand and shuffled into their midst on his crutch. *"Si,* we've thought about that. As of tonight there will be a new service at the chapel at ten bells of

87

evening each night. A sort of . . . lamentation for the newly dead.''

"Soldiers haven't been near the chapel in the past two days," Wilf piped up.

"*Hai,*" Gonji added, "mercenaries are not fond of the reminders of suffering and death."

There was a building storm of protest and grumbling, the complexity of the task ahead becoming clear.

"Michael, do you truly agree to all this?"

*Ja—da—si!*"

"Fight or die," Gonji pressed, "by the hand of Mord. Remember that he is our chief enemy, even as Tralayn so often told us. Even Klann may not know what he's about. Enough dispute now. There isn't time for it. The duty lists will be prepared today. The raiding, escort, and harassment parties will be selected and their leaders appointed—"

"What about the weapons?" Dobroczy queried. "How will we retrieve those that are at the chapel? Most of the best long-range armament sits there—"

"*Si,* Gonji," Monetto agreed, "it wouldn't do to be going in after the weapons while the children are there."

Cries of abrupt realization.

Gonji blew out a breath and scratched his head. "Many of you still have your edged weapons, and there's a lot of light armor in the city, I know that. The firearms are easy enough to smuggle. You'll have to risk that, I'm afraid. And some-how—I'm not sure how—we'll have to use the soldiers' aversion to the many coffins in the chapel to get the armament. By the by—that was a fine idea, Paille, moving the weapons and armor up and placing them in coffins."

Paille petulantly waved off the compliment from where he stood with one leg on a bench near the wall. With one thumb he made small circles on the bridge of his nose, apparently lost in thought.

"How many coffins are still in the chapel?" Gonji asked of no one in particular.

"Too many," Milorad Vargo muttered through his snowy beard. "It's a scandal. You can't even pass along the aisles." Anna patted his arm sympathetically and purred in his ear.

"There must be close to fifty," Michael answered. "There's been a steady flow of obsequies, though. Probably fewer than half still contain actual bodies."

"Hmm." Gonji sagged under the onus of unfinished planning, the chaotic nature of their operation. Yet one channel of his mind wondered at Michael's recent reversal of attitude, his sudden spirit of cooperation. For the first time his eyes now met Lydia's. She seemed reserved, calm, her eyes heavy-lidded with fatigue and resignation.

*Ah,* he thought, *she's with child.* That must have some bearing on their thinking.

She looked lovely and fragile, a delicate blossom on a battlefield. Deep inside, a brittle laugh spiraled up to mock the samurai. Gonji cleared his throat.

*"All-recht . . ."* Gonji began, unsure of the words even as he uttered them.

But then Paille snapped his fingers and blared a gravelly laugh.

"Of course!" the mad artist cried. "We solve both problems at once—the wagon movement *and* the armament caskets." Anxious heads turned in reply. Given Paille's crazy turns of mind, he might propose almost *any* outrageous . . . "Not *all* the coffins have been kept at the chapel before interment. Some chose to take their dead to their homes so that they might lie in state before burial. Well now, all the other bereaved will choose to follow suit . . ."

He cast Gonji a cunning look.

Gonji caught his meaning and nodded. *"Ah, wakarimasu*—I see—Michael, did the troops take a body count of the citizenry?"

"I don't think so. They were preoccupied with their own slain."

89

*"Yoi*—good. Then the wagons will be hitched for the purpose of moving coffins to the homes of the bereaved. If there is no interference with the movement of the first few actual bodies, then we begin moving the armament coffins to strategic locations. These will then be the first stop for militiamen when the fighting starts." Gasps and whispers of shock.

Gonji went on, gleaming black eyes mirroring the images in his thoughts. "But that may not be enough . . . we'll also have to have raiding parties to attack the garrison's armory . . . and loot the dead soldiery . . . we should be grateful for this rainspell that that—"

"It's sacrilege!" Galioto the dairy stockman cried, his face a landscape of anguish. "Some of the bodies will already be corrupting. To deny them burial is—"

"That's right," Gonji said, picking up part of the man's line of concern, "we'll have to see what Verrico and the undertaker can do about retarding corruption. And keep the coffins sealed . . ."

A farmer jumped up, storming.

"Men of Vedun—come to your senses! Listen to what these madmen are ordering. The bodies of your loved ones corrupting in your homes—"

"Sit down, Yuschak," Michael called over the din.

"—our children, our women, the old folk all led down here like cattle to the slaughter. *Eaten* by beasts from the underworld. *Stung* to death so that they bloat like fish—like—like—like Baron Rorka!"

Aldo Monetto bounded over the benches, past the bodies that parted before his charge, to stand in the middle of the fearful dissidents.

"Listen to me, all of you," Monetto said, gesturing placatingly. "Now you all know me. You know that I give my heart to the defense of the city. My loyalty to the leadership of the council. To Gonji's devotion to our cause. You know that I tilted at the great worm from the

90

tunnels. Karl and I—some of the others here—we fought with it, helped destroy it, and are here now to tell of it. It's true that it was here, there's no denying the awful reality of it. But it's also true that its carcass now lies in ruin in that very cavern where we've trained so hard. It's now a monument to our hard work. That's so, no? Mord threw his best at us, and we *destroyed* it. At the last it went down like a hog in Roric's slaughterhouse, like some quail you've seen Karl down with his bow."

He paused briefly, glancing around the circling people. "Now you also know the size of *my* family, and my love for them. And I tell you that our homes are not safe. There's no sanctuary in Vedun anymore. Some of you saw what that giant did, dragging people from their homes. I see by your faces that you'll not forget, though you pray that the memory would lie still.

*"My* children will be evacuated from Vedun. And that's . . . all I have to say."

Gonji caught Aldo's eye and passed him a slight nod of gratitude.

"All this horror," someone whined in despair, unable to stave off the stomach-twisting fear and apprehension any longer. "Our families threatened. The holy chapel become an armory." He sobbed. "Flavio would not want that—"

"No!" Gonji cried. "Flavio would *not* want that!"

He leaped down from the table and stalked into their numbers with a cold and deadly expression, as if his intent were to strike a man dead. The chatter abated, and all eyes were on the samurai.

Gonji recognized the subtle turning in the group's spirit following Monetto's heartfelt obloquy. Resignation to fate. Malleability of will. Ignoring the cautions flung before his quick-stepping mind by the conscience of the Western child part of him, he moved in among them and began to shape their nascent resolution.

"Flavio would not want that," he repeated in Spanish, in which language—one of the earliest learned—he felt most comfortable at oratory.

"Flavio would not want to see his chapel filled with concealed weapons, his compatriots' dead denied a quick consignment to their graves. His friends in armed revolt . . .

"By now you've all heard how I failed in my solemn duty to protect Flavio. What you may not know is that I would have ended my own life that very day for this grave dereliction of duty. This bitter dishonor. Had not my good friends reminded me that"—his voice shrank to a hoarse whisper—"that Flavio would *not* want that." He paused, blinked, as if awaking from a dream.

"But tell me—what *would* Flavio want? He is beyond asking—may all good *kami* convey him to his reward—so we are left with asking ourselves. Would he have wanted us to hate Klann or his captains for what they've brought to us? No, Flavio would not want that. Nor are the Llorm troops, or even those mercenaries who do what they do because they know no other way, nor are any of these to be hated. Flavio, again, would not want that—*but* . . . to hate the evil that they do, the evil perpetrated by Mord. This alone would Flavio want in this business—that we hate the evil and fight it to the death, if necessary."

He clamped his hands behind him and strode with head down as he spoke now. "Flavio . . . was a great man. A man of shining idealism and firmness of belief that he adhered to all the days of his life. He should not have died in vain if we fight now to save the seed of his ideals: the dream of peace and freedom of worship and the brotherhood of men of all nations—and *you,* Vedun, are that seed!

"You cannot live and grow in this place any longer. You would be trampled under the hooves of dragoons; your women savagely used; your children dragged to

92

befouled dungeons and hideously sacrificed to the whims of the dark powers. And, I can assure you, Flavio would not want that. No . . . he would not. I think, if he were with us now, he would have to agree with the wisdom of our plan.

"That is all that I can think to tell you."

He moved back to the table, where he leaned and crossed his arms, listening to the breathy silence as the translators finished, feeling the congealing atmosphere of bitter acceptance.

Paille shattered the sepulchral spell. "Why the long faces? Can't you see the bright tomorrow to it all? When the town is cleansed, you can all return to your lives, to a new order, free of the yoke of—"

Ignace Obradek stood and cackled trenchantly, twisting and turning to crane his head toward the chamber's dim ceiling, as if his dead eyes could see something denied the rest of them. By his side, the gloomy Paolo kept his place and let him rant.

*"Posram shié niédam shié!"* the blind wagoner squealed, barely able to squeeze the words out between gusts of mirth.

Several men brayed at the words.

"What's that?" Gonji asked.

Most of the men near Gonji shrugged. Stefan Berenyi seemed about to reply, but the cultured crystal voice stopped him short.

"It's Polish," Lydia Benedetto explained. "Sort of an old man's battle cry: 'I'll shit myself, but I won't give up.' He seems to have become the spokesman for the city's solidarity."

Gonji nodded and smiled at her. She returned it. As cool in defeat as she was in victory, she had serenely accepted Vedun's future course. Some of the men had colored to hear her unaccustomed use of vulgarity. She, for her part, was unflinching. Gonji felt a pang of warmth over her graceful combination of beauty and self-assurance.

Deep inside, he found himself shaking off the effect of her charm.

"All right—*posram shié niédam shié,* then," Gonji said. His peculiar accent evoked laughter.

"Why must such things happen?" Milorad wondered aloud, grimacing behind his fleecy brows and beard like the wrathful spirit of the north wind. "What will posterity make of all this?"

"Why did we allow ourselves to be swept along into this madness?" a man seated behind him asked similarly.

But Gonji could make no answer that would satisfy either the city or himself.

"God must have some purpose in it," Michael ventured in reply.

"It is our *destiny,* good people," Paille declared, moving nearer now.

Lydia rose with stately grace and addressed the leaders. "You've set our course, so I ask you men only one thing. Why can't we appeal to Klann to allow the innocents to leave the city without harm to them? Surely the king is not so barbaric that he would wish to see children harmed."

Gonji smiled sadly through the mixed murmurs of agreement and objection. "I'm afraid, dear lady, that you continue to miss the point. There are none who are exempted from danger now. Mord is the enemy, and he wishes for all to be destroyed, so it would seem, even as Tralayn has said again and again. If there is any hope of success, then some semblance of secrecy and surprise must be preserved."

"How can there be any secrecy with a traitor among us?" The questioner was Vlad Dobroczy, his tone filled with scorn.

Gonji's brows knit, a grim shadow darkening his features. He began strolling, speaking as the argument

94

slowly crystallized.

"Point: if security is maintained," he began, "the coward may yet be prevented from reaching Mord with the new intelligence. Or the traitor may take one too many chances and find my sword lying in wait. Point: if Mord does learn of our plans, he may delay telling Klann, since the sorcerer seems to wish for rebellious action. His arrogant complacence will provide us just the advantage we need, and then the stupid *enchanter* will wind up at the end of my blade . . ." He grinned mirthlessly, allowing time for the insults to penetrate the listeners, more certain than ever that the one they were intended for was among them. *Taunt the enemy. Cause him to lose control of his center.* "Point: if Klann *does* learn our plans, I believe his position is tenuous enough that he will be forced to try to stop our action bloodlessly, perhaps . . ."

*"Perhaps,"* Lydia repeated tellingly.

"Perhaps," Gonji said firmly, "but we must assume that he wants no more trouble. That he can ill afford it."

"Bravo," Paille said, simple and quiet. He produced a wineskin and slugged at it. "The dream of liberty is well served by you, sir."

Gonji eyed him sidelong, stroking his stubbled chin and exhaling through his nose. Ignace crowed and chattered to himself in Polish again. The samurai glanced at him warily, fearing the blind man's senile outbursts. Security seemed only a fool's hope.

"Or Klann may find out and decide to crush us," Jiri Szabo muttered on a quaking breath, at the last appending a nervous laugh full of false bravado.

"Then, Jiri," Gonji said gravely, "we'll have to show them all what fools they've been to underestimate us, *neh?"*

Slumped over, face buried in his hands, Galioto the dairy stockman fretted, "It's really happening, isn't it? *We* can suffer through it. If we're to die, we grit our teeth,

95

shut our eyes, and bear up until it's done. But the *little* ones—the children—how do we make *them* understand?''

Gonji's stomach churned to hear the very real concern voiced. He thought of little Tiva, and of Eduardo and the rest of his band of urchins. Of Monetto's children. Roric's. Of the children of a hundred other fighting folk of Vedun whom he'd come to know and care for.

Karl Gerhard ambled up to him. "This is insane, of course," he sighed. "But we're with you, Gonji."

He extended his hand to clasp Gonji's, and all the other training leaders came forward to similarly pledge their lives.

*''Domo arigato,''* Gonji said gratefully when they had finished.

*''Doitashimashité,''* Wilf replied for all, grinning. "You're welcome."

Gonji was proud to have the determined young smith for a friend and sword-brother.

But then his entire demeanor altered. His eyes became hooded as if some private thunderhead crossed his brow. The crowd watched as he turned away from them and tied about his head once again the *hachi-maki*—the headband of resolution—he had frequently worn during training sessions.

Death before failure at his purpose.

He vaulted atop the table again, glowering like some hostile stranger. He rotated in a complete circle, saw the menacing shadow beyond the unhinged catacomb door, then the anxious faces arranged around him.

"Does none of you ask the nature of the assistance I've spoken of?" he inquired cryptically. The bewildered murmuring had barely begun when he smothered it—

*"You—traitor!"* He passed an arm over the audience. "Listen to me . . ." There followed an unendurable minute in which the samurai leveled a withering gaze at every man and woman in the cavern. Some could not meet

96

his eyes, though a few held them with vapid innocence. Others quailed and shrank back, though their cheeks were reddened more by indignance and insult than a sense of guilt. Some angled defiant, scornful stares at his oriental insolence. At length he spoke again.

"Do you believe I have no suspicion of your identity, you contemptible wretch! Or of your means of communication to Mord? Do you think I bluff when I speak of my operatives, who also know what I'm watching for? Then behold—!"

Screams and outcries of alarm. People jumped to their feet as the frigid blast of demon wind roared into the cavern, fluttering the torches, extinguishing most of them.

And then they saw the huge figure that appeared out of nothing behind Gonji, a limp body slung under one arm—

"It's the—it's the killer!"

"Ben-Draba's killer!"

"Simon!" Michael called out, eyes shining with recognition. Beside him, Lydia stared in abject terror, all her fears of the rational world gone mad embodied in this charmed being who had disturbed her sleep the past year.

"Be seated, all of you," Gonji said. "There is nothing to fear."

Gradually they resumed their seats. The wind stilled, and the torches were relighted. The sentries gaped at the catacomb doorway, amazed that the eerie apparition had passed their posts unnoticed, though Gonji had challenged them that it would happen.

Behind the table, Simon slowly lowered the corpse of the mercenary. The man's neck was twisted at an unnatural angle. Eyes bulging, some of the nearer watchers clutched their throats in sympathetic horror. Simon's eyes of flint-sparked iron glanced about the room, darting feverishly like those of a cornered stray dog. Less threatening than warding, advising distance.

Gonji tilted his head in silent command, and the sentries removed the dead mercenary. He studied Simon a moment, then turned to the crowd.

"This is Simon Sardonis, a warrior whose . . . unusual abilities need no introduction in Vedun. He is our ally. Come to our aid at the behest of the good monks of Holy Word Monastery, who've suffered horrible death at the hands of Mord. There will be an accounting . . ." He let the words hang in the air a moment, then nodded to Michael.

The young council leader addressed the gathering. "We must move quickly now. First, a benediction. We'll pray for God's blessing on our efforts."

Most of the gathering dropped to their knees and bowed their heads as Michael led the prayer. Gonji joined in, assuming a Shinto prayer position. He caught a glimpse of Simon, whose lips moved silently, though his body trembled as if in pained concentration. When it was over Michael took charge again.

"First I'll call forward the pairs assigned to the alert-plan lists. All militia leaders will stay behind for specific orders. I also need you hostlers—and the founders and . . ."

"Remember,' 'Gonji bellowed, "the night after the full moon—*shi-kaze.*"

He moved to a corner of the cavern where Simon stood alone.

"How do you do that?" he asked.

"What?"

"That wind—the elemental display."

"I *don't* do that. It just . . . happens."

Then Garth and Wilf came forward, a few of the other training leaders trailing close behind, and the smith offered Simon a goblet of wine, which he accepted with a somber nod. Nervous introductions were made, Simon

98

clearly ill at ease with being out in the open among so many of the blatantly curious.

Gonji moved off with his wine to observe in silence awhile. Study their interactions. Watch individuals for telltale signs. Listen to conversations, questions. Be vigilant for—what?

*Choléra* . . .

He scanned their faces, tried to stretch out with his will, read their minds. As the assignments were discussed, he began to fancy that certain of their faces, their eyes, effused a radiance, a nimbus effect.

*The touch of the* kami *who augured death.*

He shook himself and stopped looking. It must have been the wine.

The traitor watched him, fought to stifle the roaring laughter within.

The barbarian idiot suspected nothing. He was merely a blundering, angry child who brayed and blustered about unspoken clues that were as insubstantial as moonbeams.

*Soon.* So soon at hand—the heritage that's been denied me. The life I should have been born to. And the slant-eyed fool will lead the way to its achievement. When Mord has what he wants, then I shall have what is mine.

It's all so amusing. How intriguing the game!

The traitor's throat made a small hacking sound in shackling the tittering the others would find uncharacteristic. Rancor welled up at having to avoid even so small a manifestation of the gargantuan mirth within.

They might ask. And I don't think I could resist telling them. No-no, that would be unwise, oh yes indeed. The time for the celebration will come. Very very soon now.

Him.

I don't like him, that—Simon. Who is he? *What* is he? The one Mord speaks of? Yes, that must be. But why does

Mord fear him so?

And what does *he* have to do with him? That . . . king of fools.


Paille was speaking to Gonji, dashing his reverie. "Eh?"

"I say, friend Red Blade," Paille repeated, clearing his throat in mock peevishness, "would it tax your Far Eastern sensibilities too severely to hear me out for a moment? I said that since my recovering from our night of crapulence I have been perpending our course of action, and it has occurred to me—"

Then Paille was unrolling a bundle of sheets on which were crude drawings. He began to declaim concerning da Vinci, and certain of da Vinci's military inventions and designs, and something about using some of the wagon fleet as both a diversion and an offensive weapon. But although Gonji bobbed his head in a show of earnest sympathy and interjected an encouraging word now and again, his mind was focused on the far wall where Michael Benedetto now approached Simon. Sheepishly, in that polite, light-footed manner that both belied his stocky frame and made him much coveted as a friend, Garth stepped backward gingerly a few steps and then turned softly to leave the pair alone.

Gonji watched him move off across the cavern, floppy cap in hand, then recalled something that had been troubling him.

*"Oui-oui,* Paille," he said apologetically, "that sounds well worth looking into, but you'll excuse me one moment, *neh?* Continue showing the others. I'll be back."

Paille sneered. "So, my moment is up, eh, *monsieur le samurai?* Well don't blame Paille when all your plans crumble around your ears . . ."

Gonji intercepted Garth.

"My friend, we'll need your sound military mind here awhile," the samurai said, "whether you'll be taking part in the action or not."

Garth thought for a moment, bowed wearily and moved into step with Gonji back toward the table. Gonji halted them.

"Garth, listen, something . . . I've been thinking, that I dreamed or you told me—" He fumbled with his hands in perplexity. "Anyway, I keep thinking of you when it comes to mind—what is 'the tainted one'?"

Garth's jaw sagged. *"Ja* . . . don't you remember—the Chronicle of Tikah Vos?"

*"Ah, so desu*—your parchment scroll."

"The reference to the one Klann-child of the seven that was born . . . malformed . . . strange—something. In my years with Klann I never knew him to speak of it."


"Was it necessary to make so violent an entrance?" Michael asked Simon nervously. "Some of the people were—"

"Upset by the sight of the monster that's come to them," Simon finished. He averted his eyes self-consciously, staring down at the unaccusing beverage casks along one wall.

Michael winced. "No-no, Simon, that's not at all what I meant."

"What then?"

"I meant . . . I meant that bringing an enemy's corpse in here like that . . . so cold-bloodedly—it—it bespeaks a vengefulness, a call to bloodletting for its own sake."

"Vengefulness," Simon repeated hollowly. He peered up at Michael, his eyes suddenly filled with a pitiable mixture of pain, alienation, and moral confusion. "Isn't that what you came to me and pleaded for on the day your brother was murdered?"

Michael stumbled back a pace, head hung low, a harpy

of guilt clawing at his soul. He moved slowly to the bench where Lydia sat, expressionless.

"What's wrong?" she asked gently.

He sighed. "Me, I suppose."

Her brow furrowed, but she let the comment pass. "So—Simon has come back. I suppose I should have expected it."

"If he had been welcomed as a man long ago," her husband said in a voice fraught with self-accusation, "instead of as a *thing* . . . If he had been accepted the way my poor brother accepted him, then maybe it wouldn't have been necessary for him to come now. For this. Maybe Flavio would still be alive. And a lot of other people with him."

She pondered his words. Her lips parted, but she said nothing.

A curious surprise came to them in the cavern an hour later. One that refueled Wilf's passion to get a crack at formidable Castle Lenska.

Most of the gathering had cleared to the surface. There remained a clutch of city officials, headed by Milorad and Anna Vargo, who sat on benches and clucked and fretted over the city's immediate future. Grouped around the long table were the militia captains: Gonji, Michael, Garth, Anton, Roric, Wilf, Monetto, Gerhard, Berenyi, Szabo, and Nagy. A few pairs of militiamen had been sent up to begin apprising their assigned sectors of the alert plan. The military leaders finalized their company and squad rosters and planned the synchronized raids and pitched defenses calculated to seize back the city from the occupation force with a minimum of risk.

It was decided that if the evacuation through the catacombs and the wagon dispatch could be brought off carefully, there was a fighting chance at recovering the city. However, the grim realization of the heavy reinforcement column that was sure to hurtle down from the castle (in addition to the cretin giant and whatever else Mord might be able to raise against them from the nether-worlds—which subject was tactfully sidestepped) left the leaders rather glum.

To smother their despair, Alain Paille showed the sketches of his "armored wagons," borrowed from da Vinci's designs. A small thrill of optimism gripped them when they viewed the cross-sectional drawings of large commerce wagons plated in the inside with steel from the foundries and cut through with loopholes for firing at enemies. They were topped by portable cupolas for the drivers and their accompanying crossbowmen or pistoliers and drawn by teams of armored destriers.

"Not terribly fast, given all the weight I calculate," Paille judged, "but they'll *move*. And motion will be of paramount importance, eh?"

"Rolling drum towers," Roric described them, holding up his son for a better look.

"Very nice," Gonji agreed warily, "but the practicality of their fashioning remains to be seen, *neh?*" Some of the optimism fled the band.

Through it all Simon sat apart from them, listening to their planning but contributing nothing. Wilfred began to wonder at this mystery man's role, a bit miffed at his aloofness. The young smith decided he rather disliked the man and distrusted his seeming lack of dedication. After all, what vested interest had Simon in the fate of Vedun? Who was he? What did he stand to gain? And why had his identity and purpose been withheld by some of those Wilf most trusted and loved: his father, Gonji, Michael and Lydia?

That was when they were treated to the surprise.

One of the *bushi,* a provisioner, emerged from the tunnel that led to the chapel. Breathless, about to say something. Strom's voice called out from the flickering lamplight of the tunnel:

"Hey, do ya mind?"

All heads in the cavern turned. Strom and Lorenz, who had ascended earlier with their alert list, returned now.

Each held Lottie Kovacs by one arm. Strom grinned slyly, his squirrely brown eyes searching out his father.

"Lottie!" came shouts and whispers in several voices.

Wilf gaped. "Lottie's back," he breathed, rushing forward to the slender blonde woman, mystified.

Anna Vargo was the first to observe social propriety, moving to the girl in her arthritic pain to hug her tearfully and offer her condolences. Others followed, leaving Wilf on the fringe, beside himself with curiosity and excitement.

"Lottie," Wilf broke through at last, "Lottie, how did you—?"

"*I* smuggled her in," Strom declared proudly, "true, Lottie?"

A small smile creased the girl's narrow, doleful face. *"Igen,* Strom was very brave."

"But what about—?"

*"Hold it,"* came Gonji's paralyzing shout in High German. The samurai strode forward, scowling. "Will someone tell me what's going on here?"

Wilf realized that they had all been speaking in Hungarian, keeping Gonji in the dark. He grinned and waved off the *sensei's* suspicion. "It's Lottie Kovacs, Gonji—Genya's good friend. Her father was the lorimer murdered on the day of the occupation," he appended with a respectful head bow. But his enthusiasm returned instantly. "But how did you get away from the castle? What did Strom have to do with it? What about Genya? How is she?"

"Slowly, Wilfred," his father cautioned. "Give the girl room to breathe." Garth ambled toward Strom, eyeing his puffed posturing curiously.

Lottie flicked her gaze over their looks of anticipation, blanching noticeably when she saw Gonji stroking his beard, his dark eyes riveting her. "I—uh . . . it was the night the king left for Vedun, for the banquet. I just . . . couldn't stand the place any longer. I arranged to be smuggled out in a dray leaving the bakehouse for Vedun, under some empty grain sacks. I was fortunate. There was no search. But I knew I couldn't press my luck. A search *might* be made at the main gate to the city. So I . . . I slipped out in the hills. Saw Strom. I knew I could trust him, but I feared to try to enter the city. I thought they might be searching for me. Strom hid me in the hills. He insisted on helping me steal into the city when I had the courage to try. We did so tonight. When the late herdsmen drove in their flocks, we mixed with them. That was very brave of you, Strom." She smiled distantly at him. The shepherd was red-faced and beaming.

"What about Richard?" Wilf found himself asking. "Why didn't he try to escape with you? Bun-brains had no stomach for it? And what about Genya?" he added in a rush, not allowing her to answer.

Lottie nodded mechanically, staring at a fixed point on the far wall. "Yes, Richard and Genya were to escape with me. But they were . . . detained. I couldn't wait. Couldn't bear another night in that place. So I left . . . without them."

Wilf made a gesture of understanding, but a look of unease gripped him.

"Wilf," Gonji said evenly, "tell me everything she said. Omit nothing."

Wilf blinked. He translated her tale slowly, an aura of hostility descending on them. He saw the critical looks some were leveling at Gonji. Saw the steely eyes of Simon, the eyes of a watchdog. While he spoke, Wilf noticed that Boris Kamarovsky stood at the tunnel entrance, observing nervously. Since the time Gonji had chased him and

105

Strom from the training ground, Boris had never approached within fifty feet of the oriental.

"Strom," Gonji asked when Wilf had finished, "why didn't you bring the girl through the northern hill tunnel, if you were already concealing her in the hills?"

"Hey," Strom grunted, spreading his hands in appeal. When he spoke to Gonji, his eyes fluttered and grew large and liquid, defensive. And his eye contact always engaged a point somewhere on the ceiling above the samurai's head. "I don't even know where the north tunnel comes out," he said. "And everybody told me the catacombs weren't safe anymore, true?"

Wilf saw Gonji's thoughtful expression, wondered at the samurai's suspicion. What Strom said was certainly possible. He had had no opportunity to learn of the exit of the tunnel in question, and the catacombs had been regarded as rather less than savory since the battle with the great worm.

Garth moved to his youngest son, a bit miffed at Gonji's tone. "You *could* have told someone, *nicht wahr?*" he advised with a forced chuckle. "Not like the Strom we know, eh, Lorenz?"

*"Ja,"* the Exchequer agreed, smiling and cocking an eyebrow, "he usually tells me everything he's about, if not you, Father. What's going on in there these days, dunderhead?" He indicated Strom's skull, but the shepherd waved him off.

"I just wanted to do something to help, by myself," he explained, "without maybe getting other people in trouble. Hey, everybody's always telling me I talk too much, and now you all change your minds when I keep something to myself, *nicht wahr?*" Oppressed and bristling, he pulled away from them, eyes darting in childlike hurt.

But Garth approached him and smiled, clamped a thick hand on his shoulder and nodded paternally. "Passing

106

fair courage, my son. You've made me proud this day."

Strom grinned, his mood brightening.

Lydia *tsked* and moved forward. "Lottie, dear, you look much the worse for your ordeal. You'll need a bath, and some suitable dress—"

Anna joined her in fussing over the escapee, and it was quickly determined that Lottie should stay with the Vargos at least until the evacuation.

At Wilf's side, Monetto kidded Gerhard in a hushed tone.

"Your old flame, eh?" Aldo jerked a thumb at Lottie.

A wry twist reshaped Karl's long face. "That was a long time ago."

"Last *year,*" Jiri Szabo reminded him.

"Ah, she never even looked at him once," Berenyi joked impishly. "What girl wants a hunter when she can have a 'bun-brains'?"

Karl snorted. *"Ja,* she made her decision. She'd rather have tarts on her table than fresh meat every day."

Lottie left presently with the Vargos.

Strom and Lorenz returned to the surface with Boris, and the meeting of leaders broke up. Gonji asked Garth to send for the itinerant merchant Jacob Neriah. The smith, still rather vexed at Gonji's suspicious treatment of his youngest son's valor, replied sullenly that he would do so.

Wilf monitored their chilly exchange, saw Gonji stare after the departing steps of the group that included Lottie, and worried over Gonji's strange turn of mind since their tilt with the worm-thing. How long would it be before he began suspecting even Wilf himself of being the traitor who obsessed his thinking?

Jacob Neriah descended to the cavern with much amusing ado about his shame at having had to pass through a Christian chapel. Flavio's dearly beloved longtime friend was nonetheless serenely resigned to the

107

city's commandeering his wagon fleet, if it would help wreak vengeance against the Elder's slayers. He stayed but briefly and reentered the chapel tunnel with an appeal to Yahweh for forgiveness.

His visit had been comforting to Gonji: The likeable merchant had been the first person he'd seen treat Simon Sardonis with polite disinterest and the same social grace he would tender any man.

When he had gone, only Gonji, Paille, and Simon remained.

"I'll be taking my leave now," Simon said, moving for the doorless portal to the main cavern.

"Where will you be?" Gonji inquired.

Simon ignored the question. "When you're in need of me again, I'll be about. *Bon jour.*" But when he reached the doorway, he paused and glanced over his shoulder.

"I hope you realize at what cost I've fulfilled this request of yours."

Gonji bowed to him solemnly. *"Domo arigato, Simon-san."*

"Whew," Paille breathed when he had departed. "What in the hell did that mean?" He unlidded his flagon and took a draught, sloshing wine over his tunic.

Gonji smiled wanly. "He's very frank in front of you, Paille. I think he's comfortable with madmen."

The artist sneered. "As well he might be—what was that all about?"

"I'm afraid this was all quite new to him. I doubt that he's ever been in the presence of so many people before. At least . . . not so many who mean him no harm."

Paille wagged his head. "Of what possible use will this . . . *Deliverer* be?"

"I suppose we'll all find out soon enough." Gonji's whole body creaked with every movement. His feet were swollen, his eyes red and sore, and his back, legs, and arms felt anvil-beaten. "I need sleep."

"Later, then. I'll confer with the founders first about this wagon armament business."

"Don't you ever sleep?"

"Sleep?" Paille snorted. "I loathe those little snatches of death—especially when there's work to be done." He peered into the darkness beyond the main cavern doorway. "Well, at least his French is excellent, which is more than I can say for some of us here. He reminds me, somehow, of my brother Jacques . . ."

Gonji slumped heavily onto a bench. "Paille," he said, a gleam in his eye, "why do you stay here?"

Paille's eyebrows arched. "Why, that's a silly question, *monsieur*. I have my work, of course, and the cause of freedom, which must be—"

"Stop that claptrap, and speak German or Spanish—"

*"Monsieur!"*

"With your talent you could find more lucrative work in the great cities. And it certainly isn't for friendship that you stay in a place where they regard you as an eccentric at best."

An uncharacteristic wistfulness softened the artist's mien. "Flavio," he said simply. "He commissioned a painting from me, you see, while I was working in Italia. Wrote me the fondest letter of compliment I've ever read. I decided I could do no better than to work near such a kindly patron. I would fain tell you otherwise, were it so. Such sentimentality abrades my cynical image, but—"

Gonji's indulgent smile hardened him again. Embarrassed to have so bared his soul, he said: "Go to sleep, you look terrible."

And with that he left Gonji alone.

The samurai checked on the cavern sentries and then stretched out on a pile of blankets to sleep. Found that it eluded him. The gently lapping waves of his drifting thoughts broke against shoals of guilt.

What was the last estimate of Klann's strength? *Six*

*hundred.* Plus Mord's unknowable power, wavering or not . . .

Gonji pondered what he had told them all of the evacuation on the night after the full moon, and his sense of duty assailed him over his deceit. There would be hell to pay, he knew. But it must be done this way. The interest of surprise must be served, at whatever price in the chaos that might result. But the worst of it was the dreadful consequences of Simon's learning that he had been lied to.

*On the full moon Mord would receive a fresh imputation of Satanic power . . .*

*Hai,* it had to be this way.

That was karma.

At the end of the Hour of the Dragon, just as sleep overcame him, he snapped awake with a strained cry and drew steel. Wilf stood over him, ashen and goggle-eyed.

"They just escorted my father to the castle," the smith said in an awed whisper. "Klann sent for him . . ."

## Chapter Five

Lottie sat staring absently into the crackling hearthfire. Anna crept up behind her and wincingly draped a quilt around the girl's shoulders. Then she padded to the butler's pantry, where Milorad huddled over his broth. He pulled at a chunk of brown bread and sipped a cup of mead.

"Lottie all right?" he asked, looking up when his wife entered.

"*Ano*—yes, but she's very shaken by her ordeal." She

eased into a chair, grimacing.

"This blasted rain. It increases your pain, doesn't it, *mily?*" he asked. "Beloved."

"No," she reassured him, forcing a smile, "not very much."

He drifted off, muttering into his bowl of broth, something that ended with ". . . Flavio." It might have been a prayer. He missed his old friend greatly. Leaving his meal half completed, he pushed away from the table and retrieved a cloak from the foyer closet.

"The *Japonsky* never brought back my good capote, did he?"

"Going out again so soon?"

He nodded sullenly. "I'm to join with Ignace and Paolo on this alert business. Can't see why they need me along."

"Gonji trusts your experience," she reasoned. "I think he fears Ignace's doddering, and Paolo is young and over-eager."

Milorad grunted, but his chest puffed with pride. "Get it done with, then," he said in an official voice. "Not so many houses on our list."

"Just be careful. Are you dressed warm enough?" Anna rose and rearranged the folds of his cloak such that nothing showed but his face. He impatiently pulled it open against the abrupt stuffiness.

"Anna," he said, his anguish deepening the age lines in his face, "we've had a good life, haven't we?"

She embraced him. "Done many things few will ever do. We've much to be grateful for."

"It doesn't make it any easier, does it?"

She closed her eyes and kissed him. "God is with us."

He slouched to the door, but when he opened it and stepped out into the rain, and public view, conditioned reflex reshaped his frame into the dignified, courtly posture on which he prided himself.

Anna smiled at his back, the smile melting all too

111

quickly. She moved to the table and began to clear it. When she got to the half-empty cup of mead, she raised it in her palms and drained it off at a single gulp.

His risky meeting with the confidant in the Provender's storm cellar completed, Gonji crept through the rain-slicked alleys and byways of Vedun like a nimble thief.

So many matters to attend to; so many apprehensions. And so very little time.

Sleep had come with difficulty, though his body had begged for it, and it had lasted all too briefly. His eyeballs felt burned and twisted, as if they'd been screwed into their sockets. He wore Milorad's huge, billowy capote over his tunic and breeches—plenty of room in the loose folds for his *daisho,* which he now wore almost vertically in his sash so that their telltale angles would not protrude—and the great foppish slouch hat Wilf had loaned him. This curious concession to the dandy's appointments seemed ill-befitting Wilf, who had blushed when Gonji had chuckled to see it, topped, as it was, by the splendid feather Wilf had gruffly allowed him to remove. The slouch now sagged and buckled under the hood of the capote, concealing most of Gonji's face.

Good old Wilf.

Gonji darted to the head of an alley and peered out from behind a drain at a passing dragoon squad. Few soldiers were about, driven indoors by the rain and the funerary cast of the city: much of the commerce was arrested in favor of the drawn-out process of burying the many dead. The sham seemed to be working well.

But now as he peered at the Llorm dragoons, something bothered the samurai. What was different?

Ah—the circles. A *third* circle in Klann's crest was now filled in with purpure on their uniforms and standards.

He ducked into the alley and doubled back toward the south to check in with the metal founders. A shutter cracked open above his head, giving him pause an instant, but he moved on at once. Had to be citizens, in this quarter.

He heard a bump through the rain sputter. Then something struck his left shoulder, and a noisy splat sounded on the paving stones just short of the gutter cut through the center of the narrow lane. His nose at once picked up the acrid stench.

"Damn it!" he swore low. "Damned filthy Europeans!"

The shutter slammed closed. Someone had chosen that moment to empty a chamber pot into the gutter below. Milorad was going to adore the new stain on his capote. Gonji rubbed the cloak's shoulder against a rough stone wall, grimacing at the fecal stench, and moved on.

A clutch of wagons lumbered along Provender Lane, their drivers somber and circumspect. They were escorted by a few citizens on horseback. No soldiers in sight.

As the first wagon ruddled near his alley, Gonji burst out of cover to run alongside, startling one of the mounts. He clambered up to drop into a seat beside the city's tall slender undertaker. The man lurched in surprise, did a double-take, then smiled and bowed.

"Fine weather for an interment," the man said in Italian.

Gonji scowled. The undertaker's assistant pushed his head through the burlap curtain, red-eyed from fatigue.

"Gonji!" he gasped. He was one of the *bushi.*

*"Ohayo*—good morning. What are you carrying?"

"One corpse," the mortician apprised, "one magazine of shot and powder." He showed his large white teeth.

"Whew," Gonji breathed. "Don't invite any gunfire your way, eh? And keep that casket from getting too wet. Seepage will ruin the powder, if the dampness hasn't already."

The undertaker bobbed his head, rolling in his seat as

the wagon bounced up onto a wooden bridge over a sewer culvert.

"They say Garth Gundersen's been called to the castle," the assistant said animatedly.

"I've heard," Gonji replied.

"Maybe we'll be spared the evacuation, the . . . fighting." The young man's raw eyes swerved from Gonji's. His adam's apple pistoned once in his throat.

"That's a fond hope we should maintain," Gonji said. "But in the meantime we must prepare for the worst, *neh?*"

The young *bushi* nodded morosely. The undertaker *hmmed*. Whether in affirmation, reflection, or by virtue of his sinister dispensation, Gonji could not tell.

"Drop me off at the foundry," the samurai said. The undertaker touched the brim of his black slouch.

Gonji had been forced to sit with his left side stretched uncomfortably because of the sashed swords, so he found it easy to roll off the wagon and bound into a small courtyard about a block from the foundry when they saw the mounted mercenaries before the smoke- and steam-spewing building.

"Godspeed, *sensei!*" he heard the raspy voice utter behind him as he ducked behind a corner. His tongue worked at his moist upper lip as he chanced a peek.

Three brigands. None he knew. Could they still be searching for him? No, that was silly. The scuttlebutt at the Provender was that he had gone for good. Cleared out for safer pickings like the scavenger he was. The more who were convinced of that, the better off he was.

The rain slanted down like a dirty gray curtain, soaking the city. The culverts had begun to fill, waste rising to street level. The sluice gates were opened early, and the sound of their cranking nearby caused the mercenaries to turn their heads away from Gonji's position.

He sprinted across the street and wove his way nearer

114

the foundry. He was fairly close to the Gundersens' now, he knew, as well as Tralayn's dwelling, and the mercenary garrison in the southwest quadrant. Caution.

Loping to an alley adjacent to the foundry, he slowed to a fast walk, listening intently, pulling the slouch hat's brim lower.

So intent was he on the foundry clamor to his left, that he didn't notice the mounted man seated motionless in the lane to his right until it was too late.

An electric tremor ran up and down his back, his nape prickling so that he thought he must fairly glow. He strode across the man's field of view, then angled into a doorway, ignoring the soldier's curt shout in a language he didn't know. Gonji leaned into the doorway—a side entrance to the foundry—listening to the approach of the splashing hooves. One hand on his hip, he placed the ridge of his right over his eyes as if dazed or in pain.

The mercenary dismounted and said something twice in an inquiring tone. The metallic snick of a sword being unsheathed.

Gonji felt the firm hand on his shoulder. Then the Sagami was out and up over his head in a two-handed grip, slashing the sentry from clavicle to hipbone through his breastplate. His scream was muffled by the closed buffe of his Flemish burgonet, and Gonji's finishing stroke cut it short. He dragged the body into the doorway and shooed the horse back into the lane. Cast about for some divine suggestion as to his next move.

The armed party at the front of the foundry pounded off—five of them now. *All* of them? He had to take the chance. Battered on the foundry's side door. Waited. A second, harder knock—

The door swung open.

"Holy—!"

"Quiet," Gonji growled at the founder, pushing him back and dragging the dead mercenary inside. There were gasps of shock amid a few anxious greetings. Jiri Szabo moved to the fore.

"Gonji, what—what—?"

"Never mind that," Gonji said brusquely. "What are *you* doing here?"

"We finished our alert list, so I came back here to help. I'll tell you, people are finding it hard to accept—"

Gonji snarled at him. "I told you to stay in pairs. Where's Anton?"

"Staying with the Yuschaks," Jiri replied defensively. "I thought that was only for the *alerting*."

The samurai waved a hand. "Damn it all. Is it clear outside?" he discarded Wilf's sopping slouch hat and donned the dead man's burgonet.

*"Ja,"* one of the others answered nervously.

"How goes it? What did those free companions want?"

"Just to see about weapons orders, that's all," Jiri said. "They gave us a start, though."

"How's that?"

"We were bolting sheets of steel to the insides of those wagons out front when they arrived," a large founder with a scarred face replied. "They didn't check, though."

Gonji nodded, tight-lipped. "Get rid of that body."

"Where?"

He thought a moment. "How about one of the empty coffins after the armament has been removed?"

Someone laughed coarsely. *"Ja*—if there are any left when Paille gets done."

"Eh?"

"He was here at ten bells," the scarred man explained. "We had three sides of one of those damned heavy cuploa-things riveted together when he came pounding in here and screaming at us to stop. Said something about figuring that they won't work—too heavy—something."

"Said they'd topple on turns," Jiri appended.

"Went to the woodcrafters with another crazy

116

idea—he's got 'em making *wooden* cupolas now out of those same empty coffins you're talking about!"

Gonji shook his head.

"Madman's gonna get us all in big trouble," the man judged.

"We're already in big trouble," Gonji observed.

They spoke a bit longer about matters of imminent concern. Like the others Gonji encountered during the day, the founders fostered earnest hopes of Garth's success at convincing Klann of Mord's treachery. Gonji tried hard not to shatter their optimism, but he could not help recalling Simon's discouraging reminder of how potentially volatile such a meeting would be. Gonji found himself hoping only that Garth's diplomacy was equal to the task.

He reconnoitered the city all day, commandeering the dead mercenary's steed. The buffe of the helmet snapped shut, he was recognized by no one and asked nothing. The dampering rain helped him considerably, and he discreetly avoided areas of heavy military traffic.

The heavens offered no sign that their outpouring would cease, and Gonji was reminded of the monsoon season, when most activity that was not of a vital nature came to a halt. In Vedun, such activity had barely begun.

At the Hour of the Monkey, hunger having come to him in fluttering waves of nausea, he turned into the back lane that would bring him to the Benedettos' rear courtyard. There he would huddle with Michael over tactics, insinuate himself into their evening meal, and—

The wet slosh of hooves and the jangle of bridles turned into the lane behind him. Three horsemen? *Four?*

*"Jof,"* came a shout, followed by a high voice jabbering in Low German.

*Choléra,* Gonji thought, striving to regulate his rapid breathing.

*"Jof,"* again—a man's name. They had perhaps taken

him for the brigand whose horse he rode.

He reined in and yanked the animal around to face them. Three. Flemish burgonets, shields lashed to their backs. Looking grim. He kept the buffe in place, Milorad's tent-like capote concealing the rest of him. The man who had called out was waving a soggy paper in his right hand.

They closed the distance swiftly, cantering confidently toward their fellow soldier.

Gonji emptied his mind of all thoughts but one as he clopped near: *no witnesses*. He saw where they carried their swords and spied a crossbow slung across one man's back. When they were twenty yards distant, they peered suspiciously through the pelting rain. One of them suddenly jabbered at the others. By the contortion of the mercenary's face, Gonji knew instantly that he had been pegged for an impostor.

The centermost brigand tore his cloak open and clawed for a pistol. Gonji jabbed his mount's sides and launched at him, the folds of the capote flapping like wings as he wrenched free the Sagami.

He heard a shout and the sputter of a pistol's misfire as he swung his bulk behind the horse's head to shrink the target. Then he was on top of the pop-eyed assailant. His slash tore through jack and ribcage, a crimson spray accompanying the mortal scream.

Yanking right, he engaged the crossbowman, whose blade became entangled in his heavy cloak. But the free companion's frantic spurring caused his steed to leap out of Gonji's range. The man leaned hard left, and his horse skidded on the slick cobblestones and toppled with a fierce whinny into a courtyard wall.

Gonji wheeled his mount, saw another pistol leveled in his direction, lashed the beast toward the crossing lane from which the three had emerged.

He heard the explosion behind him, felt a jolting impact

as the horse bucked under him, the shock racing straight through his loins.

Then his seating fell out from under him—the horse had been struck in the left flank by the pistol ball and went down, shrieking, to its knees. Gonji bounced off and slammed face first in a muddy pool, cracking his knee, a sudden exquisite pain erupting in his mouth as he rolled with the fall. He scrabbled for the downed *katana,* picked it up in a bleeding hand, and, stumbling once on the hem of the billowy capote, sprinted in ungainly fashion toward the corner of the intersection.

He heard the "hyah!" behind him and the splash of determined hooves. Tasted blood in his mouth, felt the stiffening of the knee as he reached the corner and turned right.

The Sagami poised in his burning grip, he took his stance and waited.

The rider swung his mount wide on the slick paving stones. Gonji had cut the short distance in half before the man caught his approach and hoisted steel. The mercenary's heavy blade arced downward. Gonji deflected it with a high parry, whirled and completed the circle with a slash that knocked him, whining, from the saddle.

The samurai grabbed the horse's reins, calmed his skittish stamping, and, cursing in a low growl, pushed himself achingly atop the animal. Riding back into the lane where the initial confrontation had occurred, he came to a jarring halt.

*"Choléra-*pox!"

The crossbowman had wasted no time righting his horse and pounding away for help. Already he could hear interrogative shouts provoked by the report of the pistol.

"Come on, you sway-backed nag," he growled painfully in Japanese, the inside of his mouth throbbing where he had bitten himself in the fall.

He rode madly on a zig-zag course back toward the

southwest for about two blocks. Abandoned the steed in an alley when he heard stamping hooves along a perpendicular lane. Wiping the blood from his cut hand on the cloak, he scaled a crumbling wall near a narrow arch. Pulling himself cautiously over a cornice, grunting, he scanned the streets for as far as he could see.

A Llorm column rode double along a lane not a hundred yards from his position. Bad. Gonji snapped open the burgonet's buffe and spat a mouthful of blood into the lane below, then dropped down with a grimace, the aching knee protesting.

He scampered westward again, away from the mounted party but into perilous territory—the granary-turned-garrison billet and the west gatehouse. But Tralayn's house was there. The nearest access to the catacombs. And the Gundersens' stables, where he had known refuge once before from pursuit.

He swung south through the commerce area. The slaughterhouse, the metal foundry. He avoided all contact, wishing to involve no citizens should he become trapped. When he came in stealthy view of the stables, he saw mercenaries about. Wilf was among them, tending their horses near the corral. Gonji skirted the place and continued on toward Tralayn's.

The clangor of a mounted party along the south bailey wall's adjacent lane—

He ducked into an ancient, scarred cul-de-sac and let them pass. Free companions, chattering gruffly. When their hoofbeats had diminished to a distant tattering, he moved on, wary of the Llorm sentries whose burgonets could be seen gliding along on the battlements.

Reaching Tralayn's house, breath huffing with the anticipation of relief, he stopped short. An armed party under Julian's lieutenant Ivar ascended the front steps. Cursing and pounding a fist against a granite wall, he doubled back toward—what? The chapel tunnel was out of the question. He'd never make it. Not now. Not with the army probably alerted—

*What in hell gave me away? I could have killed them all, if they hadn't reacted—*

More riders, shouts of command.

Gonji turned and ran, loping along the alleys, back eastward again. Hoofbeats lumbered and sloshed both before and behind him. He had to find sanctuary quickly. He bounded along a lane that backed two rows of houses, modest two-story stone houses, built ages ago, when the walls had gone up. He vaulted two low dividing walls, wound up in a small rear court that had been pointed out to him once as someone's from the militia. Whose?

He paused in uncertainty for an instant, then took the three steps of the stoop in a short leap and beat on the door. A rustle inside, then silence. Rainwater sluiced down the wall from a broken shingle on the eave's edge, fell in a silver sheet alongside the house for the rest of the eave's course.

Gonji drew a nasally breath. The door burst open. He tensed, and his hands went for the Sagami.

He stared along the wicked forte of a two-handed broadsword.

## Chapter Six

"A thousand *talers* . . ." Julian announced, walking about the headquarters imperiously. He jangled the money bag as he strode.

"A thousand *talers* to the man or group of men who bring me the Japanese. That's what the king has authorized me to offer. Have we no takers?"

The crossbowman who had just reported to the captain's headquarters in the southeast quadrant stood nearby, head hung low. He still wheezed. The others murmured among themselves over the rich prize. Salavar the Slayer eyed them evenly under surly brows. The soldier-of-fortune Gonji called "the Armorer" propped one leg on a bench and leaned forward on his thick forearms. One hand twirled the handle of his leaning battle-axe. The tendrils of his drooping mustache danced as he worked his jaws, inviting a smirk. There were none forthcoming. Some of the adventurers in the room had been there when Salavar and Julian had dispatched a dozen rebels in an alley now stained like the sacrificial bowl of the god of war. They'd seen what that axe could do . . .

"You—idiot," Julian said, pointing at the breathless messenger, "how can you be sure it was him you saw?"

The crossbowman trembled as he spoke. "I *think* it was him . . . *ja,* it *had* to be him," he added more certainly. "The way he carried his swords. The way he . . . struck his blows."

"Nobody's seen him or that Spanish chestnut he rides for *days,*" another man observed. But Julian ignored him.

"And you couldn't stop him," the captain accused in a scornful voice. "Three of you."

"I dropped his horse, I did," the man replied fendingly. "But then he—he went for help. I could hear their horses coming, so I—I thought it best to report to you, sir." He averted his eyes from Julian's piercing gaze.

"How did you know he was an impostor? What tipped his hand?"

The Flemish brigand brightened, fancying that he was being praised for his keenness of observation. "We had this thing, Jof and I. Whenever we passed each other on horseback, he would stand in the stirrups and raise both fists—like this—'' He demonstrated. Someone chortled. ''When he didn't do it this time, I . . .'' He saw Julian's look to Salavar and swallowed, reddening.

The captain's eyebrows arched. ''Children,'' he said, smiling haughtily, ''playing at being soldiers, you see. Isn't that quaint?''

Salavar hawked and spat.

''Get him,'' Julian said calmly, peering at the floorboards. ''I want him alive. Spread the word. Shoot him, if it's necessary, but bring him to me. Alive. A thousand *talers*. Get out of here.'' His voice lowered to a near whisper with this last, but the mercenaries scrambled to comply. The captain's cruelty and intractability were widely known. The spell of his saber had become legend.

Salavar cleared his throat and took up his furred helm. The vicious throwing daggers that crested it spindled the air like the horns of a bull.

''I'll roust your Red Blade for you. You can add that money bag to my month's wage. None of these sons of bitches can handle 'im. He's clever. I've heard of his moves. It'll take Salavar to—''

''And I've *seen* his moves,'' Julian shot. ''He's not as clever as he thinks.''

The brutish Slayer grunted and moved for the door.

Julian halted him. ''Salavar—I want him *alive*. Is that clear?''

The warrior turned slowly from the rain-stippled puddles in the courtyard. ''I do what I must to deal with my enemies.''

''And *I* am in command here.''

Their eyes locked, unflinching.

Salavar brayed a gravelly laugh. ''All right, Captain. You'll have your demon-eyed Red Blade, maybe minus a hand or foot.''

''That will do.''

Salavar departed, and moments later a visibly shaken Lieutenant Ivar clumped in, wringing wet but oddly oblivious to it.

"Now what's *your* trouble?" Julian inquired. "Have you heard—they think they've seen the samurai still in the city."

Ivar dismissed it with a wave and went straight to the captain's well-appointed wine cabinet. He poured himself a goblet with unsteady hands.

Julian was about to reprove him for his effrontery when he was overcome with curiosity. He held his tongue momentarily and watched his longtime subordinate drain off the cup and pour another almost in a continuous motion. Battle-hardened and not easily unnerved, Ivar now seemed a different man.

As if to himself, the lieutenant spoke. "It's no good, this place. No good for us. I knew that when I first set eyes on these mountains—" He regarded the walls as if the Carpathian peaks had shrunk to imprison him. "—first time I heard how the forests speak to one at night."

"What happened to you, Ivar?"

A half-sob, half-laugh struggled out of Ivar's throat. "You sent me to burn her house. The *witch's* house. Like the sorcerer said. I went. We tried." He looked at Julian with fever-gleam in his dark eyes. "Wouldn't burn." Turned his hand palm up as if what he related should have been expected.

"What do you mean, it wouldn't burn?"

*"It wouldn't burn!"* He trembled, but it subsided. His own shout steadied him. He squared his shoulders and controlled the pitch and volume of his voice once again. He flushed to have the captain see him so irrational.

"We tried everything," he went on in a tone more befitting a report. "Oil, dry kindling, even gunpowder. The place simply wouldn't catch."

124

"All right," Julian reasoned, "so it's the weather. The dampness took hold. So what the hell are you so upset about?"

"It's not that, Julian. Hell, it's dry and dusty as a damned tomb in there. You remember what happened at her hearing?" A whispering intimacy in his tone now. "The explosion—that—that white flash? I think the Great Spirit—*her* God—is on the side of these people—"

"What the devil are you babbling about now?"

"I'm serious, damned serious."

"What gods are you talking about?"

"*The* God. Her God. Theirs." He bobbed his head in stuttering affirmation and downed his cup, reaching for more.

"You're growing old and senile on us, Ivar. Those who lose their nerve are replaced. You're not above that, whatever you think the king owes you for long service—"

"That so?" Ivar challenged. "There's something else."

"What are you talking about?"

"The big weapons."

"*What* big weapons?"

"The ones we told you about," Ivar clarified. "The ones that hang in her parlor—*hung* in her parlor—the ones nothing mothered by womankind could wield?

"They're gone."


"Hey, *bimbo,* you wanna close that, *schnell?*"

The booming voice of Gutschmidt, owner of the Provender and its chief innkeeper, dampened the inn's conversation.

The burly brigand so addressed cast him an ugly frown that might have blighted a mulberry thicket, but Gutschmidt leaned forward over the bar and held his gaze, rock steady. The soldier looked back at the open door, where gusts of wind pelted the floor and the nearer tables with rain spray.

A few men and women at the tables called out in gentler support of Gutch's remonstrance, and the angry soldier slumpingly complied. Gutch returned to his conversation with two Landsknecht renegades.

Gutschmidt's characteristic audacity raised a few eyebrows, guffaws, and elbow jabs but little surprise among the Provender's regular customers. On a first-name basis with many of the occupying troops, Gutch was held in a position of respect by most soldiers and one of awe by many citizens. A slender man of wiry frame and average height, Gutch was dwarfed by many of the brigands he served; yet he could hold his own in surliness and was adept at handling obnoxious revelers. He was in his mid-30s, with a broad angular face, well-cut brown hair, and deep, large soulful eyes that at a moment's turning could range from fiery topaz to sensitive hazel. A dandy with the ladies, he was, and an impeccable dresser. He possessed a voice of such commanding resonance as to do any herald proud. And one other personal accouterment did nothing to detract from Gutch's overbearing mien: He was the only citizen of Vedun authorized to bear firearms. Gutch was the owner of a pair of legendary matched wheel-lock pistols of burnished steel with ivory handles into which were inlaid tiny gemstones of great value. These, few people had ever seen, and no one knew where he kept them.

Mercenaries on occupation duty came to revere and confide in their innkeepers more than they did most commanders. And Gutschmidt of the Provender was tendered his share of respect by the troops in Vedun, who had claimed him for their own.

The door swung open again, and rain licked at the floor. Two soldiers piled into the Provender with slapping footfalls, calling out greetings to their fellows and sniffing the inviting food and drink aromas. A third man followed them, quietly closing the door and scanning the inn's interior.

126

Gutch discreetly surveyed the new arrivals, as he always did, and the third man caught his attention. He continued listening to the Landsknecht's slurred mutterings as he watched the newcomer move to the bar and order an ale from the help. It took him two or three guarded glances and a little careful memory searching to realize who it was that had gone to such great pains to affect an incognito posture in the dangerous company at the Provender. The man wore a black wool traveling cloak with upturned collar and a heavy tri-corner hat. Three days' growth of beard and an eye patch completed the disguise.

First amusement, then alarm came to Gutch in alternating sensations. Slowly, with practiced skill, he extricated himself from the conversation with the Landsknechts. He poured a *kvas* for the burly lout whom he'd bellowed at moments earlier, then began to perform small cleaning tasks behind the bar with detached nonchalance.

He kept one eye on the newcomer, who now sidled to the end of the bar, scanned the inn as if looking for someone, and eased into a chair at a table where two free companions argued a point of bleary honor.

Someone was in for big trouble.


"Well, Gonji-Gunnar, you going to stand there bleeding all over yourself and dripping water on Hildy's floor?"

Gonji laughed in spite of himself and closed the door, delighted to have trusted to his poor karma and have it for once turn up a sight as welcome as Hildegarde.

"Get those things off, you sorry looking Viking," she told him in her pleasantly cadenced accent, lowering her deadly broadsword. "How many chase you?" she asked, peering out through the cracked shutter.

"I don't know," he replied, peeling off the capote, "a lot maybe. They may not know it's me they're chasing."

"Well, they come through Hildy's door today, it be the

127

*last* door for them. Next time open the pig snout on that silly helmet. I nearly run you through.''

There were few people in the city Gonji admired enough to allow such a crack to pass unchallenged. He tossed away the burgonet with a noisy clatter and obtained from her a cleaning rag with which he began to wipe the blood from the Sagami.

"Anyone coming?" he asked.

"I see a few horsemen . . . no . . . no one coming into my yard. What's wrong with you, Gonji-Gunnar? Your crazy plan not crazy enough, so you decide to get yourself killed some other way, *ja?*"

"You've heard about the evacuation, *neh?*"

"*Ja,* I hear—how come you not can speak Norwegian dialect your *Mutter* teach, eh? Save Hildy lots of trouble."

"*Gomen nasai.* So sorry." He shook his head wanly. "I lost touch with it early, I'm afraid. There's little I can recall."

She nodded understandingly and continued in German, "I watch here. You check street."

He moved through the small rooms toward the front of her dwelling, carefully skirting the coffin that took up much of the parlor floor. Gaining the front door, he reconnoitered the streaming lane. Drenched and gloomy, the street seemed quiet but for a few hurrying citizens and an occasional splashing of paired mercenaries shouting for clearance of the road ahead of them. Clearly, the thrill of a pursuit in the miserable weather had palled for them.

Gonji exhaled with relief and examined the coffin grimly.

"Your . . . husband?" he probed when she came into the parlor.

Hildegarde emitted a strained laugh and toed the lid with one foot, kicking it up and off—it was filled with half-armors and helms, unstrung longbows and cloth-yard war arrows.

She smiled coyly. "Not my husband. He been dead a long time. But he be pleased to see this."

Gonji studied her closely, seeing her now for the first time sans armor or training garb. She was a fine figure of a woman, tall and strong, proud and erect in carriage like a prize-winning Arabian mare. She wore a short, roomy gray tunic. Beneath it her breasts bobbed freely but artlessly as she tied back her auburn hair with a *hachimaki,* the headband of resolution that Gonji had introduced. Her muscular hips and long thighs were garbed in tight breeches. Between the breeches and her high-topped leather riding boots, the proper women of Vedun might have been properly scandalized. Hildegarde's eyes were of a pale blue, bright and transparent in the way Gonji had known the sky above the Mediterranean to be of mornings in early spring. Yet they somehow reminded him of the eyes of a hunting hawk, clear and implacable.

Her eyes locked with his now as she finished tying off the headband.

"They come, we be ready, eh?" she announced firmly.

*"Hai,* we'll be ready." There was no hint of patronization in his tone. Her fighting prowess was a byword in the militia. Strong of arm and sure of foot, the figure she cut with the *naginata*—the halberd—was a striking apparition in the training cavern. Nearly as adroit with the broadsword and capable with the bow, she augmented her considerable abilities with absolute fearlessness and predatory cunning and ferocity.

But as Gonji watched her stride back into her kitchen, sword in hand, he felt an abrupt attraction to her sultry mystique. She exuded a magnetic primal charm that he had rarely experienced, and he was hard put to keep in focus the fact that, unleashed on the field and ordered to fight, she was about as feminine as a battering ram.

May the gods send their hosts to piece together the woeful warrior who mistook her for a spoil of battle . . .

"You smell terrible, Gonji-Gunnar," she told him when he reentered the kitchen, "and you look like hell. Go wash in that basin there—and get that stinking coat away from Hildy's larder."

The samurai scowled and looked at his arms, sniffed his sticky tunic. He held up Milorad's capote in two fingers.

"Mud and blood and shit," he grumbled. "That's been my karma ever since I arrived here."

Hildegarde snatched the capote from him, scrubbed it, and hung it to dry near the hot stones around the cooking fire in her kitchen hearth, where fish were broiling with a merry crackle.

Gonji laved himself with the ewer and basin, untied his topknot and washed his hair, retying it properly when it was dried. The Scandinavian warrior-woman treated his cuts and abrasions with a mushy poltice that burned like saltwater, then instructed him to rinse his mouth with a diluted cup of the same evil concoction.

Doing so, he fancied that his face had melted from the mouth outward to leave nothing but his grinning skull, but he showed nothing of the shock in his expression. Hildegarde tossed her head, eyes glistening with lunatic approval, as though he had passed some arcane test.

Then, when she saw how he limped on the bruised knee, she had him remove his breeches so that she could wrap it with linen and more of the foul poltice.

"Drink," she commanded, slamming a goblet of dark, potent ale on the table before him.

When his unsubtle sniffing overtures elicited no invitation to sup, Gonji asked, "Were you just starting or finishing your supper when I intruded?"

"Now," she replied without looking at him, "you see the trout sizzling over there. And here, Gonji-Gunnar, you see Hildy culponing more. So what do you think?"

They ate until belching full, washing down their trout and rye bread with more ale.

"Wilfred been down the lane looking for you earlier," she told him while they ate. She had no idea what his comrade had wanted but began plying Gonji with questions regarding the evacuation and battle to come. Most of these were of a tactical nature, and he replied honestly, seeing no reason to suspect her motives. His answers seemed satisfactory to her—which made one of them satisfied—and she soon lost interest in conversation.

Hildegarde's moods shifted from gruffly loquacious to gruntingly laconic, and Gonji took advantage of her turning for the latter by rising from the table and performing his stretching regimen, careful to take it easy on the bruised and wrapped knee.

When he had completed his exercises under her critical gaze, he sat in the lotus position before the licking hearthfire and relaxed, drifting into a Zen meditation that was almost instantly dispersed by Hildy's switching back into a talkative mode. She seemed to have taken his mystical posturing for an invitation to utilize him as confessor.

She waxed introspective. "My Sven," she reflected, dreamy-eyed, "he was a man of the sea. I knew before he took me for wife that there would always be the other woman. The sea. She took him. Finally she took him. She does not let go easy of those who love her, the sea. So she took Sven.

"After that Hildy leave Sveden. Sweden not good these days. Denmark worse. And your mother's Norway—*ugh*. Her glory days are gone, Gonji-Gunnar. But Hildy want no more to look upon the face of the sea. So I come south, leave her behind, bring my father's harbisher craft with me. I make those—" She pointed to a small ante-chamber wherein a half-finished cuirass lay on a workbench. "—cuirasses, pauldrons, vambraces, light

131

hauberks—the kind of armor a warrior can move in. Not this crazy bulky plate that make you move like a turtle and die like one. Mine is fine leather scale and tough links of mail. *You* bought my pauldrons and vambraces, is that not so? I sell them to the barker, he sell them to you!" Her smile faded quickly.

"So I work my goods. Then I meet Eric. Eric Grimmelman. He was a highwayman. A bandit. He try to rob Hildy. He give me this." She half-turned and pulled up the back of her tunic to reveal a broad, smooth back marred only by the ugly lips of a knife scar. "I slash his leg open. So we become friends. He was my man for a time. We plunder the main roads. Merchants, travelers. We live like kings."

She shrugged. "Then they catch us in Austria. They kill Eric, hold me—big mistake. Man takes Hildy into the forest at point of pistol. Going to have some fun, you see. Make me take my clothes off. Then he take his off. I play at being weepy, then I break his jaw, take pistol and run. Join adventurers for a time. Not so different from this horde in Vedun. Not much better. I leave again. Come here. Take up harbishing again. Not too bad, not too good. Then these crazies come to Vedun. Then *you* come, Gonji-Gunnar, half-breed Viking, and Hildy's life get exciting again . . ."

Gonji shifted imperceptibly before the fire, then relaxed and exhaled deeply, abandoning the meditation.

She grew maudlin, slugging down the ale with a vengeance. "I don't care about these damn Christians, some of them. Most of them—I don't know. But maybe . . . maybe Yesus the Christ like it if I help out here, eh? These Christians need many good warriors with the wolves they draw, eh?"

The samurai nodded stiffly but said nothing.

"Flavio," she went on, "he was a good man, no? You think, Gonji-Gunnar?"

132

Gonji rose and returned to the table, rubbing his jaw. *"Hai.* He was a very good man." He stretched and yawned. Retying his *obi* about his waist, he sashed his swords and took up the capote and burgonet. The padding inside the helm was still wet.

"I've got to see how our plans are coming. The alert teams should have all reported back by now."

He moved to the tiny vaulted foyer at the kitchen door and viewed the darkening back lane. Evening descended over the Transylvanian Alps. Misty rain diminished visibility.

"You need a place to sleep tonight," she called after him, "you come back here, eh?"

He swallowed but revealed nothing of the pang of desire her casual statement had inspired. He bowed to her and smiled gratefully. Then he was off through the rear courtyard and splashing into the deadly lanes.


The traitor sat board-stiff astride a black stallion, dressed in a masked close-helmet and a cowled, silk-lined cloak, surrounded by a squad of mercenaries in Mord's private employ. Trembling with secret triumph. The game was playing itself out extremely well.

They neared the main gate, slowing as they approached a party of mourners on horseback, who in turn followed a closed wagon bearing a coffin. The traitor recognized them all, wondering amusedly at the contents of the coffin.

Were they genuinely bereaved or merely essaying a diversionary performance?

Three horsemen, headed by the formidable Salavar, clattered up on the heels of the mourners, having splashed out at a jangling gallop from the gatehouse.

Salavar ordered the small funeral cortege to halt two hundred yards outside Vedun.

This could be quite interesting. Even through the rain

133

and gathering gloom, the driver and assistant could be seen to pale as they looked at each other.

"Such long faces," Salavar intoned sarcastically as he swung down off the huge armored destrier, plucking his feathered lance from its mooring and striding up to the wagon. "Tell me—is it the rain that has your spirits down? Or the presence of so many vicious warriors? Or—my goodness," he minced, removing his dagger-festooned helm and bowing to the tearful mounted woman with mock cavalier grace. "It's a *funeral*. Now why didn't we notice that, Luba?"

Behind him, one of the soldiers laughed coarsely, and the Slayer continued walking to the rear of the wagon. His eyes narrowed, manifesting his self-satisfaction with the clever inspiration.

"Maybe it's because of the hour—rather late for a funeral service, isn't it? Open that coffin, and let's have a look at the dear departed."

The drivers began to demur, outraged, yet their eyes never strayed far from the point of the lance. The pair with Salavar drew steel, and a couple of men in the traitor's party reached inside their cloaks to prime pistols.

*Oh my,* the traitor thought with folded arms, *aren't you* bushi *in dire straits? And you have your Japanese blusterer to thank.* Guten nacht . . .

Forced to leap down from the driver's seat, the anxious men lowered the coffin to the ground. Fisting prybars with a final grim look, they began to work at the sealed casket's lid.

The traitor restrained the sudden mad urge to tear off the close-helmet and laugh in their faces. But no, there would be time for that. The laughter swelled and burst, and the traitor snorted inside the helm.

Salavar wrenched the coffin lid free of the final two nails. One of the women screamed, and some of the others crossed themselves. The Slayer peered down expectantly, flicking open the shroud with his lance.

His victorious grin fled, and he wiped his mouth with the back of a hand to obliterate the grimace he felt coming.

In the casket lay the mangled partial remains of a man masticated by the cretin giant.

"Take this thing . . ." he said, breathing in sonorous gasps, "and bury it."

Footwear was a subject of special interest to Old Gort.

Before he had become the keeper of the gatehouse, he had been a cobbler, and an excellent craftsman at that. When his poor health had caused him to abandon his beloved trade, he carried into his new job the habit of recognizing people by their footgear long before he learned to match their names and faces.

So it was that his eyes settled with lingering surprise on the fine-tooled leather boots that stirruped the saddle of the black stallion. There was no mistaking those boots, wrought by a master craftsman far from Vedun. He had seen them leaving earlier that day. But why did their owner now ride with a concealing helmet—and accompanied by brigands?

There was only one answer, but . . . it couldn't be.

Gonji would want to know of this. Oh, yes, this was just the sort of thing—

When he heard the squad leader repeat his command to open the portcullis, Gort knew his surprise had betrayed him. Even as he cranked the capstan wheel he quavered with fear. The horses walked into the tunnel, stopped. Nickering and wet pawing. The heavy thump of someone dismounting.

Gort listened to the purposeful stepping of those now ominous boots. A chill seized him as the gatehouse door squealed ajar and the wind and rain hissed in with a dank breath that coiled about the room.

Old Gort turned, affecting a shakily indulgent smile. The figure's head, sidelit in the harsh glow of the cresset lamp, shook free of the close-helmet.

The face was the one Gort had expected, but the expression was dreadfully wrong.

Dr. Verrico had told Gort that the growth that twisted his neck would sooner or later consume him.

Dr. Verrico could not foretell the future.

## Chapter Seven

From the moment he took his first step into the middle bailey of Castle Lenska, Garth knew he was dying in the way, on that day many years ago, that he had seen his father die.

His chest constricted, knotted, swelling and tightening at the same time. His breath came in short, choppy gasps, and his left arm went numb.

*Gott in Himmel,* not now, *bitte.* I must see Klann first.

He stopped and mopped his moistened brow with his cap. The pair of Llorm dragoons who escorted him paused and studied him, impatient to discharge their duty.

"Are you ill?" one of them asked in Kunan.

Garth held his chest a moment and considered the foreboding signals his body sent. He banished their concern with a half-wave and moved forward again in short strides.

Several servants, recognizing the beloved smith, dropped their tasks and rushed up to engage him with a babble of anxious voices. The Llorm escort warned them off. One servant shouted out the grim fate of the prophetess Tralayn.

Garth eyed the guards accusingly and bowed his head.

They pressed on to the king's private chambers, the smith in a state of roiling transition, his thoughts given over to disillusionment and morbidity; his stricken heart, to both palpitation and despair.

"Garth!" the king cried to see him, surging forward to welcome him into the chamber. "Garth Iorgens—*gen-kori*. Our dear, trusted friend."

Klann bade him sit in the plush red velvet stuffed chair that now faced the king's own. Garth's pain and terror held him captive, but the first sight of the tall, dark and bearded Newly Risen, with his severe, hawklike features, gave him pause. It was hard to accept the life experience and deep acquaintance of a longtime confidant abruptly impressed into the body and personality of a stranger. Garth's apprehension intensified so that he wrung his cap in his hands, wishing desperately to be at home, on his own cot, his beloved sons around him . . .

"But you're upset—Gorkin, pour for us, won't you?"

The castellan, the only other person now in the chamber, moved forward with an indulgent head bob and, filling the goblets on the silver-gilt service, proffered Garth his cup with a crafty smile that was unreadable.

They drank a toast to friendship. Then Klann came up to Garth, studied him momentarily, eyes slimming with suspicion or befuddlement. He clamped a hand on Garth's shoulder. Their eyes met, Garth fighting to stem the liquid trembling he felt in his.

"Long did I languish in that terrible insensate boredom, waiting. Waiting for my turn to clasp your hand in brotherhood, faithful Iorgens . . ."

Garth nodded shakily, parted his lips to speak. The tightening in his chest was awful. His benumbed left arm now sent tiny tingling shocks to his fingertips. His hands were moist with perspiration; he rubbed them on his breeches. Tried to speak. No words could ascend his throat.

King Klann backed away, his expression playing through a range of changes, settling on impatience.

"I shall mince no words," Klann said sharply. "I speak to you as a former loyal friend, a brother, a comrade-in-arms. Do you know that I was coming to see you and you alone when this . . . change occurred? I care not to know why it happened, or how. It has happened, and I am emerged. But I am still Klann, Iorgens. Still your former liege lord. Tell me then, and tell me true—what are your compatriots planning against me?"

His voice had soared angrily in strength and pitch.

Garth blinked with surprise, though the words had trickled down to him through a cottony muting, the warm hollow drumming of blood in his ears. His chest pulled in two directions at once. Nausea seized him, cold sweat breaking. He thought he would faint.

"I—know—nothing," he said, straining for every sound. "They plan nothing . . . against you, sire." More surely now. A bit of control returning.

Klann and Gorkin locked eyes.

"What's wrong with you, Iorgens?" the castellan probed.

"I'm—I'm sorry," Garth apologized. "I don't feel well. Bear with me, *bitte*—oh!" A slugging at his chest, less a part of him than some silent invader attacking his heart.

"Will you try to stop them?" Klann asked firmly.

Garth swallowed, strained to hear the sound of his voice over the blood-thrum that now even clouded his mind.

"I have told you I . . . don't know . . . what they're planning."

*Why did I say that? Get hold of yourself, Garth.*

"So you do admit they're plotting against me!"

*"Nein—I—"*

General Gorkin clutched the hilt of his broadsword and glared at Garth balefully, his brow a dark menacing ridge.

Garth struggled for control. *Thoughts into words. Thoughts into—* "That is *not* what I meant to say. What I believed to say—no! What I meant to say—" Now even the Kunan tongue was failing him. Was it lack of practice? or the seizure?

The two accusers stared at him in mute hostility, watching him squirm.

"I meant to say . . . that . . . *Mord* . . . *ja!* It is *Mord* who plots against you." His eyes bulged, and he drew a shuddering breath.

"Ho!" Klann laughed. "So you make a weak attempt at shifting suspicion. Who briefed you for this meeting, Garth, your dead prophetess?"

"And what's the source of this intelligence?" Gorkin asked caustically. Once a rival for Garth's position as the king's second-in-command, he tendered Garth no fondness. "Your whole being trembles with revulsion over your deceit to the liege lord you once swore fealty to. You disgust me."

"Gorkin," Klann reproved gently.

Garth grew restive, disliking Gorkin's callous, indignant posturing. *Think. Try to think.* He strove, the noise in his ears mingling with the effort of his mind to render Klann's voice a senseless hum. And then words came clearly to Garth's lips, but they scarcely resembled those his brain had fashioned.

"No one told me to say that. We simply want the sorcerer removed—*nein!*" He rose from his chair, reeling, seeing Gorkin take a defensive posture, sword drawn, Klann grabbing the general's arm.

He fell back into the cushiony buffet of the thick chair seat. *Why did I say that?*

Klann quietly ordered Gorkin out of the room. After a brief glance that seemed to question the wisdom of the move, the castellan saluted and left, the barely restrained satisfaction he felt perking the corners of his mouth. Gorkin was too much of a stickler regarding military honor to besmirch the reputation of even a former comrade. But he would relate what had transpired to the bored and jaded Lady Gorkin, who would in turn delight in relating to the other Akryllonian nationals how the European warrior Klann had so favored had as much as admitted his complicity against the king.

Garth clutched at his chest, breathing deeply. Klann had turned away thoughtfully, sipping at his wine. The king sighed long and mournfully.

"Forgive me, milord," Garth begged with great effort. "I am ill. I am speaking gibberish. Perhaps—"

"Your strain is evident. Sometimes under stress the tongue reveals what is truly in the heart."

Garth remembered things best left buried by the years. Murky clouds gathered on the edges of his consciousness, and he spoke raspingly through his fear and pain: "If I were to speak . . . what most deeply pierces my secret heart . . . then even a king such as you, milord, might quake."

Unaccustomed to him as such words were, Garth had meant them.

Klann's eyes widened, despair veiling them, and when he tore his gaze away there was a feeling in the air like the ripping of fabric. The raft of cherished memories of brotherhood and deeds shared in common bonding sundered, so that king and subject drifted apart over a sea of repelling currents.

But Klann would not allow himself to accept it.

White pinpoints flashed across Garth's vision as he massaged his stricken chest, and through them he saw the king fling his cup across the room so that it bounded against the far wall and shattered, stem from bowl. Guards appeared, and Klann cursed them from the chamber.

Then he knelt on one knee before the seated smith.

"Garth—Garth, listen to me. I know what your people fear. I know that Mord wishes to see your city destroyed, but We, *We* are king. They're all foolish to believe We'd let Mord have his way. We *need* him, Garth. Much as We despise his methods, We need him to help wrest back Akryllon from those who ravaged it. Those like him. It's useless for the province to try to pit us against Mord. Are these people so hard-headed that they'll resist rule until the violent end that must result? We're growing stronger all the time, Garth. By spring—that's all I ask, to remain here until spring—by then we'll have grown in numbers. Mord will have all the power he needs. If these Transylvanian people want to fight, well then let them fight with us! As allies! There are great riches awaiting the reconquerors of Akryllon. We'll share them with all!

"Garth—*gen-kori,* faithful friend—listen to me. Join with us. Come back to us, fight with us again, take up your former post as Field Commander—We've left the position open for you and you alone! There is none here I would trust more. We are begging you now—*begging* you, Iorgens, all the Brethren remaining within!—to take up your sword again. Think of it—you as Field Commander. Liaison between king and people. Loved and trusted by both alike. Only you, of all beings on the earth and under it, might accomplish what I ask. Might bring peace to this province through the evil winter that comes. It's on your shoulders and your conscience, mighty man of valor—"

Klann shook a finger at him, chuckling in a cracked voice, eyes glistening with emotion.

Garth was aggrieved, tormented. He could barely think, drenched with sweat straight through his clothing, sipping from his cup in mad little tips that sloshed into his beard. Pain coursed through both his arms now.

*"Nein,"* he gurgled. "It may not matter in a few moments anyway. Just . . . let the city—"

"Iorgens! We *implore* you. By the God you now espouse, and His Son who hangs on your somber cruciforms, and all your legions of angels and saints—*will you join us again?*"

A small sob bubbled up onto Garth's lips. A tear coursed his cheek.

There was, of course, the dreadful pain and the certainty of imminent death. But his head began to swim also with the lingering memories, the more recent convictions, the welter of confused voices screaming like hawkers at the market square. And the single, solid beam of revulsion, deadening the center of it all with the surety of choice it brought.

Klann was asking him to side now with the Evil One. Garth tried to say as much.

"I could never . . . join with . . . *such a fool—*"

*Nein.* The blood-chilling alarm rang in his head, and as if in signal, the seizure seemed to abate by degrees.

The atmosphere in the room fell lifeless, a vacuum. Emptied of feeling. Something had died within the king, and the mourning spell lasted a few seconds.

Garth experienced a curious mixture of cautious relief, guilt, and hopelessness. A moment's reprieve. He felt his chest, where his jerkin was crumpled and warped by the action of his white clammy fist.

King Klann stood with his back to him. A sealed vault.

"Get out of here, Iorgens," he said in a voice fired with threat.

"I have not been myself today, milord—"

Klann seemed not to hear him. "Leave us. Begone from these walls—"

*"Nein—bitte,* let us speak as—"

"Go away!" Klann's shout, as he whirled and fixed Garth with an icy glare, brought the sentries into the chamber. "Go back to your city, to your conspiring fellows!"

142

Garth stood tall, squaring his massive shoulders. "Sire, I could never raise a sword against you. Surely you must—"

"We shall see about that. The next time our paths cross, you had best be hefting cold steel."

The audience was ended. Garth turned slowly and clumped past the marble pillars of the narrow vestibule, the guards falling into step at both hands and slightly to his rear. He moved into the hall and through the corridors silently, his thoughts racing, unable to settle upon a single discrete impression. So relieved was he to still be alive; so crushed, to have earned the undeserved scorn of his former liege.

And lacing it all was the vicious memory, the certainty that it was *he* who should have been the scornful one.

In his private chamber King Klann heard the screaming counsel of the remaining Brethren within, and in confusion and frustration he fell to venting the primal rage of the Tainted One. He lashed about the room, overturning furnishings, smashing the *objects d'art* that lined the walls, crying out in anguished spirit. He tore down the priceless arras, hurled cressets and fireplace implements at the bewildered personal guards and servants drawn by their king's wrath.

And at the last, when only his chair—the high-backed, ornate gilt-edged chair wrought for the late Baron Rorka—remained upright, Klann fell into it and began to sob in many voices, wracked by the cumulative despondency of the years that ordinary men would reckon by the score.

The guard escort left Garth when he descended the short stairway to the ward, where his mare waited at the nearby livery. When he reached the bottom of the stair, he heard his name called in a familiar female voice.

143

The young hoyden Genya sidled around the gargoyle-inlaid pylon at his right. She looked pale and bedraggled in the wilting rain. And somehow—older, as if she'd experienced some ordeal. His dislike for the beloved of his son Wilfred was tempered now by a pang of sympathy.

"Genya—?" he began, awaiting her feeble attempt at speech, reaching a hand toward her, concern softening his features.

But then she was looking past him, her eyes grown wide with terror. He lurched about, cap in hand, brow furrowed.

Mord stood leering down, three steps above. His carven mask of gold shone with a glee that churned Garth's stomach. The sorcerer's head tilted from side to side at grotesque angles, as if the head of a bird resided under the mysterious mask.

Suddenly Garth realized the truth of it all, and hatred erupted in his still aching breast.

"*You,*" the smith grated through his beard with uncommon spite, "you, foul enchanter. You did it."

"Did you enjoy your audience with the king?" Mord's dirgelike voice intoned. "His Majesty does so appreciate lively conversation."

"You twisted my tongue—garbled my speech so that I spoke evil words to the king."

"Your tongue seems well oiled now, simple smith."

Garth's fingers curled at his sides, his cap crushed in the powerful clutch of his right hand. He took a step upward.

Mord lifted a gloved finger. "Tut-tut-tut. The worshippers of failed gods would do well to observe their place in the universe."

A single spark of pain in Garth's chest. He drew a whistling breath in reaction. His eyes rotated irrationally, focused again when his mind had framed the suspicion in shimmering crimson coils.

*Had the sorcerer also caused the sudden seizure?*

144

There came a surge of fear. It passed when his mind resorted to the comfort of faith. He lipped a silent prayer. The pain seemed to subside, but certainty was lacking.

Righteous wrath, however, was not.

"Hear me well, servant of Satan," Garth fumed in a simmering voice his former charges would have heeded, "though you think you've schemed cleverly, God Almighty knows your evil deeds, and you will pay for them."

"Threats?" Mord minced. "Threaten me and you threaten His Majesty as well."

"Klann knows I wish him no ill. As for you, by all that I deem holy—God forgive me—I've made no such promise." His teeth ground audibly, and the smith's mighty fists squeezed at his sides until his knuckles were pearl-hued. He blinked the rain from his eyes to keep them clear and hot.

Mord might have hissed, but the sound became indistinct in the tattering of the rain. "I should do King Klann a large favor if I were to slay you where you stand."

"Try."

Mord stiffened. There was a long silence, punctuated by the slapping, streaming wetness and Genya's panting breath.

"Soon enough," Mord declared. "To an immortal, time means nothing."

"Then you'd better begin to learn to count the days again. The Lord God of heaven and earth diminishes yours even as you plot, you—" Garth's jaw worked pointlessly, his words having run out.

"There is only one god of this earth," Mord replied. "And I, his privileged servant."

Garth wheeled and stalked off toward the sound of splashing hooves. Heading across the gloomy, near-deserted ward toward his waiting horse, he was grateful for the cleansing drench of the rain. Glad to be free of the hateful presence of Mord, and ashamed to have been so used in the malevolent sorcerer's machinations.

But then he wondered again: Had Mord, who had surely bound his tongue and made him prattle like an idiot, *also* been responsible for the seizure that had filled him with the dread of imminent death? That seemed reasonable. But how could he be sure? His father had indeed died of the heart ailment, and *his* father before him. Folklore whispered that Garth himself could expect a similar demise.

And what of it? Should the Lord be beckoning him to eternity, how might he comport himself in his present circumstances?

A tapestry of disjointed thoughts. The past. The present. His sons. Unfinished business. Vedun. His sons. His—

A brooding resolve began to form in Garth's heart as he swung aboard the mare and angled for the gatehouse.

Genya watched him go, feeling abandoned to fate. She knew she dared not look up to see that hideous golden mask that loomed above her. Yet she felt compelled, and at the last she peered up with languid despair. She tipped her chin up pridefully and met those eyes of ophidian ebon.

The dagger under her skirts chilled her thigh.

"So," Mord opened archly, "you know this blundering smith, eh? And what was your hurry in engaging him?"

She emitted a short puffing breath before answering. "He—his son—is my lover. That's all. I wished only—to convey my affection."

Mord laughed boorishly. "I feel something about you. I fancy that he's not been your *only* lover of late, is that so?"

Genya felt sickened. Loathing turned her stomach,

blackened her heart. She fought back the impulse to spit at him. *The dagger—go for the dagger . . .*

He stepped down close to her. She stumbled backward, but Mord held up a hand and fixed her with a lancing gaze of almost palpable power. She felt her feet go leaden, tingling as though they had fallen asleep, then numb altogether. She swayed a bit, then steadied, but could not pull away from his slow approach. She fancied that he smiled, though nothing could be seen of his mouth through the breathing holes of the mask.

Then he was an arm-length away, and he placed his foul gloved hand on her bosom. There was a revolting sensation of mingling flesh, and when Mord drew his arm back an inch, Genya's body leaned with it as if they were one. She felt an indescribable horror of being forever part of the sorcerer in some unspeakable way.

*Lord God Almighty—the knife . . .*

Her arms seemed under her control, but she could not find the courage. And then he released her. The feeling gradually returned to her legs.

Mord touched her brow with a thumb.

"The scarlet chrism marks you as an instrument of the Dark Lord," came the words that strobed dully through the hammering of her heart. "Rejoice! The time will soon be at hand. You shall help to prove that the life is in the flesh. The flesh and the blood—these alone, my pretty one. The spirit is nothing. You shall partake in the triumph of flesh over spirit. Be cheered. Virginal, you'd have been better, but my Master is not so biased as yours."

Genya gasped. She turned and ran madly into the ward, the sound of Mord's fulsome laughter echoing in her ears. She ran in the rain and the early twilight for an indeterminate time, those passing her—whether servant or soldier—drawing near as if to help but then strangely backing away, averting their eyes.

She gained the central keep, her composure reestablished but her thinking chaotic. Wandering into the less traveled corridors in an area of larders and antechambers, bewildered, uncertain.

Then she saw the beast named Chooch. The filthy Steward of the Larders angled toward her, wearing his perverse mind on his face. He grinned dull-wittedly when he saw her raise her skirts but halted as surely as if he'd struck an invisible wall when he caught the gleam of the blade by torchlight. His mouth contorted cruelly, and he took a purposeful step as if to test her hand, then stopped again, staring. He blinked, eyed her up and down scornfully, and hulked off into the darkness.

Genya ran a hand through her soaking hair. Throwing open a pantry door, she swept through piles of silver service pieces and cutlery with reckless clamor until she located a large shining platter. This she brought out under the light of the torch, where she beheld her reflection.

An oily red mark glimmered on her forehead where the sorcerer had touched her.

She dropped the platter with a piercing *ka-dang!* on the mildewed stone floor. She touched her brow. It felt greasy on that spot, but nothing of the substance would come off, though she rubbed at it, finally, with a frantic, tearful energy. It was part of her.

Retrieving the dagger, Genya threw herself onto the floor of the pantry. She wept for a time, shaking and sobbing like a tortured child. Then control returned.

Closing the pantry door, she rehearsed, again and again, the action of raising the blade to full arm's length, the razor-sharp point angled at her breast in both hands, and plunging it slowly and methodically down to press through her bodice and against her flesh. All the while she recited an act of contrition that she prayed would suffice.

She repeated the motions until she had drawn blood from the soft flesh of one breast, but in the end her fear

148

of the sin and her passion for life won out. She flung the dagger away.

*Get hold of yourself, Genya dear,* she thought. That's not the way. No, not at all. If the end is to come, then by the good Lord's mercy, there must be a better way. I must do what I must. I'll not go weeping and pleading; I'll be no one's easy victim. Never again . . .

And when, at length, her rage had spent itself, she was overcome by exhaustion. But before sleep overtook her, she replaced the dagger in the sheath under her skirt, pressing her hand against its firm, cold trust as she curled up in a corner. Feeling, if not precisely confident, vixenishly deadly, promising measure for measure to any who dared threaten her solitude.

## Chapter Eight

By darkfall, word had spread throughout the occupying army that the oriental barbarian with the high price on his head had variously been seen both in the eastern portion of the city and beyond its walls, in the fields and orchards bordering the river.

Some said he was mounted; others, on foot. Depending on the purveyor of the news, he was either alone or accompanied by his marauding band.

Emboldened by their numbers and their lust for gold, roving packs of mercenaries combed the eastern half of the city and its outer environs. Citizens were rousted from their dwellings as the brigands searched high and low.

Gonji knew well the direction their treasure hunt had taken, for it was his own operative who had planted the seed of misdirection that steered them both from him and from the evacuation and battle planning.

He stood peering through a shutter out into the bleak and rain-misted Street of Charity. It was nearly deserted. He was in the house of a fisherman named Miklos Zarek, a stone's throw from Garth's smithshop and stables, within view of the wagonage across the way from the Gundersens'. Most of the wagons were gone on their clandestine business, only a few scattered drays huddled about the place to avert suspicions.

Gonji leaned forward on one knee, leg braced on a chair. With his *tanto* knife he whittled from a sturdy chunk of red maple kindling. He and Zarek were alone for the nonce, a single taper casting drab light in a far corner of the dwelling's front room.

"That—what?" Zarek asked, coming up and pointing at the object Gonji shaped with the *tanto*.

"*Ninja* darts," he explained. "Darts," he added emphatically, appending a throwing motion. "If I can obtain some poison from the doctor, or the carcass of the great worm . . ."

He let it drop, as Zarek moved to the smoky cooking fire in the hearth. The flue had become stopped up, and Zarek cleared it, wiping the grime from his face as he did so.

"Want fish?" Zarek asked.

Gonji readily assented, though the meal he had shared not long ago with Hildegarde would probably have held him through the night. Zarek's trout quickened his taste buds with its aroma.

Gonji and the fisherman could share only the most broken of conversations in German—the only language Zarek knew a smattering of which Gonji could understand. Their speech was limited to monosyllabic grunts, for the most part.

The samurai enjoyed the quiet while it lasted. Soon

there'd be plenty of discussion; he'd left word with the Benedettos as to where he could be located during the Hour of the Boar.

As he ate, Gonji passed a wine jug back and forth with Zarek. Miklos was a dour, middle-aged man with thick lips and the doleful eyes of a bloodhound. He had a habit of laughing to himself from time to time for no apparent reason. A growling sound that rumbled from his throat though his lips never smiled. His wife and children had fled the city weeks ago to seek refuge with relatives in the Ukraine.

There was a knock at the door, and Zarek admitted Wilf Gundersen and two men who had been assisting at the stables of late.

"*Komban wa,* Gonji-san," Wilf greeted, bowing, the others following suit.

"Good evening. What of your father? Has he come back yet?"

"*Nein.* I'm getting worried."

Gonji nodded and returned to his dart-carving. Wilf and his friends partook of the remains of the fish.

Almost at once, the alert plan delegates began to report back. Milorad Vargo and Vlad Dobroczy arrived together.

"Not such a good idea," Milorad cautioned. "To stay so close to their garrison."

"Never mind that—are you finished with your sectors?"

Both men agreed that they were.

"Nobody can believe it," Dobroczy advised, shaking his head.

"Where's Paolo? And you, Milorad—what happened to Ignace?" Gonji's forehead creased.

Milorad blustered. "Ignace was with me the whole time, and then he was to sup with Anna and me. But surely you didn't mean for us to stay together . . . all the time, did you?"

Gonji snorted in exasperation. "Of course. Isn't that what I said? Where is he?"

The adviser scratched his head. "He . . . went to his place. I left him there. Then he was going to have Paolo bring him over."

"So where is the cocky Neapolitan?" Now Gonji directed his peevishness at Vlad.

Vlad threw his hands up. "How should I know? He was with me for part of the list. Then he just decided he had other things to do. He's a big-time killer now, figures he doesn't have to listen to anybody. Anyway, I'm not his master."

"You're nobody's master, hook-nose," Wilf called from the table.

Vlad scowled and seemed about to pursue the insult when Gonji stepped before him. "Drop it. Both of you. *I'm* speaking. Listen, Dobroczy, when I give an order, I expect it to be carried out explicitly. There is no room for error and no allowance for private interpretation of my meaning. I don't care what you feel about me personally. We are either in this together now, with you under my command, or you are my enemy. *Verstehen Sie?*"

Vlad nodded sullenly. "He's hurting, you know. That might've had something to do with his leaving."

Gonji frowned. "What do you mean? Hurt how?"

"His side." Dobroczy patted his ribs.

Pounding at the door. The room fell silent, but Gonji beckoned them to act naturally and slipped into a rear chamber. Zarek opened it and admitted a shivering clutch of wet souls that included Jiri and Greta and the Benedettos. Gonji was mildly discomfited to see that Lydia had come along when he reentered the parlor. Greetings were hastily exchanged.

"They're all reporting back now," Michael apprised. "Everything's going smoothly."

"They're dragging people out of their homes again,"

Lydia told Gonji in a flat tone. "Looking for you."

*"So desu ka?* If you like, I'll go out and throw myself on their tender mercies." He regretted his tone at once as she withdrew.

The alert teams dropped their checked-off lists of homes on the table and accepted Zarek's offer of beverages.

"Garth's on his way back," Michael said. "Someone saw him riding in the hills."

"In the *hills,*" Gonji repeated petulantly. "What the hell is he doing up there? Doesn't anyone do what's expected around here? Or what they're told?"

"Why so angry at Papa?" Wilf griped.

"We'd all *like* to know what happened at the castle, *nicht wahr?*"

Wilf shrugged in concession.

"At least you two are still together," Gonji remarked to Jiri and Greta.

*"Ja,"* Jiri answered brightly, "her father says too much. Hey—what are those?" He walked over to the window sill and palmed Gonji's handiwork.

"Darts," Zarek replied, making a throwing motion. He laughed his gravelly, unsmiling laugh.

Greta spoke. "Gonji, my mother asked me to ask you if it would be all right if she could take along a chestful of family heirlooms in the evacuation. It really isn't so very big—"

"Greta, I don't care," he replied, sighing. He asked the representatives of the craft guilds who were present how the work on the wagons progressed.

"Slowly," Jiri responded, "at the metal foundry, but all right, I think. The plates they're fitting inside the wagons take time, and there are a lot of soldiers passing by because it's so near the garrison."

"Poorly at the woodcraft shop," another followed. "That madman Paille's acting like he owns the place. Got everyone all worked up. Hell, it's not easy, this business of cutting gunloops in coffins, and fixing wagons with fittings so they can just be slapped into place when it's time.''

"Will it work?" Gonji asked.

"I doubt it."

They discussed the incident one of them had seen, when Salavar the Slayer had accosted a funeral procession and demanded the opening of a sealed casket. Somber looks passed around the room.

A soft rapping came at the door, and a single Moldavian woman entered for the sole purpose of telling Gonji, through Greta's translation, that she believed him to be a good man who would protect her sons through the holocaust to come. Through it all Gonji stood with eyes downcast and head hanging humbly on his chest. His hands were clasped behind his back, and he sighed and lipped a gentle *"domo arigato"* when she had finished.

The old woman stood on tiptoes and kissed Gonji's cheek in matronly fashion, crossed herself, and slipped out, stifling a sob. The room was struck dumb.

Greta was the first to speak. "Do you know who her sons are?"

*"Iyé,* and I don't want to." An aura of understanding and sympathy for their military leader permeated the room.

Gonji scratched his chin impatiently and sipped at his wine cup while the others exchanged listless small talk awhile. Michael and Wilf seemed similarly plagued by an itch for action, but neither spoke.

*"My* capote?" Milorad said in dismay, for the first time noticing the battered garment slung over a chair back.

*"Hai, gomen nasai, Vargo-san,"* Gonji replied sheepishly. "So sorry. It went through certain misadventures with me."

Milorad clucked and sputtered. "My best coat."

154

"I'll buy you a new one, *neh?* Whom are we still waiting for, Miko-san?"

Michael thought a moment. "Wilfred's brothers and Anton and Roric—oh, what about Nagy and Berenyi?"

"No," Vlad replied. "They're busy at the caravanserai. Lorenz and Strom worked their list."

"That's right," Michael agreed. "So just two teams, then."

"And Garth," Gonji appended.

"*Si,* of course—Garth."

There was a rash of startled gasps as Lorenz Gundersen appeared like a specter in the archway from the rear of the house.

"Well," he said, brushing the droplets from his hat and wiping his feet on a well-worn mat, "good evening, everyone. You made yourself scarce, *sensei,* but I found you."

He and Gonji exchanged curt bows.

"Took you long enough," Wilf chided without looking at him.

"We had the longest list, dear brother," Lorenz reminded.

"Where is Strom?" Gonji asked sternly.

"Where does Strom *ever* go?" Lorenz replied, chuckling. He tossed his alert list onto the table. "Out in the hills with his flock." With a courteous gesture he accepted a cup of wine from Greta, who had taken to attending on the needs of the guests when Zarek retired to a corner chair, where he sat with his cheek propped on a fist, sipping distractedly and dozing.

"And were you not told to remain together?" Gonji fumed. "Does *anyone* do what he's ordered in this territory?"

"Surely you didn't mean that I should keep him by my side for every trip to the chamber pot!" Snorts and titters attended Lorenz's arch reply. But Gonji's brow darkened,

155

and the Exchequer went on more seriously. "Oh, come now, *sensei*. You don't suspect *Strom* of treachery, do you? One can carry this security business a bit too far."

"Really, Gonji," Lydia added in support. "I myself could think of people who might be worthy of suspicion, but *Strom?*"

Milorad chortled. *"Ja,* with all due respect to the Gundersen family, I'm afraid I must agree. Treachery presumes a certain . . . cunning that I think we'd agree—"

"All right, then there *is* no traitor," Gonji stormed. "Tell me that when you awake in the night with soldiers hovering over your beds." He modulated his angry tone. "You alert people—what did you tell the citizens as you went?"

*"Shi-kaze,"* Lorenz answered at once, offering his cup in toast.

"On the night after the full moon," Jiri finished in a voice just above a whisper.

Downcast looks beset the group at the reminder of the grim business that lurked on the horizon.

A soft rapping at the door. Much like the knock of the mama-san who had come to speak with Gonji earlier. The samurai seated himself at the table. When the door was opened, the stoop-shouldered, bearlike silhouette of Garth caught the low light that crept out onto the stoop. And when the smith lumbered inside with a wet slap of his cap on a thigh, the whole gathering lurched to its feet with many a greeting and anxious query.

"First be aware," Garth said, "that I bear no good tidings. Tralayn is dead," he muttered into his beard.

Prayers for eternal rest and several anxious signs of the cross followed the bleak, though not unexpected, declaration.

Then Garth continued: "And I'm afraid that she was right all along. Mord *is* our enemy, and King Klann

156

cannot be persuaded of it, though he may even believe it himself. But the sorcerer confounded my effort. He is hateful and evil, foul beyond all our imaginings . . .''

"You let nothing slip concerning our rebellion?" Gonji asked.

*"Nein,* however . . . he does seem to know that there are subversive plans afoot—may I have some wine or ale, Miklos?"

Zarek consented in an apologetic rush, and Greta poured him a goblet.

"You're convinced that it *was* Klann you spoke with?"

"It was Klann," Garth confirmed, "though a different personage. There was indeed a new Rising after the tragedy here." He went on to describe the physical appearance of the new Klann personage and the brief personality impression he had obtained from his audience. "He seems desperate. Yet I am convinced he wishes for peace almost as much as we do. He needs the respite here."

Lydia spoke. "Then we must drop this mad plan and proceed with our normal lives. Stoically. Surely that's true now, isn't it, gentils? *Gentils?"* There was no scorn in her censure of the violent planning now, only entreaty.

*"Iyé,"* Gonji disagreed, "I'm afraid nothing is changed."

"But what would happen if we *just didn't do it?"* she asked imploringly.

Garth sighed. "The king is, unfortunately, unable to see the evil he has allied himself with. He is out of touch with the workings of the sorcerer, of his own troops. And the Foul One would find some way to assure our destruction. It's that simple. Evil has come. We must flee it, if we can. Fight it, if we cannot."

Lydia's eyes narrowed. "Even you, too, now, Papa Garth?"

Gonji also regarded the popular smith's reversal with

suspicion. And he had the sudden conviction that Klann's former general again was withholding information. He never seemed to tell all he knew.

"Why did you take so long returning?" Gonji probed.

"I rode alone for a time, troubled. I needed time. Time to think."

"Even when you carried such potentially important information?"

Garth cocked an eyebrow. "What have I really learned, apart from Klann's new presence, that we haven't already known or suspected?"

Gonji sighed glumly and went to the shutter. The streets were deserted, dismal. Here and there lights could be seen penetrating the gloom from seams in the dwellings along the Street of Charity. Two riders clopped past Zarek's house, one of them the Scottish highland rogue Gonji and Wilf had seen weeks before. His monstrous claymore stretched from just above the ground at his mount's hooves to a point nearly level with the man's head.

Not long after them came the last alert team, Anton and Roric.

"Well, the prodigals," Vlad pronounced, drawing a scowl from the bald-pated Gray knight Anton.

"There's trouble," Roric told Gonji and Michael. "Old Gort was found dead. Run through with a sword."

Gasps of shock. "When?—where?"

"In his gatehouse," Anton furnished, "about an hour ago."

"God Almighty," someone swore.

"But why?" Lorenz asked with a perplexed frown. "Why should they kill him? He was a harmless old man."

"Just the kind of viciousness they deal in," Wilf said through ground teeth.

"*Iyé,*" Gonji said, "he must have seen something . . . someone. I had him watching—I'm afraid it's my fault. It was too well known that he was watching for me.

158

*Choléra . . ."*

Ten bells rang at the square. Many would be going to the chapel for memorial services, practicing their calm movement for the evacuation to come.

Gonji sat heavily, hands on knees. "Poor Gort. If only we had the assistance of a medium now to ask him who it was he saw. Oh, Tralayn . . . if ever you exercised powers granted by the spirit world . . ."

Michael cleared his throat and gained their attention. "Well, who isn't here among the captains of the evacuation procedure?"

"Nagy—Monetto—a couple of others—" came voices in reply.

"Let's get on with the timing plan and the route maps," Michael urged, and they began to pull up chairs around Zarek's oval dining table.

"Ten bells," Gonji mused, stroking his nose. "Roric, when was Gort's body discovered?"

"About . . . eight."

"Herr Vargo," Gonji said, "when did you leave off Ignace?"

Milorad lifted his palms and shrugged. "Six? In any event, well before sunset—Gonji! Not *Ignace!*"

The samurai waved him off, and Vlad Dobroczy chimed in: "Paolo left me a lot earlier than that."

Gonji rose and retied his sash more snugly, then seated his swords in his ominous fashion. "Our wagoners have much to answer, and I'll not wait any longer."

Wilf and his two helpers pushed up from their seats. "We've got work to do at the shop, too. We'll go with you. We're not needed here."

"Wait a moment," Roric cautioned. "If all our plans are known at the castle now—I mean, let us assume it *was* a traitor who dispatched him. Won't Klann know the identities of all the leaders of the militia—?"

"And here we all sit, most of us," Anton added in

159

sudden realization.

Jiri and Greta looked to each other fearfully, and she reached out a hand to the young *bushi*.

Gonji thought a moment. "Hmm. Possibly. But it's more likely Mord still withholds more than he tells Klann, or the garrison would have descended on us in hordes by now. Still, it's probably a good idea for some of you to leave. I'll see the rest when I return. I won't be gone long."

*More crazy unknowable factors,* Gonji thought as they loped through the rustling mist and shadow-loomed darkness, his stiff knee aching a bit but the pain now forgotten.

When they reached the empty corral, the other three split for the other side of the street and kept moving at a casual pace to the smithshop's dripping canopy. Gonji waited until he saw lamps flare alight in the Gundersen home. Then he ran in a crouch to the wagonage a short distance past the corral.

Creeping past the drays, he caught the distant, muted sound of hacking, as of a hatchet, followed by soft sweeping patters. They issued from the closed and shuttered rear work area behind the wagonage office. The place was totally darkened.

A loud bang, and a spill of metallic objects.

Gonji surveyed the environs. No soldiers in sight. He tested the seating of his swords, his eyes growing accustomed to the darkness. Squaring his shoulders, he scampered to the rear door of the wagonage. More noise. He tried the knob slowly, quietly. Locked.

He took three steps backward, balling his fists, and launched at the door. His stamping front heel kick shattered the bolt and slammed the hardwood door full open.

He drew steel and called for the dim figure in the middle of the workshop to halt. A hint of ashen-gray cheekbones

160

and a gleam of eyes. The figure emitted a strangled cry and ran for the front of the shop, Gonji in quick pursuit. The man—for it was a man's voice that gibbered words of terror in an alien tongue—stumbled against an A-frame and fell, still scrabbling uselessly. Spinning onto his back. Holding up a warding hand—

Gonji stared down into the sweating face of Boris Kamarovsky.

"*You!* You little ferret! Stand up!"

Boris obeyed, cringing, jabbering in Russian. Pleading.

"Speak German," Gonji growled. "What are you doing here? Where are Paolo and Ignace?"

"I—I—I don't know, *bitte*—" he wailed. "I'm working—waiting—waiting for them, that's all—"

"Keep your voice down, fool," Gonji hissed.

Boris broke for the open door, but Gonji anticipated it, tripping him. The wood craftsman fell full length on the floor, yelping as his head struck something in the dark. The samurai closed the door and blocked it.

"I'll ask you again. Once only. What are you doing here?" His tone simmered with menace, but he sashed the Sagami.

"I, uh, I—I was helping out. I brought a hitch, a wagon hitch the old man ordered. They-ey-ey weren't here. So I waited." His eyelids flickered madly, his knees quivering like jelly.

Gonji appraised the condition of the shop as his vision sharpened. It was a shambles.

"Why did you do this?"

Boris shook like the last leaf in winter. "I—uh—" He glanced about at the ruin he had wreaked of valuable harnesses and traces. Many of these were to be used on the crucial wagons. "I just—I didn't want to *die*—" On the last word he began to sob in sporadic fits. "I'm—I'm afraid to die. I—I don't want to go away from here on a wagon—I—I don't want to go down there—the

161

catacombs—with those worm-things—"

"So you destroyed other people's chances . . ." Gonji, too, was trembling now despite his effort at control. "You had no courage to fight for your city and your people, but you found it in your gut to commit sabotage, didn't you? You disgusting little vermin—you betrayed us to Mord, didn't you?" Gonji began advancing on him.

Boris backed away, fending Gonji's accusations with fluttering hands. *"Nyet!* I didn't—really. Not you. Not the militia. Only Phlegor."

"What?" Gonji froze.

"Just—just Phlegor, that's all. I knew—" Boris whimpered, then began to laugh senselessly, though pain showed uppermost in his posturing. "—I knew he was trouble to you—that's what you'd want—to be rid of Phlegor. I—I—"

"You betrayed him to the enemy . . ." Gonji's own projected guilt over having directed suspicion on Phlegor now fueled his fervor anew. "Your friend, and your *boss."* His words crackled with contempt.

He took two quick steps forward, and Boris fell back against a workbench. The wood craftsman's voice wailed, high and keening:

"They sent me here for harnesses, I got afraid, so I did it, but I won't do it again—I'll—I'll—*please,* just let me go back, I'll take the traces, and and and—"

Gonji noticed the dark stains on Boris's jerkin.

*"Lower your voice.* Where is Ignace?"

Boris's eyes kept straying to the far wall. Tools on the walls. A shallow storage shed.

"He—he's gone. He wasn't here. I—I don't know."

The storage shed again. Gonji peered furtively behind him.

"Open that."

*"Nyet! Nyet! Let me go!"*

Boris tried to run. Gonji caught his arm and twisted it

162

behind him, walked the struggling craftsman to the shed, flung it open—

The old blind wagoner fell out with a heavy clump. Lifeless. Spidery branchings of dark blood fled the wound on the back of his skull. Boris fell to his knees, staring straight ahead, the slack form crumpled before him.

"He—he's all right. I just knocked him out . . . that's all," he babbled in Russian.

The smell of death was thick about the musty shed.

A gurgle in Gonji's throat, as if he'd taken a sudden shot to the gut.

The whine and flash of the Sagami.

Boris's head thudded dully on the floor amid the soft lap of gouting blood from the stump of his neck.

Gonji emitted one hissing breath, and then he whirled to engage the figure that pushed through the blockaded door with a squeal of wood on wood.

It was Wilf. "Gonji—what the hell's going on. *Omigod* . . ." The young smith gagged on the stench of fresh blood.

Gonji explained the shocking scene as he cleaned the Sagami.

"Come on," he commanded when he had finished, "let's get the bodies into a dray outside."

*"Then* what do we do with them?"

"You'll have to have your friends move them to the undertaker's. Or into the sewage trenches, if they can't make it safely."

Wilf grimaced. "But that's . . . barbaric."

"Welcome to war." Gonji's tone became sympathetic. *"Gomen nasai*—I'm sorry, Wilf, but they'll have to let their survival instinct guide their actions."

Wilf shook his head gravely. They both paused, flexing their hands a moment before reaching down for the corpse of Ignace Obradek.

"Poor old guy," Wilf said with a grunt as they lifted.

163

He averted his eyes from his burden. "I used to—help him here when I was a kid—he told me—the wildest stories of soldiering—I ever heard—"

"You know the business here?" Gonji queried. "The traces and everything?"

"Some."

"You'll have to try and straighten the mess."

They loaded Ignace into a dray, covered him, and went back for Boris.

*"Posram shié niédam shié,* old man," Gonji said over his shoulder, recalling Ignace's fiery words.

Inside, Gonji wrapped Boris's head in a sack and prodded Wilf into the moving of the grisly remains.

"So it was Boris," Wilf declared hollowly.

"I'm not sure. I wish I could be. It seems Paolo's shirked *all* his duties this day—if his duty still lies with Vedun."

They loaded the body. A party of mercenaries rode past when they were done. Wilf wore Spine-cleaver, and the pair of *bushi* crouched in the shadows, sword hilts gripped in clammy fists, until the hoofbeats were far down the Street of Charity. In the distance, dogs were barking, and sporadic shouts came to their ears.

"Gonji, listen," Wilf said, grabbing his arm. "When you go back, I wouldn't say—I mean, *I* understand about this, but . . ."

"I know. The facts of war come hard to the delicate sensibilities of your compatriots. I'll remember."

They bowed to each other and parted.

Back at Zarek's, Gonji lingered outside under a parlor shutter in the whispering wind and rain, composing himself, straining to hear the tenor of their conversation. Zarek was holding forth. The few Slovak words Gonji understood were not far removed from the thoughts in Gonji's own mind:

". . . of a fellow I knew a long time ago who made his

living by spying. Only trouble was he was lousy at it. Every time I'd see him, his lack of skill had cost him something. First it was his left ear, then his right ear—"

"Sounds like Paille's stories of his brothers," someone cut in.

"—the last time I saw him it was to identify which body went with his head after a mass execution he'd spied his way into."

Gonji's abrupt appearance from the rear of the house startled them. "I'd keep the shutters closed and my voice down, if I were you," he said seriously.

Lydia gasped and stood up from the sofa. Their outcries and expressions gave him pause.

"Holy Jesu Christi," Vlad breathed.

"Gonji—?" Garth muttered with darkening brow.

He looked down at his tunic and breeches. They were stained with fresh blood.

A bold pounding at the front door resounded through the house. All were on their feet now in breathless anticipation, expecting Gonji's state to have brought the new caller.

"Open it," Gonji ordered in a reserved tone.

Zarek went for the door, pale and dismayed, but the door burst open before he could reach it. It took a few seconds for everyone to recognize the visitor beneath the curious makeup and affected eye patch, the huge hat and begrimed face. It was Paolo Sauvini, posturing like a triumphant thespian.

"Got them all fooled, haven't we?"

"Shut up, Sauvini, and close the door," Michael said angrily, clumping forward a step on his gimpy leg. "What in God's name is wrong with you? Where have you been?"

"What's this all about, Paolo?" Milorad added.

Paolo slammed the door and leaned back against it, regarding the group's anxiety with bleary amusement.

"Where have I been—hee-hee-hee." His curious titter was cut short when he pressed at the pain in his side. It was clear that he'd been tipping a few.

Gonji turned away, a slow boil creeping into his carriage. His hands reached up to grip the mantel above the roaring hearthfire, his back to them.

"I've been to the Provender, you see. Done a little snooping. Gonji—*sensei,*" he drawled, appending a deep bow to the samurai's back, "you'll be glad to hear that they're searching high and low for you in the eastern sectors. Tramping through the fields and orchards, overturning rocks by the river—hee-hee!" He hiccuped and excused himself to the ladies present. Then his callow tale of bravado rambled on. "I know their strength—maybe six hundred in Klann's humble command now, did you know that? And I know a lot of other things about them. I know even the price on the *sensei's* head—oh, it's a handsome one indeed, my *sensei*—"

"A thousand *talers,*" Gonji said.

"Eh?" Paolo mumbled thickly.

"A thousand *talers—idiot!*" Gonji jerked about like an awakened watchdog. "Don't you think I know all that? Did you believe I was only bluffing when I spoke of my operatives? Why do you think Gutch from the Provender never attended militia training?"

"Too much of a fop," Lorenz observed with casual levity.

"You should talk, Gundersen," Gonji shot back.

"You asked," Lorenz replied, raising a conciliatory hand. "In any case, I *did* choose to train in the catacombs."

Gonji turned back to Paolo. "Gutschmidt already told me of the bounty on my head, and of the troop strength, *and* of their disposition and leadership. And who do you think set the occupation force on their futile hunt for me in the eastern end, *fool?*"

166

Paolo's face colored. He rubbed it, smearing the grime, swallowing back his embarrassment.

"Gutch has been plying them for information right in their midst, doing what he's been told," Gonji continued. "But *you*—you can't so much as obey a simple order. You were told what your job was, but you left Vlad to perform it for you, creating a serious breach of security. Sitting and putting on a drunk with the brigands to get your useless intelligence. And once you were in your cups, what were they able to drag from *you?*"

"They got nothing from me," Paolo roared.

"What happened to your side?"

Paolo blinked, felt the wound. "I—I got hurt, that's all."

"Taking part in that jackass rebellion?"

The wagoner's sheepish gaze was as good as an admission.

Gonji stretched up tall. "Do you know that your boss had his skull split tonight while you were off on your bold sortie?"

Mutters of shock and concern. Someone dropped a flagon.

"Oh, how awful," Lydia intoned mournfully, hands cupping her cheeks.

"Who?—what happened?—how?"

"That jackal Boris Kamarovsky," Gonji explained.

"Boris," Garth said incredulously. "What did you—?"

Gonji paused reflectively before speaking. "He joined the others in the Dark Lands this night." Seeing their horrified expressions, he bridled. "Ah, so now I have your attention again. You call yourselves educated people, and yet why is it that I can only gain your attention *when I do violence?*"

"But surely not Boris," Milorad said skeptically.

"*Nein,* of *course* not," Gonji minced. "Of *course* Strom Gundersen couldn't be a traitor. Of *course* Lydia

167

Benedetto couldn't be a traitor—" A ball of warmth burst inside him as he spoke. He was as pleased to feel her name roll off his tongue as he was satisfied with the starkness of it as an example. "—of *course* Boris wasn't a traitor. No one here is a traitor, yet we have sabotage and treachery in our midst, and all our plans are known to Mord, *neh?*"

"Calm yourself, Gonji," Michael enjoined.

*"Hai,"* Gonji said, inhaling deeply. And just as suddenly as it had begun, his outburst subsided. His face assumed its well-known inscrutable cast, and as usual he was aware that the placidity that followed his loss of temper was more unsettling to the others than the venting itself.

"So you have your traitor—Boris," Roric Amsgard concluded.

"Perhaps," Gonji replied, "but I'll reserve my judgment on that. I still entertain . . . other possibilities. Finish here and disperse. Michael, you know where you can reach me, if you need me."

With a bow to all of them and a last look at the brooding Paolo, Gonji took his leave through the rear of the house.

*Chapter Nine*

The rain showed no sign of abating.

Stillness descended on the curved bowl of the Transylvanian Alps. The sky pressed low and heavy, the clouds ceasing to move. Their gloomy roiling had engulfed the moon—it would bloom to ripe fullness on the morrow—and swallowed up the proudest peaks of the Carpathians.

168

Vedun seemed sealed from the blessed deliverance of both men and gods alike. Tension crept like a living thing from every shuttered dwelling, every seething shadow.

Gonji paused in a darkened lane to rub his burning eyes. He briefly considered all the tempting reasons why he should accept Hildegarde's invitation to return to her home for the night. These he balanced against the reasons he should not; foremost among them was his desire to maintain an angry fighting edge, a focus and concentration of his energies.

Grumbling at the inner voice, he nonetheless embraced its counsel and passed her house, moving on into the dangerous southwest quadrant to enter Tralayn's.

The late prophetess's weathered dwelling was no longer under guard. Gonji entered through the popular side window and breathed in the antique stuffiness of her parlor, mingled with heating oil. Almost at once he noticed the telling pale pattern above the mantel where the formidable broadsword and axe had hung. He approached it slowly, casting suspicious glances around the room. Now, as his eyes parted the dusty swarming shadows, he saw the evidence of Ivar's abortive effort at setting the place ablaze: splashes of oil, charred logs scattered on the floor, shredded drapery fabric, soaked and blackened.

A strange chilling sensation, the feeling that he was being watched, caused him to clear his throat, to make a few comforting noises. Without pondering the state of the house any further, he passed through the fireplace.

Thoughts of Tralayn became more generalized, splintering into thoughts of the other women who had late aroused his interest. There was Hildegarde, who inspired admiration and lust in a heady concoction; and Helena, the gentle flower whom he had shamed, whose artless overtures of love so unsettled him, fired him with a guilt he should not feel; and Lydia, the one he dared not desire yet did in futility, who made him glad for the insistent specter of imminent war.

He hardened his heart with the thought that he should allow none among them to clog his vigilance with their cloying allure. He should trust none of these people implicitly. They had disappointed him so many times.

And, his sense of duty and veracity reminded him cruelly, he had also failed them . . .

Reaching the nexus cavern's receiving chamber, he exchanged terse words with the sentries and walked to the shriveling carcass of the monster worm. He circled it, loathing curling his lips. Nodded with forlorn and senseless satisfaction at the many shafts and polearms still buried in the pulpy flesh of its many segments. Swallowed back the taste of bile when the phosphorescent glow of mineral-veined rock fell on the blood stains of its victims, those valorous *bushi* who had grimly helped dispatch this creature of the nether world.

Gonji tested the *ninja* darts he had fashioned, throwing them for short distances at quintains that remained upright on the training ground. Fair. Their weighting passable.

Tora nickered to him from among the horses bunched into a hastily erected corral near the southern valley tunnel.

Gonji dipped the three darts point first into the dark, thick pool of congealing worm venom and strode across, smiling, to speak gently to his horse. Tora nuzzled him as he stroked the doughty steed, wishing earnestly to be mounted again, in full stride, his blade bared. He could fairly feel the wind in his face and hair.

A pang of grief tugged at his heart. He might never again know the sensation . . .

Calling over the tunnel sentry, Gonji instructed him to arrange for Tora to be smuggled back into the city the next day and left at the Gundersens' stables, apprising the man of the considerable risk. The *bushi* seemed willing.

Retrieving the darts, Gonji wrapped their discolored points carefully such that he would not accidentally jab himself. Then he placed them into an inner kimono pocket at his breast.

Before he reached the receiving chamber, Aldo Monetto and Alain Paille came surging out, brightening visibly to have located him.

"Gonji, we've got trouble," the biller announced.

"The guildsmen just killed three brigands snooping around the woodcraft shop," Paille explained.

Gonji tried to slow them down. *"Ah, so desu?* One at a time now—what happened?"

"The armored wagons—" Monetto began.

The boorish artist silenced him in mid-statement. "My gun cupolas! They discovered them working on my design for the gun cupolas on the escort wagons. Now those didn't mean anything to them. They just look like paneled coffins—which is all they are in truth—"

"Get to the point," the samurai said.

"Well, it was the calthrops and spiked bulwarks that were loaded on the wagon that tipped them, of course. Ready to be driven to the lanes and alleys you designated as killing grounds and fortifications on the map."

*"Choléra,"* Gonji breathed. "Has there been an alarm?"

*"Non, monsieur*—fortunately."

"We saw to that," Monetto agreed. "We took them quietly—"

"But there's sure to be an investigation when the three are not seen by morning, no?"

*"Hai,* perhaps . . ." Gonji stroked the back of his head thoughtfully. "Nothing for it now but to see what the morrow brings."

"The damned wagon was supposed to be moved," Monetto grumbled. "We sent Boris Kamarovsky after a

171

team and harness *hours* ago. He never returned."

Gonji sighed but resisted telling them of the fate of Boris. "Send someone else. You'll find Wilf at the wagonage. He'll tell you what happened there."

They updated Gonji on the clandestine work by the militia, and soon they ascended to the chapel, where the late-night memorial service was nearly at its end. The final strains of a dirgelike hymn swelled through the wall behind the altar where the three slumped against damp rock, held back by the sentry who acted as both doorman and first line of catacomb defense should Mord suddenly decide to tell Klann all he knew of their military disposition.

Gonji exchanged words with the guard, a miller from the *bushi* who wore his straight sword proudly, in the manner a *katana* was worn. The samurai absently asked of comings and goings to and from the chapel and down into the catacombs, but all the while his thinking kept turning to the sweet sound of children's voices calling out in innocent song for the mercy of their God.

At length the service ended, and the shuffling of the exiting crowd could be heard.

"I'm going to sleep in the chapel tonight," Gonji announced. "Just till dawn."

"So close to danger, *monsieur le samurai?*" Paille asked, grimacing. "Do you dare the fates?"

"I want to be quickly available should anything break. Who's the sentry in the vestibule tonight?"

"Klaus," Monetto replied, eyebrows uplifted.

Gonji winced but nodded. "Well tell Klaus to wake me when the cocks crow. Tell him I'll be . . ." He thought a moment, smiled thinly. ". . . in the confessional on the left of the altar."

"*Si,*" the biller chuckled, "if God doesn't crumble you into cinder by morning. Oh—Helena's out there, I think. She's been inquiring after you. Shall I tell her you're about?"

172

*Iyé*—Gonji heard the stern voice of denial burst within him. Part of him wearied of the girl's insistent pursuit. Yet a gentler part of his nature strobed his belly with guilt. He swallowed hard.

"If you wish," he said softly. The artist *tsked*.

Paille and Monetto preceded him into the nave. When it was determined that there was no threat of discovery and the gathered worshipers had largely cleared the chapel, the samurai emerged from behind the altar. He saw first the great cross from the square, which had again been leveled by the troops. It glowed somberly in the light of a hundred candles where it leaned on the altar rail.

Then he saw Helena, wide eyed, a smile breaking across her lips. He rubbed his nose nervously and bowed to his friends, who departed with self-conscious glances that flicked back and forth between Gonji and Helena.

"Remember, *monsieur*," Paille said without looking back, "you are in the house of the Lord."

The merest tightening of Gonji's jaw betrayed his annoyance.

Helena came up the aisle and genuflected before the altar. She approached Gonji slowly as he neared the confessional, her eyes soft and large and faintly expectant. What followed was a clumsy exchange of signs that he remembered later as having been both uncomfortable and embarrassing. Several other people who had remained behind in private prayer studiously avoided looking at them, though their continued presence bothered Gonji greatly.

He busied himself at unsashing and stowing his swords pointlessly, smoothing out his soiled garments, and preparing a sleeping nook in the cramped quarters of the confessional—pitiable efforts at essaying the role of distracted leader. All the while Helena plied him with half-understood signs inquiring after his well being. And—worse—humble assurances of her continued affections.

173

Gonji felt for all the world like the insensitive cad to end all cads. He was burdened by karma in a way he had never experienced before. He became impatient with his conflicting feelings and all the less indulgent of Helena for it.

As he grew increasingly weary of the girl's presence and irritable with her in his guilt, he became more direct in his rebuffs of her overtures.

He appealed in a joking manner to the age difference between them—which he judged as no more than a dozen years. But there was no sense of playfulness in the hard edge of his expression, and Helena's waning exuberance reflected her dawning sense of futility and rejection.

She signed desperately that there would be more for them to communicate when the madness in Vedun had ended. The brimming moistness in her sloe-eyed gaze seeped into every crack that fissured his adamant resolve. But his face remained a blank mask that stared back like a closed book, and she withdrew from his impassable dark eyes and departed with a soft rustle and tiny echo of footfalls.

No one remained in the nave, save Gonji.

*Done. Finished. Karma. There was no other way. I cannot commit myself to a woman I do not love.*

Had he been asked at that moment how fared the good samurai, Gonji would have replied that he felt like shit. He experienced an abrupt insignificance before the infinite and unknowable forms of karma. At the same time he cursed the duality of his nature that caused him to act and then regret.

He had been too long in the West, and it had engendered in him the beginnings of a scrupulous Western conscience through association with its cultures and religions. Just one more manifestation of karma. All is karma, *neh?* Nothing but trouble, that is my lot—spies, sorcerers, recalcitrant people, rejected lovers, a price on

174

my head—

And where is my friend the Deathwind when I need the comfort of his monstrous presence?

*Loneliness among companions . . .*

From the tunnel sentry he ordered writing materials. The paper, quill, and ink were brought to him by a messenger from the catacombs, and by the velvet glow of the candles that shone through the grating in the confessional, Gonji began to inscribe the ideograms of his death *waka: The soft white blossom—/ Her eyes, markers of my grave . . .*

When he was done Gonji folded the paper into a pocket and hunkered back into the modest comfort of the confessional. Leaning into a cramped corner so that he could stretch out his battered knee, he cradled his swords against one shoulder and peered out into the nave. The ethereal aura of gold drew his eye. The outline of the crucified Christ on the tall, leaning cross.

"What will happen to these people, Iasu?" he whispered. "Am I wrong to lead them into all this? They're good people, I know. Deserving of life. I must admit that I'm very fond of them, most of them. What place does the wheel of karma serve in their lives? Will we ever reach a common understanding of the ways of the worlds of flesh and spirit?"

Gonji sighed wearily and willed his body to sleep, but more thoughts crested the horizon of blackness he tried to impose. Fears and insecurities now haunted him in the still, dark chapel.

*Julian.* Julian . . . he might be a shade faster. His tecnique a trifle more serviceable in single combat. *Iyé!* Never! His mind, unbidden, framed scenarios of the duel to come. The duel that *must* come. He succumbed to these only momentarily, arresting them, knowing that this was the worst he could do; it was a distraction and a splintering of concentration—a sure way to lose a match.

*Ushin no shin*—mind of no mind. The total dismissal of the mind's awareness of itself as a potential agent of action—this alone must be the *bushi's* concern. He must admit his fear and overcome it, plan his strategy but bury it. The planting of the seed. Instinct must ultimately rule as always.

But what was his fear?

Not the fear of death. But the fear of failure. Falling short of saving these people, failure at his duty.

He pondered his motives, deciding at last that it was at least partly his conceit and passion for admiration that made him wish to avoid death until it was over, so that he might be there, for better or worse, having given it his all, for all to see.

Then the bitter notion occurred that no one would care whether he would be there or not, that life would continue as it always did even after his death. His death might have meaning only to him. Right now no one thought or cared whether Gonji would survive, only whether *they* would, and their loved ones.

*Iyé,* he told himself defiantly, there are those who care and will remember.

And as he drifted through the hazy borderland into sleep, he dreamed of a strange forest that swelled with the chanting of distant choirs. And of trees bedecked with headless corpses that swayed and pointed as he floated past. And of Jocko, and Hawkes. And a young woman with a somber face and hair of harvest gold . . .

## Chapter Ten

Klaus awakened Gonji before the dreary dawn on the day of the full moon.

A few old women present in the pews were startled to see him emerge from the confessional to stretch languidly and mount his swords in his *obi*. He tried to hide his scowl when he saw them cross themselves in reaction to his apparent irreverence.

The samurai bowed to them solemnly and raised a finger to his lips to beg their silence, then moved quietly to a window to peer out into the street.

Commerce came to slogging life in the dawn mizzle. The city, soaked and puddled, was shrouded in fog. Visibility was limited to a block in every direction. Farmers and herdsmen guided their animals toward the gates. Early merchants plodded to the marketplace, where many of them would, they knew, present little more than the semblance of business as usual. A caravan of an itinerant chapman ruddled over the wet cobblestones. The drivers seemed wary but cheerful; they'd be less the latter when they found their wagons commandeered for the militia effort. There were few soldiers in evidence. Cattle lowed and sheep bleated nearby in the stubborn fog. Dogs began to bark as the roosters touted the sun's reticent presence in the mountains to the east.

It was *the day,* Gonji's harpy of guilt reminded.

"Did I wake you too early?" the lumpish buckle-maker fretted.

*"Nein,* Klaus, this is fine. Keep your voice down."

177

"Will you break your fast with us down in the cata-combs?" Klaus went on. "Some of the *bushi* are—"

"Shh! No. Not now." Klaus's nasally tone was irritating so early in the morning, but Gonji regretted his curtness with the solicitous fellow. Klaus seemed not to notice.

"Can I get you anything? Something from the market stalls?"

Gonji waved him off. *"Nein,* nothing now, Klaus. If your relief is here, why don't you go down and join your friends. Anything break during the night?"

Klaus launched into a tiresome recital of every trifling detail he had observed during his sentry shift. He took his job seriously and was certainly thorough, so Gonji indulged him with feigned interest. Nothing of any consequence had transpired.

"Good job," Gonji said when he had concluded. "Be off with you now, and stay alert."

Klaus bowed to him and padded off. Gonji exhaled a long breath as he watched him move away, his thoughts turning to what he had in mind.

It would be foolhardy, but he had to do it. This was *the day,* and whether by dint of his training in the Land of the Gods or the influence of the Christian chapel he had slept in, Gonji was in a ritualistic turn of mind.

He would cleanse himself for what lay ahead. And that meant a trip to the bath house.

Alerting the new chapel sentry as to where he would be, the samurai slunk off through the fog with an adrenal flush. The reckless action was akin to spitting in the devil's eye. The thrill of danger surged through his bowels as he moved from cover to cover, running in a crouch, sword hilts clutched for steadiness, wiping his dampened face repeatedly on a sleeve of Milorad's capote.

He reached the bath house without incident. The *kami* of purification smiled down on his effort.

As he had expected, the baths were empty but for the Polish lad who attended them. It would be the women's hours at the bath house for a time, he knew, but he instructed the nervous boy to turn away any who came, paying him handsomely in advance for the private service.

The attendant knuckled the grogginess from his sleepy eyes and set to work, heating the coals under the hot water with flame and bellows and hurrying to prepare the stones in the steam chamber.

Gonji removed and folded his garments ceremoniously, careful to keep both his matched set of swords and his *tanto* knife within arm's reach at all times. He performed his morning stretching regimen and a few necessarily compacted *kata*.

He laved himself in the hot water, enjoying its bite to the fullest. After a short session of deep breathing exercises and a time of meditation, he relieved himself in the chamber pot located in a small latrine at the back of the bath house. Ever vigilant for disturbing sounds from the street, he moved to the swirling clouds of white heat in the steam room, where he luxuriated awhile.

He glanced at his weapons to be sure of their position when the boy engaged in a brief, spirited argument with a group of early bathers. Gonji chuckled to hear the indignant female voices jabbering away along the Street of Hope, vaguely pleased that there were some in the city who would not allow their state of occupation to interfere with their daily lives.

The boy entered with more hot water, smiling sheepishly and flinging up his hands over the embarrassment he'd suffered. Gonji grinned and, reaching into his kimono, tossed the youth another coin.

He leaned back, wrapped in a long linen cloth, listening to the hiss of the steam, allowing it to bestow its therapeutic graces on his body. He unbound his stiff knee and found that it responded well to the magic of the heat.

Euphoria spread through him, and he tried to express his gratitude for the simple pleasures of life by composing a poem.

Then he heard the high giggling of the women, followed at once by the surly laughter of men.

At first he thought it must be the women the lad had rebuffed, returning now with their husbands. As soon as he heard the terrified piping of the boy's voice in the small lobby, he knew it must be soldiers.

*Choléra* . . .

The boy was jabbering in a loud, high voice the same words he had spoken to the women earlier, telling them the bath house wasn't open for business yet. *Gallant lad,* Gonji thought, grabbing up his swords. He let the linen wrap drop free and sprang to the farthest wall, through billowing clouds of thick steam.

A grunting, swearing male voice in the lobby. The boy's high whining tone again. A woman said something that evoked laughter. There was a sharp slap and the boy's outcry.

Gonji gritted his teeth in reflex. Soundlessly in the steamy sibilance, both the Sagami and the *ko-dachi* slipped free, their scabbards discarded along the wall.

A man's voice again, cursing. Drunk. Roisterers out to extend a long night's carousing with a few acquatic antics. Gonji swallowed and crept along the wall till he came within sword's length of the right edge of the doorway.

The boy burst in, holding his face. Red welts swelled on his cheek in the shape of a man's fingers.

Gonji hushed him, made calming gestures. The boy's tear-filled eyes seemed ready to bolt their sockets.

"Shh-shh. How *many?*" the samurai whispered urgently. "How many *men?*" He tried to remember the Polish word for man. Couldn't. He held up two fingers, three—

The boy bobbed his head in terror. Held up three and

180

two, three and two. Three men, two women.

Gonji nodded. *"Domov,"* he ordered, recalling the word for "home," and appending a thumb jerk. The boy left at once.

A woman's voice called out. "Hey, dummy!" It was Italian, as was the cry that followed, this in a man's voice, thick with drink:

"Hey, you little jackass! Where you going?"

Gonji thought he recognized the voice. From the sound of what followed, it was clear that the boy had made good his escape. More grunting and laughter. The sounds of clothing being removed with difficulty and tossed to the floor. The tinkling laughter of the two women again. Their mirth rankled Gonji. His jaw tightened with disgust.

They were in the baths now, just past the doorway to the steam room.

And then one of the brigands was inside, yanking a woman behind him. Both were naked. The mercenary flung an arm up in a mock gesture of fending off the heat of the steam.

The woman saw Gonji and shrieked.

The bandit turned, his lips describing the mouth of a funnel, hands flung before him defensively. Gonji sliced open his midsection, the force of the blow batting the man down onto the baking stones. He screamed in agony. The woman fainted in the archway, and Gonji leapt over her into the main bathing chamber.

Now it was the second woman's turn to scream as Gonji confronted the pair of startled bandits before the hot tubs. One of them was Luba, the bald, muscular brigand from the boxing matches. Gonji's eyes flared to see him.

"So the time has come, *neh?*" Gonji growled. "Come collect the price on my head, swine!"

Luba sucked in a shuddering breath and shoved the woman at Gonji, lurching after his sheathed broadsword on a nearby bench. The samurai nudged the woman aside,

181

whirled his blades in an intimidating display of shimmering magic.

The second man fisted a dirk, seemed poised to throw it. But then Luba pulled his sword from its scabbard and charged, howling with fury. Gonji sidestepped the strong but awkward two-handed arc of the other's long blade. Dancing inside Luba's overswing, Gonji slashed right-left with his blades, finishing with an inside-out crossing blow, relieving Luba of a hand and ribboning his flesh with deep wounds. The bald bandit's eyes glazed over, and he fell face first into his pooling blood.

The remaining mercenary emitted a strangled cry and threw his dirk with such wild frenzy that it crashed into a corner near the ceiling. Gonji sprang after him, but his bare feet slipped on the wet floor and he stumbled to his knees, dropping the *ko-dachi*.

His opponent still wore boots and breeches. He seized upon Gonji's misfortune and scrabbled to the lobby. He reached the door to the street, yelled for help, and a second later had his head snapped back by a blow of such force that he was knocked cleanly off his feet to land unconscious next to the benches in the lobby's waiting area.

The huge figure of Simon Sardonis appeared in the doorway as if materializing out of the fog.

Gonji descended on the unconscious man, finishing him with a single stroke that brought a moan from the sobbing woman who'd been pushed at him.

The samurai blew out a breath and mopped his face.

"You're looking well this morning," Simon said wryly, indicating Gonji's nakedness. "A fine position for a warrior to get himself in, don't you think?"

Gonji sneered and went for his clothes. The woman who fainted had by now come around to sit shuddering against the steam room arch.

"Do you kill them, too?" Simon asked in French, his

throaty voice harsh and gravelly.

Gonji's jaw worked with indecisiveness, though he knew that he would not. "We shouldn't leave witnesses to our presence in Vedun," he found himself saying, testing Simon's own attitude.

"With your traitor about," Simon answered without pause, "it's not going to matter. Anyway, infidel, we've got to draw the line somewhere. Are these local women?"

Gonji shrugged. "I think not. Probably trollops drawn by mercenary gold."

Simon strode forward with arms folded and loomed over the two frightened women. They shrank back from him, regarding him with doom-laden stares, covering themselves.

To see their horror he gave way a bit, stepped back a pace and dropped his arms to his sides.

"You've been . . ." he began uncertainly in High German, "you've been with very evil men. That was a mistake. Get your clothes, and get out of here. Say nothing to anyone about what or who you saw here. Don't make me come after you."

They scampered to their clothes, put them on and, without a look to either Simon or Gonji, ran from the bath house. Gonji watched them go with menacing eyes, then looked to Simon, who stood with his back to him.

"You could have done better than that," the samurai advanced cautiously, *"neh?"*

"What did you want me to do?" Simon spat, wheeling about. "I'm no *monster!* I could barely stand the way they looked at me." He turned away again.

Gonji nodded somberly. "Tralayn's dead."

"I know. I went to the chapel looking for you. They sent me here. There's something you have to see."

"What?"

"You'll see—at the slaughterhouse."

"Eh?" Gonji's eyebrows arched. But Simon would say

183

no more. He merely turned up the cowl of his cloak and moved to the lobby door.

"You'd better not go like that," Simon said over his shoulder.

Gonji grunted and set to garbing himself. When he was clothed and cloaked, they dragged the three bodies into the latrine, locked the bath house, and sprinted off through the dreary back lanes toward the slaughterhouse in the southern quarter. The fog dispersed by degrees, but the rain began stippling the city anew.

The streets of Vedun burgeoned now with human and animal shapes that slogged along in rain-toned iron grays and mousy browns, their muttering and barking and caterwauling muted and echoed in the ears of the pair of renegades who sped through the steep-walled labyrinth of ancient back lanes.

When they reached the animal pens of the slaughterhouse district, Simon's presence agitated the beasts into a clamorous, tossing frenzy. He growled at them, in futile anger, stirring them even more.

They entered through the rear of the long, low granite building where provisioners in bloodied aprons greeted them tersely and led them past butchers who paused and gaped before joining up at the rear of the gradually lengthening procession.

Gonji slowly brought his twisted facial muscles under control; the offensive stench of the place was something he always chose to avoid. Acquiring the taste for meat was one thing, but dealing with the physical details of the butcher's trade was something else.

The provisioners ushered the pair past the flaming ovens where waste was destroyed and led them to a preparing room hung with both fresh slabs of meat and sections for curing and salting. Many kept their distance from Simon, viewing his ominous predatory-elfish appearance askance or averting their gazes altogether.

The barking and snarling of Roric's huge dogs could be heard echoing in the chamber.

Gonji paused outside and glanced around the crowd quizzically. "Well?" he said. "What's this all about?"

"Come in, Gonji," Roric called from the chamber. Some in the crowd crossed themselves or made other warding signs. Sweating brows and darting eyes evinced their disquiet.

Gonji and Simon moved into the chamber. Roric stood flanked by Wilf, who moved forward to greet them, and Vlad Dobroczy. A few other farmers hovered nearby with creased brows, and off to one side, apart from the rest, stood Garth, cap in one hand and head hanging low.

They looked where Roric and Wilf pointed. The provisioner's dogs held at bay a large black ram, whose features caused Gonji to start. A chill of revulsion tracked up his spine.

The animal exuded an almost human sentience. Its eyes were shaped like a cat's, the irises hued a piercing yellow. Its teeth were bared, the lips drawn back not in menace at the growling dogs but rather in a semblance of ghastly smile, a grinning death's-head.

"It was found with Strom Gundersen's scattered flock," Vlad Dobroczy declared portentously. "None of the other animals would go near it. Some herdsmen saw it and came to me. I helped them drive it in."

"The damned thing's almost . . . Satanic," a butcher said, rapt by its sight, crossing himself as if in reparation for having spoken the evil name.

"And Strom?" Gonji asked of Vlad. The farmer shrugged and averted his eyes.

"Gone," Roric spoke softly.

Gonji searched out Garth, but the smith would not meet his gaze. Simon focused lances of revulsion on the eerie creature.

The event's portent was clear to all. They waited

expectantly to hear what their military leader would propose.

"Call off the dogs," Gonji ordered Roric. The provisioner complied, the straining, barking animals being withdrawn from the chamber.

The black ram tilted its head as if in amusement. When its evil eyes locked with Gonji's, its strange smile seemed to expand.

Then, snorting and emitting a guttural outcry, it charged straight at the samurai, curved horns angled for mayhem.

Klann sat back heavily in his gilt-crusted chair. His wine flagon swung loosely in his slackened grip. His officers and attendants studied him narrowly, apprehensive of the effect this shocking intelligence would have on their liege. Mord stood before the king, arms folded, reeking confidence and self-satisfaction.

King Klann stared in disbelief at the parquet floor for a ponderous moment, slumping forward, elbows on knees. No one expected the reaction that followed. The king snorted and laughed, first softly and in a thin timbre, then uproariously, imperial head flinging back.

"A revolt and evacuation?" he bellowed in an incredulous voice. "Can you believe them, Gorkin?"

The castellan's posturing and headshake clearly indicated his shared surprise.

"Stupid, stubborn, courageous people," Klann reflected, causing them to ponder his meaning. "Weapons in coffins! Can you doubt their pluck when they'd try something like this? To evacuate their innocents under fire of three entire occupation companies! Marvelous!"

A few soughings of breathy surprise were evoked from the advisers. His attitude was wholly unexpected. Mord's gloved hands levitated slowly at his sides.

"I would hardly have expected your Majesty's reaction

186

to be so laudatory," the sorcerer complained.

Klann scowled at him. "My warrior's empathy always makes me admire a people who aren't afraid to fight for what they believe. And all the while they've played at passive resistance and blank-faced ignorance of these clandestine raids." He smiled and shook his head in perverse pride. "That old magistrate—Flavio—what an actor, even to the grave! You did well to steer us to this place, Mord, and once again We've proven our wisdom in selecting it."

He chuckled, and his administrators joined in tentatively.

Mord's voice boomed with sepulchral disapproval. "You'll want to wait till the morrow's dawning, then, after I've received a fresh imputation of the Dark Lord's power. Tonight—the full moon's focus, and the faith chant which will imbue me with the force necessary to lay these rebels low."

Klann's look unnerved him. It was laced with suspicion, almost accusing. "Why do that?"

"Well to . . . to allow them to make their overture of revolt and then teach them the lesson they're so anxious to learn." Apprehension strained Mord's words.

"I think not," the king declared. "We'll worry about your . . . *additional* power later. For now, I think We'll be riding to Vedun—"

"Mi-*lord!*" the advisers entreated as a body.

"Surely, sire," Captain Sianno pleaded, "you'll not be going back there again. Not after the last time. Why, they already owe you their unworthy lives tenfold and again for sparing them after . . ." The captain's voice failed him at recounting the treacherous poisoning and new Rising.

Klann blared a belly laugh. "Think you that they'd try such a thing again? I daresay they're still whispering and crossing themselves superstitiously over what they glimpsed of our enchanted heritage. And they do need a look now and again upon the countenance of their liege lord, don't they, Sianno?" He rose and clamped an affectionate hand on the captain's shoulder. "Especially such a shifty face as that of Klann the Invincible!" Good-natured laughter leaked off some of the tension.

Mord shared none of the humor. "I must protest this venture, sire. With all due respect, it's little more than abject folly."

"Mind our tongue, magician," General Gorkin warned.

"These people have fighting spirit, Mord," Klann said. "I want to move among them for myself. I want the pleasure of announcing the new military decree. Martial law in Vedun, a city of the martial-minded, where it ought to suit their tastes. And since they're incorrigible and spoiling for a fight whatever the cost, then they can have their fill—"

Mord's head lifted imperceptibly as his tenebrous spirit fumed with delight. But it was short-lived.

"—we're going to conscript all able-bodied men into the army for next spring's assault on Akryllon! All their weapons will be confiscated, their wagons will be placed under guard, and our military governor will assume command."

"Who might that be, Milord?" Gorkin asked.

Klann gestured at Sianno. "Captain, I believe you'd be well suited for the job. Surely you must be weary of so very long in faithful battlefield service."

"If it please you, sire." Sianno's frowning lack of enthusiasm indicated his own obvious displeasure, but Klann paid him no heed.

"My armor!" Klann called out, sending personal servants scrambling. He tipped his flagon for along draught, wiped his mouth, still grinning with satisfaction. "This day bodes well—you've pleased us with your intelligence, Mord. Don't be so glum. We'll keep them

188

under the oppressive fist you favor so. Oh—and your giant, Tumo—We'll want him to go along to shackle their restive spirit, but We'll want you to remain here. Can you guarantee that he'll respond without fail to my orders and those of my officers?"

"Unconditionally, sire," Mord replied. "Tumo knows his lord, and his proper place."

"Yes, and that reminds me—no, not that one." Servants had retrieved Klann's suit of scarred battle armor. His outburst froze them midway into the chamber. "We're not going there to fight them! Bring us our finest dignitary array, and see that it's polished to a blinding sheen. This is their liege lord going to them. Their *conqueror,* not their conqueror-to-be!"

The servants shrank before his imperious mien and rushed out again, whispering accusations and recriminations.

"Now," Klann continued, "what was I saying?"

"That the giant reminded you of something," an adviser blurted in an inquisitive tone.

"Ah, so I did. Your wyvern's roost, Mord—it's empty of late. What's become of our winged protector?"

"He's . . . on something of a mission," Mord lied. "I've set him to tracking down those strangers who have helped stir the province to rebellion against you."

Klann nodded. "That Mongol bandit with the singing swords and that . . . agile murderer who eludes whole companies of archers—they're still about, you say? And Julian—where is he while they roam freely?"

The question was rhetorical, but Gorkin responded needlessly, "At his headquarters in the city, sire."

"They're about," Mord concurred, "but not so important as you might believe, milord. They merely agitated trouble in a city that was already rampant with treason."

"Just see to it that your wyvern doesn't fail."

189

"He's very thorough, sire."

Klann's resplendent armor arrived, and the servants dressed him in it, topping the gleaming golden half-armor with an ornate winged helm that had been wrought in Akryllon, a treasure of great value that drew gasps and whispers when it was placed upon the king's head.

"You are sovereign lord of the territory," Gorkin voiced in awe. "All men seeing you shall know it."

Klann viewed his servile flattery with a slightly skewed expression but assented wearily.

As he strode from the chamber, fastening his broadsword's baldric, his retainers in tow, Klann stopped and addressed Mord.

"I never did ask you, sorcerer—who was your source for this intelligence about the planned rebellious action?"

Mord's eyes smiled, widening in the black pits of the gold mask. "A citizen of Vedun. Someone who has decided that fealty to the king is of paramount concern."

"Never mind," Klann said, frowning. "I'd rather not know."

"Ah, but milord would find this person's identity especially amusing, methinks—"

"Forget it!" Klann snapped, lowering his voice at once. "Suffice it that the deed is done, and We take no special pleasure in acts of conspiracy." He marched out, leaving Mord to shrug in silence, his head tipped awry as if in condescending regard of the fumbling ways of a child.

When the room was empty, Mord's hissing laughter issued from the breath holes of his mask, rising in sibilant triumph to echo in the vaulted ceiling of the king's sanctum.

*The fool,* he thought. His Royal Multiplicity can't decide *what* he wants. I remove a soft monarch and replace him with a capricious one. Who would have thought the idiot would find their resistance commendable! This deposed nomad desires valor from both friend and foe alike! And he suspects me, yet he does nothing about it because he *needs* me so and is pleased to have been freed from limbo. Isn't that touching . . .

But now I see that I should have waited till the morrow to tell him of their insurrection plan. My worry was unfounded that Klann might not marshal his forces against them swiftly enough. No need to fret. By tonight's darkest hour my power will be such that I can begin to manipulate them all against each other when I choose. There are many of them, counting both sides, so I'll have to be careful. But I have my power—and the knowledge of the catacombs, which I'm pleased I withheld from Klann. Yes . . . before they realize what I've done, the slaughter will have commenced.

I shall have wiped Vedun from the face of the earth, and the League's compact will be fulfilled. The Necromancers will be free of the last human claim to Akryllon.

Mord's eyes clouded with mists of rage when he remembered the oriental thorn and his enigmatic partner, the audacious pair who had somehow eliminated the wyvern. His gloved fists pressed the jawlines of his mask. Then he leaned forward on the arms of Klann's opulent private chair, the chair that would be his in a matter of hours.

They would know torment, those two. They would pay the price of defiance. Whoever, whatever this Deathwind was, he and his barbarian companion would know the terror of the hunt. For tonight the Dark Master would grant him control of the Hell-Hound.

And against the Hell-Hound there was no protection in heaven or on earth.

## Chapter Eleven

"Look out!"

Black smoke fumed from the ram's nostrils as it charged the poised samurai.

Gonji drew and sidestepped in a single motion, slashing down viciously and cleaving through the creature's backbone and spine. It bleated in a subhuman voice, its legs splaying out beneath it. Two swift blows severed its horned head.

Gurgles of revulsion from the observers. A thick inky fluid leaked from the beast's gaping neck.

Gonji grimaced as he cleaned the Sagami. "Burn that thing," he said tonelessly.

They stared at it awhile before anyone moved. No one mentioned Strom's name again for a time, nor did any among them meet Garth's eyes. All the while Gonji observed their reactions, anger and anxiety welling up in his chest as he considered his next action.

"Black ram at the full of the moon," a butcher said, crossing himself. "That's an evil omen."

"We've had a few lately," Roric replied calmly.

*"Ja,"* another man fretted, hysteria stirring in the tremor of his voice and the flicker of his eyes, "this one—the evil face in the mountains—monsters in our skies—"

"We're doomed," another said, shaking his head hopelessly.

"Forget the old tribal beliefs," Roric said, "You're a Christian now. These omens can't harm you if—"

"Gonji just slew your omen here," Wilf interrupted. "And there are no more wyverns in the sky." He bobbed his head at Gonji, who didn't return the gesture but only brooded silently as he wiped his blade.

Wilf pointed in astonishment. "Gonji—the Sagami's nicked."

*"Hai,"* the samurai concurred in an abrupt tone, as if the matter were of no consequence—or of such embarrassment that he wished to gloss it over swiftly. He swept the *katana* back into its scabbard without a glance at Wilf. He shot a look to Simon Sardonis, who was moving past him.

The band fell to muted whispering when Simon knelt beside the ram's head, seized a ringed horn in both hands, and snapped it off with a powdery crumbling sound.

"Feels like your ruined crops," he said, his raspy voice causing some of them to look from one to the other. "Mord . . ."

"Michael had better hear of this," Roric said.

He designated one of the provisioners as a runner, but then Gonji shattered the tentative mood of the gathering.

*"Hai,* bring Michael here," he shouted. "And while you're out there tell Lydia and Lorenz and those others who find my suspicions offensive that there are *no traitors in Vedun!"*

"What are you saying?" Garth asked quietly.

Gonji ignored the question. "When did you last see your son?"

"Are you accusing Strom of being a traitor?"

*"Nein,* I'm asking you when you last saw him."

A red flush slowly colored Garth's face, starting at his neck. "My son is not a traitor," came his deliberate words.

"There seems to be some evidence to the contrary," Vlad Dobroczy offered from the corner of his mouth.

"Shut up, Hawk," Wilf warned.

193

"Where did you learn such haughty words, farmer?" Garth asked threateningly. "Don't move me to actions I'll be sorry for, Vladimir."

"No one's accusing Strom, Garth," Gonji said. But his unspoken agreement with Vlad hung about them oppressively.

"And what would you do if you thought he *was* a spy for Mord—*behead him like you did Boris?*"

Garth's angry words had a telling effect on the crowd in the slaughterhouse. Wilf looked embarrassed. He had advised Gonji to tell no one of the manner of Boris's execution. But he himself had told his father.

The samurai gave no sign of offense. His eyes swept downward, his thoughts preoccupied with crumbling unity and failing leadership.

"Yesterday morning," Garth said into the stillness, "at the meeting, when the assignments were passed out. That was the last time I saw him. So you have your answer. But I swear to you this—" He pointed a stubby finger at Gonji. "My son is not a traitor. He has a kind heart. There is no guile or treachery in him. He hasn't the cunning for it, God knows, and what would motivate him? I'll tell you what *I* think of this business. I think the Gundersens are being used again, as scapegoats. By Mord or whoever, I cannot tell. But *that's* what I say. The Gundersens are used and accused, and there will be an end of it. *Vielleicht* it is time for the Gundersens to fight back, God forgive me."

Gonji's eyes narrowed. "Perhaps it is," he agreed gently.

Garth stormed out into the main cutting chamber.

"We'll need you here,' Gonji called after him.

"You know where to find me." The smith's broad back disappeared around a corner on the main avenue side.

"You don't think Strom really is a traitor, do you?" Wilf asked with concern. Others also voiced their

194

incredulity.

"I don't know, Wilf," Gonji replied, rubbing his neck. "Someone is. Maybe more than one."

"I don't doubt it, after seeing this," Dobroczy griped.

Wilf moved toward him, one hand sliding along the hilt of Spine-cleaver. "If you accuse my brother, you accuse me, pinhead."

"Your opinion doesn't count," Vlad sneered, clawing for his dirk. "You see with the eyes of a brother only."

"Save it, both of you," Gonji roared. "You're going to need it."

"I can't believe it's Strom . . ."

"He *was* Boris's friend."

"It's not Strom."

Simon's throaty voice gained their attention. He leaned with his back to a wall. When he saw them all looking, his eyes flicked about the room nervously, enjoining discreet distance.

"How do you know that?" Gonji queried.

Simon stared through him a moment, then shrugged, lowering his gaze. "I just know it. I've watched him in the hills. I know his moves. It's not him."

Gonji frowned. "Then you've been watching the wrong person's moves."

Roric started a work party on the grisly task of cleaning up the remains of the demonic ram. The carcass was removed with poles and burned in the ovens while they discussed the matter in desultory fashion. As they did so, Gonji paced the room, hands behind his back, and raked back and forth in his mind over what he knew and suspected. At length he assembled them again.

"Here is what I think: I think Mord's sent us a sign that we're at his mercy. And I say we pursue the ragged remains of our plan. Let's spit in his eye—Roric, send some of your men after the leaders. Get Monetto and Gerhard, Anton, Berenyi, Nagy, the others . . . Get them here right now."

The messengers were sent out at the run. Roric had ale brought in and poured for those who remained.

"I'm going out," Simon announced suddenly.

"Where?" Gonji asked.

"To find Strom."

The reckoning was approaching. Gonji knew that Simon might indeed plan to do what he said, yet of more compelling concern was the accursed man's need to flee the company of other humans. Tonight, the full moon, many hours off. But already Simon was behaving like snared game, so urgent was his need to be alone.

Yet Gonji's own sense of urgency drove him on in the deception.

"I wish you'd wait till the leaders arrive. There are plans we *must* discuss, and you've made yourself part of this now."

Simon seemed unsettled by the others' darting glances, and he leaned back languidly against the wall where he sipped from his goblet, still apart from them.

Deep within, Gonji felt a flooding of relief.

"Well, *I'm* ready for whatever happens," Vlad Dobroczy said, offering his cup in a toast. "First the city, then the castle!" Some of them took it up. Wilf pretended not to hear him.

Gonji studied the farmer closely, curious about his new spirit of cooperation. He had no sound reason for suspecting Dobroczy, yet . . .

*The castle.*

"Wait," Gonji shouted, startling them. "Where's that girl? The one with the mourning face and cornsilk hair. I never did get a chance to speak with her. First she's at the castle and Strom's here. Then she's here and Strom's—? Strom did smuggle her in—"

"Lottie Kovacs?" Wilf interjected, his face twisted.

"*Hai.* Bring her here—if *she* can still be found in the

196

city." Wilf went to the Vargos' to fetch the girl.

"I remember someone," Gonji went on distractedly, "someone at the castle, looking down at us. A woman, I thought. She was looking down through a crack in a gallery door, but when I caught sight of her she disappeared . . . It was someone who didn't want to be seen there."

His words evoked confused mutterings and wild speculations that Gonji steered away from, choosing instead to mull over his own ideas. His eyes twitched with petulance.

Berenyi and Nagy arrived in the throes of an argument, Michael Benedetto close behind them. Not long after, Wilf returned with a suspicious Lottie Kovacs and, curiously, Karl Gerhard.

The dour archer stepped between Gonji and Lottie when cursory greetings were out of the way.

"Now what's *your* problem?" Gonji asked.

"What's this all about? Why do you want to talk to Lottie?"

Gonji peered closely at him. *"More* trouble? You and I have never had trouble, Karl. I just want to ask the girl a few questions, that's all. Something bothers me. What's your connection to her?"

"We're just friends," Gerhard replied defensively.

*"Ja,* they used to be *good* friends," the cheerful voice of Aldo Monetto called out from the doorway. "Phew! Why don't you do something about the stench in this place, Roric? You two getting acquainted again?" he asked Karl and Lottie.

Gerhard waved a hand at his friend disdainfully. Lottie made no reaction. Her small, pouty mouth held its grave set. Her eyes were demurely lidded and angled at the greasy floor. She pulled her shawl close about her.

"Nice meeting places you pick, *sensei,"* Monetto chided jokingly.

Gonji pushed past Gerhard and stood before the girl.

"Something's been bothering me, Lottie. You said you fled the castle during the confusion on the night King Klann came to the city."

"That's right," she said, shrinking back under his steely gaze.

"How was it accomplished? In a wagon, you said?" Gonji persisted.

"A grain wagon," she responded, her face clouding with the beginnings of emotion.

Gonji nodded, smiling.

"This is ridiculous, Gonji," Karl complained. "We know all this—"

"Tell me," Gonji persisted, ignoring the archer, "your boyfriend, eh—?"

"Richard," Wilf filled in.

*"Hai,* Richard. Your Richard is a baker, *nicht wahr?"*

"Not just an ordinary baker," Monetto called merrily, sloshing ale into his flagon. "A 'bun-brains,' eh?"

A few nervous laughs.

*"Ja,* he's a baker," she said warily.

"Then if you made your plan," Gonji reasoned, "and it involved a grain wagon at the bakehouse, why was Richard unable to accompany you? Exactly what happened to him?"

Monetto laughed, and Berenyi joined him.

"Richard, Squire Bun-brains, isn't exactly a tower of courage," Stefan offered sarcastically. "It's maybe a contest between him and this old man here for—"

Nick Nagy jumped up and made a move toward him. "Watch it, you little shit! Sorry, young lady." He made a conciliatory gesture, but Lottie had seemed to hear none of it. She was staring fixedly before her.

*"Stehen Sie,* all you clowns," Gerhard demanded. "You're getting personal now, *sensei."* He looked at Lottie before continuing. "The fact is that things haven't

198

been running smoothly between them lately, and . . .''
His words dwindled, but the meaning came through
clearly. Monetto fluttered his eyebrows at Berenyi.

"I see," Gonji said, strolling now, hands clasped
behind him.

"Do you have a reason for this?" Karl asked. "I
mean—*Gott in Himmel!*" Realization dawned, and his
pale eyes deepened in their sockets. "Are you accusing her
of *spying?* Her father was *murdered.*"

Lottie began to tremble. By the respectful murmuring,
it was clear that the morbid reminder had exonerated the
girl in consensus.

"I know that," Gonji allowed, his back to them. "But I
also know that there was no grain wagon, either to or
from the castle, on the night she speaks of." Rasping
inhalations. "The last piece of usable information I had
from Old Gort before he was murdered—the log he kept
for me."

Gonji peered over his shoulder at Lottie, and she began
to sob. Tears streamed down her doleful face, and her
breath hitched pathetically. Gerhard held her, burying her
face in his shoulder. He cast an angry, tight-lipped
expression at Gonji.

It seemed to the samurai that they were a curious
match, too similar to be attracted. Both fair and blue-
eyed, with the facial sets of professional mourners.

"Did you have to do that?" Karl said barely above a
whisper. There were no jokes now among the self-
conscious watchers. Only quiet anticipation.

Gonji said nothing, his face impassive. Waiting.

Lottie pushed away from Karl and dried her tears,
pulled herself up tall. A rigidity seized her. Pride or
defiance.

*"Nein,"* she said, brushing at her hair in sudden
umbrage, "I didn't escape by wagon. I didn't have to. I
walked right out, you see . . ."

There was something disquieting in the woman's manner that held them transfixed.

"Walked right out through the gate. It was easy." her tone dripped with contempt. "After all, I'm a woman. So it's easy for me. All I had to do was surrender myself to the persuasive charms of that pig who stewards the larders. Oh, of course it took time. But it gets easier after the first time. So easy—" Her voice cracked as she choked back a sob. One by one the men's gazes fell away from her searching eyes of frosted blue. "It's you big brave men who have the tough job. You have to pick up a sword and slay them. But it was easy for me. Do you—do you want all the details now?"

She paused, shaking, then glared at Gonji. "No one put a sword in *my* hand."

Lottie broke down into waves of angry tears again. Karl moved forward to comfort her, but she pushed him away and turned to the wall, hugging herself and muttering imprecations. No other sound penetrated the breathless heat of embarrassment in the room until Wilf spoke.

"Lottie—Lottie, what about Genya?"

She turned, puffy-eyed. "Genya, Genya, Genya! What are you afraid of, Wilfred? That she'll be as weak as I was?"

"Genya's your friend, Lottie—"

"*Ja*, my brave friend. You don't have to worry, Wilf. Genya would rather die than submit. She's strong. She doesn't fear death. She's too much in control for that. Men fall over each other for her attentions, and then they're afraid of her. *Nein*—not *Genya*. It's the weak that have to suffer in this madness. Genya gets her way, you bold warriors take up arms—but what am *I* to do? People murdered and tortured all around me—the evil magician following me, asking about me—my family gone—*what was I to do?*" She caught her breath. Grim resolution informed her tone. "I would not spend another day in

200

that awful place. So, *military commander,*" she railed at Gonji, "have I satisfied your curiosity? Have I made it plain enough for you? My love of life won out over my affection for Richard. Some feelings turn out to be stronger than others, don't they? Anyway—" She laughed harshly. "—he wouldn't want me . . . like this, would he?"

Karl placed his coat over her shoulders. "You needn't put yourself through this, Lottie." He cast Gonji a stern look and led her from the slaughterhouse.

No one spoke for a space. Gonji sighed, growling pensively. He felt sympathy for the woman, but her self-pity annoyed him. To his way of thinking, she had done the cowardly thing. No samurai woman would ever have submitted to such treatment to obtain freedom. Yet he knew he was being unreasonable. The damnable cross-cultural conflict again.

*"Touché,"* Simon said, stinging him out of his reverie.

*"Gomen nasai*—so sorry, gentils," Gonji said not without a trace of rancor. "From here on you can investigate your own compatriots' treachery—"

"Forget it now, Gonji," Michael said. "What do you propose? I don't believe this business about Strom Gundersen being in league with the sorcerer."

"Nor do I, I suppose," Gonji agreed, some of the men concurring, "but—"

"What did we miss?" Jiri Szabo's pleasant youthful voice called out as he padded lithely into the room. The Gray knight Anton limped in close after him. A few steps behind, the band parting to give him respectful room, Garth strode in, his broadsword belted to his waist, a baldric across his shoulder.

Gonji peered at him expectantly, adrenalin rushing to see the once mighty warrior's formidable bearing.

"Welcome again, Herr Gundersen."

Garth nodded curtly.

"We're all here," Michael declared. "Now how do we go about picking up the pieces?"

Gonji folded his arms. "Send everyone home quietly from their jobs, sector by sector. Have the chapel bell rung for services. Women, children, old and infirm to the catacombs. Slowly, gentils. Calmly. Start the alert, one team to each sector . . .

*"Shi-kaze* is now."

"You yellow devil—*you knew all along."*

Gonji glared at Simon. "That today would be the day of uprising? Of *course*. It had to be. I needed *some* measure of surprise against the likelihood that the traitor could get to Mord."

"Well you've lost my assistance, fool," Simon rasped. "Did you really think you could force me to be swept up in this? You're a *lunatic*. You say Tralayn told you of my curse. You understand that I must be far from humankind on this night, and yet you try to deceive me like this—*why?* Do you really have any idea of what you're asking?"

*"Hai,"* Gonji replied.

They were alone in the curing room, yet Simon glanced over his shoulder to be sure none in the slaughterhouse were near enough to hear. There was scurrying activity without. All were preoccupied with the imminent battle. But still Simon spoke in a whisper.

"I was right when I first saw you," he said, silver eyes staring at the samurai in disbelief. "I should have killed you that first night when I sensed the trouble you were stirring."

"The trouble preceded me here."

*"Oui?"* Simon responded in a choked voice. "Well now you can finish it yourself."

He turned to leave, batted a joint of beef out of his path. It swung creakingly on its hook.

"Why can't you do it, Simon?" Gonji called out, halting him.

"Keep your damned *voice* down." The words ground through clenched teeth.

"Why can't you use the power of the Beast against the invaders?"

"Shut up! It's impossible. Can't you accept anyone's word?"

"Have you ever tried to control it? Have you ever had reason before?" Gonji took a step toward him, emotion rising.

Simon extended a clawed hand as if he would throttle him. "Would you like to stand before me while I tried?" A mad gleam sparkled in his eyes.

"If need be," Gonji answered evenly. "Why can't you try? What are you afraid of?"

"If you need to ask that, then you *are* mad. Have you any idea what it could do?"

"We're all willing to risk that."

Simon snorted. "You presume much to speak for all these people."

"I am the military commander, and that is my right—*what do you fear.* That people will see what you cannot help being? That is the lot of all of us, isn't it?"

*"Non,* you bastard infidel!"

"Well then *what?*"

Simon roared at the top of his voice: "Because if I die on this night, it will be freed to join its demon father—*it wins!*"

His eyes gaped and his gaze drifted slowly groundward. His long fingers were balled into pale fists at his sides. A breath shudderingly passed his lips, as if a great burden had been lifted. But Simon remained adamant.

"Do what you must," he said, "but do it without me." He pushed through the sides of beef and out into the main butchering area.

"All right," the samurai shouted at his back, "go away and live forever—the lonely beast. But don't seek out human companionship the next time you're dying inside of emptiness. Go up into the mountains and *bay at the moon with the wolves.*"

Gonji's fury echoed in the nearly abandoned slaughterhouse as Simon disappeared through a rear exit into the wet back alleys, the limp from the arrow wound all but gone.

# Part II

## Shi-kaze

*"All that our hearts desire is death in war"*
                                    —Aztec motto


## Chapter Twelve


Despite the expected confusion and reluctance, the movement of non-combatants began, sector by sector.

Women, children, and elderly folk, the crippled and the ill moved through the rain anxiously in response to the surreptitious order as the chapel bell tolled in deception.

Galioto the stockman, placed in charge of the catacomb descent, ushered them in. The older people shook their wet garb in the vestibule, then genuflected and crossed themselves upon entering the nave. Some shook their heads and clucked or beat their breasts to see the irreverent positioning of armed militiamen in the chapel. The children whispered and snickered, eyes bright with anticipation. Some gawked in wonder, their parents' bewildering words of preparation still fresh in their minds.

Galioto moved them into pews amid shuffling and the slapping of moist footfalls. When the nave was near to full and the new arrivals dwindled to a trickle, it was found that this first sector of the eight—the northwest portion of Vedun—was short by several families. There was nothing to do but send out messengers to check on the absent, while the second series of tolling was begun, designed to attract the next sector's innocents.

Michael Benedetto arrived a short while later. The new council leader was the coordinator of the evacuation movement. Michael notified Galioto that military interest in the chapel service was minimal. The young Elder then limped to the pulpit with the aid of his crutch, where he led the gathering in a short benediction and a hymn.

Galioto mopped the sweat from his perpetually worried brow and aided Danko, the tanner who had lost an eye in the training, in carrying a pew over to a window. Other pairs of militiamen performed similar actions at each chapel window, where tools were laid in case it would become necessary to fortify the windows against assault.

The dairy stockman waved a weak gesture of encouragement to his own wife and smiled to his children. Then he spoke to his partner.

"Danko," he began, "Danko, how would you go—I mean, if you had to, and you could choose?"

Danko aimed his dark eye patch at him and replied in choppy Italian, *"Die,* you mean? You're asking if I had to die?"

"Shh! *Si,* I—you—you know. Would you choose a pistol ball? Or the sword? Or—?"

"Not by sorcerer's beasts," Danko snorted, his twitching grin dissolving at once. He jerked a thumb at his ruined eye. "Not by polearm again, either. Even though I know what that feels like. I guess . . . maybe . . . maybe I'd choose a pistol ball. It looks . . . quick." His breath came in sibilant gasps.

"Quick," Galioto repeated thoughtfully, nodding and rubbing his nose. *"Si,* I suppose you're right. Quick might be best. I don't—I don't think I could stand much pain."

"There's no good way."

The hymn completed, Michael gently urged the congregation forward. When the vestibule sentries had signaled that no soldiers lurked about, the catacomb door was sprung open behind the altar. An escort party in half-armor gingerly prodded the first few refugees into the torchlit tunnel just as the second sector's non-combatants began to enter the vestibule.

Some wore their fears on their faces, while others

208

managed to muster courage, or stoicism, or whatever optimistic resignation they needed to remove the children from the shapeless terrors to come. The children, for their part, went along trustingly, jostling and tittering, their small hands safely tucked into larger ones, arresting their silliness whenever they passed under the timeless gazes of the Christ and the saints at the altar.

Then a woman in the vestibule started to sob. Efforts at calming her triggered a wave of hysteria. Some at the tunnel entrance now demurred, fell back. Others sat heavily on the soft nap carpet, shaking their heads in refusal. The children caught the older folks' panic, and there was an outbreak of snuffling.

Galioto cast Michael a plaintive gaze.

Outside there were shouts and screams and the clash of steel. With the first report of pistol fire, the militiamen in the chapel drew their blades. Some threw open a coffin lid and retrieved longbows and arbalests. But the crush of bodies made it impossible for them to act.


The woman sipped from her goblet, trembling under Salavar's cruel gaze. Julian ordered her to repeat her story, but her companion did it for her.

"So he got Luba," the captain said. "You're sure it was the samurai?"

The trollop bobbed her head with certainty, but Julian didn't bother to look. He knew.

"And this other man with him—who was he? Did you ever see him around Vedun before?"

"He was a giant," the first woman muttered. Her voice shrank to a whisper. "Looked like—like paintings I've seen of . . . the night dancers of the wood. Only he was a giant."

The other woman spoke chillingly. "No one who sees this man could ever forget him."

Julian strolled as he spoke. "So he's come back,

too—*that* one. A shaft in the ass wasn't deterrent enough for him. We'll find out what he's made of."

The women had run from the bath house half-clad, badly shaken by their encounter with Simon and Gonji. One of them sat with her arms folded across her bare breasts, a man's jack draped over her shoulders. Salavar saw the soldiers who had brought them elbowing each other and leering.

He snatched a cloak off one of the mercenaries and flung it at the exposed woman.

"Put that on," he commanded. "You're not entertaining now. This is a military inquisition. *You—*" He leveled a calloused hand at the soldiers. "—stand at attention. You're not at the inn now."

Salavar caught a smirk and strolled across the floor to pass in front of them. When he reached the end man, he turned to face him squarely. His right leg snapped up and out and kicked the mercenary full in the belly, knocking him back against the wall, where he sprawled, doubling over. The second man in line turned ashen when he saw Salavar's catlike smile.

"That will do, Salavar," Julian said. "You *ladies* may leave us now," he continued, indicating the door.

The women looked at each other.

"He—he promised he'd kill us—the giant man," one of them fretted. "You can't send us out there alone."

"We've got to get away from here. Far away."

Julian rolled his eyes. "Salavar, would you care to escort these fine ladies as far as the postern gate?"

"Only to the gate?" they said as one. "But then we'll be alone on the road—it'll be night before long, and—"

Salavar grunted. "If it's all the same, why can't you have these lazy bastards ride them out. I've no time for whores now, not with high-priced quarry about."

Julian nodded. "All right. You men, see them out. Then report back to Ivar within the hour, is that clear?"

The mercenary squad ushered the tearful women out of the headquarters building. When they were alone, Julian and Salavar began loading and priming pistols, methodically and in silence. They wrapped the firearms against the rain and prepared to leave.

Salavar ran a finger along the deadly edge of his battle axe, then donned his cloak and hefted the piece onto his shoulder. He sniffed, his long mustache jiggling, and he met Julian's eyes, his own flickering with calculation.

"Listen," Julian said, "I want that oriental alive, if you find him."

"You'll get him with life left in him. Don't worry. What about this 'giant sprite' they're talking about? How much for him?"

Julian thought back to the stranger's fight with Field Commander Ben-Draba. "You bring *him* in by yourself, and you can name your fee."

"I've been known to command a good one for special cases like this."

"Just get him," the captain said, "and bring him before King Klann. I don't think you'll be disappointed."

As they moved out into the hissing rain and mounted, a rider splashed to a halt before Julian, saluted, and spoke breathlessly.

"Captain, the *king's* coming to the city."

*"Now?"* The messenger assented, and Julian went on in surprise. "But why? Why come here again after the last time?"

"He brings the 2nd Free Company—and Tumo. They've discovered some kind of rebellion plot."

Julian called out orders, and the best troopers from the 1st Free Company mounted and secured their weapons in hurried response. In moments they were pounding away from the sparsely populated southeast sector, headed for the square.

\* \* \*

Three mercenaries splashed through the lane behind Hildegarde's dwelling in the southwest quadrant, compelled by mild curiosity over the pair of large wagons parked, driverless, in the narrow street.

They dismounted and approached the wagons, shaking dripping helms and drawing their swords warily. The first soldier tossed aside the rear flap of a wagon. The short swing of an axe caved in the side of his face.

His partners cast about in alarm, raising steel in their futile defense. But the swarm of militiamen overwhelmed them with quiet speed and efficiency. In seconds the bodies were removed to a metal foundry warehouse, their horses and weapons commandeered by citizens.

Gonji strode out of concealment in an alley. He grunted a curt approval of their performance and moved to Hildegarde's back stoop. He towed a roan stallion by the reins. Tora had been smuggled to the surface, but Garth's stables were too dangerous to approach yet without risking the compromise of *shi-kaze*.

The samurai wore a leather cuirass, pauldrons and vambraces, and an old sallet with eyeslit visor designed by the famous Augsburg armoring family, the Helmschmieds. He would be momentarily unrecognizable, and that momentary delay would prove the undoing of any enemy. Wilf followed close behind him with his black gelding. He was similarly armored, albeit the young smith was topped with a cavalry Zischagge helmet of German design. Both carried their swords in their back harnesses.

The area was secured by crossbowmen and pistoliers, and men began to stream into the lane to await further orders. A company of about sixty *bushi* formed near the wagons, drawing weapons and armor from them as needed. The large draft horses were draped in leather armor, and Paille's coffin-cupolas were unloaded and affixed to the tops of the wagons. They were hinged in several places with cutaway sections from which pistols

212

and crossbows could be suddenly unleashed. The sailcloth cover was slit along the sides of the wagons where gunloops had been cut in the plate-armored insides.

Wilf went over tactical assignments with the fighting squads while Gonji entered Hildegarde's home.

The samurai found the Scandinavian warrioress honing a halberd on a whetstone in her kitchen. Several militia personnel were in the parlor, selecting armor and stringing bows.

Hildegarde grinned to see Gonji.

"Well, Gonji-Gunnar, we fight well this day, isn't it so?" She ran a finger down the vicious edge she had wrought, nodding with deadly satisfaction.

"*Hai,* we fight well this day or never again." He exchanged curt greetings with the busy men in the parlor, then returned to the kitchen. He took great comfort in Hildy's confident courage. She would lead ground troops in the important function of dividing and harassing Klann's horsemen, throwing them into disarray and establishing killing grounds in Vedun's mazes of ancient walled alleys and byways.

"Come here, Gonji-Gunnar," she said, laying aside the halberd.

The samurai moved toward her with curiosity. She placed her arms around his neck and kissed him, long and passionately, then stepped back, tossing her head and laughing at his discomfiture.

Gonji affected annoyance, unsure of how to act in his complete surprise. After first ascertaining that none of the others had seen, he rubbed his chin and scowled unconvincingly.

"Stand fast there," he said. "Is that any way to treat your superior?" He tussled with the flaring of lust that unsettled his thoughts. It was an emotion out of place, out of time, in their present circumstances. Yet not altogether regrettable.

Hildegarde laughed again to see his expression. "You feel real warm, Gonji-Gunnar," she said softly, taking up the weapon again. "Some of them, they say you be cold. They be wrong, no?"

Gonji met her smoldering eyes for an instant. "Let's see how warm we can all be when this is over," he said, the fatalism he felt mocking his words even as he spoke them.

He cleared his throat and stepped to the parlor arch.

"Let's go," he said.

They followed him out solemnly into the rain of the rear court, where the militia squads assembled. Wilf strutted before them, hands behind his back, declaiming in a command voice that caused Gonji to smile discreetly.

"—a lot of different kinds of armor and dress here," Wilf was saying. "Take a look around you. Know your fellows. Particularly you archers. We don't want you dropping your friends—" Nervous chuckling spread through the attentive band.

Gerhard and his archers moved up to Gonji. Rain rattled on Karl's dark steel hat, which was of the design favored by the English longbowmen. He kept tugging and adjusting his black glove and archer's ring as he approached Gonji. The hunter tilted his face up to the shedding sky.

"Not good," he said grimly. He still seemed to bear Gonji ill will over Lottie's embarrassment.

"Mmm. That can't be helped," the samurai replied. "But it aids us more than it hinders. You'd better ready your bows."

The archers removed their strings from dry pockets and helped one another string their bows.

Gonji stood front and center and addressed the anxious company.

"This is it now. Be strong. Act on command only, without hesitation. We take the city back, or we clear out. Remember—*ushin no shin*—mind of no mind. Don't

214

think, don't plan with too much deliberation. Let your arms practice guide you in battle. Let's move—and may your God and all good *kami* be with us this day."

The foundry warehouse doors sprang open, cavalry troops bounding out and forming in a double column. Gonji and Wilf mounted and joined with the other leaders in heading up their bands.

Gonji smiled and saluted to Garth, who sat glumly astride his destrier, a broadsword on his back and a battle-axe slung beside his saddle. The smith wore his old Klann armor, *sans* the coat-of-arms surcoat. He raised a hand and nodded to Gonji. Lorenz sat behind him, armed with pistol and rapier, bowing shallowly to Gonji, eyes alight with anticipation.

Two more armored wagons arrived. Pistoliers and bowmen took up their places with them. Hildegarde set off with her infantry column at an easy run. Messengers sped to other quarters of the city, where militiamen awaited the order to attack.

"*Shi-kaze,*" Gonji said, low and fiery, determination in his searing gaze.

The warrior parties split and clattered off toward their combat assignments. Within minutes the sounds of gunfire and the clash of steel could be heard from various points in the city.

The postern's replacement detachment—three Austrian mercenaries—arrived at the gate and dismounted. They moved quickly under the shelter of the gatehouse and shook their wet helms and cloaks. The relieved soldiers emerged to greet them. There ensued an exchange of rapid chatter.

Something was afoot in the city. The relief party had noticed an inordinate amount of sudden activity. Shops were closing throughout Vedun. People hurried about suspiciously. Many wagons rumbled through the lanes at

215

something more than accepted safe speeds. And the king was coming, scuttlebutt said.

The relieved men were advised to first check into the unusually rushed traffic at the chapel down the street, then report to Julian and Sianno.

They were glancing in the direction of the overflow crowd of women and youngsters lining the chapel steps when the body of the Llorm rampart sentry crashed to the cobblestones not twenty yards from them.

The six drew weapons and looked to the crenellated walls as they ran to the downed sentry. A hundred yards off, a second Llorm crossbowman dropped to the allure, skewered by bowshot from an unseen sniper.

The next thing they saw was Wilf's form hurtling at them from the rostrum at the square nearby, teeth clenched, naked sword blade brandished behind him. Paolo and Monetto followed on his heels.

They spread out to engage the *bushi,* and two of them were struck dead from the rear, Gonji's *katana* lashing through light armor with deadly surety. The remaining four split into pairs, roaring their defiance at the rebels.

Wilf yowled a bloodcurdling *kiyai* and snapped his sword through a brief snatch of flashy *kata* that momentarily bewildered his opponents. Then he leapt between them, beating their blades aside, mortally wounding them both in the space of a heartbeat. One mercenary's arm, severed betwixt wrist and elbow, lay at his feet.

He breathed through flaring nostrils like an overwrought racehorse, more from the adrenal rush than the exertion, and looked to Gonji.

But the samurai was already moving away from his slain enemies toward the square, where gunfire could be heard in the Ministry building, and the screams of children at the chapel.

"Well, you sure didn't neep my help," Monetto said at

Wilf's ear. The biller then bounded to the great wheel that cranked the open portcullis down. "Somebody haul up the drawbridge," he called over his shoulder.

"I'll get it," Klaus shouted indulgently, lumbering up on his huge horse to comply.

A band of six mercenaries pounded through the Street of Hope, Vedun's nexus of commerce. Slowing to assess the anxious people clustered around the chapel entrance, they caught sight of the rebel band at the gate and spurred ahead. They stopped and wheeled their steeds, readying pistols and bows when they saw Gonji and some of the other *bushi* riding toward them.

A crossfire of shafts from behind the bell tower and the alleys at the farther side of the avenue felled them in seconds. A few rebels dismounted and finished the work with fear-grounded savagery, seizing the dead soldiers' mounts and armament.

Gonji swung the roan across the broad square to the Ministry and Chancellery, where the pistol fire had by now ceased. Outcries and jostling issued from Alwin Street, and the leading edge of another sector's innocents appeared in the square, surging to the chapel.

"Secure the chapel, and keep those people quiet!" Gonji yelled as he rode. Garth shouted back affirmatively and took a squad of men with him to protect the chapel throng.

Lorenz appeared in the Ministry entrance and signaled to Gonji: the building had been taken. Fortifying troops appeared in the windows with crossbows and a few fire-arms.

The samurai returned to the gate to find Wilf staring out the ever shrinking portal, as Monetto and Klaus cranked the drawbridge shut.

The smith's breathing was tight, his muscles tensed. "Castle Lenska," he said, as the road beyond disappeared from view.

"First the city, *then* the castle, young warrior," Gonji reminded. "Stick with me now. We've work to do. *Monetto—*"

The bearded biller came in response. Gonji's eyes shone as he scanned the square.

"Get your men up on the ramparts—more Llorm coming." He pointed up to the walls, where burgonets and Klann-crested surcoats pounded along the allure, crossbows at port arms.

Monetto nodded and barked orders at his small squad. Hefting their own arbalests, they scaled the stairways to engage the enemy.

"Where in hell are those armored wagons?" Gonji shouted, waving an arm. Two of the wagons thundered out of the alley in reply, gun ports opened and weapons angled. Pikemen formed their staggered lines of defense. Farther up the road, redoubts were hastily built of grain sacks, tables, and shelving from the market area. Gerhard's archers were deployed in small deadly firing pockets, their shafts laid out for rapid launching.

Combat began on the walls, small numbers of men exchanging arrow and quarrel fire. Other such outbreaks of fighting could be made out on distant wall sectors, archers on the ground harassing the Llorm sentries.

"Get that hostler at Wojcik's to start assembling the wagons. North sector first." Gonji cast about with animated intensity, surveying the incipient action.

"All secure," Garth bellowed from far down the street.

Gonji nodded curtly. *"All-recht.* Garth's in charge here at the square. Don't fail him, worthies. Paolo—you hold that gate, come demon or Death himself! Keep the people flowing through the chapel. We'll worry about the west gate later, when the wagons are assembled and ready to roll—what in hell are those drag-asses at Wojcik's *doing?"* He craned his neck to the northeast, wagged his head.

"Come on, Wilf, we've business," he shouted. "We've got to see how the others fare."

They started off, paused briefly to watch a fresh clash between Garth's infantry lines and a hesitant column of mercenaries. Seeing Klann's troops lose heart and break ranks before the organized defenders of the square, the pair of *bushi* darted into the lanes, charging and weaving through the age-old maze of Vedun on a hellride to the south.

Klaus jogged up to Paolo with a metallic clangor, a grin on his sweat-streaked face. He leaned his polished axe on one shoulder. Raindrops sounded off his helmet like the rattling of a tin drum.

"You're the boss, Paolo. Just say the word, and I'll do what you want."

Paolo's eyes smoldered as he observed the distant fighting, a crowd of screaming non-combatants now hemmed into an alley, cut off from the chapel.

He sneered as he looked over his shoulder. "Just stay the hell away from me, idiot!" Paolo ran off toward the bowmen at the fountain.

"Whatever you say, Paolo," Klaus replied dutifully, returning at once to the gatehouse, where he joined Jiri Szabo in selecting what Gonji would have thought the most useful defensive arrangement.

They took turns peering through the tiny gatehouse grating at the north road that wended to the castle. Now and again a bolt would shatter on the stone facing or a sharp report of a discharged pistol would echo in the vaulted passageway, causing Jiri to wince and clamp his teeth shut.

"I don't blame you," Klaus said upon noticing. "It scares the hell out of me, too."

"What are you talking about, Klaus?" Jiri snapped.

The young founder made an indecisive motion, swallowed back the bitter taste in his mouth, then ran out into the square without another word, his wing-shaped shield slung before him.

Klaus watched him vapidly for a moment, then marched to the grating and stared at the road, all the while practicing sword draws and hilt grips, knowing his *sensei* would be proud.


"Heeeere they come!"

The breathless scout wrestled his steed to a halt before the marshaled cavalry line.

"All right, good," Nick Nagy said. "And the Provender?"

"Most of the soldiers are gone from there now."

Nagy nodded. "Then get back to the Provender and tell the boys at the caravanserai to move like hellfire. When the column passes, they get all the wagons hitched and down to the square—move out!"

The scout saluted raggedly and spurred off in compliance. Up and down the ranks the rebel cavalrymen passed anxious looks. Some stifled tears of terror, beating their breasts and thighs in supplication or private efforts at steeling themselves for the fray. Death was near at hand for many, they knew.

Thus far, their timing had been splendid.

They had held back while the sounds of conflict wafted to the southeast sector, the most sparsely populated area of the city, where Julian had set up his headquarters and many mercenaries were billeted. The majority of the troops had ridden off toward the sounds of battle. The sector's non-combatants were then escorted to the square by mounted militiamen without difficulty. The headquarters had been taken in a lightning attack, with but few casualties.

But now the cavalry's deadliest assignment had begun: They must keep the eastern troops occupied while the wagons were moved from the Provender and Anton and Roric's party attacked the armory in the northeast.

They sat now in a double rank in the broad, weed-tufted clearing once used for equestrian sports, more recently for drilling by Klann's troops.

"Everybody check your gear," Nagy ordered, walking his mount before them, helm in hand, gray hair matted and tangled in a fashion Berenyi would have commented on in less desperate circumstances.

"Archers—string your bows," Stefan called to the rear rank. They dismounted and rushed to aid one another. "Get your pistols primed, you lucky gun-wielders—oh, hey—that includes me, doesn't it?" He fluttered his eyebrows as he flourished his long-barreled wheel-lock piece.

Nervous laughter came in response to the younger hostler's jest as the cranking of spanners and tamping of charges disturbed the rain shudder. Pistoliers, hunched over their guns to guard the precious powder from the wetness, were reorganized to spread their firing points.

"Can't believe we're sacrificing all our toil—" A farmer named Balasz grumbled. "If we evacuate, there won't be a thing left—"

"You archers know your duty," Nagy called over the heads of the front rank. "Two volleys over us when we charge, then cover us when we draw back."

"You mean *retreat*," Vlad Dobroczy cut in wryly.

"I said *draw back*," Nagy growled. "That's a tactic, not a flight. And we do it on my or Stefan's order—"

"—I could've had two hectares of arable land in the north," Balasz continued, "and I kissed it off to stay here because—"

"Aw, shut up, Balasz," Dobroczy said, cursing, two mounts away.

The pounding of hooves came to their ears, though their enemies were still out of sight. Someone whined a prayer along the front rank. The archers hurried back atop their horses.

"Remember," Berenyi said out of the corner of his mouth, "you archers have to cover old men's mistakes."

"You're at attention over there, Berenyi," his elder partner reminded.

Berenyi ignored him. "This is historic, boys. First engagement of the 1st Rumanian Hussars. We want Paille to have something good to scribble about this—"

Now the mercenary force poured into view across the grounds, emerging at a trot in a double column from Provender Lane. Halting with a jangle, reforming their array, spreading wide and thin for a skirmish.

"The bird in flight—the *hawk,*" Nagy grated, recalling for them their training. "Advance with the beak, hit the prey, withdraw the beak, and enfold them with the wings. Everybody got that?"

Nagy strapped on his helmet and drew steel from his back harness. The mercenaries charged at a gallop with a bloodcurdling howl. A hundred yards separated them.

"Archers—ready!"

"Jesus God Almighty!" a man screamed. "I can't do it! I'm sorry—I—I just *can't.*" He broke from the rank and wheeled off.

"Steady in those ranks," Nagy ordered, feeling their flagging spirit.

"He'll be back," Vlad declared. "There's no way out."

"Now!"

On Nagy's roaring command, they rumbled forward with blades and polearms extended hungrily, a shrieking *kiyai* icing the tilting ground from sixty throats. The rear rank archers launched their first volley into the rain-drenched sky, then their second, slowing the mercenary charge, dropping men and mounts among the skirmishers.

Pistols exploded on both sides, some misfiring in the dampness. There came a spanging of lead balls off shield

222

and stone. More men fell, one being unhorsed among the militia by the recoil of his own piece.

The 1st Rumanian Hussars' center sagged to lure them in. The flanks swept up and around like the wings of the hawk. The two lines met with a splintering shock of steel and leather and the screams of the injured and battle-maddened. Sword and shield, lance and mace, axe and pike met with a shuddersome collision of wood and metal, pitching bodies and bucking steeds.

"Watch your ass, there, Berenyi!" Nagy cried out as he tilted with a snarling foe in brigandine and Flemish burgonet.

Berenyi slipped a blow, lurched his steed into his opponent's, and downed the man with a passing slash.

"Don't you worry about me, old man," he yelled back as he rode toward an outnumbered pack.

In minutes the slightly outmanned mercenary troop was put to shambles. The militia, smelling imminent victory, fought on harder.

"Holy shit," Dobroczy swore as he and Stefan wheeled about in search of able enemies.

They looked to the head of Provender Lane, where Captain Julian Kel'Tekeli sat, Salavar and a small contingent of Austrian brigands with them.

"Hell, I'd love to get a shot at *him*," the farmer declared, hastily cleaning and reloading his wheel-lock.

"Yeah," Berenyi agreed. Nodding to each other, they pounded away from the fray to the eastern wall, riding through a back lane that paralleled Provender.

The remaining mercenaries broke free in disarray and lashed out wildly to gain space, then dashed back across the equestrian field toward their leader.

"We run 'em down, Nick?" a man shouted in high-pitched battle glee.

"No—form up here." He looked back to the second rank, who dutifully unleashed a fresh fusillade at the backs of the departing band.

"But they got that blasted captain with 'em," the man appealed. "We could—"

"No, I said. It don't look right. Anyway, we got our strategy to follow."

"Aw, hell—"

"You wanna tell Gonji you got yer own way to fight this battle?" Nagy asked him. The dissenter lowered his head and said no more.

The mercenaries across the grounds took to cover as the rebel archers sent off another salvo. Julian sat in defiance of them astride his magnificent black roncin, seemingly scanning them in search of something.

"What's he doing?"

"Probably looking for Gonji," Nick replied. "Hey—where's Berenyi?"

No one seemed to know. Heads were lowered mournfully when they glanced over the strewn corpses of men and animals. Nagy dispatched a party to pick up the wounded, anxiously covering their progress.

"No Berenyi?"

They shook their heads and helped the injured onto mounts. Gunfire cracked in the distance.

"Jesus, Nick—look!"

A double column of Llorm cavalry poured out of the distant lane under Captain Sianno, crossbows hefted before them.

"Let's go," Nick shouted. "Let's get out of here. You know what to do. Split into your squads and lure them into the alleys. Move! Stefaaaaan!" he roared to the skies.

A crossbow quarrel tore through the clavicle of the man riding next to him as the Llorm advanced in a disciplined formation. Nagy was the last to flee the grounds, shafts and bolts rending the air all about him as he clung close to the saddle.

He did not see Julian's lieutenant, Ivar, fall from his

horse, a victim of the pistol volley fired by Berenyi and Dobroczy. Nor did he see the squad of wildmen, led by Salavar, that drummed through an alley in pursuit of the bold pair.


"Open that blasted door—Captain Sianno's order."

The three mercenaries on duty in the armory looked from one to the other indecisively. The sounds of gunfire and sporadic din of steel weapons could be heard in the indeterminate distance.

The man in charge, seated at the desk, nodded abruptly.

"Hold on a minute," the guard at the door said through the grating. He could see his fellows milling about on the grounds before the armory. Perhaps a half dozen mercenaries, muttering apprehensively, checking their armament.

The iron bolts slid aside. The door creaked open. The lone Llorm messenger pushed through impatiently. He moved to the desk and fumbled inside his cloak. Threw a rolled paper onto the desk.

The duty officer unrolled the order, a second man leaning close beside to read it along with him. It said:

*"I am Anton of Udvary, come to you with compliments of Baron Rorka."*

Both men gaped and lurched backward. Two pistols exploded in the tight room with an ear-splitting discharge, felling them. Anton spun and drew his sword.

But the man at the door had remained suspicious. He reacted at once to throw home one bolt and extract his own saber. Hobbled by his leg wound, short on leverage, Anton was hard pressed to stave off the other's desperate attack.

Two sparking clashes of steel. Then Anton's Llorm burgonet flew off under a heavy blow, his bald plate cut open so that blood leaked down to his eyes, obscuring his vision.

The two men cursed and grunted in the close-quarter combat, while shouts and thumps and the whickering of arrows resounded without, mixed with the barking of dogs.

A heavy beating thundered off the oaken portal. Anton's voice was called outside. A smashing of window grating and shutter wood came to Anton's ears, and a sudden burst of gray light haloed his opponent as Anton went down under his press, holding back the descent of death with both hands on his sword hilt. The larger mercenary bent Anton backward over the desk, inching down toward his unprotected throat; cursing him, nose to nose.

Anton felt numbness in his bad leg. He gained the man's midsection with a twist of his knee. Pushed off with all his remaining strength.

The mercenary stumbled back and screamed. A long, blood-freezing mortal howl. Anton stared, pop-eyed, as the man fell forward, slow and wavelike, from the dark red point of Roric's halberd, where it leaned on the smashed window sill.

Anton gathered himself, stanching the blood flow dizzily with a shredded cloak while he unbolted the door again. The *bushi* rushed in, one of them attending on Anton's scalp wound, while Roric plucked the armory keys from the body of the duty officer.

A wagon ruddled up to the entrance. Dead mercenaries, spindled by shafts, lay all around in blood-swirled puddles. Roric's huge dogs still worried one of the corpses.

"Hurry up in there," someone called in.

"By the saints, Anton!" Roric exclaimed, looking at a corner of the blood-stained wall. "There are powder kegs down here. With all your shooting, you might have—"

"I know where the damned magazines are," Anton countered. "I am a knight of the blasted realm, you know."

*"Ja,* the last," a man added. "Let's get the weapons and get *out* of here."

Bows, shafts with various tips; arquebuses, pistols, shot, and powder were rushed onto the armored wagon. Many firearms were brand new ordnance, still unshot, gleaming with oil.

A second wagon rattled up through the rain and gloom of gathering twilight. The woeful sounds of small skirmishes neared the armory.

"Julian's coming! He's heading up at least five and twenty!"

"And look—more Llorm! Coming from the north garrison!"

Roric assessed their status. They were barely twenty. "Leave the rest," he commanded. "Let every God-fearing soul run like the wind. We'll deal out weapons as we go—"

And then crossbow quarrels and war arrows were lacing the armory area from far-off rampart sentries and approaching dragoons.

Two men fell from atop the wagons, across Roric's field of view. He helped Anton into one wagon, tossed up an arquebus. Then he mounted and spurred off beside the wagon's cover, calling out to his dogs. The heavy coaches were slow to accelerate, but valiant archers provided cover fire, while men within the coffin-cupolas and gun ports began firing.

Roric and Anton escaped with barely half their tiny command, some men falling from the rear as they departed; others, the less fortunate, being unhorsed by enemy fire and bad footing to await, with glaze-eyed shock, the rumbling juggernaut of pincering troops.

Leading an ever diminishing band of *bushi,* Gonji and Wilf drummed through Vedun on a harrowing timed route designed to view strategic checkpoints and assess the

227

rebellion's progress.

Fighting from horseback as they made their way, hastily ushering non-combatants toward the chapel when they could and hustling them into safe havens when the streets were impassable, they wove through the city on a scythelike path that would supposedly parallel the timed sequence of action and provide them with an overview.

Gonji experienced a foreshadowing of doom.

The refugees moved too slowly, too tentatively. Disorganized, and sometimes without military escort. The cavalry and armored wagons were too slow in reaching the escalating combat at the square. And for some reason the wagons from Wojcik's and the Provender had never arrived. Without their transport, the women, children, sick, and elderly would be on foot in the uncertain territory or, perhaps worse, trapped in the ominous catacombs.

The militia fared best in the mazes of canyonlike back lanes, the alley killing grounds, and in the blockading of selected culvert spans. Hildegarde's pikemen were especially efficient, exacting a toll of shortcutting troops. Yet the main roads were still firmly in the grip of the well-armed and heavily manned garrisons.

And now, a new threat: One sector's innocents had already reacted to spreading rumors that the evacuation plan had been abandoned.

The traitor's cankerous work had begun to rot the core of their planning.

"Over here," Gonji yelled to his men in Spanish, indicating an alley off the Street of Charity littered with dead men and mounts. "Let's see what gives. Let the horses rest a moment, and you can reload your guns."

They picked their way over the carnage, made a tight turn to the right. The alley seemed quiet, deserted, their hoofbeats echoing sharply up the walls.

A slap of feet preceded their leftward swing, and they

hefted their weapons cautiously.

A creaking of ropes, then a swift rush of wind from the ponderous bulk that fell across their path, slaming down in the alley with a boom of timbers and a great splash.

A rustling of several figures moving as one—Wilf's steed whinnied keenly and threw him over backwards in the mud—

"Hold it—hold it!" Gonji shouted.

"That's Gonji—and Wilfred! Hold your fire, everyone."

"God damn it, Janos," Wilf swore, reclaiming his equipment and steadying his skittish horse. "You knew that was us."

Janos Agardy moved out of the shadows with his ungainly stride, using a wicked-looking *guisarme* in lieu of his cane.

"On the contrary, friend Wilfred," he said, "we must be ever on the alert for deceptions. Your battle guise gave us pause. Are you hurt?"

"I think I broke my back," the smith answered, twisting delicately.

Archers and polearm-wielders stationed in every window and niche of the alley laughed and relaxed. Gonji scanned their faces. Many women; several old folk; some, like Janos, crippled from birth—these were the stubbornly valiant and high-spirited citizens who had refused to be dismissed from action out of hand.

Janos was their leader. Undaunted by his club foot, the shy and gentle poet had surprised everyone by demanding to remain in the city and fight along with the other young *bushi*.

Everyone but Gonji. For the samurai had learned to recognize the courage and anger that grew out of a lifetime's subjection to the mean spirits of the insensitive. He looked up to the windows. A toothless old man winked and grinned at him over the steel-tipped bolt set in a tightly gaffled crossbow.

Wilf walked up to the great wooden barrier that bristled with foot-long sharpened spikes and shivered. Two mercenaries were still impaled on the spikes, the timbers stained with blood in roughly human patterns.

"We, uh, thought it was a properly ghoulish touch," Janos offered by way of apology, some of his people chuckling. "That is the way these things work in warfare, *nicht wahr?* Intimidation?"

Gonji nodded. "Where's Laszlo?"

"His party has the far end. No one passes this alley, unless, of course, the *sensei* orders otherwise." Janos grinned.

Gonji's ears seemed to perk, his brow furrowing. "Mount up, Wilf."

"What is it?"

"Just mount and *ride.*"

"Where to?"

Gonji had already spurred back toward the main street. "Back to the square."

Janos gestured for luck. "God go with you." He shuffled back into the shadows, motioned for the block-and-tackle crew to again raise the spiked barrier. Then he saw the girl peeking down through the second-story shutter thirty yards down the alley. Janos swallowed, paling.

"Go on," a man said at his side, nudging him. "Tell her."

"I *can't,* Bela. She's a queen. A goddess."

"And you might be a dead poet by tonight."

He looked at his friend, knew the truth of what he spoke.

Janos moved out of the shadow into the center of the alley. Heart galloping, he breathed in short pulls through his nose while he found his voice. The girl peered down, half-smiling. Curious over his strange expression. She waved weakly. Long golden hair lapped her shoulders, curled about her white throat. Her eyes widened.

"Giselle—Giselle, *I love you,*" Janos called out in French, louder than he had expected. His friends chuckled excitedly over his boldness and whispered encouragement. "Giselle," he went on, pushing himself up with the polearm in his waxing confidence, "I've worshipped you from afar too long. Now I've come to beg your love before you—"

Giselle registered surprise, half-turning. Then she was shoved aside. A scowling, unshaven face appeared where Giselle's had been.

*Like a thunderhead masking the radiance of the sun,* his poet's soul told him. But Janos held his tongue.

"What in hell are you blaring about down there, cripple? Do you want to bring the whole goddamn army on our heads?"

Janos blanched, but he stilled the trembling of his jaw and spoke again. "Sir, were it in my power I would send a holy angel to whisper on sweet, silent breath—"

"What *is* this rot?"

Janos cleared his throat and puffed his chest. "Your daughter's hand, sir—my time may be short. If she will have me to spouse, then I shall ask of you her hand in—"

"Are you out of your mind, leadfoot? Get all these crazies out of here before we're *all* murdered in our homes."

"Sir, when next the bell tower sounds, this sector will be evacuated according to plan. Are you prepared to see your daughter safely to chapel?"

"She's not going anywhere, and neither am I. Now stop this before I—"

"You have a duty to perform," Janos said earnestly. "As do all family men here."

"I don't need a cripple to tell me my duty."

"Sir," Janos persisted with gentle firmness. "I will

have an answer from you with respect to Giselle's—"

Janos almost didn't see the clay pot descend through the gathering darkness. He leaned out of the way at the last instant. The pot shattered on the cobblestones behind him as the second-story shutter banged into place.

Janos stood tall and dignified.

"Passing fair aim, sir . . ."

Klaus gaped through the grating, stumbled backward and fell. He started to run from the gatehouse, but his fascination caused him to call out to Paolo instead, first softly in a cracked voice. Then louder, a nasally bellow.

He inched up to the grating again and stared without.

Klaus had not been near the square when the cretin giant Tumo had last done his savagery in Vedun, and for Klaus's part, the tales of destruction and mutilation had done his appearance scant justice.

A slavering, loping behemoth. A spiked ceiling beam cradled on a cattle-hind shoulder. Beside him rode the king himself! And behind—a long, long column of crack Llorm troops from the castle garrison.

Before anyone came in response to Klaus's alarm, the embattled rebels atop the wall spotted the relief troop. Soon the cretin giant's clanking plate armor could be heard as he bounded toward the walls ahead of the rest.

On the square, the rebels were finally giving ground. The Hussars had not arrived in sufficient numbers to help, and the wagons had been waylaid. Only a third of the evacuees had reached the chapel.

The defenders fought valiantly to hold the square, but it was useless. Their spirits flagging, their numbers thinned, dissension spreading over the crumbling of the plan, many now left their posts and bolted for home. Dispirited warriors, frustrated, confused, and fearful, now called out accusations of incompetence by the war council, especially Gonji. This, despite the steadfastness and bravery of the majority.

Garth Gundersen had done wonders to hold the chapel grounds against increasing opposition. Wielding his broadsword and battle-axe in a manner none would ever forget, he inspired his charges to lofty heights of heroism. And Karl Gerhard had continued to fire his four-man longbow with telling effect even after his hands and arms had begun to cramp from the strain, such that every volley caused him considerable pain. And Aldo Monetto's lithe squad of athletes had managed to keep the Llorm rampart sentries pinned and preoccupied all the while.

But it had not been enough. Because of losses, confusion, unforeseen difficulties, and failed courage, the Hussars had been unable to link with the *bushi* holding the square. The backup of the evacuees had caused many married militiamen to lose heart and refuse to turn out.

The crushing blow was the mortally wounded messenger who told Garth on a dying breath that Klann had known their plans: occupation troops had cordoned off the wagons in all three locations even as the rebellion had begun.

Only the armored wagons rolled in the city. Of these, two remained at the square, immobilized, their draft teams dead in the harness, their ammunition gone. A third had been captured by Llorm. Another had caught fire inside and gone up like a lightning ball in the central city. Still another had fallen victim to militia confusion. The harassment squads had weakened the supports of a culvert span, but instead of a column of occupation troops, a steel-plated wagon now lay in the trench muck. The final armored wagon, with Anton aboard, fought its way across town to finally reach the marketplace, only to find the militia slowly giving ground at the square.

And now the death kiss to their costly efforts: Tumo clambered over the wall with a bloodthirsty bellow, sending Monetto's rampart-defense team leaping and scrambling for their lives. The rebels fled the gatehouse area, and Klann's troops rushed along the wall base to open the portcullis and drawbridge.

While half a hundred Llorm dragoons threw a cordon around the great wall that stretched to the west gate, the rest poured into the city, Klann himself, his imposing winged helm looming like a standard of doom, riding at their center.

Tumo tore into the fleeing defenders, crushing everything that moved. Monetto narrowly missed a sweeping arc of the massive spiked truncheon, diving beneath its swing as the man who ran beside him froze an instant too long. His shriek was scissored by the gouging blow that impaled him, then flung him, lifeless, into the fountain wall.

Tumo roared in glee, bounding through the square, stomping and smashing, amidst the scurry of terrified men on the blood- and rain-soaked flagstones, the yelping of dogs and neighing of maddened steeds. Cattle and sheep broke from their pens nearby and scattered through the city.

While hurtling bodies surged past them for cover, Karl Gerhard and his archers held their positions and launched their volleys now at the giant and the king. But Tumo's armor admitted few shafts, and the beast's rapid movement made picking the small vulnerable areas impossible. A ring of Llorm regulars threw shields up around Klann.

The clash of steel, screams of the wounded, and outcries of women and children at the chapel filled the air. The dragoons began to run down the rebels who fled on foot.

The crews who manned the immobolized armored wagons abandoned them just as Anton's wagon rumbled into the square after its perilous battle run through Vedun. Only Roric and three horsemen, plus the butcher's dogs, still rode in escort. They pulled up from the west, assessed the situation. Roric met their eyes, nodded somberly, and gave the order to press an attack.

They headed straight for Tumo, firing from wagon and saddle as they charged, howling.

The cretin giant turned and awaited them, braying in expectation.

A flanking attack by Llorm dragoons, harried though it was by the archers' alert cover fire, hit Roric's berserker attack broadside in full charge. All four horsemen went down almost in concert in a cacophony of gunshots, clacking arbalests, screaming voices and metal, and tumbling carcasses.

Roric's deep voice could be heard, urging them on, until the trample of hooves and falling bodies silenced him.

Only the missile-spindled armored coach and Roric's faithful dogs hurtled on.

A lead ball fired from the wagon tore through Tumo's unprotected jowl, blood coursing his cheek, and the heavy *thuck* of a steel-tipped quarrel penetrated his breastplate. He screamed like an injured titan child and ripped the bolt from the corpulent flesh of his chest.

Most of the fighting ceased in the square, save for that of Garth's hemmed-in faithful, as Roric's snarling dogs tore into the giant, almost human in their directed wrath, as if avenging their downed master. They opened vicious wounds in many places where Tumo's blubber oozed between his armor couplings, on his porcine hands and the backs of his legs.

But in the end the brute's monstrous size won out. Whining in pain, he whirled one dog by its tail, dashing it to pulp against the Ministry steps. When the second dog had been rent, hind limbs from body, its head bitten off in rage, Tumo turned his attention to the rumbling wagon.

The startled draft team veered sharply in fear of his charge, lurching the heavy coach over a pile of bodies at a redoubt. The wagon leapt in the air and snapped an axle when it struck the ground, sending it swerving out of control in the rain, shaking up the men within.

Anton ordered them out the rear while Tumo pounded the team senseless. The men broke across the broad street, dragoons bearing down fast. Tumo swept up the last man out, as Anton's roaring arquebus sent down two Llorm and mounts at once, throwing the pursuers into scattering disarray. But their continued firing dropped the running rebels one by one, until only Anton, skipping desperately on his bad leg, reached the cover fire in the alleys.

Tumo shouldered the wagon over onto its side on the third try. He tossed away the dead militiaman and began battering in the sides of the armored wagon, more insistently as the steel plate interior resisted.

The materiel within, bought at such great cost, clattered around inside, useless to the militia.


Paolo and his band admitted Monetto and his surviving men behind their pitched position on Alwin Street.

"Look at it," Paolo said excitedly, pointing at the cretin giant. "If it keeps punching like that . . ."

"What are you talking about?" Monetto asked.

"There must be black powder in that wagon."

Monetto's eyes widened in understanding.

"Watch that big lumbering ass ignite it," Paolo said through gritted teeth, tittering in a high pitch.

They watched breathlessly, awaiting the explosion that never came. Captain Sianno arrived and called Tumo off. The idiot beast sulked away, disappointed to have its sport ended.

Paolo ground out a curse, echoed by the ragged men behind him.

"What do we do now, Paolo?" came Klaus's voice.

The wagoner sneered, his expression altering when he felt his reinjured side wound. The old saber cut dealt by Julian bled anew.

236

"Why don't you go out there and feed the giant," he said, cruelly shoving past Klaus.

"I will if you will," Klaus replied with unaccustomed indignance.

Paolo ignored him. "Let's fall back," he said in frustration. "It's all over here for now."

Gonji and Wilf arrived at the market area. Blood-spattered, their armor rent and gouged in spots, at least one of their men *hors de combat* though he clung gamely to his mount, their spirits sagged to see the militia in full retreat. Many warriors passed them, rabbit-eyed, nostrils flaring.

There was little pursuit through the streets, Klann having wisely held most of his command at the square. There would still be killing grounds and snares extant in the maze of the city interior. Plenty of time for the occupation force to clean out pockets of isolated revolutionaries later. For the nonce, all that mattered was that the gates were held, and the entire north wall arc.

Gonji spotted Gerhard's archer squad running madly southward, chased by a mounted knot of mercenaries with whirling blades. Shouting to his men to dismount and scatter in the alleys, he bounded off to intercept the pursuit.

Nearing the rear of the mercenary pack, he shouted: "Run, you men! I'll handle these louts!" He removed his sallet as the hunters reined in and looked back, casting them an obscene gesture.

Impelled by the dancing image of the reward on Gonji's head, the band of six howled and wheeled off after him.

When the samurai zig-zagged back through the alley where he had left his men, he found to his dismay that only Wilf lay in wait in a crumbling niche, sword at the ready. The others—whether from fatigue, injury, or abject defeat—had ridden off.

Gonji nodded to Wilf in encouragement, saw the deter-

237

mined battle fervor in the young smith's eyes. Spanked his horse away.

When the greedy adventurer band stormed past, vigilance clouded by their gold-lust, the flashing steel of the ambushing pair took their horses' legs out from under the leaders. The mercenaries piled on top of one another, men and mounts entangled and heaped like freshly plowed earth. Seconds later, only warm, twitching corpses lay in the alley, a blockade of flesh.

Gonji had to pull his friend from the scene. Wilf's eyes were glazed, as if he were experiencing a vision.

"Gonji," he said, resisting, "we can go now, can't we? To the castle, if it's over here—"

"It's not over here."

"Klann's brought the whole damned castle garrison. Why can't we—?"

"Wilfred!" Gonji shouted in his face. "Get hold of yourself. Come to your senses. We've got to remain clear-headed now."

When Wilf had snapped free of his bedazzled, fearful reverie, they scaled a wall and skulked over rooftops and arches toward the square again. They made their way to the roof of the millinery shop, peered over the ledge at the scene below.

An awful moment.

Gonji seized Wilf's arm.

"Wilf," the samurai said gravely, "make your decision. Do you want to go after him? If so, I'll go with you. But it must be one thing at a time."

Wilf stared down, horror-stricken, at the chapel grounds. His breath hitched as he spoke raspingly: *"Nein . . . wouldn't—wouldn't do any good—the castle—that's all that's left."*

Gonji nodded deliberately, his jaw tight and his brow creased with intensity. "I'm not so sure."

\* \* \*

Lydia's heart skipped a beat when she saw Klann march down the chapel's center aisle. She knew what Michael would do.

Her hand clamped down hard on his arm that held the primed pistol under his cloak. They were in the third pew. She fervently prayed that her husband would not be recognized as one of the city leaders in the excitement of the moment.

Michael's free hand grabbed her wrist and squeezed. She wouldn't be able to stop him. When Klann mounted to the altar and tried to spring the secret panel—

Klann stopped and faced the weeping, shrinking congregation. Many beat their breasts, or slumped in despair, holding their heads. Hands on hips, he leveled a stern gaze at them.

"How well you might pray for those foolish rebels among you, people of Vedun," he said. His voice softened. "And for your honored dead."

A woman wailed long and keeningly in the rear pews, rising and shaking her fists at Klann. He peered at her with an unreadable facial set.

A dragoon along a side aisle toed open a casket, then called the king over to him. Klann looked inside at the armament, lifted his gaze to where the dead sentries were being cleared from the vestibule.

"For all the valiant among you," he whispered, such that only those nearest could hear.

Then he strode from the chapel.

Lydia sighed in profound relief. But a curious expression washed over Michael's features.

"He didn't know," Flavio's protegé breathed in surprise. "He really didn't know about the catacombs. Or the entrance tunnel here."

"Or didn't care," Lydia was saying. "Michael, maybe he doesn't wish to harm any—"

But Michael was moving away from her, speaking to

239

the mournful refugees.

Klann watched his army sort out the remnants of the melee at the square. The weapons were seized and loaded onto the amazing wagons, which were drawn near the fountain and ringed with heavily armed troops, who looked worn by their ordeal with the surprisingly capable militia of Vedun. Tumo sat with them, growling as a soldier patched his wounds with strips of a blanket.

Thunder boomed in the Carpathians, and the rain slanted in the buffet of fresh gusts of wind.

Klann examined one of the wagons, shaking his head in disbelief at the cleverness of the design.

"No one saw them build these?"

His officers lowered their eyes in embarrassment. The king next picked up a sword of recent forging. A *schiavona*. He executed a few passes with it, slashed nearly through a hitching rail.

"Superior to those they made for us?" he asked.

"Doubtless, sire," Captain Sianno agreed glumly.

Klann shook his head again, removed the winged helm and rubbed his face.

"What happened to Mord's overrated intelligence?" Klann grumbled in Kunan to his officers. "He said nothing of this. And the revolt was supposedly scheduled for tomorrow. We arrived not a moment too soon—damn him to the flaming Pit! All this could have been avoided." He eyed the city garrison leaders. "That was good work, Sianno. And Julian—well done."

"What about these rebels, Your Highness?" Julian queried, waving a hand over the heads of the captives.

Klann thought a moment. "Detain them for now, I suppose," he said, expelling a weary breath. He spotted the huddled party of rebels on the Ministry's steps, Lorenz among them. Some were badly wounded. "Use their Ministry building for a detention center—"

"And these, sire?" a dragoon asked. He headed a party who pulled injured rebels from the carnage. Among the litter-borne was Roric, barely conscious, both his legs shattered as well as one arm.

"Seek out their surgeon," Klann ordered. "Have him attend on them. For our wounded, have our own surgeons—"

"Sire, with all due respect," Julian disagreed, "this one is one of their leaders. It is our opinion that an example is needed here."

The king was annoyed by Kel-Tekeli's insinuation of timidity, clear from his tone. "All right, Julian—then crucify him."

Julian saluted, smiling thinly. "And that one, milord?" He jerked a thumb back down the street.

Klann stiffened. "Come with me." He mounted and clopped through the sloppy square, through blood-mingled pools, picking his way over bodies and debris. Julian and Sianno followed.

"Tell me, Julian," the king said without turning, "where are the oriental and that lithe murderer?"

Julian forced down the lump in his throat. "They're either gone or . . ."

"Or?"

"Or they'll be dead by morning, sire."

Klann grunted. "Morning, then. Because they're not gone. I can feel their presence. Even now . . ."

And then they reached the chapel grounds, and the duty Klann dreaded. From deep within, the Brethren tendered their angry counsel. But he shook them off, unheeding.

Garth Iorgens still knelt, prayerfully, eyes closed, where he had now for the past half hour. Splattered by mud and the blood of many he might formerly have called sword-brother, the smith had been forced to surrender along with his remaining few sturdy *bushi*. They had been hemmed into their redoubt by their reinforcement troops,

241

the dragoons hesitating to fire upon them, knowing Garth's former status with Klann. But there had been no way out. No other way to save the survivors but to surrender. And so he had thrown down his stained axe and sword and instructed his charges to do likewise, and then he had fallen to his knees in the redoubt amid the lifeless forms of those fellow citizens who had died under his command.

Garth opened his dark eyes, rosy-hued now, and stood unsteadily. He locked eyes with Klann, their mutual resentment almost a palpable thing. Some of the Llorm, the older men, turned their glances away.

"You . . ." Klann began, quaking with emotion. "Whom I called *gen-kori* . . . so you could never raise a sword against me? This is how much your word can be trusted." He swept his hand over the carnage.

Garth's jaw worked, but he said nothing. Head hanging, shuddering, he was led with the others toward the Ministry building.

"Let it be known," Klann declared loudly when they had reached it, "that Captain Julian Kel'Tekeli is hereby promoted to Field Commander of the Royalist Force of Akryllon, for distinguished service in having suppressed the Vedunian rebellion."

There was applause, saluting and handshakes. A brief, not altogether sincere cheer spreading among the mercenaries within earshot. Julian seemed both relieved and surprised by the battlefield commission. His chest swelled with pride as he accepted the honor he had so long coveted.

"And *this* rebel leader, sire?" Julian asked when the brief ceremony had ended. He angled his head toward Garth.

Klann's smile melted. He had hoped Julian's pride in the appointment would channel his thinking away from Garth. But the soldier's arrogance, a family trait, would permit no compassion to either enemy or rival. And Garth was both.

At length Klann was forced to answer, his subjects' eyes on him. He gazed up into the rain, the impenetrable darkness. Night had fallen, and the clouds grew thick, devouring the mountain peaks.

"You're Field Commander now," Klann said. "You deal with him."

Garth's eyes clamped shut a moment as he accepted the finality of his fate. Then his round, bearded face reddened, his ears bright with anger.

The king had swerved his mount and ridden off toward the main gate, his shield-bearing escort again forming about him. Garth's bellow of rage halted him.

"Klann—*where is my son?*"

King Klann wheeled toward him with a perplexed expression. Julian had drawn his saber and ridden toward the smith as if to strike him dead, but Klann stopped him and stared blankly for a long moment. Then he made the connection. A look that might have been grief or pain pinched his face.

"If the fates smile upon you," Klann said to him in Kunan, "then he's dead." With that he yanked his steed around and trotted off ahead of his escort.

Tears streamed down Garth's face as two mercenaries dismounted and bound him on Julian's order. They helped him onto a horse.

"Captain Sianno," Julian said, his gleaming teeth in smug display, "you may have the honor of dealing with this turncoat. Hang him in some . . . shameful place. From a sewage culvert, perhaps. Someplace where the king need not be troubled by his sight. It seems our liege lord finds his presence disturbing. And that will never do."

Sianno cast him an ugly scowl, but saluted stiffly. Another mercenary joined the first two, and they began

243

the slow, dismal ride westward along the Street of Hope, toward the sluice gates.

When he passed Lorenz on the Ministry steps, Garth lipped him silent words of comfort. Lorenz seemed beside himself.

When the hanging party was half a block away, Lorenz suddenly pushed past a guard, shouting after his father. He sprinted straight for a mounted mercenary, taking him by surprise, dragging him off his horse. But the soldier clung to his leg, and two more arrived quickly to wrestle him to the ground. One of them placed a rapier point at the soft flesh of his throat.

"*Nein*, Lorenz!" Garth shouted, anguished. "*Bitte*, no more."

"You don't have to worry, papa," a brigand laughed. "We'll take real good care of him."

"*Ja*, Mord's always in need of men who can't hold their tongues."

"Like that craft guildsman—"

"Big man with a big mouth—"

"Mord knew how to cut him down to size, though, eh?"

They all roared at the jest as they bound Lorenz, hand and foot. Garth, his mount dragged away by the reins, could only crane his neck in horror until he was guided left into a crossing street and the scene was lost to view.


Roric Amsgard sagged from wooden beams leaned against the postern gatehouse. In great pain, he complained little.

Late in the Hour of the Dog, a whistling hiss parted the rain, and the sleek arc of a cloth-yard shaft ended in Roric's breast.

Whether the mercy stroke was launched by friend or foe, whether in sport or out of compassion, no one was able to discover.

## Chapter Thirteen

"The moon is full tonight—but where is it?"

"It's waiting," another *bushi* answered his partner at the window as he sat binding his leg wound, puffing.

"Gonji," someone called from a corner of the darkened parlor, "didn't you say the sorcerer would have new power at the full of the moon?"

The samurai peered cautiously from another window, an angry scowl on his face. "I heard a lot of things about the full of the moon. None of them seem to matter anymore," he appended bitterly.

They had gathered boldly in Flavio's splendid but now battered manse, which lay near the marketplace. Parts of the chapel, the bell tower, and the rostrum at the square were just within view. Several of Flavio's magnificent leaded glass windows had already been wantonly smashed in the fighting.

Outside, the rain continued, and a stiff wind drove debris before it in the streets, whipped the draperies through the broken windows. Within the house were Gonji, Wilf, and several fatigued fighting men, as well as three women and five children from a scattered sector movement.

Refugees were reportedly in hiding everywhere: homes and shops, meeting halls, even the bath house. The city ran foul with soldiers seeking out pockets of rebels, less earnest about their duty and more besotted as time crawled on, for the militia had gone underground, Gonji's order having spread swiftly to ears only too willing to hear it.

But soon the search parties would be organized into house-to-house, building-by-building investigations.

Animals roamed the streets, barking and bleating forlornly in their confusion and fear. Dogs bayed in the distance for dead masters. At the square: the occasional bellow of the cretin giant.

From an extreme angle at one second-story window, Gonji had made out one pork-barrel knee of the beast where it sat among the captured wagons.

"Does warfare ever change?" Wilf asked of the unresponsive darkness, slumping forward on a high-backed chair. He seemed alternately anxious and calm, crumbling and defiant. "Those endless moments before engagement . . . then the—the way time gets squeezed, flying past when the fighting begins . . . the parched mouth . . . sweating hands . . . that panic you feel when you know death is suddenly *this* close . . ."

Gonji stared impassively from the edge of the window.

The rear door from the servants' quarters opened and shut, causing weapons to be hefted in readiness. Aldo Monetto burst into the room.

"They told me I'd find you here," he said to Gonji. "How goes it?" Curt greetings were exchanged, and Monetto was offered a cup of wine and some of the same stale bread and dried meat the others ate. He accepted them gratefully.

"Listen," the bearded biller said between gulps, "Klann's gone back to Castle Lenska, and taken half the dragoons with him. Maybe more. They're going to conscript every able-bodied man in the city into Klann's army when this is all sorted out."

One of the *bushi* laughed harshly. "That's why they didn't just kill everyone they captured, eh?"

Monetto nodded somberly. "Oh, Wilfred—I just heard. I'm afraid they—" He licked his dry lips. "—they took your brave father and—and hanged him. God rest his blessed soul." He turned away, unable to take the look that dawned on Wilf's face.

The young smith hung his head. "I suppose I knew. Expected it when we saw him . . ." His voice cracked, and he angrily brushed aside a tear. "Why hang him? The bastards. A lot Klann cared about his past service."

No one spoke for a space, then Monetto came up to Gonji at the window. "Look, Gonji, I—well, I have a feeling we'll not be seeing each other alive again and I—I just want to say it's been great to work with you."

Monetto's eyes flicked about apprehensively, and he extended his hand. Gonji took it slowly, bowing to the faithful militia leader.

*"Domo arigato,"* he replied. "But let's say little of dying for the present. There is still much to be done."

Monetto shrugged. Someone snorted and grumbled about the futility of it all, tiresomely recapping their grievous circumstances. Gonji allowed the man to prattle, knowing the need for the venting of their terrible frustration. At length, though, he commanded the frightened man to cease.

The wind began to lash the city with increased power.

A troop of ten Llorm dragoons splashed past the manse. When they were as far as Milorad's house, a short distance along the *Via Fidei,* a hard rapping sounded on the portico door.

"It's Gerhard," someone shouted, and another voice hushed him to silence. The dour archer was admitted at once, the ornate front door quickly shut and barred.

Gerhard shuffled into the parlor, soaking and haggard. He dropped his helm, gazing around the room at the huddled refugees as his eyes became accustomed to the darkness. Ignoring their expectant greetings, he flung his beloved longbow against the wall, following its flight as if it were some despicable thing.

"What news, Karl?" Monetto asked his friend.

Gerhard frowned in Aldo's direction. He strode to a sofa, flopping down heavily, sullen and withdrawn. He unbelted the sword and empty quiver from his back. Monetto repeated his query, more urgently.

"Michael and Milorad were called into conference with them. You all heard that?" he asked.

They assured him that they had.

"I don't know what else, then. Oh—Michael says you were right. Mord must not be telling everything he knows. Klann didn't seem to know of the catacombs."

Karl blankly eyed the parquet floor as he spoke, and it took Gonji a few seconds to realize the archer was addressing him.

"He came to the chapel," Gerhard continued, "but he gave no sign of knowing about the tunnel."

"Or maybe he didn't want to," someone reasoned.

Gonji's eyes widened. *Choléra*. Then one way or the other the innocents in the catacombs may be in grave danger . . ."

Monetto belted his axe and sword. "I've got to get home. Check on my family. Just get word to me there when you need me. Karl—maybe we'll see you later, *nicht wahr?*"

Gerhard sighed and nodded weakly. Eight bells sounded at the square, and the archer pulled himself erect in his seat.

"Oh, yes," he breathed, "and they're going to kill one hostage each hour until Gonji and Simon surrender themselves."

There were gasps of horror in the manse, and even Gonji betrayed his emotion. He strode forward, fists clenched at his sides.

*"Simon,"* he hissed through his teeth.

"What will you do?" a woman asked in Italian. "The hostages will die, and perhaps the women and children in the caverns—"

"Hush, Lucia—"

Gonji's eyes blazed as he considered a course.

"There's only one thing to do," came the eerie voice from the shadows beyond the parlor arch.

Pistols and steel sprang into itching palms. A woman screamed, and the sobbing of children followed as they clung to their mothers for security.

"Simon!"

A rampant wind fluttered the drapes at the opened window of the dining room, where he had entered. Seeing the fear of the refugees, he remained in the cloaking shadow.

"You," Gonji growled, slipping the Sagami half out of the scabbard, but returning it almost immediately.

"Save that," Simon advised. "You'll need it. Come with me."

Gonji moved to the dining room, a few of the *bushi* following. They were struck by the strange shifting, rearranging that had already begun to transform Simon's features. Only Gonji appeared rather disappointed, expecting something . . . different.

"That's . . . all there is to it?" the samurai inquired.

"Never mind that," the other responded, his tone more gravelly than usual. His manner was fraught with urgency. "Just come with me."

Gonji locked his thumbs into his *obi*. "Why should I go anywhere with you?"

"For the sake of these people, that's why. Don't play coy with me. You have no idea what we're risking."

"Where are we going?"

"We're leaving Vedun—"

Wilf sucked in a breath and stepped forward, slack jawed.

"—for the nonce."

Garth clopped along at the center of the hanging party,

249

not feeling the rain, the chill. Benumbed now, considering the events of his life and embracing his faith. Knowing that in moments he would confront his Creator, wondering whether he would be permitted to ask the Lord God why he hadn't been felled by the great seizure before he had had the chance to spill so much blood.

His hands, twisted and bound at the center of his back, tingled from strictured circulation.

Sianno turned them into an alley, narrow and littered, a place children had always been warned away from, as it dead-ended dangerously at a sewer drain.

So this was to be the place of his execution.

*Lord God of all, give me the courage to—*

"What's that?" Sianno grated, halting them. The three mercenaries drew steel and wheeled their mounts to and fro, casting him questioning glances.

"What, sir?"

"What did you hear?"

"I'm not sure," the captain replied, gazing with narrowed eyes into the darkness. "Came from up ahead there."

They peered into the blackness before them.

"Maybe we should hang him somewhere else," a brigand judged, chuckling nervously.

"You two ride ahead, but be careful."

The pair demurred a second, then walked their horses ahead warily, swords upraised. Only the dim lights from nearby dwellings cast what humble illumination the alley could claim.

Garth watched them ride, momentarily heartened. The sensation was short-lived. *Rats, probably,* he thought. Garth had held for a time the faint hope that they would blunder into a militia ambush, but this forgotten alley had never been considered in the rebellion plan. Besides, if rebels attacked, Garth would surely be the first to go.

*Dear God, protect my beloved sons from . . .*

The snick of steel behind him. A strangled outcry cut short by the crashing descent of a broadsword and a cry of mortal terror. Garth turned in time to see the spurt of blood that erupted from the remaining mercenary's neck.

Then Sianno was riding up to him, dirk in hand, slicing the bonds. Tossing him the dying man's saber, calling orders to him in a voice that seemed lost in the pounding of blood in his ears.

Garth caught the saber but almost lost it, the feeling returning to his hands only gradually. He kicked through the alley, a length behind Sianno. They were on top of the bewildered scouting team in seconds. The two men's hesitation in the face of their superior's charge cost them their lives.

And then Captain Sianno, Garth's comrade in a time long past, was seated across from him, breathing hard through flaring nostrils.

"Don't think I'm doing this out of compassion," Sianno said. "You think I'm soft, is that it?"

Garth was shaking his head dimly, lost for words.

Sianno went on. "Well, you're probably right. I am going soft in the head with the passing of years. All of us are. You, especially. What the hell did you get involved in something like that for? And don't think this is for Italy, either. You were just doing your duty then, I know. But I remember . . .

"Julian Kel'Tekeli for Field Commander. *Fie* on the Kel'Tekelis! Arrogant bastards, one and all. And Julian's the worst, the little cur. He was just a pup when you and I fought for Klann in the noble days. When all this meant something. When we really believed . . ."

He caught his breath and dismounted. Garth did likewise. They stood looking at each other for a long, nostalgic moment. Garth smiled after a while, and they clasped right hands warmly. Then Sianno drew away, broke the eye contact.

"Iorgens," he said sadly, "I know a terrible injustice has been done you—"

"Don't," Garth fairly pleaded. "For the sake of sweet memory. Let's think only of those days when we rode together in the name of righteousness, of an ideal."

Sianno bobbed his head. Garth winced to see the captain slice his own arm open with a wicked slash of his dirk, letting the blood drip across the front of his weathered breastplate, staining the seven interlocked circles of the Klann crest.

"Part of my cover," the captain explained, smiling wryly.

"Is that really necessary?"

"It will be in this case. Our old friendship hasn't been forgotten. That's why that sadistic popinjay sent me to carry out your execution." Sianno waxed serious. "Do you think you can lie low awhile? Or better still, flee this city? It's no good for you here, Garth. No good at all."

"*Ja . . .* awhile," Garth allowed.

Sianno studied his expression before sighing and nodding heavily. He patted the muzzle of his gray roncin affectionately. The animal nickered and pawed the mud.

"Do you recall the mount you gave me that day when mine went down?"

Garth looked puzzled, then remembered. His eyes crinkled merrily.

"Grandsire of this trusty fellow," Sianno related, his expression sagging.

The captain drew his sword again, and Garth gasped to see him strike the steed's skull. It went down to its knees, whinnying in shock and pain. A second blow silenced it. Its twitching carcass shuddered in the rain.

Sianno stared down, grimacing.

"But why?" Garth demanded.

Sianno's voice was strained. "They also know how much I love this horse . . ."

252

At length they remounted. Sianno clamped shut the buffe of his burgonet when he sat astride a bandit's horse. His left arm was coated with blood, and the tasset and boot of one leg, where he had knelt into the blood of his roncin for dramatic effect.

*"Gen-kori,"* Sianno said ominously, though he used the Kunan term of affection, "should we meet again, out there . . ."

Garth nodded in understanding.

Gonji's swords described a great X in his back harness as he stood with the apprehensive *bushi* in Flavio's well-tended garden. Atop these he slung his longbow and the nearly empty quiver with the few remaining envenomed war arrows.

Simon moved apart from the rest, the hood of his traveling cloak pulled up. He shivered as if from an attack of ague.

Wilf's eyes were on Gonji. He looked hostile, as if feeling betrayed. "You can't go now," he said in an anguished voice.

"Just be ready to move when you get the word," Gonji ordered.

"There isn't going to be any word," Wilf despaired.

Tumo blared in the square, causing them to stiffen as if movement might allow the giant to sniff them out.

"We must stop this madness," a woman fretted from the doorway.

Gonji bowed to them and took two steps, paused and glanced around the company. "Don't allow yourselves to get stiff—keep moving—take heart—we may yet get the people out of here—"

"Come *on,*" Simon growled in a chilling voice.

"What about Mord's giant?" one of the warriors begged.

"That's a giant, not a god," Gonji snapped, pointing

toward the square. "He can *die* . . ." And then he and Simon were off at a run through the back lane.

They took to the walls, scrabbling along at a crouch. Over rooftops until they were facing the square, a hotbed of troop activity. They could see the armored wagons—three of them—into which the confiscated weapons had been loaded.

The cretin giant sat in a blubbery heap among them, grotesquely gnawing a whole raw pig. The couplings of his body armor had been unfastened, such that huge rolls of fat protruded from the sides and spilled over his broad belt.

Gonji halted Simon.

"We haven't time for that now," Simon argued.

"They need it," Gonji said stubbornly, nocking one of the poisoned shafts. "What made you come back?"

"Look about you," the other rasped from beneath the hood. "The fine shambles you've made. I knew in your infidel's pride you'd be laying part of the responsibility on me."

Gonji flinched imperceptibly, scanned the square for observers, pulled slowly and aimed from behind the roof's retaining wall.

"And there's something I want you to see—"

But the twang of the release cut short Simon's words. The shaft hissed through the drizzle and struck the giant's breastplate at a poor angle. It stuck but failed to penetrate to the flesh of his chest.

Tumo roared in surprise. Soldiers took note. Shouts of command as they darted in all directions after the sniper.

Simon grunted with pain, scrabbled away across the roof. "To the west gate," he growled over his shoulder.

"Then what?" Gonji asked.

"Over the wall where the land begins to drop away—and make sure they see you. Then meet me at the north tunnel."

Gonji rubbed his itching nose and nocked another shaft. At the fountain: Tumo casting about in mindless confusion on his barrel legs.

The samurai rose above the wall, fired. And was spotted.

Tumo blared and stumbled backward as the poisoned shaft thucked home in the pulpy flesh of his side. He tore it free with a howl, the worm venom already darkening the white flesh, bruiselike. But even the deadly substance could not reach the giant's vital organs or circulatory system before it was diluted in the massive layers of fat.

Gonji bounded over an arch and skipped across the slick, narrow ledges of the walled lanes, finally dropping to the paving stones and making his way to the west gate. He saw the gate cranking open, the small drawbridge over the moat landing in place. At least a dozen mercenaries manning the gatehouse. And beyond—an indeterminate number of Llorm sentries.

A dragoon party clattered through the gate. Simon Sardonis appeared out of the shadows and raised his arms before them like a haunter of the dark. The mounts, trained war chargers though they were, neighed and bolted, throwing the gatehouse into a frenzy.

And then Simon was dashing through the center of them, slashing with his broadsword.

Gonji heard pistols crack amid the chaos as he bounded for the stairway to the allure. He crouched in the gloom until the two Llorm crossbowmen passed overhead at the run. Then he took the steps by twos, felled a sentry with a shaft that struck him between the shoulder blades, and hang-dropped the fifteen feet into the waist-deep water of the culvert.

He sloshed out, unhurt, and loped through the brush that bordered the Roman road, saw the guards whirling in dazed confusion. Simon had taken to shadow again. There were few Llorm stationed outside the gate now, but more could be seen galloping around the distant curve of the wall.

Gonji checked his armament. A lone dragoon pounded past, reining in not far off and panning the forests to the north of the road. Gonji raced from concealment, twenty feet off when the Llorm finally heard him.

The dragoon managed a single strangled sound before the *ninja* dart pierced his throat under the open buffe of his helm. The samurai slashed him twice in the blink of an eye and dragged him, already dead, from the saddle. He calmed the peevish steed and towed him to where he had left the longbow.

Scooping it up, flinging away the empty quiver, he spurred to the center of the road, where he made a broad gesture of farewell to the small band of mixed Llorm and free companions who regarded him uncertainly. He raised his sallet with cavalier elegance and bowed.

Recognizing him, they spurred toward him with a vengeance.

"*Sayonara,* Vedun," he cried. "It's been great fun!"

With a "hyah," he wheeled the animal. Before he had made three strides, Simon again leaped from the brush at the valley side of the road to spook the lead mounts, sending them and their riders crashing in a wet clangor that sprawled over the road, slowing their comrades.

The enchanted misanthrope sprinted for the forest that sloped upward to the northern foothills.

Gonji yanked to a stop and watched. An alert adventurer, dismounting to steady his hand, squeezed off an echoing shot. It struck Simon with an unmistakable impact as he reached the trees.

Gonji scowled and raced for the northern trail that wended through the pine forest, the route by which Klann's human force had attacked Castle Lenska a month before.

* *

Simon's breath wheezed alarmingly. The black hole at the small of his back shone in the bleak light of the full moon, which had risen now to search them out through the gray wadding of cloud and the black steepling pine boughs.

The tethered horse began to whinny and strain at the bit. Simon clutched the hood shut with one hand like a leper. Gonji watched in rapt fascination, mesmerized by the coarse hair growth at the back of the now enlarged hand.

"How can you do anything tonight, hurt like that? Someone's got to remove that ball from your—"

"It won't last," the voice replied, now a totally alien voice, from the hunched figure. "And neither will you. Now see—see what you must—and then begone, quickly—"

A bristling hand shakily indicated a berry thicket. Simon withdrew the hand in pain.

Tight-lipped, Gonji marched to the thicket, his hand warily cupping the pommel of the Sagami. In the bush lay a mound. On closer inspection: a body. A dirk protruded from its back.

He looked over his shoulder, suppressing the chill. Simon was on his knees, doubled over, his breathing labored. Yet he seemed to be growing somehow, bulging like a filling sail on a brigantine.

Gonji stooped and turned the body, sucking in a breath.

It was Strom. He laid the shepherd on his side and examined the dirk. There were a hundred like it in Vedun among the citizens alone.

"Strom," he whispered. "But why—"

A half mile below, the voices of soldiers could be heard, chattering in several languages.

"You've seen it. Now take your ruminations away from here." Simon's voice was a rattle of winter-dried branches.

257

Gonji's heart hammered in his chest, his jaw working as he pondered. "Lorenz? Boris? One of the herdsmen? The soldiers? Who?" he wondered aloud. "And *why?*"

Clumping hooves and muted voices ascended the trail below.

"Stay, man of the East," came the eerie, malevolent voice. "You're halfway into your grave . . ."

Gonji whirled and drew steel. Such a voice could not have issued from Simon. But there was no one else.

The horse shrilled and bucked, tearing the bit from its bleeding mouth, stamping insanely into the woods.

At one shoulder of Simon's cloak, a great rent appeared as if the fabric were shredded by the claw of an invisible presence.

"I'll be—I'll be at the catacombs first—" Gonji said, backing away.

*"Non, monsieur—*wait—" Simon's harsh voice again. "The scrawl—read the letters—on the ground." He pointed at the body of Strom again, then fell face first, racked by convulsions.

Cautiously, Gonji knelt again and checked the ground around the body. Near where Strom's head had lain, there were letters gouged into the ground. Two of them, his reed pipe still protruding from the second. The first was an *M*. But Strom had died before he had completed the second. Or had he? It was either an *I* or an incomplete letter. The start of a lower curve suggested a *U* or an *O*.

*MI*— Michael? There were also three Mikloses and a Miskiewicz Gonji knew in the militia.

*MO* or *MU*—?

"Get away from me—*now.*" Simon's voice was a barely articulate growl. "If I can," he gasped, "I'll signal . . ."

"And if not?" Gonji snapped, wide-eyed.

Simon hurtled into the forest on all fours, groaning.

*"Block those tunnels—"* The words came to Gonji's ears like the voices one sometimes imagined in the crackle of a lonely campfire.

## Chapter Fourteen

The small band of *bushi,* weaponless now, who had boldly appointed themselves personal bodyguards to Michael, Lydia, Milorad, and Anna, led the remaining city leaders back to the Benedettos' house.

When the doors and windows had been secured and they had waited sufficiently long enough to be sure there would be no search of the premises, they descended to the cellar and rearmed from the weapons cache secreted there.

Lydia clasped her hands before her and sighed to see the fortress her home had become.

"Well," Michael told her as he loaded and primed two pistols, "Klann's troops seem convinced it's over."

"Isn't it?" she said airily and without conviction. Michael ignored her, and she busied herself by straightening the room.

"They say Simon came back. He's with us now," the new council Elder went on. "He and Gonji made a great show of leaving the city. But they'll be back later. This time—this time we win."

"Can anyone really win?" she needled. Their eyes met. She smiled at him. "I was proud of you, somehow, when you spoke to Klann. So strong, so defiant. I almost really can envision you in one of those Llorm surcoats. Except for your crutch."

"I'll never wear the crest of Klann. No one here will.

You know that."

"I know," she said. "You'll die first."

She followed him into the kitchen, where he peered through the curtains. Producing a brush, she began to work at her hair. "When they've come back and . . . done what they're going to do, do you really think we'll be able to ride away from here?"

The question surprised him. "You will, anyway."

"Oh, so you're going to stay behind. Go down with your men. Very noble."

"You know you really are like my mother," he said, leaning both hands on a sill. "The way only she could be at those times when it seemed terribly important to her to grind my father into meal."

"I know—bitchy."

Again he was mildly surprised. He turned and looked deep into her pale blue eyes.

"It's because I love you, Michael," she said simply. "And I don't want to see you die."

He snorted. "It's because you want to be right. Always so very right."

She came close and placed her hands lightly on his damp back. "Will you concede," she asked gently, "that I was at least partially right? That you had it in your power to prevent all this?"

"I don't know whether anyone could have prevented it," he replied reflectively. "Anyone who would have wished to." He thought a moment, adding: "I thought you didn't want to flee Vedun."

"Of course I don't—didn't. It seems there's no other way now. I want our child to live."

"So you can tell it how its father made sausage of his talents and ambitions, despite the predictions of his mentors?"

She drew back. "Our child will know what a great man his father was. Of course," she added softly, "it would be

260

nice if you'd be there to tell him yourself . . ."

He took her hand and pulled her close. They held each other a moment, silently, sharing each other's warmth. At length Lydia set about preparing a light meal.

Michael gazed through the shutter into the lowering sky, where the full moon blazed in triumph.

Aldo Monetto set his children to playing a game in their bedchamber after putting their confused fears to rest regarding the fighting and screaming that troubled them. He kissed them all with a prayerful desperation none of them would be old enough to understand for some time. Refusing their request for the "Papa the Jester" performance he sometimes did for them, Monetto joined Sylva in the kitchen for a brief, quiet time.

He scaled the attic ladder to find Gerhard observing the street sullenly.

"Kind of quiet out there now, eh?" Monetto said.

To which the archer grunted, shifting, his face beset with angry creases.

"Maybe you ought to check in at Michael's, or Flavio's—" Monetto began, but his friend interrupted him gruffly.

"Why don't *you* go out there and check in?"

"Hey, I'm sorry. You think I won't? I just thought—"

"Sure," Gerhard said wryly, "send the guy with no family to worry about. That makes sense."

"That's not what I meant, asshole. Anyway, you're part of *this* family, aren't—"

"I did my part today. Now I'd like to lie back and let somebody else get their hands bloodied."

"Oh, so I didn't get bloody enough for you, eh?" Monetto fumed. "What the hell do you think I was doing up on that wall—?"

The heraldic cry from the rooftops in the northern quarter smothered their bickering.

*"Men of Vedun, behold the sign! Your Deliverer is at hand. You shall know the Death Angel by his works!"*

Soldiers passing in the streets below, recognizing the voice, belly-laughed and called out in mocking encouragement and mimicry. Some slugged from wineskins, secure in their numbers.

*"Beware the Angel of Death . . ."*

Monetto shook his head, eyes crinkling with disbelief. "That Paille. Amazing, eh? Karl, what's bothering you?"

"That's a stupid question, *nicht wahr?"*

"You've just been . . . strange lately."

Gerhard frowned. "Can't imagine why. Nothing strange happening in Vedun."

*"All-recht,* forget it," Monetto snapped. He drew away from the attic shutter, clambered back to the ladder. "Think I'll go out and see what Paille's drinking . . ."

"Anybody heard what happened to Stefan yet?" Nick Nagy whispered louder than the others.

The newly arrived messenger shook his head.

"At least you're safe from his insults, Nick," someone offered by way of a distracting jest.

"That's true, that's true," the old cavalryman jokingly agreed, the pain in his face belying his words.

The Hussars were scattered all over the city, many out of touch with the leaders' plans. Some had abandoned their mounts in courtyards and alleys and fled on foot. Others, like the fifteen with Nagy in the barn near the south wall, awaiting some word of action that they could trust. Their weapons at the ready, they sat with their weary steeds in nervous vigilance. When the soldiers finally came, they would wish they had instead stumbled into a vipers' nest.

"So Gonji's left the city?"

"Just a diversion, they say—"

"No news at all of what the war council will do?"

A warrior snorted. "Probably none of them left alive."

"Michael and Milorad are. I know that. They went before Klann."

"The devil, you say?"

"Then they're probably dead by now, too."

"Hey, Nick—I think Magda's staying with the Kolodyis."

"That's good," their leader rasped above the others' low chatter.

"And your wife's at the chapel, Victor."

"Thank God."

"If we don't hear something by ten bells, I'm getting out of here."

"You're not going anywhere," a stern voice shot from the darkness.

The double doors creaked open, and the posted sentries raised and pulled their bows. The click of pistols being cocked—

Two *bushi* peeked in, holding up staving hands. "Hey, hold your fire!"

"Any of you men seen Berenyi?" Nagy asked, scrambling toward them.

"Don't you worry about Berenyi, you old fart," came Stefan's familiar voice. He limped in, wet and rumpled but apparently in one piece. The wrap on his injured hand hung in tatters. He was unarmed.

"Well it's about time you'd report in," Nagy carped, masking his relief. "What the hell's the matter with you, riding off on your own like that? When you have a tactical plan, you follow it."

The backslapping welcome of men who took profound comfort in the living faces of comrades drowned him out.

"I've seen Michael," Berenyi said. "We're to wait for Gonji and that Simon character to spread the word, somehow. Then we hit them again."

"Jesu Christi—"

263

"Did you bring anything to drink, Stefan?"

"What the hell do I look like? Somebody send for Gutch."

"Stefan," Nagy called, "what happened to Vlad?"

Berenyi seemed thunderstruck. "He—he went down . . ."

"What happened?"

"Just . . . gone." Berenyi moved away from them, slumping down in the straw with exhaustion.

The sentry sat dozing on a boulder behind the spearhead-bristled redoubt in the northern hill tunnel.

*"Shi-kaze."*

Startled, he raised the pistol from his lap and fired, the recoil rolling him backward off the rock. The lead ball struck the top of Gonji's sallet with a sharp whanging sound. The samurai fell back slowly, dreamlike, landing with a heavy thud on his tailbone.

The echoing report brought the sentry's partner at the run, arbalest readied to unleash a deadly bolt.

"Holy Mary, Mother of God—*that's Gonji!*"

Screams and shouts of alarm wafted mutedly into the tunnel from the main cavern. Galioto scrambled in with two other men just as the sentries cautiously approached the downed *sensei.*

"He—he shot Gonji," the second sentry cried.

"Oh, Jesus—Gonji," Galioto swore, moving up shakily.

The samurai waved them back and peeled off the sallet gingerly, looking dazed. Saying nary a word, he shuffled into the cavern, hollow-eyed, carrying the creased sallet, breathing in shallow gulps until he was certain he was truly unhurt.

He felt his head. A tender spot, knotting up. Behind him: accusations and recriminations. A man weeping.

He surveyed the catacombs as he strolled with throbbing skull. There were hundreds watching him, some calling out hopefully or in apprehension. Women, children, the aged and infirm. Hundreds. Yet still not all the city's non-combatants.

He moved to a water trough and washed his face. As if the pistol shot had been a signal, his other injuries came back with nagging mindfulness: He laved the grime from the cut on his hand; rinsed his mouth where he had bitten himself in the horse fall the previous night.

"Oh God, Gonji," Galioto muttered behind him, face contorted with worry. "I don't know what to say to you to—"

"Forget it."

"I knew I should have stationed myself in the tunnel. I knew there—"

"How are the people faring?" the samurai said in a blanketing voice.

"They're afraid," the dairyman whispered, swallowing. "I can't blame them. Gonji, what's happening in the city? There's been no word."

Gonji recounted the battle and the powder keg situation in Vedun.

"Oh no," Galioto breathed as he listened. "You can't—you can't spare me any more men down here?"

The samurai shook his head sadly. "We're thinned too much up there as it is . . . too damned much."

"But what—?" Galioto had begun to fret in a whining voice, but he composed himself and spoke more conspiratorially when he saw the anxious faces that peered at them in the torchlight. "What will happen to us down here if . . . if the worst happens up there? What if we never get word to evacuate? If the wagons never roll? If we're sealed off down here—?"

"Then," Gonji said firmly, staring out over the heads of the innocents to where the blackened carcass of the great worm crumbled back into the earth that had cradled

265

its misbegotten spawning, "then you'll just have to fight your way out. Go south, on foot, if need be. Rush these people to the mountain passes, then westward to Austria. Find them sanctuary . . . somehow." Gonji studied the man's face, saw the panic creeping into his eyes.

"What if there's another monster? That one's mate, or—"

"I have every confidence in your fighting ability."

Galioto blanched. "I—why? Why us? Why does it have to be us?" His lips trembled, and he shut his eyes, turning away. "I keep thinking how Pete Foristek died—why *us?*"

Gonji spoke with arresting calm. "Because you're here. And no one else. Just you. And it's your duty." He saw the resignation that gradually deadened the evacuation leader's near hysteria. Galioto hugged himself tightly, then thrust forward his jaw and nodded resolutely.

The samurai smiled and clasped his hand. He tossed his head in the direction of the tunnels.

"Have bonfires built at the redoubts—"

"Wha-a-a-t?"

Gonji held up a stifling hand. "Set them ablaze and *keep them burning all night.*"

"But *why?*"

"Because your lives—*their* lives—may depend on it. When you get word from the surface that it's safe to move, douse them and get these people to wherever the messengers tell you."

"What about the rest?" Galioto pleaded. "There must be hundreds up there yet who—"

"We'll get them down here," Gonji assured, "or out through the gates. Something."

They exchanged well wishes, and Gonji went to the vestibule chamber, where he found Paille, tipping a wine bottle between efforts at catching his breath.

"I see you've been busy," the samurai said, surprising

266

him. Paille choked on his wine, and several people cleared out of the samuria's path.

"What has happened to *shi-kaze?*" the artist snarled in a fierce whisper. "The *bushi* have all gone to shivering in their warrens. The evacuation wagons still sit under guard at the wagonage, the Provender, Wojcik's."

"Steady yourself, Paille."

The wild-eyed aesthete bridled but clammed up as another noisy group of refugees hurried in from the chapel tunnel.

"Well, at least they're still coming," Gonji said.

"You think I'm drunk?" Paille bawled. "That's what they think as well. The soldiers. But Paille's done his patriotic duty." He held up a sheaf of papers, his in-progress *Deathwind of Vedun* epic. "No jejune chronicle, this. Listen to me—they've left that mooncalf giant at the square, but half the Llorm's detachment's been pulled outside the walls. Seems they're very concerned about you and Simon trying to return—"

"Then it worked," the samurai said with tight-jawed satisfaction.

"Humph! Not for fear of you so much as for Simon. That's the value of a good Frenchman. It takes half an army to watch him."

Gonji spat and grabbed the wine bottle out of Paille's hand, taking a swig. "Rather good wine, for you."

Paille ignored the insult. "Gutch trotted out his best for tonight."

"Those wagons of yours—I must admit, they're a marvel."

The artist snorted and retrieved the bottle. *"Oui,* and now, thanks to your brave *bushi,* they're full of occupation troops."

"We'll get them back." Gonji remembered something and reached inside his breastplate and tunic. He gave Paille the sweat-soaked but still legible fold of paper.

"What's this?"

"Remember the poem? My death *waka?*"

Paille took it reluctantly. "So it's come to that." It was a glum statement. "What would you have me do with it?"

"See to it that it's inscribed on my tomb." He shrugged. "The place that marks my body, my memorial, whatever—whatever these people decide to do."

Paille scowled. "Probably won't be anyone left alive to remember you. But I'll keep it. I'll add to it your sonnet by Shakespeare, and the snatch of Cervantes you never let me read."

"That's good," Gonji said, rubbing the sore spot on his skull. "The *kami* of good fortune sometimes withdraws her smile without warning."

Paille waxed sullen, withdrawn, and they parted without another word.

Gonji ascended alone through the tunnel to Tralayn's house. Donning the dented sallet as he sneaked through the spattering streets, the thought suddenly occurred how very much the helm resembled the war helmets he'd worn in Japan many years past. How many warriors in helms such as these might rally to his side in these perilous times . . .

If he were only in *Dai Nihon.*

The streets were quieter now, much of the activity centered around the city walls, as if the occupation troops were more concerned with defending against attacks from without.

Gonji made it to the stables. They were unattended. He crouched down the lane while a party of Llorm dragoons, fatigued and jabbering in their native tongue, watered and wiped down their own lathered steeds before pounding away on fresh mounts.

He slipped into the stables and found Tora blanketed in a dark stall. Tendering his brief affections to his beloved Spanish stallion, he went into the house, sword bared, to retrieve his kimono, which Wilf had laundered and stored for him.

He spun, nerves crackling, when he heard his voice called.

Garth peered up at him from the cellar door.

"Garth! They said you were—"

"And so I would be," Garth agreed, "if not for the lasting power of good fellowship. But do come down here, *schnell,* before we're visited again."

A lone oil lamp offered its forlorn orange glow in the stygian darkness. The cellar was cold and mildewed. They sat on the stair, facing each other, finally breaking out in short bursts of lunatic laughter to find themselves alive together in the midst of so much death. Gonji touched a finger to the dent in his sallet, and Garth chortled madly, crossing his arms over his middle. He stopped abruptly when a tear coursed his cheek. He rubbed it into his beard.

Gonji saw the redness that rimmed his eyes.

"Garth . . . Garth, where is Lorenz?"

The burly smith stared thoughtfully into the dark corner, where the great chest lay. "They took him. Those mongrels Klann calls warriors. That's not how it used to be. Not in the days of glory, when men fought for things that seemed worthwhile."

"Arrested him?"

"They beat him—he never wanted any part of this, Gonji—"

"Then he'd be at the Ministry? With the other prisoners?"

"Of course. Where else? God, my back aches . . ." His peevishness had altered to distraction without the slightest transition. Now it changed again to low-keyed anger. "They . . . they spoke of taking him to Mord. And something Mord had done to Phlegor."

Gonji experienced a chill at the memory of the late guild leader.

Garth panted as if in sudden panic. "Strom—gone. Lorenz—gone. Wilfred—"

"Wilf's *all-recht*. I saw him not long ago. I—" He bit his tongue when he caught himself about to speak of the way he'd found Strom. It was better, he thought, not to know.

"Things won't get any better, Gonji," Garth mused. "Julian Kel-Tekeli's been appointed Field Commander. A young savage who delights in viciousness and hangs those he fears . . ."

Gonji's eyes narrowed to see the fires that lit the smith's vision. "Will you be lending those powerful arms to the cause again this night?"

"Aren't there still children to free?"

Gonji stood slowly and bowed to him. *"Mein freund,* may we seek out one another in the next life and waste no time resuming our friendship." They shook hands warmly.

"What will you do?" Garth inquired sympathetically.

*Julian. Mord. Julian, Mord . . .*

"Seek the satisfaction of honor, I think." *Julian and Mord.* "You must tell Wilfred . . ." He sighed. "Tell him that when he goes after his Genya, he must search out Simon. Seek his help. Or else, do what he must do . . . alone."

He turned to mount the stairs.

"You know Wilfred," Garth said. "He'll not settle for that."

Gonji stopped, shoulders bunching, for a second. Then he left the cellar.

He emerged into the lane behind the shop, smelling manure and damp hay. The rain rattled maddeningly off his sallet. He carried the rolled kimono under an arm, his lips twisted with loathing.

*Julian-Mord-Julian-Mord . . .*

Hatred drove the blood in Gonji's veins.

270

*Whatever his skills,* the voice of Master Oguni came,
*even the consummate warrior can be but one man. One
target can be engaged at a time. Only the fool overreaches
the nearer for the seductive glory of the farther . . .*

Black smoke roiled across the pale disc of the full
moon. Several houses in the southern quarter had been set
to blazing by searching troops. For what reason, Gonji
could not tell. He approached the nearest, set his kimono
on a sill, and peered out from the shadows.

A mercenary band splashed away at a gallop, whooping
at people who watched from windows, terror in their eyes.
Flames sputtered and sizzled from the small dwelling, the
rain turning them to inky smoke on contact. Three mercenaries stayed behind, dismounted, passing a wineskin
back and forth. Several people lay dead in the street
outside the house, among them a woman and a child.

"Come on out, you sons o' bitches," a soldier roared at
the stricken observers, who quickly ducked inside their
homes in fear of being next. "You want to fight? Come
on."

Teeth clenched, Gonji sprinted up behind the three, his
*katana* flashing. By the time one of them had turned, he
was two steps from them. He tore into them with a growl.
In four strokes, the three were laid low, their swords still
on their hips. Only one was alive, thrashing and gasping,
Gonji's slash having fulfilled its intention.

"You bastard!" the man cried, whimpering, the hiss of
the flames drowning him out. "I can't move my legs. You
yellow bastard!"

"Keep your voice down," Gonji said, standing over
him. He glanced about, a terrible calm in his manner. He
heard his name whispered from nearby shutters.

"Where is Julian?"

"Julian'll cut your guts out!"

"Where is he?"

"Will you—will you let me live, if—if I tell you?"

Sobbing now. His manner shifting.

*"Nein."*

The brigand emitted a whimper. "The Provender," he whined. "He'll cut your—" He drew his pistol, though it was empty. A second later, Gonji's blade silenced his last cry. A muffled scream came from one of the houses.

Then a gloomy stillness blanketed Vedun, the heavens withholding their outpouring for endless seconds. Only the crackle of the flames could be heard in its wake. When it passed, a sudden violent wind shook the city, tearing at Gonji's clothing and armor, flipping his sallet back onto his neck. The rain sliced across the plateau in buffeting sheets.

By the time Gonji had retrieved his kimono, the flames in the house had been extinguished.


*Chapter Fifteen*


*Hour of the Boar*


Gonji left word with militiamen at the slaughterhouse that he could be found at the home of their late boss and training leader, Roric Amsgard.

He found Amsgard's widow in bitter mourning, several friends and *bushi* making a strained endeavor at comforting her. She seemed disconsolate, clutching her younger children about her for a raft of security. The oldest Amsgard son, of whom Roric would have been justly proud, diverted his siblings and doted on his mother as best he could. The stoical manner in which he bore up under the loss cut Gonji to the heart.

The samurai made a somber effort at offering his condolences, for Roric had been a close friend and a fine comrade. The widow appeared to bear him no rancor.

Michael and Lydia arrived soon after receiving word of Gonji's whereabouts. They were accompanied by Wilf and Anton the Gray knight. They were dripping and chilled, apprehensive of the next action.

"Thank God for this rain," Anton said.

*"Ja,"* Wilf concurred, "we weren't even stopped."

"Well," Michael said glumly, "you're still the military commander. They're awaiting your further orders."

Gonji nodded, distracted but warmed by their continued faith in him. "I think you'd best keep hold of the mantle of leadership. You're the better administrator and coordinator. I've another duty now. Simon and I must set the works in motion. It's now or never."

Wilf cocked an eyebrow suspiciously to hear his words. "I'm going to fight alongside you, right?"

"For the moment, I've another duty for you."

"Wait a minute—"

"Am I not your superior?" Gonji snapped. The young smith backed down a bit, anxiety flickering in his dark eyes. He twisted at the hilt of Spine-cleaver. Gonji went on more sensitively. "You're my most trusted friend and warrior, Wilf. My second-in-command. It's no good for us to be caught together, you understand that. Later we'll link up with our commands. You're in charge of the entire western half of the city. I wouldn't have anyone else. I want to know that when those wagons are moving they'll make it through the west gate."

Wilf pondered the business, unconvinced, while Gonji sent messengers after Jacob Neriah and, to everyone's curiosity, an obscure archer from the militia, the father of the little girl Tiva.

He turned to Wilf again, gestured for him and the others to gather in an antechamber. Cups of mead and ale

273

were passed among them, and Gonji spoke in a low voice.

"Wilfred, you must join your father at the stables and be ready to liberate both the horses and the wagons from across the way. There's no minimizing the peril of your task. The west gate is crawling with troops, and the garrison at the old granary in the southwest corner will have to be destroyed before the innocents can move. We've purposely left the western sectors for the last movement. They're the closest to the gate. Those who can will be moved through Tralayn's house into the catacombs. A solid defensive posture will have to be maintained, of course. I'll leave it to you to mount your parties and decide how to do it, so sorry." He smiled wanly, exhaling and slumping into a chair, where he sat with hands on knees. "Those who can't get to Tralayn's will have to join the wagon caravan while it is still in the city. And I'm afraid they'll have much company—"

"Too much," Anton grumbled.

*"Hai,* I've been to the catacombs." He shook his head. "Spread the word that the *bushi* should be ready to move, but only on order. Until then they must stay indoors. That goes for everyone, Miko-san. Select your sector-alert people from those on hand here. Pockets of *bushi* in hiding will have to pursue the tactical plans as they come, whatever their number and armament. We can only wish we knew better our remaining strength, but . . ." He lifted his palms in helpless resignation.

"We've still got the majority of our fighting men, I believe," Michael declared.

Gonji nodded. "It's chaotic, but it will have to do. And listen—Simon will stalk the city tonight. I have no idea what he'll do, or what he'll be—"

Lydia gasped and crossed herself in the doorway.

"—but the people must not fear him when they've received the order to move. Everything depends on that. No time for faint hearts or stalling." He rambled on with the fragmented plan, trying to touch on all that troubled him. Before long it had become rather like a last will and testament.

Noticing Wilf's look, he stopped and stood. "You have your orders. Fight well, my friend."

The young smith frowned, mouth working as if he would speak. But he only took Gonji's hand firmly. They bowed deeply to each other, and Wilf departed, a bit ashen in his fear of the samurai's ominous attitude but for once uncomplaining.

The others followed him out with words and gestures of prayer and well-wishing, until only Anton remained with Gonji.

The knight cleared his throat and affected a bluff posturing. "You know I, uh—I didn't like you at first," he said with downcast eyes. "Not sure I do *yet*. But I know the cost of doing what you do. For people who can't understand your ways. That's . . . sometimes the soldier's lot when he fights far from home, ain't it?" He sniffed self-consciously and flexed his shoulders. "Shit, I'm no good at words."

He made as if to leave, but Gonji halted him and bowed.

"It's a great comfort to side with such as you, Anton, whatever our differences." They shared a smile, the nervous atmosphere dispelled. Gonji espied the bandage that wrapped Anton's scalp wound. "That bald head of yours makes a good target, *neh?*"

"There'll be hell to pay for this, I'll tell you."

They both chuckled, and the knight joined a group of militiamen selecting and honing weapons. Gonji called for a ewer and basin. He closed the door and stripped himself, then began laving ceremoniously in preparation for what was to come. Reflections of his life came to him as he pursued the ritual.

When the itinerant merchant Jacob Neriah and Tiva's

father had both arrived, the Benedettos brought them into the tight chamber, looking on with curiosity. Through the doorway, Gonji could see into the Amsgards' parlor. Roric's widow seemed trancelike, catatonic. An elderly man knelt before her, speaking and motioning with measured calm and kindness. Beside her a woman wept and plied the beads of her rosary.

Gonji bowed to the two men. Jacob stood shaking, eyes shut. Tiva's father, a stern-visaged man named Vaclav, gazed at Gonji with smoldering distrust.

"Jacob, I want you two to descend to the catacombs, and when the signal is given, you will depart in advance of the evacuees to prepare a place for them in Austria."

Jacob nodded but seemed perplexed. "Yes, yes, I think I can arrange that. I own property and have many friends in Vienna, but I—"

"I just think a delegation should precede the main body, that's all," Gonji said defensively, staving off their questions.

"What about my daughter?" Vaclav asked.

"Tiva goes with you, of course."

The archer looked surprised. "How do you know her name?"

Gonji turned and began fussing with his weapons. "I became acquainted with Eduardo and his little band of urchins. She's a wonderful child. Now be off with you, both of you, I've no more time to bandy words."

With a look to each other, they excused themselves, Neriah offering up a prayer to the God of all for their deliverance and for revenge on the marauders who had so ravaged the province.

Gonji sent a puzzled man to move his armor to the Gundersens', and before the door closed behind him, he caught a glimpse of Lydia in the parlor, a smile perking her lips.

He laid his weapons on a mat and knelt before them in

tunic and damp breeches, barefoot, his topknot precisely tied, the *hachi-maki* about his brow. He meditated for a brief while. Bending forward, he reverently drew the Sagami, clucked and exhaled, a dismal frown on his face to see again the nick Simon Sardonis had made in its graceful sleekness.

The door cracked open, and he heard the sibilant rush of air that passed Lydia's lips.

"No-no, do come in," he said, rising and replacing the Sagami. "I . . . wanted to speak with you anyway."

She entered and closed the door, lowering her eyes demurely. "That was very kind of you," she said in a voice just above a whisper, "sending Tiva away like that."

Gonji grunted. *"Someone* had to smooth the way for the refugees." Seeing that she was unconvinced, he abandoned the deception. "Some people would call it favoritism, *neh?"*

"Mmm. Too bad we can't move all the children off like that. But I suppose there isn't time."

"No time and no more individual escorts to spare—by the way, congratulations on the big belly," he said. "I never thought to tell you before."

She smiled and sat on a stack of packed belongings the Amsgards had prepared for the evacuation. *"Gracias.* Gonji, tell me something. I know that what we're doing now is beyond questioning. We must leave Vedun for now, but . . . was I not right all along? That none of this should have been allowed to happen?"

Gonji peered at her through slitted eyes. He bent over, hands on his thighs, and licked his dry lips.

"Perhaps," he allowed. "Immature men, blustering and posturing to prove their toughness, *neh?"* He smiled crookedly, and she laughed curtly to recall her angry words. They had been spoken so long ago, it seemed.

"The city is ruined," she reflected. "What else can

happen now? You can add my prayers to those of the others who hope you've taught them well. Do you know what I think? I think you're basically a good man. An educated, refined man who simply tries too forcefully to win the love and admiration of others. And the results sometimes are not what you would wish. Violence, distrust—"

"If you'll pardon me, *gomen nasai,*" he interrupted sourly, "let's skip the journey through my soul until another time, eh? You've rather missed the mark anyway." He chafed at having a nerve exposed, but the irritation swiftly passed. She looked serenely lovely, and in the expectation of what would soon come to pass, he determined to acknowledge what was in his heart.

"You know I, uh—" He scratched the stubble along his jaw as he groped about the garden of unseemly words.

"Please," she said, rising and moving near, "please don't." Her eyes were soft and liquid, aglow like the morning sky after first frost. Full of pleading. "I know the words you would say to me, but saying them would only spoil them. Keep them in your heart," she whispered.

She reached up and held his face between her hands. Kissing his cheek lightly, she turned and whisked herself from the room with a rustle of skirts. The door closed soundlessly, leaving Gonji alone, flushed and bewildered.

*How do you like that?* he thought in embarrassment. Damn it all, woman! How dare she presume to know my feelings so well! Have I been so careless, Spirits of my Fathers, even with all my pains? I'm about to join my ancestors for reasons I'm not even sure of . . . I try to pledge my love to a woman, and before I can even say the words she sends me off to my death with a pat on the ass like you would a horse!

Gonji pondered it all for a space, blew an exasperated breath, and dismissed it, emptying his mind as he knew he must.

He lashed on his *tanto* knife and remaining poisoned darts, donned his kimono, tied his *obi,* and sashed his *daisho* at their threatening angles.

*I shall depart Vedun as I entered it . . .*

Moving out to the parlor, Gonji surveyed the street that coursed east-west across the entire southern stretch of Vedun. The rain fell in torrents, and the culverts were rising, but the clouds seemed to be breaking over the mountains to the north, and the full moon's glow grew stronger as it spanned the sky on its course. Stray animals wandered about aimlessly, some foraging in the gutters for food.

At that moment, Salavar the Slayer splashed past the house, headed toward the west gate. With him were three heavily armed adventurers.

Gonji ground his teeth as he watched them ride out of sight. He turned and bowed to all in the parlor, taking up a borrowed cloak.

"Soon now," he said. He appended a sign of the cross for all to see. "We'll need the help of all gods that be, this night. Farewell, all of you."

The tower at the square sounded eleven bells.

They wished him well and sent him off with their prayers. He caught a fleeting glimpse of Lydia as the rear door's click banished him to the driving rain and cloaking darkness. Then the *waka* came back to him. The poem he had composed upon thinking of her on a sleepless night during the training:

> She is the blossom
> that blooms by night.
> I am the sun.
> The moon is her light.

Bracing himself against the shivers, he sprinted off into a bleak lane that ran awash with streaming ruts. He slowed to a fast walk, taking to the eaves for protection from the rain.

Behind him followed the one who had watched and waited for him, knowing he must leave sooner or later. Stealthy. Longbow wrapped in sailcloth to protect the string until it would be put to use.

Lady Olga Thorvald sidled up behind the brooding Klann at his dais. She reached her hands around the chair carefully, a smile curling her red lips. Her long, painted nails met at his eyes.

"Can you tell who it is from the touch alone?" she whispered. "Owwww!"

The king grasped her hands at the wrists and twisted them outward vigorously. She pulled away, her hands thrust around her sides as she squeezed at the pain.

"Did you have to do that?" she cried.

"Yes, We can tell from the touch who it is," he said without looking at her. "The touch of the vixen, the viper."

"That's not what you once called me. You had many names for me when once I shared your bed, names of affection, attributes shouted in the heat of your lust!"

He turned, glaring at her, rising from the gilt-inlaid chair. "You forget again, scheming bitch—is your head chiseled of the same stone as your cold heart? That was another king. Another time . . ."

"A more grateful one," she spat, "one who would have rewarded faithful service. Do you know what I've done for you?"

He stood looking at her, his emptied goblet trembling in his clutch. Her long flaming hair had been brushed in sultry waves that caressed her still shapely shoulders, her full bosom. Seductively undone at its front, the spring-green nightgown his brother had once so favored flowed gently along her outline, shifting with every breeze.

His lip curled in disgust. "You make me sick," he growled. "Leave us!" He hurled the goblet at her, missing by inches.

Tears streaming from her angry, confused eyes, she stormed from the chamber, past the embarrassed sentries. Once in the central hall of the keep, she saw the sorcerer approaching at a quick pace.

"Mord," she shot, "you've played me for the fool."

"Whatever are you talking about, dear lady?" he replied impatiently, looking past her. The clock in the great hall tolled eleven vibrations through the castle's stone skeleton.

"I've done what you've asked. You swore you'd mend the rift between myself and His Majesty. When will you fulfill your part?"

"Lower your voice, please," he commanded in his voice like the rumble of a desecrated tomb. "You're making a spectacle of yourself."

"I want the bargain completed, Mord," she threatened, "lest I tell the king of your treachery."

There followed a short, deadly silence.

"Whatever are you talking about?" he asked simply.

"You know," Lady Thorvald replied, steeled by her desperate anger. "And tomorrow, *he'll* know. Am I making myself clear?"

Mord laughed, low and minacious. "Tomorrow things will be different. You'll see. Tomorrow you'll be united with the king once again."

"We'll see," she replied, stalking off.

Mord would have killed her straightaway for her idle threat had he not been troubled by matters of more pressing concern. He hurried to the chamber but was halted by the sentries.

"Out of my way," he ordered. The sentries crossed their pikes and stood fast.

"Sorry, sir. No one permitted to see His Highness."

"On whose order?" he bellowed.

"His physicians," the Llorm guard answered, holding his gaze steadfastly.

The inhuman bellowing rage that issued from the closed chamber door answered Mord's next question. It was followed by a thundering crash and shouts of warning in human voices.

*The Tainted One again.* The primitive child, mindless and enraged.

*Damn the stars!* Mord thought. It was time for the chant, yet the garrison and the civilian population would do nothing about it until Klann had given his sanction. Mord would have to do something soon. He *must* have the fresh imputation of mana, must command the power to control the Hell-Hound.

For the spirit of the territory had been awakened by the moon. Moved to fury beyond rational direction, it stalked somewhere very near. Too near, for the sorcerer's comfort. Yet he knew that if he could destroy its corporeal existence, the enigmatic spirit would be allied to him.

*Chapter Sixteen*

*Hour of the Rat*

Gola the Butcher, they called him.

Or so he said. And why not? Hadn't he sliced two rebels to dog meat that very evening? sent their women into hysterics with his handiwork?

So he had, and there'd be more kills on the morrow.

He'd see to that.

Gola sat bleary-eyed, pulling at his wine, the single night guard watching over the sleeping mercenaries in the old granary in the southwest. Relishing his brutish memories. Listening to the snoring of the fatigued and drunken adventurers who lay skewed on the blanketed floor or overhung their cots.

In his stupor, not altogether sure he wasn't asleep and dreaming himself, he watched the slow buckling of the oaken doors. The bending of the door bar from the strange inward pressure. His imagination whirled and eddied, fashioning shapes of things which could cause such a phenomenon. Chuckling at thoughts of night-fiends he'd heard described over campfires.

"Password," he growled, propped on one elbow. There came no response, only a brief stay of the buckling. Presently it began anew.

Gola scowled and slipped his saber from its sheath.

Nothing he envisioned in his dim fantasies prepared him for what cracked the doors, splintering them at their seams. His reverie had been an inadequate rehearsal. He saw a rushing mound of fur for an instant, then the glint of firelight off razor-edged surfaces. Then he saw no more.

He was the first to die. Twenty men died with him.


Gonji leaned against a wall inside the three-sided sand-stone outbuilding before the Provender's veranda-topped corral. He collected his breath as he cleansed the Sagami's blade. Three men lay dead at the corral; three more, inside the stables. There were no more bandits in his way.

The rain eased in its force. The jammed corral and stable were alive with stamping, neighing horses. The violent events, the night's foreboding aura-*something* had moved them to skittishness.

He wiped his face and peered around at the front of the

283

noisy Provender. How many soldiers? He expelled an anxious breath, eyes narrowing at the grisly sight of the naked forms hanging upside down from the inn's signboard.

Three more brigands rode down from the north, tied their steeds with the jostling animals lined before the smoky yellow light of the Provender's windows. Two drunks emerged, exchanged surly greetings, mounted and trotted away.

Gonji could feel the staring eyes of the small party of Hussars in hiding, two hundred yards away. Chafing at the bit. They had accepted with grim reluctance Gonji's order that they must hold back until it was time to perform their given task, only half understanding the point of honor that dictated what he must now do alone.

One of the newly arrived brigands stopped at the door and brayed a laugh, giving one of the corpses a spin. It was Vlad Dobroczy.

Gonji gritted his teeth and slid past the cover of the tethered steeds when the soldiers had gone into the inn. He wiped his eyes with the hood flaps of the cloak, blinking back an angry sting. The two *bushi* had been obscenely dealt with before they had been killed. Feathers from Salavar's lance had been pinned to Vlad's flesh with a small dagger. Freshly felled game on display.

The samurai peered through a window, hand on hilt, counting.

Sixteen free companions, two Llorm regulars, as near as he could make it. And Julian, leaning over the bar.

He steeled himself, fists clenched as he made a brief prayer to the *kami* of strength. And made his move.

The small sack of gold sailed across the room and clinked on the floor at Julian's feet.

"I quit, soldier," came Gonji's voice from the doorway.

Tables and chairs grated and careened all over the inn

284

as the troops lurched to their feet, sweeping out pistols and blades. Gonji threw off the cloak and drew both his swords with a flashing twist, stopping them in a hypnotic instant.

"Halt! Stop right there!" he cried in German. "If those pieces aren't loaded, primed, and spanned, then you best lower them now and back off."

Sweat coursed from his armpits. His anxiety was reflected on the rapidly sobering faces of the troops. Some could not remember reloading their touchy ordnance; all had seen the havoc the endless rain had wreaked with their black powder.

There was a breathless pause. Only the two Llorm continued to approach slowly, swords held before them, and Gutschmidt sidled along behind the bar softly.

Julian turned with deadly calm. He looked at Gonji in amusement and, lost for words, began to laugh.

"Arrest that . . . man of honor," the captain said at last, still laughing. Some of the men moved to obey, but Gonji leveled his blades at them.

"Stay your hand, or you die," the samurai said earnestly. "My fight is with Julian now, your well-bred master. I've come for him alone."

"You contemptible cur," Julian sneered, drawing his own pistol. "This one, you'll find, is primed and ready."

Gonji took a breath, prepared to charge, when two clicks sounded behind the captain.

*"Ja,"* Gutch said, "and so are these. And I'll lay ten-to-one that you're the first to go."

Julian half-turned. Gutch sat atop a high stool, pearl-handled pistols braced on his knees, aimed at the captain's head.

Julian laid the wheel-lock on the bar carefully. "I'm surprised at you, Gutschmidt. I thought you were a man with more class than to side with this . . . inferior. We'll take this up later, you and I."

"That's gonna be real tough with a big hole in yer head, goatsucker."

Gonji smiled thinly and drew himself up tall, suddenly a figure of menacing command. "Draw back," he warned, "and let me pass."

"Seize him!" Julian shouted.

The brigands began to shuffle uncertainly. The Llorm urged them along. Gonji's rotating blades cut the air with slow, balletic grace, warding them back with the promise of flashing death.

"Hold on," someone said in their midst. The free companion moved forward. Gonji recognized him at once. It was Stanek, the man whose lip Julian had split in almost that very spot when he and Gonji had first crossed paths. The bandit ran a finger along the scar above his chin.

"I'd like to see this," Stanek continued. "I'm sure the captain would like to prove himself before his men."

"You mutinous pig—arrest Stanek, too!" Julian roared, his face reddening now. The two Llorm took a step, but Stanek flourished his swordpoint in their faces. They backed away. The others followed, falling toward the walls. Julian's eyes widened in astonishment.

*"Take that man!"*

*"Si, mi capitan,"* Gonji said, smiling ferally, replacing his swords in their sheaths. "Seize that man! Charge, you cowards! Attack them! Do my dirty work! You never do anything dangerous for yourself, do you, Julian, you swaggering coward!"

Someone behind him ran out into the street. The sound of a horse splashing off. Gonji paid it no heed.

He began to walk slowly toward Julian, narrowing the distance with measured strides. His left hand gripped the Sagami's hilt. Sweat broke out on the captain's forehead. He rubbed his palms on his breeches. His saber dangled at his left hip.

"Seize him—obey me—I'm the great Captain Kel'Tekeli," Gonji went on acidly. "Even your men want to see what you're made of." He stopped, the distance halved. "You know, I've been wondering about your prowess in battle since that fencing bout I was so foolishly lured into. I've been wondering about your guts. Your willingness to die. Are you willing to die, Captain? I am. Let us see who's more comfortable fighting under the certainty of death . . ."

Mesmerized, Julian began to tremble slightly, sweat rolling along his well-formed jawbones as the samurai began to stalk him again.

They were in engagement distance. A draw, and their blades would mesh.

"For insulting me and my family—for murdering my master, Flavio, and committing sundry crimes against the people of Vedun, I am going to kill you."

Julian's open right hand reached delicately across his front to where he knew the saber grip would be. But then the moment was past . . . They were too close. Impossibly close for sword engagement. Neither man could draw cleanly. And still the oriental moved closer. His nose was a hand's width from the captain's.

"You bastard," Julian whispered to stave his quaking. He grasped the saber's basket hilt.

Gonji's left hand brought the Sagami up. His right caught the forte inches from its point as the blade twisted horizontally, inside out, over the top of Julian's draw and across in a silver lick. There was an instant's resistance and a soft tearing. A scattering of droplets just behind the blade's arc, a tiny shriek of air escaping.

Then a lap of blood that gouted onto the hem of Gonji's kimono.

The soldier behind Gonji saw the samurai's shoulder blades rotate and his arms flap—he had hit the captain.

287

The man puffed out a breath and advanced, broadsword aimed at the wanted man's back . . .

The Austrian highwayman at the left saw what he thought was the gleam of a dagger, then the captain's stiffening. Then blood. He kicked a chair out of his way and charged . . .

The brigand with the clearest view, standing just to Gonji's right, groaned to see what happened. Somehow the samurai had unleashed that deadly blade and sliced the captain's head half off so that it fell on his chest like a wet gunnysack. Hair standing on end, mouth a screaming rictus, he aimed his primed pistol.

Pandemonium reigned.

The explosion of Gutch's pistol caused Gonji to blink as he continued turning to his right. He saw the pistolier's face shatter, the gun in his hand cracking off an errant shot.

Gonji whirled and caught the *katana's* hilt in both hands. An underhand, upward snap of his wrists unhinged the jaw of the onrushing swordsman. Another pistol exploded, and there was a crashing of pewter on the shelf behind the bar.

The tumbling of furniture and splatter of falling cups—shouts and stamping feet and a metallic din—

Gonji began to move, darting and striking like an asp, motion his only chance against so many. He ran down a backward stumbling pistolier who raised his hands to stave the charge and tumbled over, disemboweled. The samurai leapt atop a table and back down to the floor, striking down another bewildered swordsman with a vertical slash.

Gutch's second pistol barked and bowled a man backward with the ball's impact. The samurai hurdled the falling form and charged at two bladesmen who barred his way to the door. He froze an instant, drawing their swings. His whirling steel whanged off both blades, parrying them aside, but then he felt the motion behind him, whipped a high parry over his head and bound an overhead slash.

He heard the hiss of an arrow, helpless to heed it, as he twisted the *katana* down and under his armpit with his right hand alone. The attacker shrieked in his ear, skewered through the chest.

A man plunged toward him, and Gonji slashes him needlessly through the neck—a Llorm—a war arrow embedded in his back.

He ducked an arcing *schiavona* and sliced deeply into the attacker's thigh. A pistol cracked—Julian's, in the hand of Gutch—another sleek shaft parted the air and sheared a brigand's hauberk and ribcage, knocking him off a table and onto a companion. Gonji's fanning left-right sequence finished his foe.

Now one cursing bandit was surging for the bar, where Gutch had brought up a rapier and was calling him on. Another bolted from the Provender; his yowl of pain followed seconds later.

The remaining six assembled, panting and perspiring, some of them nursing small injuries. They glared at Gonji, who stepped lithely at their center, *katana* snapping before him from hand to hand in a display of confident skill that terrified them, made them reticent to advance.

The clash of steel from Gutch's engagement—a cloth-yard arrow sizzled and chunkered through the flesh between Stanek's shoulder blades, emerging from his clavicle—

The five remaining revelers were ignited. With a howl of battle-frenzy they stormed down on Gonji.

The samurai moved as they did, whirling and taking on the startled man at his left rear, slipping his lunging blade and slashing down through his shoulder so that he fell, blocking the man next to him. A wrist-twisting high parry, and he was breaking from their midst, gaining more favorable ground. He felt the fiery line of cold sweat and stinging pain as a mercenary's swipe tore through the back of his kimono, opening a wound in his lower back.

Running past the bar, where Gutch and his quarry dueled over the counter, spilling goblets and snarling. Bounding over bodies, he leaped over a forest of upset benches and stools behind a table. They would have to pick their way through to him.

Coming from right and left, they went down under Gonji's flailing, sparking steel. A circular parry and jaw-splitting upward slash—a high block covering his apparently unprotected back—two lunging feints and a roaring *kiyai,* energizing a ripping slash that knocked a man off his feet. Then up onto the table, the Sagami singing off two blades, swatting them aside as the samurai sprang over their heads and landed with sword at the ready.

Hurling his clan's war cry at the ceiling, Gonji descended on them with sword held upright like the sting of the scorpion, driving them back in their flinching fear, slashing the first man such that he spun like a weathercock, while the second took the full brunt of a charging lunge, gurgling a choked scream and slamming backward into the table and over.

Gonji turned to the bar. The mercenary held both hands at the spot where the innkeeper's rapier still stuck in his breast. Red wetness dripped between the goggle-eyed brigand's fingers.

Gutch brought his face near the enemy's. "Hey, bimbo, you're bleeding all over Gutch's doublet." He pushed the soldier's face away, sending him reeling off the rapier's point.

Gonji exhaled with relief and fell back onto a stool, head hung low. He assessed the carnage. The Provender lay awash in blood, its scent thick and cloying, churning his stomach. He grimaced and removed the *hachi-maki,* shuffled to the body of Julian and dropped it thereon.

*"Danke,* Gutch," he said bleakly.

*"Ja*—now look at my place."

"Well done, gentils," came Paolo Sauvini's voice from the doorway. "And you needn't worry about the one who tried to go for help." He stood posturing like some hero out of picaresque fancy, hand on hip, longbow leaning beside him, his brown cloak's hood framing his glowing face.

"You—so it was you again—idiot!" Gonji growled, eyeing him angrily. But he sighed and added wearily: *"Domo."*

"Hey, you pinhead," Gutch grumbled, "every time you come in here you're lookin' for trouble. What do you think you are? You better get that twinkle outta yer eye, Manfred. This ain't no game."

Paolo cast him a wry look and fell into step with Gonji, who was gazing out into the street, listening.

"Pass the word, gents," Gutschmidt was saying at their backs as he reloaded his pistols, "the Provender is now open to business—*for citizens only.* Good luck, boys."

Gonji executed two quick, efficient cuts that freed the dangling bodies of Vlad and the other militiaman.

"Let's go," he said grimly. He and Paolo mounted two of the tethered horses. The rain was dwindling to a spray again, the enshrouding cloud breaking over the mountains. "Where's your wife?" he asked.

"She'll be okay," Paolo replied, shrugging.

"Then I take it you want to ride with the city defenders—"

He never finished. The Hussars had broken from cover to begin freeing and hitching the wagons. Now Berenyi and Nagy were shouting from down the street.

"Mercenaries coming down Charity!"

"How many?" Gonji shouted.

"Hell, I don't know," Nick Nagy bellowed.

"Take a stand and stop them," the samurai commanded. "Archers, set up a crossfire—"

"We haven't got many—"

"They'll have to do." Gonji fought with the reins to steady his nervous mount. "Berenyi and Nagy, get those wagons hitched and rolling. Half back here to pick up stray refugees later, the other half split between the Streets of Faith and Charity. Roll them to the marketplace. Then get them going from Wojcik's—all of them—"

The mounted mercenary party emerged from the Street of Charity. At least five and twenty, but they were already besieged from windows and rooftops as the militia holed up at the eastern end began to turn out. Crossbows laced them with bolts. They went down howling, horses rearing and tumbling, throwing their column into disarray. Chamber pots and other heavy objects flew from windows to smash in their midst.

But now the Llorm sentries on the walls were converging above and behind the Provender to launch arbalest volleys down at the rebels. Some fell from the rooftops, others dashing for cover.

"Damn—you're sliced open," Paolo shouted, seeing Gonji's bloody kimono back.

"It's not what it looks—come on." They surged ahead to meet the leading pair of cavalrymen, taking them down almost simultaneously.

Paolo shouted in triumphant glee.

"Never mind that," Gonji cried impatiently, casting about for an orderly plan to the rapidly spreading chaos. He ordered Paolo to alert the militia leaders to turn out their *bushi* in full force, concentrating on the key strongholds, particularly the square, where the armored wagons and confiscated weapons were being held.

"But the giant!" Sauvini objected.

"Don't *worry* about the giant. Distract him, draw him

off—something. We'll deal with him later—*I* will, if you can't handle it."

Paolo looked offended, nodded resolutely. Then the savagely wounded rider approached up Provender Lane from the south. The adventurer clung to the neck of his frothing steed, whose eyes bulged hideously.

*"Monsters!"* the wounded man was screaming. "Monsters attacking the garrison—"

Thirty paces from where Gonji and Paolo sat with drawn swords, the horseman tumbled off the falling mount, bouncing hard before landing face first in the mud. He was knocked unconscious. They could see from their vantage the flayed and bloody flesh on his left thigh. The horse was dead, its flanks gouged.

Gonji stared back along Provender, eyes straining at the distant darkness. The *thuck!* of a crossbow quarrel landing beneath him scattered his thoughts.

"Get going," he snapped as he kicked his mount into a gallop.

Paolo watched him dwindle as he rode in the direction from which the rider had come. Then a wounded mercenary was on top of him, swinging his mighty battle-axe for a strike.

*Chapter Seventeen*

Wheeling his steed into the byway from which he thought the wounded harbinger had emerged, Gonji rode with all the speed caution would allow toward the hoarse cries of orders in military voices.

His breath hissed between his teeth and his heart

thrummed blood past his ears as he wended his way south-west, shortcutting dangerously through an antiquated alley canyon that outletted into the color and grace of the Italian district. In the drizzle and din he could make out the idiot blaring of Tumo. Gunfire here and there, and the clash of steel. The city was coming to desperate life, aroused to a realization of its dire peril. Lamplight flared houses bright with illumination as he clattered past windows.

Shouts and cries. Now and then the sound of his own voice being called as he rode past. Whinnying horses in the distance that loomed ahead darkly, full of the animal terror they projected only when threatened by fire or predators.

He thundered by several scurrying bodies who paid him no heed, exchanging one ineffectual sword clash with a passing mounted adventurer. Then he swung left into a lane in the slaughterhouse district. And saw.

A Llorm squad or the remnant of a column had established a hasty pitched position. Drays and furnishings torn from houses, a few animal carcasses—these were being heaped together by desperate, sweating men who growled and cursed their fate.

But there was no exchange of volley, no clash of arms at all in the dim lane. Torches in spots played over fevered eyes and tortured brows. So enraptured was he to see their desperate action, to hear—as they heard—the savage snarling that echoed from the next crossing lane, that Gonji didn't so much as raise his *katana* in challenge.

He watched with fascination, skin prickling, as a few mercenaries in the troops' number banged on doors, begging entry. A bureau drawer, dropped from a high window, plunged downward onto a Landsknecht's helmed skull.

Gonji laughed, a curt, humorless trill. Then he locked eyes with the Llorm commander. There followed the strangest of tacit communications, both men realizing as one that they were not enemies for the nonce; rather, they were allies in the struggle between human and supernatural forces.

He inched his steed forward gingerly, seeing the archers along the blockade ready their arbalests, knowing that they might spindle him in a second should they choose. Knowing that they would not. For the snarling of the Beast was at the crossroad now, its fell shadow spanning the lane in moonlight as it sniffed and sensed the strength of the ambushers.

Gonji held his breath, seated behind the double line. He had just caught sight of the butchered sheep and pigs on which they had hoped it would pause to feed when he abruptly realized his exposed position—tallest object at the forefront now.

And then the shadow was withdrawn, and the Beast was looming on a rooftop above the defensive line, snarling in unbridled fury. And leaping into their midst. Four hundred pounds of streamlined power and cunning, canine teeth in jaws that could shear the leg of an ox. Black foreclaws and hind talons gone red with gore. A thing fashioned of solidified nightmare that walked upright like a man, though the shoulders were surmounted by the head and ruff of a wolf larger than any spawned in nature.

It raked through the paralyzed Llorm like a scythe. Two bolts rent its golden fur and thick hide. It howled to the moon and tore them free as if they were straw, then resumed its attack with renewed wrath. Some men dropped their weapons and fell back, staggered by the sight. Others broke ranks and ran, streaming prayers from raw throats.

Gonji's horse bucked and threw them. He looked up from the grime. It bore down on him, a bare-fanged dynamo of primordial power whose eyes were the red orbs

295

of the demonic energumen within. Simon's soul was subordinate to it this night. Clearly, he hadn't exaggerated the consequences.

His nerve ends flaring, Gonji scrabbled through the muck, past trash bins and onto a rear stoop. He turned on an elbow, the Sagami held overhead defensively. The werewolf had leapt onto his struggling horse and was savaging it. Men ran in all directions.

Gonji beat on the rear door of the house, calling out his name in identification. The last thing he saw before he fell through the opened portal was the steel-trap snapping of wolf jaws that crushed the steed's neck.

He lay on the storage room floor, smelling spices and musty larders, his ears ringing with the almost sentient mortal plaint of the horse. He had heard the sound before. A stallion downed by the Black Forest's nocturnal hunting fiends . . .

"A torch," he gasped. "Do you have a torch?"

Voices jabbered. A man's, a woman's, an older man's. He thought he recognized a face. Language unknown—

"Do you have a trap on the roof?" he was shouting.

And then, dreamlike, he was carrying an ignited flambeau, and ascending a rickety ladder. Emerging to the sounds of human terror. The crackle of the mist that worried the flame. The coppery taste in his mouth. Blood. Or fear.

At the roof's ledge. The Thing below. Huge and muscular. Golden-blonde. Broad at the shoulders, slender at the waist.

Feeding . . .

*"Si-moooon!"* Holding the torch out over the street.

Red eyes panning up. Pink lips drawn back over darkly dripping fangs.

"Remember yourself!" A bellowing issued from the next lane. He heard it only later, in memory, so intense was his concentration on the creature below. "Remember meeeee!"

He patted his chest. An instant later he sucked in a whistling breath and backpedaled, drawing the Sagami again. The Beast scaled the side of the house with a scrape of chitinous nails and padded toward him in the crouch that preceded the spring. Dripping talons rotating with anticipation—

*"Sim—"*

Gonji hurled the torch and dove through the narrow aperture, the woman's shriek passing him as he fell. He thudded on the attic floor, a sharp pain in his side. The werewolf's bestial head and arm groped for him. It growled maniacally in frustration, the great shoulders unable to pass the hatch.

In an instant it was gone.

*"Obor,"* one of the men yelled from the floor below. Gonji recognized the word *giant*.

From a second-story window they observed the brief clash of monstrous foes. Tumo hooted a challenge at the werewolf, tongue slavering over flaccid lips and splay teeth. He hefted his spiked club on one round, plate-armored shoulder. The Beast circled him warily, blood-stained jaws dripping saliva. Its back was arched, ruff bristling in warning.

Tumo brayed and smashed downward with the bludgeon. The werewolf slipped the resounding blow easily and bounded at the much larger attacker, ripping a chunk of whitened flesh from Tumo's forearm, blood streaming from the wound.

The cretin giant reeled with the pain, its wail keening in the ears of the wincing human observers. With the strength of a bull elephant in its humanoid frame, the wounded giant seized the snarling Beast by leg and ruff and flung it thirty feet to slam into a cornice and drop to the rutted cobblestones.

It shook itself and, with a final growl, disappeared into the shadowed lanes in search of easier prey.

*"Choléra,"* Gonji breathed, watching the Llorm escort try to prod the giant after the creature with polearms. It slapped at them, whimpering, wagging its head negatively. Before it padded back the way it had come with great splashing footfalls, helm ridiculously askew, Gonji caught sight of the large white patch peeking through its armor at the spot on the ribs where his poisoned arrow had pierced it without serious effect. There was no satisfaction in the discovery.

*Kami,* he prayed, if only they could hit the square while it's undermanned, the giant absent . . .

He pushed past the questioning citizens and made for the street, where he bounded astride a straggling horse amid half-hearted notices of his presence.

He galloped off for the stables, spreading panic as he went, calling out disheartening words to bewildered occupation troops. By the time he arrived at the stable area, he led a long retinue of pursuers, the effect being that he brought reinforcements against the already beleaguered rebels fighting for control of the southwest quarter.

His appearance was such that his own men very nearly opened fire on him when he dismounted in full stride before the smithshop.

"Hey, that's Gonji—" Wilf cried, staying the archers.

"What the hell'd you bring *them* for?" a warrior called out from the wagonage window, firing his pistol in the next breath.

Gonji kept running against the grain of the splashing cavalry troops who crisscrossed the broad space between the Gundersens' livery and the wagonage. He sliced a dragoon off his horse, kept racing, zig-zagging through the mud between the pounding hooves of the disorderly free companions. The *bushi,* seeing him, took heart and fled their cover for a bolder tack.

Wilf took down another with a similar hit-and-run

298

tactic, roaring in mirthless battle glee. Near him, Garth, armored and helmed, exacted a toll with his broadsword and Frankish axe. Now throwing with deadly accuracy, now delivering punishing blows, bloodshed marking his wake.

A *guisarme* flashed over the samurai's head just behind Wilf's shout of alarm. A trailing rider aimed his wheel-lock over his steed's ears. It sizzled and misfired in the dampness. Gonji ducked instinctively, *katana* whirling in an arc that took out the horse's forelegs. Two short, choppy blows finished the spilled mercenary.

Gasping for breath, Gonji sprang for a corner of the corral, where he knelt, sword on his shoulder, for a moment's much-needed respite. When he saw the figure huddled in the shed behind the wagonage, he angled toward it, mayhem in his eyes.

*Oh no, no, no—not yet. Not there, too many—uh-uh. No, not for you, Arvin. You've got to wait for a good spot. That's all. Maybe one backing up. Right onto your sword. Hee-hee . . . No. No, it wouldn't matter. You could never—You couldn't bear to watch anybody die from so close, could you, Arvin? Could you? Not even her . . .*

*So let's just wait till they're all looking to save their asses. Then we'll just creep up to the allure when the soldiers are busy, and then over and—*

*O my God. O Merciful God in Heaven. Not him. Not him. Not—*

"Jesus save my immortal soul!"

Disheveled and soaked, bleeding and blooded, begrimed and aching with present pains and the certain expectation of those to come, Gonji advanced toward the cowering figure at the wagonage shed. He recalled the face from the catacombs, but not the name. An undistinguished trainee like so many. Shock of hempen hair. Pale blue eyes effusing reluctance. Sallow skin and sunken cheeks. Wiry frame that seldom exerted full effort . . .

Lips spreading to reveal clenched teeth, Gonji sprinted at him, sword trailing in a stiffened right arm, chasing him from hiding and out into battle, where his friends and neighbors fell to buy him precious moments of freedom.

He stopped when he heard the man's piercing cry in a strange dialect. But he heard the name of Iasu, and knew what must have been meant, feeling a mixture of contempt and pity, and then nothing more.

The fighting folk of Vedun turned out in increasing numbers, though their tactics were egregious at first and strategy was hatched on the run. The thinning troop strength at the western end was pressed back steadily toward the all important west gate through which the wagons must roll—when and if it became safe for the evacuees to turn out of their homes, though it was known that some already had, and with certain disastrous results.

The immediate stable area cleared of occupation troops, work parties saddling mounts and hitching what few wagons were available at the place, Gonji purposed that he must move to the square. The armored wagons and weapons caches must fall back into the hands of the militia, if there was any hope of seeing the evacuation through.

And Simon. The Thing that was Simon—

"By all the saints and heaven itself, Gonji," a warrior swore when he entered the Gundersens' dwelling, Wilf racing in close behind.

"Gonji—?" Wilf began, but he was drowned out.

"He's a *monster,* for Christ's sake! Is that what you've brought us as a Deliverer?"

"You might as well have asked *Mord* to help us," another man griped.

"Shut up, you cowards," Gonji fired back. "He'll

300

bring it under control—''

*''He?* Who in the hell *is* he?''

Garth heaved in through the door, blood-spattered from boots to beard. He flung his helm on the floor and grabbed a proffered flagon. ''That's Simon Sardonis,'' he wheezed between gulps, ''and you'll be speaking kindly of his pitiful soul while you're in my house.''

Gonji nodded to him. *''Domo,* friend.'' He stripped off his filthy, tattered kimono and quickly laced on his pauldrons and vambraces; the back harness for his swords, and the low-brimmed, eye-slitted sallet he'd come to like. He obtained help in stringing his longbow.

''Can he do it, Garth?'' Gonji asked softly. ''Bring it under control?''

''Who can say?'' The smith shrugged.

Wilf grunted. ''So you knew about this, too, *nicht wahr?* Nice that you share things with your family—''

*''Stehen Sie,''* came Garth's impatient remonstrance.

''That's our Deliverer,'' one of the grumblers took up again, ''the one you promised us—a goddamned raving monster out of some peasant's fever-dream!''

''I promised you nothing,'' Gonji shot back, ears reddening at once in acknowledgment of the half-lie. ''Just the possibility of success in this business if you all did your part. It was, so sorry, if you will recall, your late prophetess who promised your God's Deliverer. So you will, *dozo,* take your belly-aching to Him—or her—in the future.''

He pushed past the man, lashed a quiver of war arrows to Tora's saddle and rolled his kimono behind. He mounted his chestnut stallion with a sigh of relief to at last be reunited with the brave steed. A half dozen men joined him.

*''Domo arigato,* Wilfred-san.'' It was Wilf who had readied Tora in faith that the samurai would be along to use him.

"Still Wir-fred," his friend joked, mounting beside him. "What's your problem?"

"Let's go, smart ass."

"Where to?" Wilf reared his destrier anxiously.

"The square," Gonji answered over the sound of beating hooves.

"The innocents—" Garth cried at their backs, "—take care for their protection above all else—"

Then a line of skirmishers, Austrian renegades, for the most part, howled with bloodlust and spilled from lanes and over fences and garden walls to the east.

The *bushi,* now firmly ensconced in homes and shops of the livery area, leaned out from windows and barricades to draw their beads.

Gonji, Wilf, and their small escort clattered away under fire, one man among them crying out and slumping over his horse's withers, keeping to the saddle for as long as he could. Falling, finally, when the bell tower was in sight over the rooftops.

The stable battle raged anew. Horses stampeded, some falling under fire. Others were recaptured, penned and tethered, only to be dispersed again in their panic as the metal foundry exploded with a stunning shock wave that blew windows and doors from the structures in the south. A pillar of rich flame and billowing black smoke blotted the moon's anemic disc, affording but a moment's respite from the struggle.

Men and women cried out in pain and death amid gunshots and the din of steel, the slosh of plummeting bodies and the shrilling of frenzied animals.

In the mud and blood of the slipping, sliding carnage, the man began to feel himself drift.

He saw, though his eyes were shut, the faces that passed over him, peering down in an instant's grief or satisfaction, only to shrink away quickly as survival demanded.

The great pain and stress were departing now, a numbness supplanting them. He tried to speak, fancied that he heard a voice in response, then felt a sensation as if he were crossing a relentless current, engulfed in a black wave. Then it was gone. He experienced a mild euphoria, knowing that the moment of crisis was past. He would be all right.

He gazed down at the face, feeling pity for that one less fortunate than he, when he realized that it was his own still and mud-spattered countenance that he looked upon. He wondered at the grave expressions of passersby, earnestly wishing to convey to them that there was no fear now. He was merely sleeping. In a moment . . . in a moment . . .

He lifted slowly, resignedly, unbidden reflections of his life filling his sphere of transcendence as if they were his new body, the substance of what he was.

Then, with a last look to what had been called him but was not, he lofted above the silent, futile strife of the battlefield and moved toward the pinpoint of light so very far away. The end of life's struggle and quest.

A pleasant, buoyant withdrawal.

## Chapter Eighteen

### Hour of the Ox

Two pairs of mercenaries, growling in argument as they cantered along the narrow alley in the north sector, swung carefully through the sinuous channel, blades held out to scrape the walls and keep their distance where the labyrinthine turns were darkest.

The first two passed under the arch. The second pair never saw the hurtling Aldo Monetto until he had dropped between them, spilling them both from their startled mounts. The bearded biller regained his feet first and downed the nearer brigand as he attempted to rise. The other was momentarily lost to view behind a stamping mare.

Then he saw him, broadsword drawn, teeth bared, over her haunches. He hefted his axe before him, ready for engagement, breath coming in ragged gasps.

Ahead, the lead pair fought to turn their steeds in the tight quarters, cursing. One held up a pistol, cocked it. Gerhard's armor-piercer shaft, fired from the roof above, lost eight inches of stole in steel plate and leather, flesh and bone. The second man looked up in time to see the sleek trajectory of spindling death.

Monetto leapt over the top of the mare's saddle, crashing downward but missing with his axe. The bandit hurled an oath at him and darted around the horse to stab at the rebel, who ducked and swung low, opening a deep gash in the soldier's leg. He yowled and struck the mare with the flat of his blade, causing her to rear and stamp. His flinch laid him open for Monetto's gut-splitting blow.

Monetto sucked in a cold breath to see what damage he'd done. His foe screamed and kicked on the soaked ground.

"God," Aldo cried, his overhead chop ending the man's suffering. He fell on one knee and covered his face. "Verily, friend—verily do I ask your mother's forgiveness . . .

"Hey, Aldo—you *all-recht?*" Gerhard lowered his bow to the alley and hang-dropped down seconds later. He scanned the downed enemies and nodded succinctly. Monetto had begun to gather their armament, his face drawn with grief.

"You're unhurt—*ja?* A good wheel-lock piece here," the archer said, grabbing it. "So she said we might pull it together again," Gerhard continued. "So what do you think?"

Monetto shrugged. "Lottie's a nice girl. You're a nice jughead."

*"Nein,* come on, *dummkopf,"* Gerhard pressed, eyes shining, "do you think I'm too old for her?"

"Does she think so?" Aldo moved past the arch to where a terrible wheezing issued from a downed victim of Gerhard's deadly longbow. A sucking chest wound. Hopeless. Monetto frowned.

*"Nein."*

Monetto trembled slightly as he knelt to disengage the pistol from the dying man's belt. "I guess . . . I suppose it won't make any difference—your ages—ten years from now," he spoke absently.

*"Ja-ja,* that's what I've been thinking." Karl coaxed one of the horses, calming it, swinging astride.

"How different, an unhorsed enemy," Monetto said low.

"What?"

Aldo swallowed, checked the pistol. Loaded and primed. He gazed deeply into the man's pleading eyes. Laid the pistol gently on his belly. "I can't offer you any words of good cheer . . . a prayer maybe . . ."

"Aldo—horses coming down the street!" Gerhard clucked the steed into a trot toward the sounds in the Street of Hope. There was fighting at Wojcik's Haven.

With a last look at the downed enemy, Monetto scaled to the rooftops again and sprinted across the crenelled alley wall in pursuit of the archer. He reached Hope Street to find Gerhard swearing at a hysterical cluster of noncombatants who scurried toward the square.

"Not now, you idiots," Karl shouted, fighting the reins. "Stay indoors until you get the order—"

A roaring band of soldiers galloped by, swinging at anything that moved. The people fell back into doorways and the spaces between buildings, but one woman was trampled, her family screaming her name. Gerhard drew back and nocked a shaft, dropping the rearmost rider. A pistol ball shattered sandstone beside him.

*"Gesu!"* Gerhard swore.

"O my God," Monetto echoed.

A straggling mount bolted past. A Llorm dragoon was bent backward in the stirrups, lolling over the animal's haunches. His head was gone.

The people broke into the streets again, mingling with a few sheep and a solitary cow in a bleating chaos the two *bushi* tried to sort. Then another tattering of hoofbeats. More soldiers, rotating their blades wildly overhead.

Gerhard spurred into the street, roaring in horror. Monetto bellowed helplessly—

A child sat crying in the sewer at the center of the wide avenue. Horsemen bore down on him. The archer nocked as he rode, snapped off a shot that struck the lead horse in the skull. Horse and rider slammed down, rolling, hooves high.

Karl leaped down, dragged his unwilling steed before the child and reached down for him.

A dragoon's saber slashed him from behind, cutting three inches into his neck and tossing his helm six feet through the air. His eyes glazed over as he fell, blood spurting.

"Noooooo." Monetto vaulted a cornice, hit the ground, tumbling, and came up running, falling, scrabbling through the mire to reach his friend and the child.

"Karl—you're *all-recht,* Karl—there's nothing to fear—" he sobbed. But then there was everything to fear.

Gerhard's horse whinnied and clambered off. And the Thing the soldiers had fled stalked Aldo Monetto, alone now with the child in the Street of Hope.

A clutch of wagons, freed from Wojcik's, rumbled to a halt behind the lone *bushi*. The lead coach skidded and overturned with a crash. But Monetto could only stand and stare, paralyzed with terror. He had lost his axe somewhere. Now he drew his sword dimly from its back harness, holding it loosely at his side.

"Now, don't cry, child," he whispered, hearing the voice of the tot he straddled. "Aldo has a little one . . . just your size at home."

He heard voices shouting behind him, but he could only stare at the monstrous shape, hulking and rippled with sinew; the snarling jaws, fangs bared and slavering; the black talons; the golden fur, streaming blood from shaft and lead ball.

Monetto bent slowly and pointed the sword at the bestial creature's heart. With his other arm he enfolded the tiny child. He began to lose control of his bladder.

*"God in heaven will not permit this,"* the biller hissed.

An arrow skidded by the werewolf, shattering on the cobblestones, and as if he'd been struck, the nightmare beast fell, doubling over, eyes suffused with an inner fire.

There was a long moment of terrible struggle, as the Beast seemed in its death throes. Simon's soul, aroused to righteous wrath, wrenched in struggle with the energumen's controlling animus. The whispering *bushi* and fleeing refugees began to inch closer, watching with dazed ambivalence the scene of profound bloodless violence.

And then the energumen, craven seeker after comfort that it was surrendered in its satiety, having known its fill of flesh this night. The red glow faded from the demon canine eyes, and the silver glint some of them recognized at once washed into them, flickering with gathering reason and intelligence.

"Simon," Monetto whispered through quivering lips.

*"I . . . am . . . man."*

"That's him—that's Ben-Draba's killer—Simon, they call him—it can't be—"

Some moved closer, encouraged despite the fear that simmered just below the surface.

"I *told* him . . ." the werewolf rasped in its voice like a barely intelligible growl, ". . . not to move . . . until all was well. *Why?*"

Tears rolled down Aldo's cheeks. "He—he couldn't wait," was all he could offer in reply. He dropped the sword and bent to pass the quaking child to an old man. Then he fell heavily in the sewer on all fours.

Nikolai Nagy eased forward from the wagon escort, the rest of the Hussars keeping their distance.

"What have I done?" Simon asked. *"Tell* me."

Monetto shook his head weakly, a sob choking off any reply as he cradled Gerhard's body. His hands were smeared with the brilliant archer's blood.

"Can we . . . get 'em rolling now?" Nick Nagy asked meekly.

Llorm dragoons splashed toward them from the east, arbalests clacking. A wagon driver screamed and leaped from his seat, clutching a steel-tipped bolt's stole.

The dragoons slowed and fanned out to see the werewolf's menacing turn. The Hussars were deployed for a skirmish.

The dragoons halted, watched with uncertainty how the werewolf ignored the citizens. It scooped up a dead man's blade in each taloned fist and stalked toward them, massive back muscles bunching with lethal promise. In his wake, the 1st Rumanian Hussars charged, and for the first time, the disciplined Llorm troops were seen to retreat, bewildered by the night's events.

Monetto, kneeling beside Gerhard, observed the great golden man-wolf through puffy eyes. Wondered at the supernatural power that allowed it to keep pace with galloping steeds. In its ghastly, wounded state.

"How long can he live . . ." he wondered aloud. ". . . shot through like that?"

"What is he, Aldo?" a man asked behind him.

"That's our Deliverer," he said. He heard himself laugh in a lunatic voice, quivering as he babbled on: "Don't you know? It's *shi-kaze*—the Deathwind." He fought back a sob, trying to feel what he thought he should feel, striving for control. "This is it now. *Shi-kaze*. The evacuation."

"*What* evacuation?"

Monetto's face went ashen, the man's words sobering him at once. "The catacombs—your families—" he tried to clarify.

"Jesus, what's happening?" a woman puled.

Moments later, after a hurried exchange, Aldo stared off toward the square. "Oh no. Oh dear God, no . . ."

The people in the north central sector knew nothing about the evacuation.


Garth Gundersen lumbered over the scattered corral rails, grimacing and wheezing, trying to recapture his breath. He leaned the Frankish axe on his shoulder to rest his thews, but kept running, circling an upset dray and the twitching, dying draft horse beneath it.

He bellowed at the militiamen who converged in triumph around the downed soldier who held up a warding blade.

*"Nein!"*

They stayed their blows, puzzled.

Garth pulled up to them, nostrils flaring. Shafts whistled by. He looked down at the injured Captain Sianno, who gasped through grinding teeth, one hand clutching the arrow that had torn cleanly through his ribcage.

"So, Iorgens . . ." he whined, ". . . you've saved the

". . . final blow . . . for yourself. Finish it . . . finish it, then . . ."

"Pick him up," Garth said levelly.

"What?" one of the *bushi* cried in disbelief.

"Pick him up and carry him into my home. Take his feet."

They looked from one to the other. "You're out of your mind, Garth—"

By the look in his eyes, they reasoned that they were quite possibly right. One of them bent to take Sianno's booted feet.

They lay the wounded Llorm officer on the worn sofa-bed in the Gundersens' parlor-dining room. Garth dismissed the man who had helped him.

"What are you going to do?" Sianno hissed. "It's—it's too late for me. You like being one up on favors?" He groaned and clawed at his side.

"*Ja-ja.* Lie still."

Garth propped him on a pillow, gave him a cup of *kvas*. The captain drank, choking at first before swallowing a mouthful and exhaling with a harsh suspiration. Then the smith removed his helm and brushed the sweat from his brow. He grasped the stole of the war arrow in both sinewy hands—

"No!"

Snapped it cleanly in half with a flex of his powerful arms. Sianno cursed in Kunan. Garth eyed the red arrowhead that protruded from the back of his old friend's ribs.

"Leave it—will you?" Sianno rasped, pushing at Garth's hand.

Garth held a big fist before Sianno's eyes. "See this?"

"You don't scare me, you—you muscle-bound ass—I faced it before—got back up, didn't I—" He lurched with pain.

"You want to try me again sometime, don't you? Now

310

hold still." Garth seized the bloody shaft and yanked hard downward.

Sianno screamed and arched his back. Then he collapsed, unconscious. Garth grimaced and tossed away the broken missile. Obtaining a poltice and water, he cleansed the wound, praying silently that his efforts would not be in vain. He bound it with some difficulty, using his own linen shirt.

After a time Sianno came to, groggy and in considerable agony. Garth refilled his cup and mopped the man's fevered brow.

"You're a fool," Sianno complained with closed eyes, shivering. "By the gods—what they've done to you—"

"*Ja-ja,* just be still," Garth told him, a weary, downcast set to his face. "Or I'll have to gag you."

The bell tower began to clang its alarm in the distance.

*"Choléra,"* Gonji swore to hear Monetto's jabbering intelligence. He moved away, sword in hand, as Monetto caught his breath and guzzled water from a skin thrust at him.

The samurai stared with shining eyes out across the square, where the mounted knight Anton led ground troops against the occupation force's pitched defense of the weapons cache and armored wagons. The drawbridge and portcullis were agape. Reinforcements stationed outside the walls were stayed in their effort to pour through by fusillades of war arrows fired into the gatehouse, which by now resembled the hide of a porcupine.

But Gonji's mind's eye fixed on the consequences of his error. "Another goddamned mistake," he growled, infuriated with his lack of foresight. He should have checked the sector once his suspicions had crystallized.

But why? Why had he done it?

Wilf laid a hand on Monetto's shoulder. "You're

sure—about Karl? That he's dead?''

"Of course, I'm sure," Monetto snapped. "Do you want to check for yourself?" His expression changed to see the hurt in Wilf's eyes. "I'm sorry. I'm just—"

Wilf nodded sympathetically.

"—it's just that he and Lottie, they—" Monetto shook his head in bitter frustration. "They were just getting back together again, you know?"

Gonji turned to him. "I never got to tell him that I was sorry for treating Lottie like that."

"Ah, he knew. He was just hardheaded, that's all . . ."

The bellowing of the cretin giant came to their ears from somewhere in the central district.

"Where is our monstrous ally?" Gonji asked. "You're sure he's in control now?"

"*Si,*" the biller assured. "He was with Nick Nagy and the cavalry. They're fighting a Llorm party near Wojcik's. The wagons are tied up with them. I circled around it to get to you."

"*All-recht,* let's go," Gonji ordered. "Monetto, you get back to the north central sector and make sure those poor people understand that they're leaving *now*. Come on, Wilf." He strapped his sallet on tightly and leaped astride Tora. The young smith mounted beside him.

"Now what?"

"We've got to turn out the evacuees—all of them. Get them moving through the chapel, through Tralayn's, onto wagons—whatever the hell we have to do to clear this city."

They rode into the center of the square battle, where Gonji ordered Anton to seize the area at all cost. He sent a messenger to Galioto in the catacombs to start the innocents out into the valley to await the wagons. Then, enlisting a small band of mounted *bushi,* they surged off under shot and steel to clear the chapel and the marketplace for the passage of the city-bound evacuees.

312

They encountered little resistance until they reached the long market district. There, a harried company of militia footmen, fighting with polearms for the most part, found themselves pressed by the desperate remnant of a free company.

The brigands had fought their way up from the south, thinned as they sallied forth by family men who fired down on them from dwellings as word of the imminent evacuation spread. Skewered and shot, clubbed and dashed by plummeting furniture and cooking pots, the adventurers charged into the rebel line at the market stalls. Driven, they were, by the vision of their army's main strength, with whom they'd link at the square.

Decimated by the militia pikemen's tactics, they plunged through tents and stalls, trampling tables and wares and the bodies of the unfortunate who blundered into their path.

They emerged into the Street of Hope to find Gonji and Wilf awaiting them with their small force, weapons drawn for engagement. They paused for an instant, hearts sinking to view the intimidating charge led by the formidable samurai. Then they rose to meet it with a howl of hysterical fervor.

Gonji experienced an instant's nostalgic sympathy for their plight. He envisioned himself in similar circumstances just before he slashed their leader from his steed.

The skirmish was brief and furious. Gonji and Wilf lost half their party to the adventurers' desperation. Then it was over. The stragglers were run down and slaughtered by the pinch of infantry and emerging family men.

For now the market square was theirs. Gonji fought Tora's excited curvetting, scanning the field. Nagy and the Hussars rumbled up from the east at the head of the long wagon retinue, looking embattled, shafts spindling every coach. But they seemed in goodly strength.

"You pikemen," Gonji called, "hold this area. Let's

get the people moving through the chapel. Secure a path. Get archers up here." To Nagy: "Nick, how many non-combatants have you?"

"Not many," the old hostler roared back. "Hell, we had to fight all the way—"

"Split your column and send back half the wagons for those who can't reach the chapel on foot."

*"What?"* Nagy tore his burgonet free. His tangled gray hair bristled as he squinted at Gonji. "We just fought half the goddamn garrison to get here. I'll be damned if I'm gonna—"

"Just do it!"

Cursing and slapping at his thigh, Nagy reluctantly wheeled off to comply.

"Let's get moving," Gonji shouted, "back west. *Shi-kaze!*"

They angled back through the city's maze of antiquated thoroughfares and side lanes, battling at the run, spreading word of the evacuation and coaxing frightened fighting folk out of hiding.

When they slowed to rest their steeds as they crossed a sewage culvert, Wilf caught up with Gonji.

"Who in hell was supposed to alert those poor fools in the north central sector?" he called at Gonji's back.

The samurai tossed his head back, his manner peremptory. "I don't know—forget it." But it was a lie, for the north central sector alert had been entrusted to Wilf's brothers, Strom and Lorenz.

## Chapter Nineteen


Paille hunkered in the bell tower, assessing the battle below, thrilling to the ferocious movement of men and animals and the tools men had fashioned. He fancied that he was witness to a movement of epochal, far-reaching consequence, and that he occupied a pivotal part in it.

So it was that he drew poetically elliptical parallels between the raging elements and the wild human conflict they backdropped. His pen fairly flew, scarcely able to keep pace with the images in his head: the rain and wind and blood; the mud and trench offal; the clash and thunder in darkness; the screams of the terrified; the forms of the dead and dying.

*The price,* he wrote, *of freedom* . . .

The stench of death thickened in his nostrils. At first he thought it must be the wine he sloshed, heightening his sensibilities. He had known such effects before.

But never such a shape as this that loomed up through the belfry hatch to pierce his soul with its demon eyes. The monstrous canine head, the head of a golden wolf, seemed to grin as he gripped his dagger and raised it defensively. Paille's eyes strained at their sockets. The wine jug tipped and sloshed.

"What—what manner of Beastie might ye be?"

When he heard the voice that came in impossible reply, he felt the warm trickle spread through his breeches.

"Just another . . . Frenchman," the creature rasped. And an instant later it was gone.

Paille rose shakily and leaned out the belfry to see what

ensued. *"Deathwind,"* he whispered. "The Deathwind—"

"The DEATHWIND, Vedun!" he screamed in his herald's voice. "Your Deliverer is come! *Shi-kaze! Shi-kaze!"*

He shredded his shirt and waxed the strips from his guttering taper. Stuffed them into his ears. Then he swung down the bell ropes and clanged the alarm signal the city heard only in times of dire emergency.

Anton saw his men fall back from the awesome sight of the Beast that stormed from the bell tower, hefting the giant sword and battle-axe that had hung in Tralayn's ancient house. Mute omens of this day. Of unknown origin but clear and terrible purpose.

The stiff resistance formed by mixed Llorm and mercenaries retreated in horror before the werewolf's attack. Seven-and-a-half feet of looming fury, gyrating those huge, verdigris-stained weapons that had become legendary in the taverns.

Anton winced to see two mercenaries shredded in a single blow of the giant double-edged axe, their bodies sundered and cast aside in pieces. He heard Paille's mad pronouncement from the tower, followed by the din of the alarm bells. He remembered what he had been told to expect this night—as if any expectation could have prepared him for this.

And slowly, not certain that he was doing the right thing, he urged his resisting steed forward, rallying his troops around him. The militia began to press in as Simon's bestial attack drove the shocked occupation force back through the gatehouse to reassemble.

The weapons and armored coaches were again in the hands of the militia. Bolts peppered them from the walls, and an occasional lead ball from a well-tended pistol found its mark in their numbers. But Anton held them steady, and the weapons were furiously disbursed.

316

Draft horses were brought from tether, some falling under fire before they could be hitched. But finally they were readied for movement, manned with pistoliers and bowmen, weapons nocked and primed behind steel-reinforced sides and coffin-cupolas. Armored drivers and assistants took up traces under the portable hoods affixed over their seats. Extra horses were lashed behind, and Paille's adopted brainchildren were on the move.

One moved east to join with Nagy's Hussars; another, west to the evacuation gate with the refugee wagons. The third Anton kept at the square to help hold the position.

At the chapel farther down the street, Michael Benedetto stood on the steps, trying to bring order to the stampede of women, children, and aged who streamed under the comfort of the cruciform spire. Sporadic fighting played out around their caterwauling movement. Gunshots boomed at the ruined marketplace.

Anton spurred his bucking stallion toward the gate-house, calling out orders. The werewolf's raging attack exacted a toll among the scattering troops. Bodies, armor, and horseflesh piled in mounds about him. But steady fire from troops who kept their distance began to slow the Beast. He bled from a score of wounds. Now and again he would howl in agony and wrench a quarrel or shaft from his hide.

The knight's horse threw him at last. He struggled to his feet and hobbled to the gatehouse. He waved for men to assist the werewolf. Those few hardy souls who dared fight on foot amidst the carnage helped but little, lost in their brutalized fascination for the werewolf's savagery and over-cautious about avoiding his whirlwind death strokes.

A squad of Llorm crossbowmen crouched atop the allure above the gatehouse to fire a volley down at Simon.

"Archers!" Anton cried, pointing, but they responded too late. The arbalests clacked on order, two of them striking the Beast-Man in the back at acute angles.

He shrilled and spun down, kicking and rolling in frenzy. Hauling himself under cover of shadow, he painfully worked the bolts free. His silver eyes blazed up at this tormentors. But instead of hazarding a leap up to the allure he had once vaulted as a man, Simon seized his weapons and slunk off along the base of the girdling wall, limping badly, head hung low.

Anton followed his movement, brow furrowed with amazement. "He won't last long," he said to the man at his side. He spat, the stench of blood and viscera nauseating him. "Not like that. Off to die in some . . . ditch."

"Or the blasted giant will get him," the other ventured.

Anton nodded grimly.

"Do we drop the portcullis?" someone called from the gatehouse.

The knight peered out the gate in judgment, where the mercenary company gathered in force, joined now by another Llorm dragoon contingent.

"Sonofabitch—*no!* Let 'em come. The more come through here, the less to hit the wagons." He looked back toward the west. "Good luck, Gonji," he breathed. Then: "Come ahead, you bastards!"

Before his challenge was completed, a tremendous explosion in the east rocked the entire plateau, shifting the ground beneath their feet, some men falling, others unhorsed. Volcanic flames bloomed over the eastern wall, smaller concussions following.

"Christ Almighty . . ."

He scanned the ramparts in response to the shouts of alarm all about him. As if the thunderous explosion had been a signal, the reinforcements outside the walls had scaled to the allure and were dropping to the streets and descending the stairs in waves, each wave covered by the fire of the next. Some canny leader among them, espying

318

Anton's strategy, had eschewed the killing ground of the gatehouse for this new tactic.

And the enfilades of bow and pistol and arquebus fire were directed not only at the defenders of the square; some missiles fell among the innocents pouring into the chapel as well.

"Get that wagon moving—fall back toward the chapel—*protect those people, for God's sake!*"

The blaring roar of the cretin giant sounded in the distance over Anton's frantic commands.


The explosion in the east shattered what remained of William Eddings' modest life. All that had afforded him scant sense of belonging in the hostile cosmopolitan city of Vedun.

Glassware crashed about the sundrier's tiny shop, bursting into shards. Trinkets, knickknacks, and cheap jewelry fell about him where he knelt, rocking back and forth in his lament, inconsolable. For his tearful petitions had failed to move Providence to breathe life back into the limp form of his father.

Now he was alone. He'd last seen his brother John among the armed family men escorting non-combatants to the chapel. Among them had been John's wife, Sarah. But there'd been fighting. A nightmare. People screaming, dying. For all he knew, they were dead now, too.

They'd left him alone.

No, they hadn't left him. They'd been taken from him. Just as that dragoon in the mud had wrested his father from William's life, John and Sarah had been torn from him by order of that yellow bastard. That imperious oriental barbarian.

But the bloody dragoon had paid dearly. Yea, William of Lancashire had discovered that he could kill after all. Could kill and *had*. And would again.

As soon as he found Gonji.

Another party of mounted mercenaries bolted their steeds through the front door of the millinery shop, whooping with destructive glee as they tossed their torches. Fabric caught fire in spots, as the free companions continued riding through the wider rear door, slashing at any *bushi* who impeded them.

Some men tossed buckets of water on the swiftly spreading blazes. Paolo spun, sighted along both pistol barrels, the crashing reports blasting two brigands from their horses. They fell to the buckling floorboards to be trampled by their fellows or sworded by frenetic rebels.

"How do you like that, you sons of bitch-es!" Paolo roared after them, clearing the spent charges and frantically reloading.

"Good shooting, Paolo," Klaus called from across the room, where he clanked about in the remnant of his heavy, shining armor, his battle-axe on his shoulder as if he were out on a simple jaunt after kindling.

"Who asked you?" Paolo jeered.

Two more brigands pounded through. One threw a dagger that caught a rebel in the thigh. He spun down, howling. Klaus lumbered forward and swung his axe gamely. The mercenary deflected it with a cursing parry, his return blow falling short of the buckle-maker, who tripped backward and landed with a metallic clangor on his backside.

Paolo's single loaded pistol barked, the lead ball tearing through kettle hat and cranium. The rider's mount whinnied and tossed the corpse next to Klaus. A warrior slashed at it needlessly, weeping with madness.

"Either get them or stay the hell out of the way," Paolo blared at Klaus.

"Sorry, Paolo. I—"

"Next time I'll just blow *your* goddamn head off—look out!"

Two more yelping adventurers galloped through with clacking arbalests—a third—the sharp report of a wheel-lock—a militiaman dousing a fire screamed and clawed at the back of his neck as he fell face downward—

Another—flinging his torch onto the bolts of silk veiling, triggering a pistol that sputtered and misfired, burning his hand. Klaus's axe chopped horizontally—a horse shrieking and slamming down, kicking in pain. *Bushi* falling on the downed soldier with pikes—

The free companions were playing pheasant-shoot with the trapped bunch in the millinery shop. But now their own numbers were considerably thinned. Their powder was failing them all too often. Now they'd wait for the flames to force the rebels out into the open.

The cannonading blast from the east quaked the shop, knocking loose objects from all the shelves. They collected themselves and pressed their fight against the creeping flames. Assorted hats and headdresses lay everywhere.

"How in hell did I ever get stuck here with you?" Paolo grumbled as Klaus moved in beside him.

Out in the street the mercenaries suddenly came under fire from nearby homes. The sector's evacuation had begun. Women dumped chamber pots; men tossed stoves from upper floors. Household objects cascaded to the streets. Dirks and shafts began to whistle through the drizzling rain.

"Good shot, Petra!" Paolo shouted, as a woman with a crossbow spilled a rider at full gallop. "How do you like that?" He raised his pistol and fired, missing an Austrian highwayman, cursing and tossing the piece aside to aim the other.

"Shit, there's fighting at the chapel now," one of the *bushi* on the second floor called down.

Paolo dropped a passing mercenary. "You just earned your pay," he called at the falling man.

"What was that explosion?" Klaus asked.

"They did it after all—the *Hussars,*" Paolo spat in contempt. "Berenyi and Nagy and those jesters. Said they were going to send up the armory. Wouldn't trust me. Had to be one of the precious officers. Their leaders. Screw them all!"

He spannered a wheel-lock, dropped the spanner and stooped to retrieve it.

"More water!"

Two mercenaries stormed in the rear door with swords and shields. Klaus and another man hurried to engage them. A harpin's vicious needle point disemboweled one brigand. The other, finding no opening in Klaus's figure-eight axe pattern and spotting the pistol in Paolo's hand through the smoke, retreated at the run. Klaus helped the other militiaman overturn a tall section of shelving in front of the door.

"Will you stay the hell out of my field of fire?" Paolo yelled.

Klaus returned, apologetic. "You're a good leader, Paolo. Even Gonji knows that."

"Screw him, too—oh, look—" He pointed at a band of evacuees, married men in armed escort, moving toward the now embattled chapel. They were carrying a woman who had just given birth to a child, the midwife jabbering as she ran with the swaddled infant. "She *would* have it now—"

A steel-tipped bolt zipped out of the darkness, tearing through Paolo's throat. His head snapped back as Klaus screamed. A single high whistle escaped the rent in Paolo's throat. His eyes glazed over. Blood gouted from the wound. Then he lay still.

"No, Paolo! Nooooo! You can't die now. It's not fair. You've got to lead us—" Klaus's sob turned to a choked growl as he grasped the pistols and ran into the street, pounding toward two wheeling mercenaries. Both wheel-locks cracked as one, their unfamiliar recoil jarring his wrists.

322

One soldier was struck in the leg. The other spurred off. Klaus threw the weapons in his lumbering dash. He reached the wounded man, waited for the horse to stop its frightened stamping. The man's saber sang off Klaus's heavy body armor. And then the gentle buckle-maker was dragging him down from the saddle, beating him with his gloved fists, wrestling the saber from his grasp. Strangling him until his tongue protruded, swollen and mottled purple.

He never even bothered to retrieve his battle-axe from the smoking millinery shop before he mounted the dead man's horse to pound eastward after his partner.


The 1st Rumanian Hussars howled as a body, clinging to their startled mounts, when they saw the violent fulmination that scattered the armory all over the now evacuated northeast sector.

"How do you like that—the little shit *did* it!" Nick Nagy shouted with pride, blinking at the blinding secondary bursts. "Well, that's one I suppose I gotta congratulate him on."

They continued with the task of herding evacuees into wagons. More privately owned carts, coaches, and drays arrived all the time as the plan gathered momentum. Mercenary ranks were thinning, it seemed, and more important, the soldiers-of-fortune seemed progressively less willing to see a fray through as the night wore on. Only the Llorm continued to fight tooth and nail, and the occupation army was concentrating its strength nearer the gates, which aided the procedure of picking up stragglers. For the first time during *shi-kaze,* old Nagy was feeling optimistic. There was just a chance that—

"Oh, Nick—look."

Nagy turned in the direction the warrior indicated. Stefan Berenyi's roan destrier pounded past on a frothing hellride. The young hostler's body lay slumped forward in the saddle, tangled in reins and stirrups. Festooned with shafts and bolts.

The animal ended its nightmare ride fifty yards beyond the horrified Hussars, where it collapsed and rolled twice, breathing its last. Berenyi's lifeless body lay twisted beneath its carcass.

## Chapter Twenty

Wilf skidded to a halt in the street, raising his *katana* high in both hands, moist palms spread six inches apart. He slashed as the dragoon rode past, nearly stomped by the crashing hooves that spattered him with mud. Something struck his helmet, dazing him an instant, white specks dotting his vision. He looked up to see the soldier doubled forward, broadsword falling from his slack hand.

The young leader whoofed out a breath and sped for cover at the other side of the street, his own livery in view down the street behind him. Ahead to the west: the besieged west gatehouse, their next vital objective.

As he caught his breath, he experienced a pang of fear for his brothers. Strom—unseen for days—the black ram found among his flock. Lorenz—detained, or hauled away—no one was sure.

His own recurring fear swept over him again. The fear that he would not make it. Would not live to invade the castle fastness in the mountains to rescue his Genya. Caution urged him to run off and hide. Wouldn't it be wise to conserve his strength for the castle assault?

*Nein.* Gonji would have been mortified to hear such thinking. The survivor was he who took the threat to his survival by the horns.

He looked up the street and saw his father, fighting like a demon. He swelled with pride. What a warrior he must have been in his youth. Beside him, still aboard Tora, fought Gonji. The samurai occasionally pressed at something that hurt his side, only when he thought no one was watching.

Wilf cast about for a horse. His black gelding lay dead a block behind under the smithshop canopy, whose struts it had knocked loose in its fall.

Another dragoon pounded through the moon-glinted puddles. Sucking in a breath, Wilf charged out of the shadows. The soldier veered his mount, but Wilf closed the space swiftly. His circular slash undercut the *francisca's* vicious swipe.

He dragged the injured mercenary down and rolled onto the animal, kicking off for the west gate with the others.

He caught up with them in the midst of the wide killing ground before the gate, strewn with the bodies of horses and men, the dead and the pleading maimed, unknown enemies and boyhood friends. He gagged momentarily at the sight, tossing the reins from side to side, unsure what to do, where to strike. Thanking God that he was not in command, that no decision of how to sort tactics from this chaos would fall to his responsibility.

When he looked around him to see how few militiamen remained alive in the environs of the gate, an overwhelming sense of futility suffocated him. How many warriors left? How many family men would depart with the wagons? How would they ever mount a besieging force to deal with the castle garrison and its formidable defenses?

A sensation of betrayal. It quickly passed. *Nein*—Gonji did not lie to him. Did not deceive him in his passion to save Genya. There would be a way. Somehow. Gonji would know.

Then it was all forgotten. He saw the pitched defense set up by the renegade German Landsknecht detachment. The *bushi* who fell before it. The Landsknechts were deployed in two ranks; the front leveled lances from between tall escutcheons that covered them completely. Shattered arrows lay uselessly about their line. The second rank coolly launched their own shafts from behind them, additionally covered by crossbow fire from the Llorm sentries on the allure.

The militia took to cover, thwarted for the nonce. Gonji pranced Tora at the head of the lane that outletted to the killing ground, momentarily indecisive.

But then, as a sudden stiff wind swirled through the city, the werewolf was loping along the allure, diverting the startled crossbowmen, shredding them with fang and talon. A grisly nightmare. A forest fiend come to prey.

Nothing he had heard quite prepared Wilf for the sight of men unlimbed, screaming, their torn bodies used for battering their fellows off the walls. Some lost heart and dropped outside the walls for temporary safety. Others held fast in their duty, to their mortal chagrin.

Arrows from the contingent outside the walls whickered between and above the merlons. Some struck the raging Beast, but it was scarcely slowed, a spectacle of supernatural fury.

Only part of Wilf believed this thing to be Simon Sardonis. No man could become such a thing. It must have stretched to at least seven feet in height and an unguessable weight of pure animal sinew. The head was the head of the largest wolf he had ever seen, and it walked upright like a man. Naked and covered with a golden coat and black-tipped ruff, it was streaked with blood. But whether its own or that of its victims, Wilf could not tell.

No, this thing could not be man, could not be spoken to or trusted as one might trust any man born of woman. Yet

326

he could not deny that its eyes were indeed the eyes of Simon Sardonis.

He shook off its spell and, in his fashion, decided that the less he pondered the phenomenon the better. There were other things more meet for human thought.

A long line of wagons careened up the street now to join those the *bushi* were using for cover. Many of the new coaches carried refugees who could not reach the chapel and those whose duty had kept them in Vedun. The Benedettos rode in the lead wagon.

The draft horses stamped and swerved to a halt to catch the scent of the werewolf, whose snarling rage in their proximity unnerved them.

Now the Beast was dropping into the midst of the Landsknechts, sundering the ranks. The pinned militiamen charged and launched their volleys. On Gonji's order, ashen-faced archers skirted the sentient creature and mounted the stairs to the allure. They fired down into the reinforcement troops outside the walls.

Through spotty clashes and occasional pistol fire, the militia at last took control of the west gatehouse. The evacuation procedure was about to begin. The night-fiend that strode with the deliberation of a man lowered the short drawbridge and readied to open the gates on Gonji's command.

Wilf looked for Gonji, breathless with anticipation. So near. So very close to his desire—but *how?* How could it be done?

"The god-cursed bastards," someone cried.

From farther along the walls, where troops had scaled to mount a fresh attack on the rebels, flaming arrows sizzled through the mist to lob downward among the wagons.

"Get loose armor—grain sacks—*anything*," Gonji ordered. "Cover them over. Bring water buckets from the

327

troughs. Keep all the children's heads down. *Simon*—let's see what we're facing—''

The huge figure, its erect canine posture eliciting gasps and mutterings all along the wagon line, cranked open the gates.

Outside: a gauntlet of waiting cavalry.

''Do you want to try for Tralayn's?'' Michael yelled down.

''There's fighting,'' someone apprised them.

''The *giant's* there!'' another voice called in finality.

*''Iyé,''* Gonji announced softly, ''there's no time. No other way. The best chance is still through the gate. Galioto will have his hands full as it is.'' He sent messengers to order the tunnels barred to further entry.

''Well, that's the end of that, then,'' Michael observed. ''Maybe we'd better stay back with you and—''

''No, my friend. They'll need you to lead them . . .''

Gonji exchanged wistful goodbyes with the Benedettos. Mercifully brief. As he assembled the escort party of family men, it seemed to him that the backbone of the militia was about to depart. Somehow, during the training, the illusion had been that a majority would remain behind to take back the city. Futile, ill-conceived hope, it was clear now . . .

He tossed up curt well-wishes to the people as he moved along the wagon line. More carriages, coaches, and drays arrived, some under embattled escort. But Gonji was encouraged to see the occupation force diminished and disheartened, their deployment in disarray.

He passed the Vargos, greeted them. Lottie Kovacs sat between them, almost catatonic. He wondered whether anyone had told her of Karl's fate yet. Two wagons farther back, Wilf was embracing Genya's parents in the bed of an open dray. He sighed deeply, felt the pain at his side, briefly wondered whether a rib was broken.

Screams of children. A quilt, struck by a fire arrow,

sprouted in licking flames. The children were grabbed by helping hands, the fire smothered.

"Those are children, you bastards," a man's voice bellowed at the walls.

"No—let it burn," Gonji said, running alongside. "We'll send it back to them. Just cut it out of line."

They led it to the head of the line, flames spreading slowly to the damp wood, the draft horses becoming skittish. The armored wagon pulled up behind, and people brought up casks of oil for fueling the flames when they were ready. Others tied loose horses at the rear of wagons. Every manner of transport would be needed.

As the wagon line closed up, Gonji saw Helena, seated beside her mother, who held the reins of a coach. The girl gazed at him anxiously. He strode in front of their team, and Sophia tried to lurch the wagon past him. The samurai seized the traces and glared at her.

Helena sat trembling, lips quivering as if she would find the speech long lost to her. Gonji swallowed, felt the eyes on him. He fancied that he signed, *Maybe I'll see you again,* but as soon as he saw the warmth her eyes radiated, he knew he had unintentionally pandered to her wishes. He could not recall how one conveyed the concept of "maybe," and he was increasingly certain that "I'll see you again" had come out as a more positive "I'll be back."

Helena touched her lips with her fingertips, reached down to touch Gonji, but Sophia lashed the team forward to tighten the wagon line. The samurai leaped aside, annoyed at the old woman's intractability, vaguely wondering whether he hadn't secretly wanted to sign to the girl just what he had.

"The refugees are assembled in the valley," the relay man shouted from the walls.

Simon bounded toward Gonji, growling in defiance at the animals and citizens who reared back from him.

"Stupid fools!" he grated in his intelligible doglike voice. "I'll help them past the north road. That's all I'll do."

Gonji held his gaze steadily, though the sight of the Beast's multitude of wounds caused others to turn away.

"And Mord?"

Simon hissed. It might have been a laugh. He looked down at his blood-matted fur. "I'll do all I can to fulfill the *sensei's* wishes," he snarled, bolting away with a howl that needled the innards of the onlookers.

"God's curse is on him," a woman fretted.

"For *what?*" Gonji challenged without singling out the accuser.

Then the flaming wagon was doused with oil, flaring it anew. The shrieking draft team was guided through the gates, a rolling bonfire parting the marshaled troops. Simon retrieved his weapons and charged into their number, bowling over an entire squad. Archers fired down into them in rapid volleys. The armored coach rumbled out next, dispensing death from cupola and gunloops.

The evacuation was on. The married militiamen shouted their goodbyes and pounded out in determined escort.

"Pick up those valley people," Gonji shouted. "Leave none behind. Don't look back—don't look to the forests—the Death Angel runs with you! Keep looking ahead! Don't stop until you burn the bridges of Buda and Pesth!"

He mounted again and rode toward the gate, taking up his longbow, caring not to ponder what now lay ahead.

When half the first party of wagons was through, Tumo tumbled from a side lane, bellowing in pain and primitive anger from his many wounds. He ran riot among the wagons, overturning the first he chanced upon, slamming down horses and men, smashing and killing any he could reach, gouging and biting like a titanic enraged child. His forearm and hand, where the werewolf had bitten him, were coated with blood and grime. The flayed flesh was bound with a woman's nightdress.

The family men's desperate volley of shot and shaft drove him back near the discarded oil casks. Miklos Zarek and Gonji shared a sudden inspiration.

Zarek rode past the giant, who turned and reached but missed him. Passing the casks, Zarek slowed and arced his double-edged axe down hard on a lid. It shattered, oil leaking and swirling over the wet ground. The samurai followed with a torch, guiding Tora near enough to taunt the monster into giving chase.

He pulled up at the far side of the oil spill. When Tumo reached the slick, he skidded and slammed down comically. Gonji flung the torch into the midst—

The cretin giant blared a pathetic animal cry. Parts of its armor caught in the blaze—its boots, the leather and hemp fastenings. And its exposed flesh was seared in spots before its frantic, gargantuan rolling and subsequent whale-dive into a flooded sewage culvert snuffed the tormenting flames.

Tumo's beady eyes sought out Gonji. And then his mercenary escort party rejoined him. Together they bore down on the samurai.

Gonji stamped backward astride Tora, unleashing his bow. He had time for one poor-angled shot that caromed off the giant's breastplate. Then he became aware of his sudden vulnerability.

A pistol cracked off a shot that burned through the air very near.

"You men—come with me," he called to three *bushi* nearby. They guided their steeds in his wake.

He heard Wilf call his name. On foot. No time to wait for him to mount. He galloped on. His last impression of the west gate area was a dismaying one: Many unmarried militiamen abandoned the plan and bolted the city with the first wave of evacuation.

\* \* \*

Gonji had no idea where to lead the cretin giant. But the farther from the west gate the better. There would soon be more wagons pulling through, and cover fire was dwindling fast.

They rode in circles through the lanes, Gonji and the other bowman in his band hitting the giant and his small mercenary escort with harassing volleys. One free companion was dropped from the saddle, and an occasional cloth-yard shaft pierced Tumo's armor, giving rise to a yelp that did little beyond further stoking his rage.

Cutting through lanes and alleys, across gardens and courtyards, they were dimly aware that they were spiraling toward the north quadrant. The square, and its uncertain situation.

A pistol ball felled the man to Gonji's left as they emerged into the square. Gonji and the others split off in three directions, the samurai making for the rostrum and fountain. The giant's companions took after his men.

Small skirmishes sounded in the environs, but the main concentration of fighting had by now moved far down the Street of Hope, well past the quiet chapel.

He heard his name called here and there as he clumped past to guide Tora up onto the rostrum that had once served as a boxing palaestra. He wheeled. Very bad. Soldiers clattering through the gatehouse on his right. And coming straight at him on all fours—the slavering cretin giant.

They bounded off the rostrum, rounded the fountain and made for the now silent bell tower. Gonji unloosed his quiver and threw a leg over Tora's crest at the run, scampering for the tower entrance. Gained the ground floor. Slammed and barred it.

He heard Tora's whinny and the giant's roar. A stamping and sudden gallop. *Dammit, horse—save yourself.*

The door burst inward with an ear-splitting explosion, a huge meaty fist retracting, raw and bleeding.

He meant business. *Well, Gonji-san, you've never had trouble making enemies* . . .

He took the steps three at a time to the second landing. They spiraled upward toward the belfry. A barred grating admitted moonlight at the far side. Tumo's face appeared at the aperture, straining to peer through the darkness.

Gonji froze. Nocked swiftly and silently. *Hai*—The grating blasted inward from the strike of an enormous palm heel. Gonji's shaft stuck at the base of Tumo's thumb, shearing through the soft meat to plunge out the back of the colossal hand.

Tumo shrieked insanely and withdrew the hand. Gonji sucked a breath and tried to pass the grating—the hand speared through, becoming entangled in the bell ropes as Gonji stumbled back and lost the bow somewhere in the black, sooty stairwell. The bells clanged in a broken chiming. Gonji covered his ears against the echo. He found the bow as the hand disengaged itself.

The Sagami whined from the back harness, slicing bone deep into the forefinger.

Tumo's scream electrified the night.

Clambering past the window, hugging the stairs, sure that he'd be squashed like a beetle—

Silence for a moment. The third landing. He calculated his height—good. It could not look in now without climbing.

A scraping below. The giant thrust the corpse of a woman through the broken grating. He used it as a flail, slapping about a short while. Gonji's lip curled. He wiped away the sweat from his brow.

As he bounded past the third grating, it gave way under the force of a hitching rail. Tumo twirled and scraped it inside the bell tower like a cook mixing batter. The bells vibrated with discordant half-clangs.

The rail was jammed in hard, and a thumping concussion rocked the tower, followed by an ascending abrasive sound that came from everywhere at once. A blubbery arm bulged against the window, past it—

Tumo was shinnying up the bell tower in undulating rolls of quivering fat. A growling, maddened humanoid slug.

The pulpy flesh of a thigh bulged a foot inside the third level grating. Gonji bounded over the boards and plunged the Sagami eight inches deep and ripped an arm's-length gouge across his vision. The giant bellowed in infantile anguish and squeezed the tower with all its might.

Masonry crumbled and stone caved inward, spidery cracks shooting up the walls.

Gonji scurried up the curling stairwell, passed the hideous, bloody face. Its cavernous mouth blared like a demon herald, blocking his ear. He kept running upward, notching another war arrow, kissing the stole as he reached the belfry.

His heart beat at battle tempo. A section of wall caved in below him, and a great bleeding arm reached in, slapping about. He glanced down—back up—past the now clamoring bells—a hand gripping the belfry portal—the terrible torn face, red tongue lashing across malodorous splay teeth—

He pulled back mightily, grunting with the pain, and fired.

His cloth-yard arrow penetrated the cheek just below the left eye, the head emerging through splintered bone at the eye socket.

Tumo's mouth gaped as he fell, shaking the tower's foundation at the street below. Gonji roared in triumph at the arch, watching the screaming beast whirl about in the darkened square like a sunstroked scorpion. It tore the shaft from its ruined eye and bowled over in its pain, scattering horses and men.

334

With any luck, Gonji thought, the arrow had struck the brain. Death would follow.

But now he pushed off his self-congratulation, gathered his shaken wits. His ears were blocked, his head ringing. He assessed the situation from his vantage: Many more wagons rumbled through the city; Anton and his doughty souls had disappeared altogether from view; mounted skirmishes could be seen; flames consumed several dwellings and shops; the armory was a smoking hole. To the east, the river was swollen to overflowing, engulfing its banks, swirling around the engorged moat that cleansed sewage.

He turned and looked to the north, to the mountains and the distant battlements of Castle Lenska. A sinuous line of troops descended toward the city. The castle garrison had been turned out, as expected.

But what could be done about it? How many *bushi* remained alive in the city? And how might they be assembled?

He cursed his lack of foresight, then dismissed it. There would have been no sure way to plan. With a despondent notion—his friend Wilf in mind—he skipped down the stairs to the hole the giant had broken high up the tower wall. He dropped through to the cobblestones at the rear of the demolished bell tower, racing through the shadows. Already, inquisitive soldiers were ambling toward it, not altogether eager to discover what creature might have dealt so rudely with their giant—if not the werewolf itself. For all had seen its work.

Gonji found himself alone in the north quadrant. The postern gate was in occupation hands again, with many troops milling about for the relative comfort of numbers. And soon the castle garrison would be here as well.

To his great relief, Gonji found Tora pawing near the chapel. He gave thought to descending to the catacombs, recalling at once that he had given the order to seal the tunnels from the surface.

"Shit," he whispered, rolling astride the Spanish stallion. "Looks like you and me, old boy—*hyah!*"

Clinging low, never turning in answer to the shouts behind him, Gonji rode with a vengeance toward the shambles of the market stalls.

## Chapter Twenty-one

### Hour of the Tiger

They stood in the middle bailey ward of Castle Lenska, the officers and advisers breathless, the messenger slumping in a state of exhaustion, his helm slipping from his grasp.

All awaited the king's reaction.

Klann paced slowly before them, still in his armor. His hands were clasped behind his gleaming backplate. A terrible calm beset his long, bearded countenance.

"There's no end to them, is there?" he said quietly in Kunan. He turned on them suddenly, the serenity driven before his rage. *"Has the whole world gone mad?* Monsters, you say? They've raised monsters against us? Have we not monsters of our own, Mord?"

The sorcerer's golden mask angled down at his feet. He offered no reply in his defense. General Gorkin, standing beside Mord, moved away a pace, contemptuous of him, as if to divorce himself from association with Mord's failure.

Rain pattered about the king as he gestured vigorously. "Turn out the garrison. Hold back one

Llorm company to man the battlements. Get those lethargic free companions moving—"

"Only two mercenary companies left here, milord," an officer reminded him.

"Where's Julian during this madness?" Klann grumbled. "Where is my fine new Field Commander?"

"I fear he's . . . dead, sire," the messenger reported somberly.

Klann ground his teeth. "And Sianno? Send for Sianno. I want an accounting of how—"

"Captain Sianno has been reported . . . missing in action."

The king drew his sword and rifled it across the stone courtyard, striking a horse's hoof. He moved toward his waiting steed, his personal guard falling in around him. Mord, too, fell into step.

"Sire, you're distraught, but there's no need to take the entire garrison into Vedun—"

"Get away from me, Mord. It's your erroneous intelligence as much as anything else that allowed this. You said it would be done on the morrow."

"Yes, I admit they deceived me. They advanced their schedule. Possibly to cause just the sort of precipitate action you're pursuing."

Klann slowed and became more attentive. "Why?" he asked suspiciously.

"The chant. The Dark Lord's faith rite. They know I'll be imbued with fresh mana this night. That I'll have the power to put an end to their insurgent ways, as soon as we've essayed the ritual. You see, I have just the demonic agency with which to stamp out their little rebellion. All you need do is direct the garrison and the civilians to join me in the ritual for the next hour and—"

"I don't trust you, charlatan," Klann interrupted. "Where is your moronic giant? And the wyvern—whatever became of it? Still on its pleasure flight?"

"Grumble you may, sire, but please recall all I've been able to do for you in the short time since we've been associated. You know that Tumo was raised unto me in the full of the moon last winter. Only the conjunction with the solstice caused his . . . curious imperfection. You know, too, that the quality and number of the faithful is vital in this matter. And when have we had more believers in our community than now?"

Klann thought about his words, shook his head. "Speak to me of it later. For now I ride to Vedun."

Mord raised his voice to an insolent forcefulness that evoked frowns from the elite guard. "We need to perform it *now*—I shall be useless to you without it if the moon passes from phase."

The king swung into the saddle. "You're useless to me now," he said. "Later, Mord. Trouble me later."

The sorcerer folded his gloved hands inside his sleeves, shoulders relaxing as if in resignation.

A band of mercenaries marched across the ward, pausing to bow before the king. Among them was the man they'd brought with them from Vedun.

"Ah," Mord began with obvious satisfaction, "our informant."

"*That* one?" Klann inquired, perplexed.

"Yes, milord. More faithful to you than his sire, eh?"

A sour look crossed the king's face. "You've been deceived again, Mord . . ."

And with that he pounded away at the head of his command, through the gatehouse and on toward the barbican, leaving Mord to muse over his comment.

Salavar pulled to a halt before the darkened alley, a field of blood, littered with corpses. In places the fallen were piled so high as to allow them to repose nearly upright on their feet. Carcasses were skewered on calthrops and spiked redoubts. His two surviving men

338

drew up alongside.

The Slayer snapped his double-edged axe, bloodlets flinging off. Both he and his destrier were splashed to the ears with gore, red flecks dotting his beard. He removed his fur-brimmed helm and breathed a great weary sigh. The killing had been good. Many of these citizen soldiers had fought well; some even died nobly. And the more who did, the greater the honor heaped upon the Slayer.

His one regret was that he had been tracking the oriental bandit all night, yet never crossing him, always finding the quarry just beyond his reach, arriving a shade too late. Either the samurai hid himself well or he was already dead beneath some tangle of bodies.

"This is it, eh? This is what's got you all so scared?"

One of the mercenaries agreed readily. "I think there's only one left now, but what a hellion!"

Salavar snorted. "I can see that. Well, go in and get him. I haven't time to waste on—"

The sizzle of a shaft. Salavar instinctively threw up his shield. The man on his right was torn backward by the impact, out from under his morion helmet to lie writhing in the street. The armor-piercer arrowhead protruded six inches out his back.

"Son of Satan!" the other man cried. "What strength!"

"Try *daughter,*" Salavar corrected. He started to laugh. "That's a *she*-demon—a *woman,* you fear, all you brave bastards. Get in there and bring her out to me—" He saw the fear in the man's eyes. "Duck behind your nag's crest. You've got a pistol, you friggin' coward."

The brigand brought his piece alongside his helmet and uncertainly clucked his mount forward toward the deadly blackness. Salavar gurgled a laugh and calmly loaded his arquebus and wheel-lock, watching from behind his propped shield.

The nervous subordinate halted his steed at the head of the sinuous alley, licking dry lips as he crouched low.

Hildegarde's battle cry froze him as she skipped forward, her scalpel-sharp halberd glinting in the full moon's rays for an instant before tearing through the brigand's throat. His pistol fired wildly. With a great flex, the warrioress lifted her foe from the mount's back and tossed him among the broken bodies. With a snarl at Salavar, she disappeared into the shadows again.

"Sonofabitch," Salavar swore. "All right, gentle lady, you've earned a tilt at Salavar." He rode forward, arquebus propped on the shield's top edge.

He could hear her soft footfalls as the darkness engulfed him. A helmet bounced off the wall to his right. He spotted it instantly for the diversion it was and aimed his great firearm to the left. Hildegarde surged at him as the arquebus discharged its tumultuous blast.

The *bushi* screamed and spun away, her left shoulder in ruin. Salavar's destrier fell under him, her razor steel having sliced open its neck. The Slayer hit the ground and rolled, losing his shield and helm in the fall but coming up with his lethal axe at port arms.

Hildegarde breathed hissingly somewhere in the shadows. The arrogant mercenary saw his helm on the ground but dared not reach for it.

With a banshee wail, Hildegarde charged him, the halberd leveled for disembowelment. He parried it downward, binding it on the stones, lunging forward with animal grace in the next motion. She leapt back, barely evading a smash to the face, and brought up the halberd's head with a swipe.

"Arrrghhh!" Salavar grabbed his inner thigh. His hand came away darkly wet and coppery to his nostrils. His leather legharness came loose where she had cut the strap. He tore it off and flung it at her.

"Bloody bitch—you'll pay for that. You know where I'm going to plant this axe?"

Hildegarde cursed him in her own language, her voice

340

labored. He took note of the bits of meat and blood flecks at her shattered left pauldron. She was fighting him with little more than one arm. Galvanized, he whirled the battle-axe at her in a figure-eight, clashing with her, pushing her back.

A wild blow aimed at her head struck a wall with an explosion of masonry, and her quick reply cut his ribs. He roared with shock and pain and thundered forward. Hildegarde gave ground, her strength beginning to fail with the blood loss, the strain creasing her face.

She tried a desperate lunge that Salavar slipped, her point digging into soft stone, catching. The Slayer's powerful blow split her haft with a sharp snap. He came on for the finish as she stumbled back.

Hildegarde pressed her savaged shoulder a second, then picked up a downed militiaman's broadsword. This she held in both hands in an *iai-jutsu* reverse guard. Salavar looked at her contemptuously and pulled his wheel-lock from his belt.

Gritting her teeth, Hildegarde danced from side to side, howling a battle cry and charging. The pistol's report echoed through the alley. The Viking warrior-woman spun and fell, where she lay still.

Salavar breathed a sigh of relief and tested his wounds. Then he came up to her prone form.

Her arcing blade hamstrung him. He pitched backward, roaring. Hildegarde tried to rise but couldn't get off her knees. Couldn't reach him with an overhead blow.

The wounded bandit clawed at his boot. He cocked his arm from where he sat, and the small dagger tore into her abdomen, just below the protective line of her leather breastplate. Bleeding profusely and in the throes of agony, Hildegarde shrilled a cry that lasted the duration of her remaining moments of life.

She scrabbled forward on her knees at the desperately

crawling man, catching his ribs with a headlong lunge of her sword. Ripping upward through cuirass straps and flesh to lay open the whiteness of bone.

With her last breath she withdrew the dagger from her belly and, finding an opening between his warding hands, plunged the slim blade into his eye.

The relays passed the alarm along the windows above the alley: Laszlo's defenders had given way; a Llorm troop had crashed through to ride, by ones and twos, through the gauntlet of the remaining old folk who fired down on their heads.

"The wagons are here—out in the lane!" came the cry from the head of the alley defended by Janos Agardy's determined band of aged and handicapped. Escape was imminent. Janos saw brutalized eyes gleam with desperate pleading in his direction. Relief was so near, and there was little left to defend.

"All right. All right, then—the people left in the dwellings first—*look out, there!*"

The first two Llorm crashed through, slashing down upon their heads. Janos fell back against the wall, nearly trampled. He saw one Llorm fall. The second dashed the brains of his old friend the fisherman, with whom he'd sat at the river in days past when none save he would have the company of a clubfooted child.

He grimaced and choked back his sob. "Get moving, you people in the houses," he cried. "Your work is done. Now *flee* . . .''

He heard Giselle's frantic voice from the window down the alley as another Llorm lurched through aboard a spastically jerking horse.

"*Janos*—my father—he won't leave—"

He took a swipe at the horseman, missing, saw Giselle yanked from the window by her long, radiant hair. The shutter slammed and bounced open.

342

Janos called two men to accompany him. Screams and bellows behind them. They battered the rear door of Giselle's dwelling until it gave with a snap of timbers. Janos lumbered up the stairwell, *guisarme* before him.

"Open that door, sir."

"Get away from here, you God damn cripple! I'll kill you!" The muted voice was choked with fear.

"Sir, this sector has been evacuated. The last of the people are boarding the wagons now. You must transport Giselle to safety."

The door swung open, and Giselle's father stood with heaving chest in its frame, a broadsword brandished in threat. "We're not going anywhere."

"Sir, you must get Giselle to safety and then join with the other militiamen to escort—"

"I'm not going to die fighting for that god-cursed Jappo." He warned them back with twitches of his swordpoint.

"As a Christian, sir, I cannot ask you to fight. Nor will anyone else. But you must save Giselle from the army's reprisal. The wagons are here now. They won't wait. And it will not be pleasant for those left behind. Surely you must understand that. Soon even we shall be abandoning our post. Think on it, sir, but swiftly."

He did, and a moment later he threw his cloak about his shoulders and tossed Giselle her mantua. "Come on, girl," he said bitterly, starting down the stairs, slapping aside the harpin wielded by his neighbor on the landing.

"She'll join you momentarily," Janos assured, leaning forward on his *guisarme* and smiling at her.

"God damned infidel's got everybody crazy," her father grumbled as he departed. "Even the cripples."

"Giselle," Janos began, trembling but holding her bright gaze, "I've only a moment to convey to you a lifetime of yearning. Since we were children I've loved you, worshiped you from the respectful distance one

343

would tender an angel. I've written songs to your lips, to your eyes, the halo you wear when the sun smiles at your passing. But now there is no more time for song. I must speak plainly while I still can . . ."

"I've heard your lovely songs," she said, "but I never suspected I could have inspired them. I fear you exalt me too much. Your songs sing of divine perfection. Look here—" She passed a slim hand across the small scar high on her left cheek. "Do you remember the day I fell, how I cried?"

"I cried with you, and then my tears became tears of joy—if you will forgive me—it was a perverse comfort to see that you could bleed like other mortals. But that scar is God's gracious, holy flaw! Lest you be thought a goddess, untouchable to any man . . ."

Her brow creased, and she looked at him with a mixture of wonder and warmth.

"*Janos*—the cavalry says they must move now. They're under attack, and the *giant* is thrashing about, very near now—"

He snapped out of his reverie and tugged her by the arm, guiding her to the balustrade. Her eyes were on him as she descended.

"Grant me this, Giselle," he said desperately. "Not that I may have your hand. I dare not ask for that. But only tell me that I may be counted among your legion of suitors. I've seen them, and paled before them. But I'm a fighting man now! Ready to charge over the heads of your retinue from my humble rearmost position!"

She leaned across and kissed him. Her eyes were moist and sincere. "You're more than among that fancied company. You're foremost—there is no other."

Janos threw up a fist in triumph and ushered her out, personally escorting her to safety aboard the last embattled wagon. He waved to Nick Nagy as he rode by, then returned to his charges, lashing about with a

344

vengeance, a song soaring from his chest as he fought valiantly, though his heart was far from the battle.

Giselle peered back at him as she was spirited off, part of her wishing to leap from the wagon to remain at his side. Heartsick, her stomach in knots, she deplored the years wasted on flirtation and romantic flummery. Feeling, for the first time, a profound mutual concern and a sense of completeness, now sundered by events too large to control. She scarcely heard the conflict rage around her.

She would not see Janos again. She would marry in Austria a man of modest means and properties, bearing him three children and living out her life comfortably, deeply loved and needed, and, in her reflective moments, resignedly grateful and content. He was a compassionate, understanding man, her Hans. He indulged her the cenotaph on their land, raised to a forgotten poet, and inscribed with the curious epitaph: *God's gracious, holy flaw*. Hyacinths flourished about the memorial site, and fresh-cut lilies were laid there weekly.


Klaus splashed onward through the Street of Faith, his quarry still in sight but pulling away. He cared not that he had left his axe and helm behind, his only armament—the slender misericord at his waist—more a decoration than a weapon in modern warfare.

The red-eyed buckle-maker swung right onto Provender Lane, taking scanty note of the ugly black cavity of the armory, still billowing pungent smoke and hissing flame, an untended bonfire.

Klaus thought only of Paolo, struggling with the reality of the death of the man he'd tried so hard to befriend out of admiration and respect. He saw the brigand's laughing face. He'd laughed when his companion had shot the bolt through Paolo's throat.

Laughed and pointed like a leering ape. The man who'd fired the shot had paid the price for his sin. God had given Klaus the strength to kill him.

But the other had laughed and cursed and galloped off. Klaus would catch him and drag him down as he had the other and make him understand the terrible pain of loss that twisted his insides such that he couldn't think straight. It wasn't nice to laugh when a man's friend was killed.

The bandit pulled up in front of the Provender, swung from the saddle and strode inside. Either he had forgotten about Klaus or it was a trap.

*Ja,* that's what Gonji would have said. A man too sure of himself was laying a trap. Klaus would have to be careful. But, then, what did it matter? Paolo had been careful, hadn't he?

Klaus dismounted fifty paces from the Provender. The area was deserted now, or seemed so. Only the dead here now. So many. An uncovered graveyard.

The pistol report from the Provender froze him in his tracks a second. Then he pushed himself on, heart racing, wishing his armor would stop clanking as it did. He peeked through a smashed window, only shards of the expensive swirled glass remaining. He remembered at what cost it was said those windows had been imported from Frankfurt—

Nothing moved inside. There was an awful stench of death and strong drink that clogged his nostrils. He eased inside through the wedged-open door.

A sudden movement at the far end of the bar—

*"Jaaaa!* What the hell you doing here, bimbo?" Gutschmidt roared from behind the barrels of two pistols. "You're still alive? Gutch can fix that real quick,—*boo-hoo-hoo!*" the innkeeper blared the exaggerated laugh he reserved for surly, overbearing moments. There was none to share the aggressive mirth.

346

It died on his lips.

"That soldier killed Paolo, Gutch," Klaus said disconsolately. He shuffled over death and debris to the warm body. A large rift split the man's face.

"Well, what did you want me to do—save him for ya?" Gutch began to clean and reload a pistol. A rank of long barrels lay primed on the bar, another on the shelf below. "Paolo's dead, eh? No surprise in that."

"He was a good man. A good leader," Klaus eulogized in his nasally voice.

"Sure—*ja-ja*—now why don't you get lost? You're bad for Gutch's reputation." He splashed water in his face, toweled off, and ran a long comb through his sweat-soaked hair. His doublet hung over a chair, his silk shirt torn and blood-stained.

"I—I don't know where to go, Gutch . . ."

"You want Gutch to tell you where to go?"

Pistols exploded outside amidst war whoops, and still intact panes of glass shattered inward. Klaus hit the floor next to his late foe, and Gutch ducked behind the counter.

"Here we come—and there better be some *service.*"

A spate of laughter. "We'll serve ourselves. Come on, Darusz—"

A big-chested brigand burst inside, pistol still smoking. Two bandits followed, angry war helms dripping. They spotted Klaus peeking up at them.

"Hey, there—!"

Gutch's pistols boomed, clouds of smoke fuming, as Klaus pushed himself up and stumbled, lurching toward the surprised looters.

Two bandits went down. Gutch seized another wheel-lock. "Get outta my line of fire—"

Klaus met the trailing mercenary before the door, twisting from the sword slash that dented his back plate before lunging forward like a steel cannonball to pinion the man's arms. They wrestled on their feet, slamming against the wall and pushing and tugging each other over one of the fallen bodies. Gutch bellowed and swore, moving along the bar anxiously.

Then Klaus locked a leg behind his opponent, remembering the technique taught by Gonji, and plunged him backward. He landed atop the man, breath huffing out of both of them. Klaus staved the sword arm from his vulnerable skull as he fought out his misericord.

The needlelike blade pierced cuirass and flesh. Falling again and again, until the mercenary shuddered and died. Klaus wheezed as he pushed himself to his feet unsteadily. He dropped the misericord and backed away, sobbing.

Gutch breathed a sigh of relief and leaned forward on the bar. "C'mere, jughead."

Klaus shambled over the wreckage.

"Rhine wine," the stylish innkeeper said, pouring out two goblets. "These Slavs don't know what's good. Here."

*"Danke,* Gutch."

"You got nothin' to do, eh? I could use some help around here. Got a feelin' this place is gonna be crawlin' with swine pretty soon. And not the payin' kind. Why don't you stay and help get the place cleaned up for the customers?"

"Sure, I'd be glad to," Klaus offered solicitously. He set his goblet down. "Do you want me to start with the furniture or the bodies?"

Gutch eyed him sidelong in haughty disapproval, trying to decide whether the buckle-maker was crazy or merely simple. He shrugged. "Finish your wine first."

Klaus offered his cup in toast. "It's you and me against all of them. We can handle them, *nicht wahr?"*

*"Ja-ja*—let's not overdo the you-and-me business. It's bad for Gutch's image. *Prosit."*

An hour later the Provender had become a temple of foreboding. Corpses, propped in the windows and piled before the door, stared out onto Provender Lane with dead eyes. Tables, chairs, and broken casks were heaped at the windows, topped by oil-soaked rags. Thin lines of black powder snaked back from them to the rear of the bar, where Gutch and Klaus sat on stools, the buckle-maker emulating the posturing of his new compatriot.

Torches burning in cressets behind them, weapons arrayed on the bar, they awaited the anticipated influx of business.

Bounding over the body of the Scottish Highlander, his seven-foot claymore beneath him in death, Gonji pounded up to the wagon caravan escorted through the south central sector by mixed cavalry and footsoldiers led by Monetto.

"The castle garrison's on its way," Gonji told him.

To which Monetto replied, "It's about time, eh? God, what a mess."

"Are any sectors cleared? Completely cleared?"

"I think the whole north end is evacuated," the biller replied. "They got moving fast once they believed what was happening. The explosions and fires woke them up pretty fast. It's the damned center of town that's the problem."

"Anton may still be stuck there, defending useless territory," Gonji mused. "What happens if the drain sluices aren't open in the south and east along with those that admit the river water?" he asked disarmingly.

Monetto looked puzzled. "Well—we'd have a flood."

"*Hai.* Where?"

The biller thought a moment. "The city sags at the center. The big culvert that splits Vedun would overflow first. What do you have in mind?"

"Slow the pursuit. Get to Anton fast. Tell him to with-

349

draw across the culvert spans. Collapse the wooden ones, blockade those of stone. Anything that will slow the big reinforcement troop. We need time to get people out. Then take a small party with you and open the wash gates. Let the Little Roar pour through. Vedun could use a good cleaning anyway."

Monetto galloped off, and Gonji led the wagon caravan the rest of the way. They splashed through the small lake the bloated moat had become, encountering little resistance once beyond the gates. Most of the troops had fallen back toward the north, fearing the werewolf's return.

Gonji could hear the Beast's chilling howl in the forest as he leapt atop an overturned wagon, rapidly sticking his shafts in its side.

"Gonji," Wilf called from down the street, cutting across the wagons' path to reach him. "The garrison's turned out of the castle. Now's the time to take it. Where is the siege party?"

"Patience, Wilf," he urged, firing at the swarming mercenary band that hit the escort from the northern curve of the wall. Passing citizens and the cavalry escort cheered to see Gonji's inspiring pose. He continued launching, dropping bandits into the muck, though each shot pained his injured side. Plenty of time for pain to be an annoyance tomorrow; tonight it was life-affirming.

Mercenaries seeing him began to angle toward him. He watched a woman drop a free companion from her wagon with a well-thrown dirk. It was Magda Nagy. She ordered her driver to slow before the samurai.

"Go! Don't stop here," he cried, firing and tearing a Spanish rogue off his whinnying steed.

"Gonji, you seen Nick?" she asked.

"He'll be along. Get out of here."

He heard well-wishes in Slovak dialects, farewells from friends and strangers alike. And like their vain hopes of retaking the city, more militiamen streamed away with the caravan.

"Make sure the valley people are all aboard," Gonji reminded.

An archer atop the wall cried, "The castle troops are at the north gate. Fight well, men!" One of the family men, he spotted the wagon his family rode and dropped aboard with a last wave.

Decimated and disorganized, the attacking mercenaries fell back from the wagons and moved to join with the reinforcements at the postern.

Gonji was thinking how few Llorm seemed to be left in the city garrison when he heard the thunderous wash of water through the sluice gates.

"Good," he grated. The bellowing of the cretin giant came next from not far off. "Not so good."

"Hey, you men!" Wilf began chasing a band of single *bushi* who were pounding out along with the wagon troops.

"Let them go, Wilf," Gonji ordered.

"We need them later," the smith roared over the distance. He kicked his steed toward the samurai, who rejoined Tora. "Who the hell's going to be around to attack the castle?"

"Unwilling men are no good," Gonji explained.

Wilf's insides were in turmoil, his voice at near hysterical pitch. "Well then how many will there be? We should be riding there now. Let's go when these wagons are through."

"There are more people to be picked up. More wagons. I've seen them—"

"Aw, the hell with those wagons. They've got enough—"

"That's enough of that, Wilfred," Garth shouted.

Wilf exhaled long and slow. "I'm sorry, *bitte*. I'm tired, and when I see those cowards riding out—"

"There are no cowards here today," Gonji said evenly. He watched Garth and another man load the injured Captain Sianno aboard a stopped wagon, amazed at the smith's blend of courage, compassion, and honor.

"You just be still and lie there—" Garth was saying, chuckling at the captain's ill humor. "—when Klann gets you back, he won't know you. They're going to make a real European out of you."

"How *do* we besiege the castle when it's time?" Wilf was asking calmly. The last of the wagons were clattering through the gate, their wheels spouting sheets of water.

"You'll see," Gonji told him absently. Tumo's bellow was nearer now. "Nothing to do here. Time to start riding, men—"

"Where?"

Tora wheeled and tossed anxiously, catching Gonji's tension and the scent of the giant. The samurai counted heads as the *bushi* gathered, shaking his own as he did. "We're going to comb the town for stragglers. Let's go."

"Stragglers?" Wilf queried. "You mean warriors for the raiding party?"

"I mean trapped innocents." He kicked into a gallop, the rest following.


Mord grabbed General Gorkin by the shoulder. The castellan, seeing who it was, twisted free as if averting an alighting spider.

"Forgive me, General Gorkin, but I believe it's time to begin the troops and the Akryllonian people on the chant ritual. Why don't you gather the people in the castle's chapel? I think that would be a fitting touch, now that I've prepared it."

Gorkin stared at him coldly, waiting a long time before replying. "When the king returns, I'm sure he'll give the order."

"I'm afraid that won't be soon enough," Mord

352

retorted, almost allowing the panic to seep through his tone. "You see—the full moon—it will drift from phase soon—it must be done now."

"The king knows your situation." The castellan turned away.

Mord grabbed his arm. "You're in charge in his absence. Do you want to bear the responsibility for—"

Gorkin snapped his arm free. "Go piddle among your potions." And with that he marched off, his boot heels resounding in the empty corridor.

A sibilant hiss, as Mord added still another name to the list of those to be dealt with. He hurried off for his tower to do what he must, though the danger of it far exceeded anything he had attempted before in all his centuries of arcane gramarye and dark invocation.

Reaching the tower, he threw open the ground level iron door, and a rush of bodies tumbled past, lurching back from him so that they might avoid so much as a brush of his cloak.

The hostages—all those still alive among the captives from Vedun. The experimental subjects for his work at separating the remaining personages of Klann. Freed from the dungeons. Mord laughed to see them scurry through the wards and into halls and towers like rats from a listing vessel.

Fools. Where did they think they could run? And their panic was misbegotten: He had no further use for them. No more need for the deception of working hard at undoing a spell that was irretrievably binding. Tonight he would triumph. Even now the city was being laid waste. Later—King Klann himself. Then both he and the Akryllonian League of Necromancers would be satisfied in their age-old passions.

Just as soon as he had received his new imputation of power. More power than he had ever dreamed could be his, as the Dark Master had promised.

*If Klann would see the people through the ritual . . .*

Yes. Yes, of course he would. He needed Mord. He wouldn't fail him. There was no need to panic. The blunderer would bring about his own destruction. And if he was too slow? If the moon's phase passed?

Then human sacrifice would have to suffice for now. *Much* human sacrifice, starting with—

The girl. He felt her presence and smiled, moving through the pitch-black corridors of his tower unerringly, descending into the dungeons, rife with the sounds of subhuman suffering. Past the cells of groaning half-men, pausing at the chamber where she tried to hide like a foolish guilty child.

"Come out, come out, my dear. *Dance* for your master."

He manipulated with his gloved hand, as if pulling invisible puppet strings. She pirouetted out before him awkwardly, struggling all the while.

Genya glared at him hatefully.

"Let them out, did you?" he smirked. "Valiant to the last. But now you're underfoot till I need you. Come along . . ."

He fluttered his fingers, causing Genya to shuffle along behind him like an automaton. "Have you tried to bolt the castle? Did you find it impossible to leave me, your new betrothed? An insubstantial, invisible membrane, you see. A womb—or a tomb, if you prefer. It restrains you from straying too far from me."

He walked her to the highest level of his tower, locking her in a tiny, barren chamber with a single narrow window grating through which the plateau and part of the city could be seen far off against the southern mountain range.

Genya gasped to see the flames in Vedun. The misted night wind carried the fearsome sounds of conflict.

"Such power," Mord's bass voice rumbled. "Would you have believed any single being could have wrought such a thing? A fitting finale to a life of minor enchantment. For soon I shall soar to greater heights. Transcendent. A new epoch lies in wait. So the Dark Lord has said. You shall help to bring it about." He hung the keys on a hook just out of her reach through the door grating. "Practice the spell of levitation while I'm gone," he taunted. "See if you can unlock the power that resides within you . . ."

He hurried down to the dungeons. In his chamber of spells and magick artifacts, he brooded momentarily over the ambitious invocation he would essay. It worried him. The Hell-Hound was not his to control. Not in his relatively weakened state. He could invoke it, give it substance in this realm, and set it on its relentless course. It would unswervingly track and destroy the enigmatic presence in the territory that so troubled both Mord and his Dark Lord. But it could not be destroyed by any power on earth; nor would Mord command it.

His appeal to his Master for guidance fell on deaf ears. He was disturbed until the huge, musty tome of spells began to move on its stand, the leaves flipping open of their own accord to land on the invocation he considered.

His evil mind smiled. From within the protective pentacle, he performed the difficult ritual. At its conclusion, the diamond-shaped glass within the oracle atop the blood-stained altar began to spin. Mord gazed into the netherworld, seeking, searching through that despondent realm where he had been told only the failed would ever reside. Never the competent servants, who would live on to serve, immortal.

He saw it in the chaos, and called it forth. Wolverangue, Spawn of Satan. The Hell-Hound. A sight to make these mortals curse their mothers' wombs for having ever birthed them.

Next—he concentrated on the glowing key that lay among the retorts. The object that radiated the aura of the tormented spirit. The glass clouded. In another facet the being appeared, and Mord started, despite all that he had been given to witness. It howled through the forests to the west, running beside . . . the women and children of Vedun.

Mord laughed insanely at the propitiousness of the timing. Surely the Dark Master rejoiced in his Palace of Awe.

The facets merged, became one. Then the diamond crystal shattered, and Mord was thrown from the pentacle. He lifted himself up in shock and fear, trembling. And suddenly he felt the slow dawning of terrible betrayal. The mocking sensation of having been a pawn. Deceived and abandoned.

## Chapter Twenty-two

### Hour of the Hare

"Holy Mother of God, Jiri—it's a *flood*," Greta observed needlessly, hands at her throat. "Look—all the trenches are overflowing."

Jiri Szabo seemed bewildered by it all. It was all beyond comprehension, past anything he had prepared for. He leaned against the sill in the upper floor of the guild hall, feeling choked and helpless in the grip of his fear.

"Look at all the troops coming," he breathed in awe.

"It's King Klann," she added, "riding at the head of them. Jiri—please—we've got to get out of here. I don't think there are any militia people left."

"No—look," he said, pointing. "Anton. That's Anton

down there. They're—they're blocking the culvert spans. Oh, good idea, old knight . . .'' He felt for the sword at his back, snicked it out and gazed on it with passionate eyes as he had countless times during the night. "I'd better get down there. But what am I going to do about you? Damn, Greta, why didn't you leave with your parents?''

"I told you, Jiri," she repeated again hoarsely, "I wanted to be with you. I couldn't stand the thought of you dying alone somewhere. Not knowing . . .''

"That's the warrior's lot, Greta, you've known that all along . . .'' He made to move off for the stairs, grimly but tentatively, face a mask of conflicting duty and concern for her safety. When Greta tried to hold him back, he pulled away all the harder. When she surrendered in despair, Jiri would reconsider his battle eagerness and turn to comfort her.

They had been recreating this cyclic scene all night.

Their rehearsals had not prepared them for the reality that invaded their sanctum. A surly voice, speaking German:

"Ho-ho! Look what we have here—''

Greta muffled her scream with the back of a hand. The two brigands eased into the loft, glancing about warily to be sure there was no one else present. One of them held a primed pistol; the other, a stained rapier.

"—two little pigeons, snug in their nest—'' He removed his kettle hat and tossed it on a chest. The guild hall's upper loft was used for storage of unsold goods. Cabinets and wardrobes were strewn about the place.

Jiri's stomach fluttered with terror. Greta clung to him, trembling as he eased her toward an armoire.

"Now you hold it right there, boy." The pistol jerked in emphasis. Jiri froze. The bandit undid his jack and heaved an exhausted breath. "You don't want any trouble in your little perch, do you? Move away from her."

Jiri shook his head, eyes gleaming.

"Know what I think?" the other soldier said archly. "I think we got a fighter on our hands. Now step away from her, boy, and I'll give you a fight." He twirled the rapier point. Jiri's broadsword was still sheathed on his back.

Jiri and Greta began circling away from them as the pair approached slowly, menacingly. An uneasy ballet.

*"Move away from her!"*

"No!" Greta shrieked, leaping at the pistol-wielder when he was within arm's length. She latched onto his arm and wrestled it for dear life.

"You little bitch!"

The pistol barked off an errant shot, and the brigand slammed Greta down, tussling with her as she clawed and beat at him.

Jiri's knees buckled, but he recovered at once to see his beloved in danger. His broadsword flashed as the rapier lashed out at him.

"A two-handed man, eh?" his opponent jeered. "Let's see you stop a modern fencer—come on, boy—let's see what you've got—"

Jiri was hard pressed to defend against the slim blade's stinging attacks, giving ground, backing toward the window. He tried to remember everything Gonji had taught, then tried to empty his mind as he'd been advised. Under fire, none of it made any sense. He heard Greta's shrill cry and a tearing of fabric. He growled and roared a *kiyai,* trying to press an attack against the impossibly long blade as his man laughed at his impassioned effort.

And then the other man screamed horribly and rolled out from behind a cedar chest. Greta's poniard, the blade she had learned to use in the catacombs and carried strapped to her thigh, was embedded in his back. Greta covered her mouth to see what she'd done and kicked backward on the floor.

Jiri's opponent reacted with shock, suddenly looking

trapped. The young *bushi* whipped his blade through a flashy series of baffling blade exercises, growling with the gyrations as he'd seen Gonji do so many times. The bandit backed two steps, then chanced a lunge that Jiri parried almost by accident.

His wrist-twisting riposte cut the man's upper arm to the bone. With a strangled cry, the Frankish highwayman dropped his rapier and backpedaled from the loft.

Breathing hard, Jiri leaped after him, shouting down from the landing hysterically. "Go on—get out—if you come back, there's more—I'll—I'll kill you next time—"

He ran back into the loft and slammed the door, pushing a heavy chest in front of it. Then he dropped on his knees beside Greta, who stared at the corpse in abject horror.

Jiri looked at the dark, wet stain on his blade.

"I sliced open his arm," he said in awe.

"I *killed* a person," Greta wailed.

They clung to each other for a long time, quaking.

"Jiri," she said at length, "Jiri, it's all wrong. I didn't know it would be like this. We're going to die, I know it—"

"No, we're not," he assured in an effort at comforting her. They listened to the sounds of gunfire and bowshot, galloping and shouting, for a time.

Jiri moved to the window and peeked out. Klann's large reinforcement detachment fired across the overflowing culvert at a running band of rebels. He gasped to see the enemy's numbers.

Then Greta was beside him, wide-eyed to view it all. "I don't want to die without knowing love, Jiri. There's so much we'll never do. Never see. Hold me. Let's never leave this place. They—they won't find us here . . ."

They lay together in the darkness, distraught and afraid. Listening to the sounds of battle and the rush of river water through the flooded streets below their window onto Hell. Clinging fast, sharing each other's warmth, they surrendered to the bleak promise of imminent young death.

In the midst of death and darkness, they dispelled their confused fears, making love for the first time.

At length Jiri drew up on an elbow, gazed vapidly at the corpse of the man Greta had slain. Shaking his head with abrupt resolve, he rose.

"Come on," he said with quiet determination.

"What?" she asked uncertainly, wincing and turning away from the sight of the dead man.

"We're leaving."

Jiri obtained a coil of rope and, drawing the reluctant girl by the hand, removed the barrier and cautiously descended the stairs. They emerged into the street behind the guild hall, found a wandering horse, and rode double toward the eastern rise of the girdling wall, thanking God that they encountered no resistance. They offered not a word to the frantic citizens who questioned them as they passed.

Splashing through the flooded trench and gaining the wall, they climbed to the allure and secured the rope to a merlon. Greta placed her arms about his neck and laid her head on his broad back for comfort. Before he lowered them outside the walls, Jiri took a last look at his home.

"I've got to take care of Greta now," he said, as if Vedun itself had demanded a parting rationale. "I'm just not ready . . . just not a warrior yet. I'll be back. Someday I'll be back."

They dropped into the head-high water of the drainage moat and dragged themselves onto the soaked ground. Heading for the bridge over the Little Roar, they plucked fruit that remained after the harvest and pressed on, leaving certain death behind them for uncertain life ahead.

The battered *bushi* in Gonji's band fought their way into the central city, men dropping out along the way to check into their homes with promises that they would return. Many rode wounded in the saddle, but there was nothing that could be done for them save for numbing pulls at skins of water or heady drink or crude efforts at self-bandaging.

They reached the central culvert, which had overflowed the retaining wall. Water from the swollen river rushed past, driving rubble and floating corpses through the broad street. The only passage was close by the structures that faced the culvert.

Anton pounded up to them, a mixture of relief and wrath contorting his features. "It's about goddamn time!" he swore at Gonji. "Look at them—"

His men reeled in their saddles, exhausted. They had finished their heavy task, blocking or destroying what bridges they could, buying time in slowing the coming pursuit.

"They're out on their feet, for Christ's sake. Is there anything else you want from them before they drop?"

"They've got to be alive to feel exhausted," Gonji observed.

Anton sneered at the samurai's philosophizing. "Well, what now?" he growled, throwing up his hands. He fought his steed's peevish stamping in the rumbling water.

Klann's reinforcement troop poured across the flooded street beyond the culvert. The king fanned out his crossbowmen, calling out orders from between the personal guards who held shields before him. A gallery of Klann crests spread across their field of view.

"Jesus," someone whispered, "we're going to be trapped here—they'll be at the west gate—" A few men broke ranks and sped off.

Wilf hurled imprecations at their backs. "Damn you, cowards."

Gonji ordered them into the cover of the next street as fusillades of quarrels arced sleekly down on them. Garth was the last to move, staring over the rushing cataract at Klann a moment before galloping off.

The soldiers had begun to ford the culvert, slow going. But many were moving off in search of unblocked spans, of which there were many.

"Not much time," Gonji assessed. "Let's get the rest of the people evacuated. No one left behind—come on."

Wilf grumbled behind him as they rode, fighting small skirmishes, men dropping by ones and twos. "We blew it—the timing—we were too slow. We should have ridden out an hour ago. Into the hills. Let the relief column pass us by—*attacked the castle while it was undermanned!*"

Gonji reined in, wheeled and faced him. *"All-recht,* so you're *right!* So I failed you, too—you needn't feel special. There are plenty of dead people here who'd say I failed them more than you."

They glared at each other, and another warrior rode between them, gesturing placatingly. "Hey—we *couldn't* do anything about the castle. Look at us. How many are we? There's no use torturing yourselves. *There's* our enemy—across the water—"

*"Ja,"* Wilf agreed despondently, "how many are we?"

A pistol's report from a side lane snapped them out of it. The sizzle of the ball raked the air past Gonji's ear. Tora lurched, and he fought the steed for control. They scanned the lane, saw wagons bounding by toward the west. It took a moment to identify the defiant figure, clad in black, seated astride a mare with smoking wheel-lock. It was William Eddings. He made no effort to flee but only sat leveling hate-filled eyes at the samurai.

"Grab that man!"

*"Eddings*—have you lost your mind?"

Two men rode up to him, swords bared. Gonji cantered up, grimacing at the Englishman, who held his steely gaze.

362

Gonji had seen such loathing before. His men waited for an order.

"Take his pistol," the samuari said quietly. Eddings began yammering and sobbing, his spite clear, though Gonji could understand almost nothing of the language.

"He says he'll do it again when he gets the chance," was all one of the men would offer by way of translation. He tried to reason with Eddings but was shouted down by the irrational sundrier.

"Well?" another *bushi* asked.

*"They're coming across!"*

They charged off in escort of the wagons without another word, separated now from the main body. Gathering stray militiamen as they went, picking up screaming evacuees, they fought broken parties of mercenaries who were ever less eager to skirmish. Content to pick them off as they clattered by. Outbreaks of pillaging and burning could be seen as the occupation troops sensed the rout, the general breakdown in order.

The *bushi* could do nothing about it. Escape was of paramount concern. They fell grimly, silently, past the fear of death.

As they sprang and bounced over the carnage and debris in the shattered city, dragging aboard the wounded, they let loose the dead to make room for the living. Gonji watched his friend Garth alternately clash with ferocity and mete out kindness to the unfortunate. He repeatedly stopped to aid the wounded and the lost. Gonji was overwhelmed by his strength both physically and spiritually, his mercy and humanity.

Some of the Hussars' horses, driven beyond all limits of endurance, dropped dead in their tracks. Fallen men doubled up with friends when no riderless mounts could be had.

Gonji shouted a warning to a man up the street who struggled with the weight of a wounded compatriot. A mercenary behind the smashed counter of an open-fronted lorimer's shop fired his pistol, downing the militiaman with a cowardly shot. Both men fell.

Outraged, Gonji stormed inside the shop aboard Tora, taking the reloading bandit by surprise and dashing his brains with a blow from the Sagami. Another brigand ran from the rear of the shop for the relative safety of the street. A poisoned *ninja* dart caught him in the side. And then Gonji jumped Tora over the wrecked counter and back out to rejoin his ragged command. He fought with a spate of uncontrollable rage when he viewed, in a passing wagon, the young boy Eduardo, holding a sword over the form of his wounded father.

Occasional confusion over identity aided their flight. Once Miklos Zarek rode laughing from a side lane, having sent a free companion troop back east on the trail of a phantom rebel band. But the gauntlet continued to tighten as they pressed their wild ride, Llorm dragoons beginning to appear in the distance along crossing avenues, having forded the flood.

The west gate was in sight. A wounded rider, pressing in his side, saluted Gonji and blurted the news that a large troop of dragoons was on its way around the walls to block the west gate.

"We'll never make it through," a mounted woman cried out.

They spurred onward, teeth clenched and swords flailing.

They could see the *bushi* who vainly tried to hold the wall above the gate, under fire of Llorm crossbows now as they readied for a charge of swordsmen along the allure. The lead men met. A slashing madman at the head of the *bushi* fought like a demon, pressing the adventurers back.

As they neared, someone identified him:

"Paille—it's that crazy Paille!"

When they hit the gate, the wagons rumbled through,

water cascading up from the spinning wheels. They came under attack at once, the married militiamen fighting it back gamely, their desperate need firing them. Tragically fallen men strove with their last breaths to cover the evacuees' escape. Women and children huddled tightly in the beds of the wagons.

A cheer went up as an armored wagon bounded along the wall from the north, the men within blasting and launching from every gunloop at the thinning pursuit.

But now a new menace: Tumo, bowling up from the south, maddened with pain and rage, spinning and smashing with flayed and bloody barrel fists. A few desperate *bushi* engaged the cretin giant with bow and pike.

"The blasted beast won't *die,*" Gonji fumed. "Get these people out!"

Paille fell on the walls, and Monetto came up close behind him. He stayed the killing blow intended for Paille with a disemboweling axe-cut. The attacker's head was severed with the next berserker arc.

"Cover Monetto," Garth shouted below, archers firing up at the retreating mercenaries. "Let these innocents go, you *barbarians,*" the mighty smith roared.

Monetto lowered Paille to waiting hands below. Gonji pounded up and dismounted.

The artist's chest leaked blood, but he was raking out something from under his jack.

"What the hell were you trying to prove, Paille?" Gonji asked.

"Never mind that," the eccentric poet gasped. "Look what they've done . . . in their ignorance . . ." He pulled out the thick sheaf of *Deathwind of Vedun* manuscript. It was pierced and bloody now. He cradled his wounded masterpiece. "This is what they think . . . of a great work . . ."

"Damn thing saved your life, Paille," Nick Nagy called

365

down from horseback.

"I told you you should have called it *Red Blade from the East,*" Gonji recalled.

"Arghh—I don't believe in your infidel omens." His breath rasped.

"Don't let them forget the valor you saw here, Paille," Gonji said somberly as they carried him to a wagon. "Write of brave men who battled beasts out of nightmare."

"I shall write of—of courageous souls . . . who fought for freedom. Not of monsters . . . lest rational men think me mad."

The wagon pounded away with a frantic lashing by the fear-maddened driver.

Tumo blared a challenge and threw a dead horse at his attackers, stooping to seize a crawling man and rend him before their eyes. The armored wagon, waved up by Garth, rolled forward to tilt with it. An enfilade of arquebus and pistol fire from within staggered him, striking vital areas in his damaged armor. Tumo bawled a great cry of rage and terror and loped off to lick his wounds.

The wagons were gone, all save the last armored coach. And the remaining *bushi* were pincered by troops from inside the city and without.

"Let's get out of here," Gonji cried. Monetto dropped to the street with his two surviving men. The samurai himself found his body so ached that it took two tries to roll aboard Tora and join their flight.

With the sounds of pillaging and burning behind them, attacking troops hitting them from side and rear, and the certain knowledge that there must be people left helpless in their wake, they made their bitter escape, feeling no relief. Feeling nothing but the blind urge to survive.

They continued to fall as they splashed westward along the road, running game now for the archers who trailed close behind. The armored coach caught fire, and those who rode in escort of it fell back from the rolling fireball it became. Some of the team that manned its armament still trapped inside, it plunged over the hillside to explode in the valley.

Gonji halted and turned at the thunderous report, men flying past. Anton and Nagy were the last in the column, and they slowed to urge him on for his life. But the pursuing troops had yanked to a jostling stop.

The howling of the werewolf wafted on the wind from some indeterminate distance down the Roman road.

The samurai cursed to himself to see the belching smoke and flames that roiled up from the city. Wheeling back, he saw the knotted clump of men waiting for him, Wilf at their center.

The young smith's eyes were red and swollen. "That's the castle road up ahead," he said, pointing along the bend.

Gonji inhaled a deep breath. *"Choléra,"* he breathed in exasperation. "You're unbelievable, friend . . ."

He looked back. The pursuers, pushed by their officers, were beginning to resume the chase.

"Hyah!" He kicked Tora onward at a gallop. He gave it no conscious thought in his bone-weariness, was aware of no decision on his part, but when he reached the north trail he swerved right and loped up into the hills. He heard Wilf's gurgled shout of triumph somewhere behind him. Then he was guiding them off the trail and into the rugged forests, still tracking upward. Their steeds complaining with every stride, they circled upward, higher and higher, until they again crossed the potentially dangerous trail and headed for the northern tunnel to the catacombs.

The samurai gave way to let them pass, having no idea who still followed. What he saw both surprised and troubled him.

Wilfred—Garth—Aldo Monetto—the erstwhile coward

named Arvin—the hate-driven William Eddings—and Miklos Zarek, slumped over his mount's withers, near to death.

They tethered their steeds a safe distance from the concealed tunnel entrance and helped Zarek to the now abandoned, though still fortified tunnel.

Barely dragging inside, they collapsed almost as one. There was sobbing, but nothing spoken, and the merest effort made at comforting Zarek.

Deathlike sleep overwhelmed them.

It would be dawn soon. There was no cheer in the thought for Genya. She longed to be a bird, to slip between the bars of the window grating and—

The clink of keys startled her. A tremor of terror chilled her to the core of her being. She turned, her back to the wall, and sucked in a cold breath to see the familiar face in the door's loophole.

"Lorenz," she whispered.

He smiled, tinkled the keys before his face, then held a finger to his lips. The lock scraped and clicked, and the portal squealed open.

"I've come to bring you freedom," he said, stepping inside and leaning back so that the door slowly swung shut behind him. "To *rescue* you, if you will . . ."

But then he studied her face, saw the fear in her eyes, and his smile faded. His urbane manner fled before a dawning malevolence, as of one betrayed. "So you know."

She ignored the remark, licking her lips with an equally dry tongue. "Where is Mord?" she asked, gathering her composure.

"What is that mark you wear on your forehead?" he asked with childlike inquisitiveness. He ambled toward her, his mood changing to amusement. He was freshly scrubbed and scented. His garments were new, down to the polish of his imported riding boots.

"Lorenz, what's happened in Vedun?"

He stopped and held up a hand. *"Listen*—can you hear?" he whispered dramatically, eyebrows lifting. "The night wind tells the tale."

Genya's tears began to stream. "What—what's become of Wilfred?"

Distaste etched his cruel mouth. "Wilfred," he repeated with disdain. *"Really,* my dear, is he truly so important? Isn't he just one of many who look upon you with hunger?"

She felt panicky, sweat breaking out, beading her face, her palms. Lorenz was quite mad.

*"Why,* Lorenz?" she sniffled. "What could they possibly offer you?"

"Come now, my dear," he fawned. "You're no ordinary peasant. I've always known that about you. You understood games of power and influence. I've seen you utilize that knowledge. It's for *power* that I strive, for the position my abilities warrant . . ." His words were filled with bitterness now.

"For the lofty birthright I was denied."

She sobbed, unable to comprehend this strange and evil transformation of a person she thought she knew. "So much death and destruction," she said. *"Why?"*

"The deaths of *peasants,"* he exclaimed. "Of common men. Blacksmiths and shepherds and simple-minded tinkers. Inferiors and barbarians all. And there I was in the midst of them, raised by them in a cloak of secrecy so that they might bleed me for my gifts like leeches. Can you imagine? With *my* noble heritage? Is it any wonder I found it child's play to become the chief administrator of their economy, to cause their community to thrive?"

She was perplexed, trying to piece it together. "Herr Gundersen . . . is *not* your father?"

*"He is the father to fools—and a king of fools!"*

She blinked and stiffened at his outburst, which cooled as suddenly as it had been stoked.

*"Nein,* not their king," he amended calmly, "merely their jester. You really don't know it all, do you?"

Genya started to shake her head, but checked herself and gathered her strength. "Lorenz, you were always so gracious. *Bitte,* help me to get away from here. If I could just get to Wilfred, I feel I could be free—"

*"Wilfred*—bull-headed, uneducated Wilfred—what do you find so attractive in him? Don't you know what I could give you? Haven't you ever seen how I've looked upon you, studied your ways, knowing that only *I* could be a fair match for your cleverness?" He grabbed her hair in both hands and yanked her head back. A small outcry escaped her parted lips. "That only I am fit to be your consort? Has Wilfred ever done this for you?"

He squeezed her close, a hard, smothering embrace that forced the air from her lungs. His lips traced a moist path along her throat.

"I—love—Wilfred," she cried, twisting in his clutch.

"Then you love a *corpse,"* he snarled.

*"Nein*—if he were dead, I'd know it," she cried out, feeling his hands claw at her back, raking, tearing.

She reached under her torn skirt, finding the sheath, the dagger's hilt. With her eyes shut tight, a confused prayer in her mind, she drew the blade and stabbed at him, cutting through his doublet and shirt, notching his ribs.

Lorenz screamed and flung her away. She fell to one knee, the dagger held before her threateningly. He began to laugh. A cold, eerie sound. As if she'd abruptly been forgotten. He turned and gripped the window grating, pressing his face against the rusted iron.

Genya eased out, locked him inside, and fled the tower.

Lorenz cackled and strained to peer down at the fragment of the tiny, smoldering city he could make out by pushing until his face was a hideous distortion.

"All gone—all dead—no more deceivers . . . Morning's coming. A new day, a new me . . . Yes, Your Highness, I did sleep well.

"And you?"

## Chapter Twenty-three

Throughout the night Simon Sardonis loped through the forest on the north side of the Roman road, covering the loading of the non-combatants. The elements raged in concert with his actions, the wind and rain following him, adding superstitious terror to the physical effects of his assaults.

Staying clear of the wagon teams as much as possible to avoid catalyzing their animal fear of his huge lupine form, he terrorized Klann's troops, stampeding their mounts, running amok among them; now with axe or sword, now with fang and claw. Bounding into their midst from unexpected places.

Not far behind him ran failing courage; the soldiers' trepidation soon caused them to become less interested in the fleeing wagons than the easier prey in Vedun.

The duty stations shifted with the movement of battle. As new waves of wagons broke from the city, fresh troops would give chase awhile, only to find the Beast slavering out of the forest to level the unfortunate, his speed an awesome blur at first.

Though they struck him often with bowshot, they began to lose heart, believing him invulnerable. He would tear their shafts free with an agonized howl and come at them again, seemingly invigorated.

371

They did not suspect how badly they had hurt him, despite his supernatural resiliency. He fought on in severe pain and gnawing fear, his strength waning with the passing hours. More than once he thought to retreat, lest he die and thus fail to achieve his vengeance, freeing the Beast's corpus to fall under its soul's control, unleashing it upon the world unchecked.

But he gambled on God's mercy, knowing the people's need of him, drinking in the rare and strangely wonderful sense of belonging, and reveling in the energumen's now buried frustration and wrath.

He fought on in his pain, knowing that it purchased life for the innocents of Vedun. He found himself longing for their safe passage, though they feared him as much as the pursuing troops.

And there were few losses along the road to the west.

When the last wave of wagons had passed a mile beyond the north trail, the escort party led by Anton and Nagy joined in exhausted rejoicing with the Benedettos, who had hung back in their wagon, along with a squad of anxious cavalry.

"Did everybody make it?" Galioto fretted, brow creased.

Nagy cleared his throat. "Most did, I guess."

Anton passed him a wineskin. "It's not as bad as it might have been," the knight judged.

"Bad enough," Lydia replied wistfully.

"A lot of good young men left back there," Michael added.

"Too many," Nagy agreed, looking back along the road and thinking of his dead friend Stefan.

Anton hummed thoughtfully. "What's the matter, Nick? Nobody to call you *starý baba*—old grandma—anymore?"

"Nobody but women, brats, and old farts left," Nagy mused.

"Everybody out of the catacombs?" another late arrival asked.

*"Everybody,"* Galioto assured emphatically, as if he'd been accused of failure. "I went back three times and checked—" He rambled on for a time, repeating the details until he had assured himself of their confidence. When he was done he rode off with some of the men to rejoin their families.

"We'll be back, Vedun," Michael said in a voice just above a whisper. A few turned to regard him in surprise.

Then someone spotted the eyes.

"Look—the *werewolf.*"

Simon's angular eyes gleamed in a stray moonbeam, staring down from the wood, motionless.

"He still unnerves me," Lydia breathed.

They saw the eyes turn away sharply as he scrambled back east several yards with a rustling of foliage. The clumping of hooves sounded behind them.

"Let's get out of here—"

"Wait," Michael commanded. Something was happening on the road between them and the approaching band of soldiers.

A dark blot appeared, swirling like an inky cyclone. Their vision could not penetrate the growing stain in the air. They saw the soldiers now, jangling to a sudden halt, their commander cursing at their failing courage. And then they, too, saw what began to take shape in the blackness, swathed now in red flames that emitted no sound.

The sound that did come caused them to cover their ears.

*"Oh my God—"*

There was a wailing of souls in torment, and around the darkly glowing saurian apparition, there appeared the reaching, pleading forms of the eternally lost. A forgotten corner of damnation had been released to move among men.

373

The mercenaries broke their ragged ranks and began fighting the loyal but outnumbered Llorm, having had enough of this mad work. They battled back along the road toward the valley trail that would take them to the southern curve of the Carpathian range and out of this forbidding territory. They would join with many more who had already made that despairing decision.

*"They've opened Hell!"* someone screamed, pointing, in the Vedunian party. And when it began to move, their panicked steeds would wait no longer. They were borne away on hooves that scarcely touched earth, peering back in horror until they disappeared around a bend in the road.

Simon saw the dark shape begin to move, blacker than the night, amidst the whirling chaos that accompanied it. He was struck with a terror he had never known before.

Something sparkled where eyes might have been. It was gazing at him as surely as if he stood before it. The trees could not hide him. He instinctively knew that nothing in nature could. For it had come for him.

*Wolverangue,* the energumen's soundless voice formed upon seeing it through his eyes. There was no rejoicing in the possessed spirit's recognition, though it tried to mask its own demon-fear.

The Hell-Hound began to move, and the trees flared in its passing, though they were drenched from the long rain. Slowly it stalked upward toward him, its footfalls searing the ground with unearthly smoke and flame.

With a prayer for his immortal soul's deliverance, Simon moved down to engage it, circling it cautiously. Uncertain of what it was he engaged. He was shaken to the core by the wailing of the damned that cavorted about it like satellites, their torment increased by the sight of the natural world they could not gain again.

With axe and sword the werewolf laid into the Hell-

Hound, and before he had seen the first blow pass through it without effect, he understood the futility of his effort: Wolverangue did not live in this realm, nor could it be destroyed here.

His weapons cut a swath through flaming air again and again, each time emerging from the vaguely reptilian blackness hotter than the last. Until the axe and sword began to glow with a dull redness, too hot for him to grasp. He growled and looked in wonderment at the smoking of his palms, smelling the scent of singed hair.

Wolverangue's yellow eyes suddenly glowed, stoked by Hell's furnace. Tenebrous teeth and hooked claws took shape at its extremities—not in one place but many—and the werewolf was seized and borne aloft. Flaming needles seared his body in a hundred agonizing spots. He roared and struggled to escape the grasp, fearing that he would be dragged down into the Pit with it.

The Hell-Hound began to take more definite shape, solidifying as it more surely gripped its quarry. Simon lashed out, tearing with the savagery of the doomed predator, fur and skin burning black wherever they touched. He had to get free from the agony which by now would have rendered any normal man insensible.

Pain-maddened, he twisted and kicked, flipping backward out of its clutch, to land on his muzzle. He shook himself, vision filled with flashing lights.

Unhurried, the Hell-Hound stalked him, tireless, pressing toward the end for which it had been invoked with evil calm. Glorying in the chance to wreak destruction while it moved across the face of the world. Along its burning path, nothing would ever again grow. A charred scar for the world of man to mourn and avoid.

Simon took up the sword again, howling in desperate fury, the weapon now cool enough to wield but heavier than it had been: dawn approached; the slow and painful transformation had begun.

He poured all his remaining strength into a tremendous twisting blow. It struck the creature's lower portion without a sound, but the impact jarred Simon's teeth, and the blade sheared in half with a shower of sparks. He was left holding the hilt and a jagged fragment of forte.

The demon's fulminating breath descended to his nostrils as the unspeakable mouth gaped wide to engulf his face.

A wave of heat singed the fur of his head—he bayed in mortal terror—smelled the stench of burning flesh—

And thrust the broken sword upward mightily. It lodged in the spreading maw of the Hell-Hound with a blinding red iridescence, and though it appeared to the grounded Simon to float in the air of its own accord, it stayed the descent of the gaping mouth.

Wolverangue paused, confounded. The cruciform hilt, wrought in the ritual fires of holy men in a Vedun long past, began to glow with a blazing white light too bright to gaze upon. The Hell-Hound's yellow pupils receded, the claws and teeth and nebulous form followed, whirling smaller and smaller. An imploding vacuum, a vortex that dwindled to a ball of black fire. And vanished into nothing.

Simon lurched in pain, not caring whether it had been the holy symbol or the dawn's first flicker that had banished the demon back to the Pit. He knew only that the agony of return was upon him.

Running madly in his effort to smother the pain, dragging the battle axe behind him unconsciously, he bolted across the road and down through virgin thicket into the southern valley. He ran until he could run no more, until he fell and tumbled into a stand of larches beside a boulder-strewn brook, where he screamed his pain into the bubbling clear water for the space of half an hour.

Crisp, cool morning sunshine filtered through the dizzily spinning branches overhead when he recovered his sight. Pale light played over the scores of punctures and vicious burns that covered his naked form.

Healing scar tissue had already begun to form.

"How do you like it?"

Simon Sardonis blinked awake in the lengthening shadows of late afternoon. A gentle breeze ruffled the trees, but no life buzzed or twittered near the brook. His head felt squeezed in a vise, and his body protested every movement. But most of the pain was gone. It would return, he knew, when night fell . . .

He rose on an elbow, wondering for an instant at the voice he had heard. Then he knew what it must be, just before he saw it.

It was the rarest of occurrences: The energumen, the possessed spirit that cohabited his body, whose own body was that of the werewolf, had parted from him. It sat on a boulder now with the legs of a goat tucked under the teated body of a cow. Its head was that of a pig with dirty needle teeth, the horns of an ox protruding from its temples. The thing rarely departed his body for two reasons: Moving in the physical world, it knew only frustration at having no capacity for sensory experience of its own; and worse, there would always be a struggle when it attempted to return. Thus, it reserved its comings out for moments when Simon was extremely weakened. It had chosen its timing well this day.

Simon heard the voice in his head again. The voice, it seemed this time, of a dwarf with a cleft palate.

"I said how do you like it?"

"It befits you."

"Oh, this?" the demoniac spirit said, raking an eagle's talon over its strange body. "Just something I cobbled together. Filched it from a farmer here, a peasant there, an old woman who will cry for want of milk today—" Its laugh was a staccato trilling; a bumblebee and a bullfrog in harmony.

Simon stooped and drank from the brook, dispersing with an act of willpower the bizarre illusions that floated past. He thought of how hungry he was. When he turned and looked at it again, the energumen was slurping at raw entrails.

"I know what your mother likes," it rasped in a sing-song cadence.

Simon sighed and slumped down against a tree, closing his eyes.

"I think I found out something about you last night," Simon said, smiling with quiet satisfaction, running his eyes over the healing wounds.

The demon hissed, "Well, I know everything about you, ass licker—and here's something for you—Wolverangue is going to kill you tonight. It can't be destroyed in this realm, you know. Oh no-no-no—that's fixed by the laws that be. Do you know who made those laws? Aren't you grateful? Why don't you curse His name?"

Simon ignored it and went on. *"Oui,* I think—correct me if I'm wrong, and then I'll know I'm right—I think that you've been taught well by the Deceiver. You've been deceiving me all our lives. I felt a certain . . . panic when you thought the Thing would drag us into the Pit last night—"

"He will, he will. Wolverangue will drag you down to perdition, and then I'll be free to roam the world and . . . do those things you'd like to do when you're being honest with yourself."

"I think," Simon kept on, "that you've masked the truth about the Beast's death, guarded it all this time. Made me believe I was a slave to it. Must have taken you one hell of a continuous effort. First of all," he ticked off on his fingers, the demon babbling all the while in a sound like a child fluttering his lips, "I found that I *could* win control over the Beast in the full of the moon. Did that make you . . . uncomfortable?"

"Have a drink." The energumen waved its eagle talon in a rotating movement and performed one of the minor kinetic enchantments it was capable of: a torrent of water from the brook and a cascade of pebbles pelted Simon where he sat. But it could not know the merest touch of the objects it threw, to its great anger, and the power could last but a short time. The attack slowed and ceased.

Simon wiped his face and flicked the stones from his lap. "My . . . aren't we childish today? But allow me to continue. Second, do you know what else I think? If I were to die in the body of the Beast, so would you. You would not be freed, as you have suggested to me so often. All your urgings that I throw myself off promontories and into bonfires . . . I have observed that when *you* command the Beast during the full moon, you're rather careful, for all your savagery. So I reason thus—"

"The Hell-Hound will flay you," it sang in a woman's voice, the voice of one who had once caused him a grief and shame he would never dispel. The voice nagged on in normal discourse: "Why don't you give it up, my darling, dearest Simon. All the agony. The life of an outcast, shunned by men and filthy animals alike—how can you go on like that? Men hate you, beasts hate you, the birds in the trees—where are they? They won't come near because you're here now. You're hated by all. All save me. I pity you, and with good reason, for I know your suffering—"

"Of course you do," Simon replied, "because you feel everything I do. You fled me today because you couldn't stand the pain. Don't you think I feel your squirming when I suffer? Don't you know that *knowing* the certainty of your pain is all that sustains me in my darkest moments?"

"How can you know what I feel?" the woman's voice railed. "I feel nothing but what I wish to feel, and you grant me too little of that with your stubborn asceticism.

379

When you die, I can live, and I can see no point in your going on. *Here—*"

A rustle in the branches overhead. A noose dangled from a sturdy larch limb.

"—here is surcease of pain, the sweet endless sleep of death. Eternal, insensate. A balm to your weary heart. *Emptiness . . .*"

"You hate me most of all, don't you, demon or devil or whatever you be? For I deny you true life, as long as I cling to mine."

The voice became masculine, a thundering cathedral boom. The spirit sprang upward on its borrowed goat legs, and an eagle talon reached skyward. *"He* hates you most of all, and He's deceived you. How He must laugh—why don't you curse His name and be done with Him?"

"By the holy name of Jesus, be silent!" Simon commanded.

"That's the one! Why don't you curse it for what He's allowed to happen—*look at you!*"

Simon clamped his eyes and ears shut and prayed in fervent faith. "By the God who created both of us and His Son who has died for mankind, *I command you to be still!*"

The energumen shriveled and disappeared, the animal parts falling atop the boulder, withered and dried.

The ensorceled man gasped. His eyes widened with the realization of a dawning hope. When he turned, the thing was behind him, a tiny girl now, but sexually mature. Simon jumped in spite of his knowledge of its tricks.

"Exciting, wasn't it?" The woman's voice again. "Had you ready to apply with the Office of Inquisition, eh? By the way, how do you like it?" The thing began to fondle its new body.

Simon scowled with revulsion at its perversity and leaned away against the tree. "Don't bother to tell me

380

where you got it."

"Hah-hah! You might go there at once, eh? Actually, it's only an illusion this time, enhanced by the dark desires of your own soul, of course. Ah, the pleasures the flesh offers. Why don't you give it up? You don't know what to do with it anyway unless you're . . . properly led . . ."

The noose fluttered before him in the tree.

"Come-come now—up and in."

Simon grasped the rope. He swallowed. "You'd like that, wouldn't you? It would set you free if I spurned God's gift."

"What gift has He given you?" it sneered.

"The gift of life, for better or worse. You see . . . I know the truth now. Only if I take my own life will you be freed."

"That's what you think, is it?" the demon asked wryly. "That's what you've reasoned—your great revelation. Such a philosopher, you are," it minced, cartwheeling into the brook across his view.

*"Oui,"* Sardonis said reflectively, "and if there is a way for you to live independently of me, then there must be a way for me to free myself of your cankerous presence."

"Such talk."

"I shall find your demon father and wring the truth from him one day—"

"You had him once," the energumen taunted, the reminder always a stinging one for Simon, "and what happened?"

Simon turned away from it again, blotted its voice from his mind. "I shall find him and destroy him, and somehow that will destroy you—*I know it.*"

"He's your father as well, you know," the voice offered seductively.

*"My father died by his hand!"* Simon stormed.

The energumen cackled. Its voice became that of a nun who had tutored the orphan during his monastic youth in

France: "Fresh sacrificial meat, he was, that's all—"

"I'll destroy you both, if it be God's will, because I know now that the samurai—the others—they're right—"

"There is no universal will but the Dark Master's."

"Call him by his despised name," Simon said acidly. *"Satan*. The Despondent One. The Lost Angel—"

The woman-child tumbled in front of him and squatted, producing excrement so vile that he was forced to cover his face and move off to the brook. He began to wash, fighting back a sob, feeling terribly alone. His fatigue caused him to hate the endless struggle with every fiber of his being.

"Tonight you die," came the foreboding voice.

"And you with me," he answered without looking back.

"Go ahead. Find out." The energumen began singing a ribald drinking chantey.

Simon experienced a moment's doubt and bitterness. Then he remembered: the taunt it could not bear. A thin smile creased his lips.

"Demon," he said without looking at it, "what is your greatest sadness?" The song ceased, but there came no reply. "Shall I remind you? Do you think you can know my griefs while I am ignorant of yours? We share *all* unguarded thoughts. Let me ask you this—what is your name?"

He heard what sounded like a whispering wail in his head.

He turned, and it was gone. The woman-child, the excrement, the noose—all evidence of it had vanished from the woodland delve.

"Hiding?" Simon pressed in a loud voice. "Do you think that can spare you from the truth. *What is your name?* You *have* no name! You are *nothing*. You will live a captive within my body, nameless, purposeless, leaving no mark of your passing on earth. Until the day that I die and take you with me—"

The energumen shrieked inside Simon's brain until he thought it would burst. It attacked him and fought to return in its nonentity's shame. There ensued a fierce spiritual conflict, and during its brief time Simon realized that if he could best it, he would be rid of it forever. But in his weakened condition, he could not resist its invasion, and the thing again took up smoldering residence within Simon's being.

He fell on the ground, exhausted, beating the earth with his fists. He knew he must decide a course of action, for all too soon night would fall and Wolverangue would seek him.

Prostrating himself and pouring out his terror in a long, humble petition for guidance and protection, he felt a resurgence of determination, of will to live, of courage to face the agony to come. For although his multitude of wounds were healing with the remarkable rapidity he'd grown accustomed to, he knew what the transmutation at sundown would do. They would burst to bleed anew.

At length he decided his course. Hefting the battle-axe, he started off on foot for Castle Lenska. On the main road through the valley, he chanced upon an abandoned steed. Grimly determined to test his stubbornly held convictions for validity, he spent some time trying to coax the horse to come to him. It came as no surprise that it instinctively fled from him; but this time he stayed with it. For an hour he circled around the horse, a sturdy destrier, talking to it gently, moving ever nearer, careful to avoid startling it. It began to accept his presence.

An hour later Simon sat aboard the steed, the great axe lashed beside him. And to his delight, his pains had served up an added serendipity: a half-full wineskin and a pouch of food. Grateful for the transport in his wish to conserve strength, though horsemanship was new to him and he was still unclothed, he guided the mount northward.

There was much ground to cover before the horse abandoned him at sunset.

# Part III

## Hour of the Dragon

*"And when there is no more to be desired, there is an end of it"*—Cervantes, *Don Quixote*

## Chapter Twenty-four

For several hours in the tunnel the only sounds to be heard were those of pain and grief and utter exhaustion.

None of them could even mount enough concern for security to act as a sentry. They collapsed, disdainful of comfort. Garth wincingly tended Zarek's wounds before falling backward in surrender. Monetto tried vainly to light a fire, flinging away the materials at last. Wilfred, Arvin, and Eddings simply abandoned all effort, drifting off into private misery that soon became deep, merciful sleep.

Had any enemy discovered them, they would have been pinned between the invader and the bristling spearpoints of the tunnel redoubt, though none of them would have cared.

Gonji sat apart from them, knees drawn up to his chin. He was the last to sleep and the first to rise.

About noon the samurai awoke to the sound of Zarek's moaning. Minutes later, Monetto started, a strangled cry breaking off as his vision cleared. His expression clouded with gloom when he remembered his circumstances. He looked to Zarek, nodded to Gonji, and scrabbled for the tunnel exit.

He came back a moment later. "Sunshine," he announced with cautious optimism, as if to dispel the horror of it all. Seeing Gonji's lack of expression, he moved to tend on Zarek. "The caravan must be well on its way by now," he continued. "Wonder if Sylva's got the little ones in hand."

"You don't belong here, Monetto," Gonji said blankly.

"Your place is with the caravan."

To which the biller responded gently. "Karl would have wanted to be here. But he can't be. So I am." He placed an extra blanket under Zarek's tossing head before peering across at Gonji. "Sylva would want me here . . . helping. She's a great manager of the children, you know." He looked away.

Gonji cast him a curious glance as he rose.

"Where are you going?"

The samurai had begun clearing a path through the redoubt. "I forgot something. I'll be back."

"What?"

Gonji paused before he disappeared. "I left my mother's sword in the heart of Vedun . . ."

The last thing he saw in the tunnel was the baleful stare of William Eddings.

He tramped through the desolate catacombs, pressing at the insistent pain in his side. Ascending to the surface, he moved through Tralayn's house full of ghostly memories, strapped on his sallet, and eased out into the southern quarter.

Vedun looked like a plundered graveyard. Looters ran amok, tearing homes apart for the valuables left behind in the evacuation. Few took notice of him in the excitement of the rich harvest. Most who did gave him wide passage, the fight knocked out of them by the night's events. Some merely took him for another scavenging mercenary. And the few who saw that it was Gonji and momentarily entertained notions of revenge or glory or gold quickly abandoned them when they saw the menacing flicker of the dark eyes under his brooding sallet brim.

It appeared that Klann's mercenary companies, the workhorse of the diminishing army, were ravaged by death and desertion. The dead city was a feast for carrion birds and men alike; its halls and houses, a meadow sprinkled with treasure.

The afternoon sun strobed him warmly as Gonji mounted a stray horse and clopped sullenly toward the smithshop. The sky was burnished blue, clear but for a tracing of cirrus clouds in the west. The rain had fallen over the eastern edge of the world.

Animals wandered near the livery area, bleating and lowing. Dogs howled over dead masters. Two of them fought over forage in an alley as the samurai rode by.

The city's wet mantle had begun to evaporate. Odors of smoke and waste and corruption asserted themselves. A single night's madness had rendered it unfit for human habitation.

Gonji dismounted at the rubble before the Gundersens' home and sidled into the smithshop. It had been plundered of riding gear. The stables housed a motley lot of broken nags, all the good horses having been stolen or ridden out by citizens.

He entered the house, hearing scuttling sounds within. He drew the Sagami silently. In Wilf's bedchamber, a lone brigand sat on the cot, pulling on the stylish Italian riding boots Gonji himself had bought and later disdained.

The samurai leveled his blade at the surprised man, who froze, hollow-eyed. He reached for one of the two pistols thrust into his belt. The Sagami's point stopped a half inch from his nose.

"Take them out with two fingers," Gonji directed coldly, "and lay them on the cot. Then take off those boots and leave this place. Don't ever let me see you again. You've violated the home of my friends."

The man gulped and complied in a rush, anxious to be gone before his reprieve was withdrawn. He reached for his own boots, but Gonji stopped him.

"*Iyé*. Leave them."

He seemed about to protest. Gonji slashed his boots into neat halves with two sharp blows and returned his swordpoint to engagement between the man's eyes. He was on horseback, galloping away, seconds later.

The samurai took up the pistols. They had been loaded and spannered. He grinned to himself and shook his head. Then he stuffed the wheel-locks into his *obi,* still tied at the waist of his cuirass.

The hatch in the floor that led down to the cellar had gone undiscovered beneath the worn rug that concealed it. Gonji descended the cool, clammy stairs to find his mother's *wakizashi,* her gift to him, still wrapped in the spot where he had left it. He drew it. Saw the high gloss on the blade where Garth had mended it. He ambled to the large chest that contained the memoirs of the smith's days in Klann's service.

Planting the blade in the lid of the chest, he climbed out of the cellar, replaced the rug, and departed.

Not even a token effort at martial law was enforced in the streets of Vedun. The looting continued, drunken soldiers braying in celebration of their prizes. Perhaps all the captains of free companions were dead; perhaps they were numbered among the pillagers. He noted at least one party of the hated Ottoman Turks, sniffing about the ruins. Soon there would be more, and a new order would lay its stranglehold about the Carpathians. Gonji could not bring himself to care.

He rode on glumly.

The flood waters had receded, the exit sluices having been opened. Bloated bodies, their skin mushy and gray-mottled, lay about the walls of the central culvert. The dead were everywhere, in every imaginable attitude; piled and twisted, some still straddling the saddles of downed mounts. No Llorm were about. Nothing had been done in the way of clearing the carnage for future habitation. Only the looters. And tomorrow they, too, would be gone, their work finished or not. For no one would hazard to move amidst the decay. There was none to bury Vedun.

He spotted Tumo's massive spiked truncheon in the

debris and wondered whether, farther on, he would find the cretin giant finally among the dead. And the grim thought came: *Was it I who fought here only last night? Or someone who used my sleeping form in some kingdom out of nightmare?*

Passing the smashed market stalls and gutted millinery shop, he saw a band of thrill-seeking wastrels setting houses afire while they drank and cavorted before the spectacle. One of them pointed him out to the others. They began to follow, hurling insults at his back.

He wheeled the steed and aimed both pistols into their number. They shuffled to a halt.

"Looking for bounty?" he said in Spanish. "Who will pay it, swine?"

"Hey—you got a point there, slant-eyes," their leader agreed. With mollifying gestures, they backed away from him and returned to their sport. He rode off, turning south into the next main street.

Gonji found himself approaching the manse of Flavio. Bandits were loading a wagon with the late Elder's furnishings: his ornately carved mirrors; the decorative, leather-upholstered Italian dining set at which Gonji had supped; his huge, hand-loomed tapestries; silver services and gold ornaments.

They saw the angry pistol barrels before any of them recognized the impassive face. The band froze and looked from one to the other.

"Leave it," Gonji ordered in High German, cocking both wheel-locks.

One of them started to gurgle a laugh. It rose to a gravel-toned guffaw, the others taking it up slowly. There were six of them, all sporting firearms.

"Aw, give it up, mate," the man said in disbelief. "What's the sense of it anymore?"

Gonji blew a large hole in the center of his forehead.

The others lurched and dropped what they were carrying,

some clawing for their pistols.

"Who dies next?" the samurai inquired calmly.

It was clear that there were no volunteers. Slowly they dispersed, glaring back at him as they mounted and clopped away. Gonji put up the pistols, knowing the futility of it all. They'd be back later for their spoils. He sighed wearily.

"Hey, you men!" a man's voice cried from the portico. "I can't save this man!" It was Dr. Verrico, Vedun's surgeon. He held his hands before him. They were covered with blood, as was his apron. He looked like an employee of Roric's slaughterhouse. He had been working at gunpoint over the severely wounded companion of the departing bunch, who lay dying on Flavio's settee.

He blinked to see Gonji, his brow darkening. "Oh, so it's you. The *sensei*," he growled. "You think this exonerates you?" He pointed at the staring dead man in the street. "More killing? Where do I begin, oriental butcher, eh? Show me which of these men you need to raise from the dead, and I'll start to work! Well? No lofty words of exhortation to valor now? What's wrong? I say to you, which ones shall I patch together for your use?"

Gonji turned, gritting his teeth and kicking the horse into a trot, forcing back the sting of the tears and the sick feeling at the pit of his stomach. Verrico called imprecations after him until he had turned into a side lane far down the street.

"*You are the Deathwind you seek!*" was the last pronouncement he heard behind him.

Not long after, he passed the fallen forms of Gerhard and Berenyi, which someone had laid side by side on a flagstone walk. *In war, men fall,* he told himself, but there was no consolation in it.

He continued eastward, drinking in the brutalization of it all, trying to achieve a surfeit of it, or an understanding, a relief from the confusing sense of guilt. In *Dai Nihon,* no such feelings would have been attendant on the aftermath of a conflict. But he was not in the Land of the Gods now.

He knew these people, their ways. And he could not disperse the feeling that he had brought evil karma into both their lives and his.

He reached Provender Lane and saw the heaped bodies without, wondering whether someone weren't enjoying some perverse jest. But the corpses stacked at both sides of the door like entrance columns were all slain soldiers. Entering warily, he found Gutschmidt and Klaus, packing satchels.

"Gonji!" Klaus exclaimed heartily, almost in exhilaration. His armor was gone. He moved forward to bow to the samurai, who returned the greeting in perplexity. "You made it," Klaus continued with sincere relief.

Gutch nodded to him. "You did good," the innkeeper assured. "You got 'em out. Now what—for you, I mean?"

Gonji glanced around the inn. It had been cleaned and swept, looking ready for business, except that most of the beverage casks were gone. "I don't know," he responded dimly. "What about you?"

"Me and Gutch tidied up the place," Klaus answered for him. "We thought we'd head west and check in on the townspeople. You know—see what their plans are. Then maybe we'll head to Augsburg or Frankfurt for awhile. We've got all Gutch's good stuff loaded out back so that—"

"*All-recht,* bimbo, I'll do the talking," Gutch cut in. "And let's belay this 'me and Gutch' business. I said we'd see, *nicht wahr?*"

They exchanged small talk for a space, Gonji bemused by it all. Of all the unlikely friendships to develop out of the night's grim events, this one was the strangest he could imagine. But he was briefly glad for the sound of their good-natured banter.

"Do you need all those pistols?" Gonji asked, indicating the long row on the bar.

"Help yourself," Gutch offered.

"You have powder and shot?"

Klaus chortled in his nasal voice. "Do we have powder and shot, he wants to know!"

They loaded a pack horse for him with the weapons and ammunition. At length they shared a parting toast from Gutch's finest stock. The samurai left them. At last sight they were lighting the funeral pyres outside the Provender. "Gutch leaves nothing untidy," the stylish innkeeper explained.

And then Gonji took a last turn through the maze of ancient alley canyons, counting the dead *bushi* who had held their posts to the end to buy time for the evacuees. He soon abandoned it when the task had begun to make him feel as unclean as a gravedigger, the lowest of the untouchable caste in his homeland. And just when the morbid analog occurred to him—that by his arguably poor planning he had, in fact, *become* akin to a gravedigger—he found Hildegarde.

He stared down at her a moment, then left the horses to drop on his knees beside her lifeless form. What began as a quiet meditation ended as an emotional storm. He clutched at himself and curled up beside her, weeping bitter tears and trembling in the alley. He'd known no such moment since his youth.

He felt lonelier than ever.

Monetto set his food aside when Zarek fell into his hysterical delirium. The end was nigh. Garth rushed up with him, rubbing his palms helplessly on his thighs.

"I don't want to die," Miklos repeated again and again, tossing from side to side in his fever sweat. *"I'm afraid to die! Not yet—not like this—I'm not ready—I'm not ready!"*

Monetto panted with apprehension, desperate for something to do to ease the man's travail. He tried to give him water, but it wouldn't pass Zarek's throat.

Arvin sat a good distance from the dying man, hands over his ears, banging his head against his knees. Eddings mumbled to himself, eyes averted. Wilf watched, arms stiffened behind him as if he would spring should they call for his assistance.

"He's coming for me—*and I'm not ready!*" Zarek screamed.

"Miklos—Miklos," Aldo comforted, grimacing and supporting his head, "call out to God, man. Scream His name—beg Him to take you to His breast—"

With a final arching of his back, Zarek breathed his last in Monetto's arms.

Gonji returned in time to see the man sag back onto the tunnel floor. He glanced about at all of them grimly, dropping his gaze to share their long silence.

At length he spoke. "Garth—come with me, *bitte*. There's something . . . I must show you."

"More secrets?" Wilf asked petulantly as they shuffled off through the tunnel toward the forest. "Are there any left?"

They paid him no heed, Garth eyeing Gonji anxiously, his aching heart signaling to him in precognition. They gained their steeds and clumped through the forest circumspectly, arriving at the place where Strom's flyblown corpse lay under a bush.

Gonji walked off, allowing Garth space and time to vent his pitiable grief, Gonji himself being touched in a way he had rarely felt in such matters.

When he returned he found Garth still struggling with spates of choked sobbing as he knelt beside his son. When the smith's sorrow had been spent, Gonji spoke with great difficulty.

"Garth, I . . . I would take my life by my own hand, if it would spare you the burden I must add to your grief. I think . . . *choléra* . . . I think it must have been Lorenz who murdered Strom. Can you tell me why?"

*"Nein,"* Garth replied, anguished, shaking his head in denial. "It cannot be . . ."

Gonji recounted the evidence against the city's Chancellor. Garth still refused to accept his son's guilt. Gonji sighed and showed him the partial word dug in the mud, Strom's reed pipe still angling out of the uncompleted second letter.

"What do you suppose he was trying to tell us?" the samurai asked gently.

Garth extracted the pipe, cleaned it absently as he thought, and a slow burning anger clouded his brow. His cheeks began to redden.

*"M—"* Gonji read, throwing up his hands. "—something."

*"'MU,'"* Garth said with certainty. *"Mutter*—mother." His tone was filled with an uncharacteristic contempt.

Gonji's eyes widened. "Explain, *bitte*. I thought your wife was—"

"I prayed she was. *How* I prayed she was. Oh, I never truly believed it, but I prayed that it might be true . . ."

Gonji folded his arms, breathing shallowly, absorbed.

Garth's voice drifted back over the years.

"When I was a young, brash, officer under Klann, you see, I thought the world was mine for the taking. I had my choice of any number of women to take to wife. And of all the beautiful camp followers and titled ladies from among the Akryllonians themselves, from all those I might have chosen in conquered duchies and principalities, I chose perhaps the worst. Olga. My Olga. Lady Olga Thorvald was the most beautiful and exciting woman I had ever seen. Always too beautiful, too damned desirable for anybody's good. Not so different, perhaps, from Wilfred's young hoyden Genya. You understand? I forced myself to pretend that her appetite for the attentions of men would stop at innocent flirtation once we were married. I was a fool. A young, lovesick fool. A warrior out in the marches, fighting campaign after glorious campaign, sometimes is not equipped to fight the battles in his own life, *nicht wahr?* Once, we sailed off in search of lost Akryllon, while Klann's people, the army's families, remained on a sympathetic island kingdom. When I returned, Olga was heavy with child. She gave birth to Lorenz not long after. She tried to convince me that he was mine. But I knew. I knew that he could not be.''

Garth fell to silence for a time. Gonji grew impatient.

''Why have you and your sons maintained this story about your wife's being dead all this time? Why was Strom murdered? What has happened here, Garth?''

The smith peered at his dead son's body. He shuddered. ''They didn't know, at least until recently,'' he breathed with remorse. ''I explained to you, I wasn't sure myself. I only hoped that it were true. But now . . .''

''You're losing me,'' Gonji pressed.

Garth struck his palm with his fist and coughed out an angry sob. ''Gonji, I feel great affection for you, almost as much as for a son. But as God is my witness, I declare that He must have set you the lonely task of breaking old men's hearts—''

Gonji was taken aback; he hadn't needed that. ''There are a lot of broken hearts back there.''

''*Ja-ja,*'' Garth agreed sharply, ''but none worse than mine. It must be that . . . that you're right. But I can't believe it. Olga and Lorenz. He was always her favorite. He *would* have been the one she would have sought out. Yet he gave no indication of knowing. *Why?* What could they possibly have had to gain? How did she even learn that I was here in Vedun? I took such great pains to close the book on my former life.''

He saw Gonji's confusion and suspicion, and went on. ''*All-recht*—the whole story, then. When I knew that Lorenz was not my son, I determined that I should not

397

make the innocent bastard pay for his mother's wrong. I loved him as my own. But I was given in those days to ill temper and a vengeful spirit. In all fairness I must say that these dire consequences are as much my fault as Olga's. Though I persuaded myself that I could forgive her infidelity, my pride drove me to take steps against her ever hurting me again. I took her repeatedly, brutally, I suppose. I quickly impregnated her with Wilfred, and then with Strom. All the while watching her mounting hatred for both me and my sons—"

"And Lorenz," Gonji interrupted on sudden inspiration. "Is he . . . *Klann's* son?"

Garth laughed harshly. *"Nein,* that's the irony of it all. If it were true, this might make sense. But one of the unfortunate side effects of the enchanted coupling of the seven children was that they were rendered sterile. The House of Bel dies with the last Klann personage. I fancy that it was Olga's exalted opinion of herself, as well as her attraction to Klann's kingship, that ultimately did drive her to his bed. It would have been like her to entertain the notion that she alone among all women might defeat the spell and deliver him an heir. By the time of which I speak, I know that she had approached him, but he resisted her charms out of friendship for me. This, of course, was the royal personage I served, whom none of you saw. Had he lived, Mord would never have worked his filth with this army . . ."

He drew a deep breath. "It was during the end of Klann's true glory years, when the quest seemed noble, when the Llorm force alone outnumbered the army you saw here, when small kingdoms were won as easily as the peaceful city of Vedun. We were marking time in a duchy on the continent. Lorenz's true father tracked us down, maddened, demanding him back as his sole heir. He was a minor prince, a fop and a dandy, given to womanizing and a life of dissipation. His family suffered a curse of madness transferred through the males of its line. I think he would have left it lie had the madness not been upon him. Surely Lorenz could not have been the only child of his seed. But he wanted him, tortured, I supposed, by his memories of the red-headed seductress. So he came, making his demands. And faced with the truth, sneering and posturing before me, I killed him in a violent rage. Him and all his party. Klann was angered that I had brought us to war with the island kingdom, forcing us to move on. And Olga— Olga began to fear for her own life. In hatred and fear, one does what one must.

"She seduced Klann at last while he was still furious with me. I knew it, though I made no issue of it with the king. Perhaps all that kept him from my simple, expedient murder was the fact that we shared so much. His sense of gratitude over my shielding his life—who can say? But not long after, while I was on a campaign, I received word that Olga had died suddenly, that the mages and surgeons had been helpless to save her. By this time I had become sufficiently sickened by my own brutality. I had begun to find killing so repulsive that I was considering resigning my commission. It took little urging to convince me to retire to raise my sons. Klann was going to set me up with a house, a piece of land, and a generous stipend to sustain us comfortably. And, I suppose, to ease his conscience. But I suspected the truth of it all, though I wouldn't admit it. So I left without word to anyone as to where I could be found. I journeyed here to Vedun, befriended Flavio, became a follower of the Christ, and said nothing more of my former life.

"But I knew. Deep inside, I knew what they had done. That was why I wished to avoid the banquet. I hoped that Klann's invitation to the chief blacksmith had been made in ignorance, out of some need for service. Then when I saw it was a new Klann, I began to hope that he would not know me. And most of all I hoped and prayed that I had been wrong all those years, that my suspicions were unjustified.

*That she—was—dead.''* He sighed raggedly. "It seems all my hopes and prayers were in vain."

"You could have brought your suspicions to light before," Gonji advised gently.

"What man enjoys admitting to *himself* that he's been a cuckold, much less to others?"

Gonji nodded forlornly.

The smith stared off into empty space. "I just can't believe they would conspire to cause such misery. Fratricide. Klann wouldn't endorse such—"

"You forget," Gonji reminded, "it seems it was *Mord* they conspired with."

Garth grimaced and cast him a look of disbelief. "Maybe she did it all out of vengeance. But can one woman carry in her heart so much hatred? And *Lorenz?* I must know," he said softly. "I will have an answer. Leave me now, *bitte,* to bury my son."

Gonji bowed to him, heartsick to see his renewed grief, and backed away to rejoin Tora. His face bore a repugnant set. He felt numb. Unsure of whether his feelings had died or were merely rallying for a new onslaught.

When he returned to the north tunnel, he found the others eating and drinking in sullen silence. Zarek's body was gone. Monetto tended a cooking fire. Gonji avoided their eyes as he obtained some of the salted beef and fruit, steering clear of the concoction Aldo was stewing. He was glad that Wilf kept to himself, offering not so much as a greeting his way.

The samurai sat cross-legged apart from them and ate quietly. His swords were laid along his right side in a minute effort at peaceful respite.

William Eddings suddenly charged for the pile of pistols Gonji had brought from Vedun. Seizing one, he cocked it and aimed at Gonji.

"Hey, what are you doing, you fool?" Monetto shouted, leaping at him. He wrestled the pistol from his grasp, the

400

hammer clicking uselessly. It hadn't been loaded.

Gonji watched without reaction.

*"Flavio would not want that,"* Eddings roared in Spanish, mimicking Gonji's pronouncement from the speech he'd given them at the alert meeting. Then he began stalking Gonji, railing at him in English, his sword drawn in tearful wrath. Monetto tried to stay him, but Eddings threatened him back with the saber.

Arvin sat nearest Gonji, slumped forward on his bent knees. He was the only one among them who understood English.

"God damn you to *hell,* you bloody yellow devil!" Eddings cried in his ire. "My father is lying back there with a broken skull because of you. I never even had a chance to bury him. Hundreds of people *dead.* And all because of *you.* You and your swaggering bravado—*Flavio would not want that!"*

He postured before Gonji in imitation of his well-known strut, grasping his saber in the manner of a *katana,* flourishing it mockingly through a few techniques Gonji had taught. "Hold your blade higher—stiffen your arms—complete the circle . . . I don't even know what became of my brother and sister-in-law. I'll never see them again. All because *Flavio would not want that."*

"Take it easy, Eddings," Arvin said sternly. "I saw your brother and his wife leave with one of the wagon lines."

"Who asked you?" Eddings fumed. "You lousy *Francais*—you'd bloody well hang yourself as soon as tell an English subject anything close to the truth."

"You're not an English subject anymore, Eddings," Arvin replied. "You gave that up, remember? It's no use blaming him. He told us often enough what the cost of freedom would be. After that our destiny was in our own hands. Sometimes there's nowhere left to run to find freedom. Sometimes you just have to find the courage to stay, each man for himself, somewhere inside him—"

"What the hell are you trying to say?" Eddings demanded.

Arvin shrugged and looked away. "I don't know."

"You—*Jappo!*" Eddings continued, poised to spring like an adder. "*Yoi-suru*—ready! Just like in the catacombs, eh, *sensei?* Stand up and cross with me. I'm bloody mad enough now. You didn't like my form then. Well, try me now. *Stand up.*"

Gonji continued to sit, staring at a point before him, emotionless. Eddings began to tremble. An angry puff of breath whined from his throat. Wilf was rising slowly to move behind him. Monetto stood by, breathless.

Eddings blinked back tears and turned. "Give me those pistols!" he cried. But Monetto lithely bounded over to them and dropped the satchels on the other side of the redoubt.

The distraught Englishman cast about, back and forth, irrational. Then he charged Gonji with a mighty roar, saber held high. Wilf tripped him as he went by, and he and Monetto fell on him, holding him down until he had surrendered in a sobbing heap.

"You should have let him finish," Gonji told them.

Monetto rose, chest heaving. "Now what in hell is that supposed to mean? We've got enough problems around here without you wallowing in self-pity, *sensei.*"

Arvin saw Gonji stiffen, wondering how the warrior would take to Monetto's audacity. But the hard line of the oriental's eyes softened as if with relief.

Monetto bobbed his head. "You told us what to expect. There were no surprises. No one twisted our arms to stay. Even you can't anticipate everything. So stop acting like you've . . . disappointed a bunch of children or something—I don't know," he finished in a rush, turning away in embarrassment.

Arvin lay his head back, eyes closed. "That's right, Gonji," he said in French. "What happened would have

402

happened even if you hadn't come. Maybe worse, *n'est-ce pas?* No one fought more courageously than you. You frightened me out of the fear of death, I'll tell you. There's no scarier sight than that sword of yours in . . ." He was hardly aware any longer that he was speaking loud enough for the others to hear. "You see, it's always been like that with me. I've never had the courage to deal with the ugly things in life. My wife was dying, you know. There was nothing anyone could do. No one but me. She lay on her deathbed, calling out my name, begging me to stay at her side during the final ordeal . . . squeeze her hand . . .

"I couldn't even do that, you see. I—I just slunk off and drank myself into a fine painless stupor until—until word came that it was all right for me to crawl out of my little hole—" He broke down in waves of quiet tears, and he could feel the others looking away, trying to distance themselves from his burden. But at length Arvin recovered and spoke again.

*"Merci, monsieur,"* he thanked the astonished samurai. "I can only wish you had come sooner . . ."


Garth returned, pale and dour of countenance from his ordeal, and the others looked from him to Gonji and back again for the explanation that was not long in coming.

The valiant blacksmith sat on a stone and called Wilf to him. Speaking low but making no effort at excluding the others—save for Eddings, who could not understand and seemed not to care—he recounted to Wilf the tale of woe he had told Gonji. The rest listened in grimly.

He finished, and there was not a sound for a time.

"I'm so very sorry, Garth," Aldo offered in earnest sympathy.

But Wilfred became outraged. "How *dare* you? How dare you keep this from us all these years?"

"Wilfred, I—"

"I know why," Wilf bellowed. "It's because you wanted

nothing to tarnish your image—the pious and humble smith. Don't worry, everyone—I'll survive—I'll crawl away from those who've cuckolded me and change my name and dig a hole somewhere and drag everyone I can in there on top of me—"

*"Wilfred, that's not fair,"* Garth shouted.

"Don't tell me what's fair, old man! Have you been fair to me? To poor Strom, God rest his soul? *Nein,* you've been too busy turning both cheeks to make God smile on you by pampering the bastard son you loved more than your own, who went on to murder my brother and my city. Here is Strom, my idiot shepherd; ah, and Wilfred, my thick-headed apprentice—aren't they lovable? But *this— this* is Lorenz, my shining star, the brainy one in the family." He spat noisily. "Son of the madman *who screwed my wife!"*

The tunnel echoed with the sharp slap that snapped Wilf's head. The others winced.

Wilf turned to him slowly. Garth's face shook, flushed with anger and regret.

"Don't ever hit me like that again," Wilf said, deep and minacious. *"Why,* Papa?" he accused, scowling with confusion. "Why did you give Lorenz the best of everything? Privileges, education, encouragement to advance himself in the world. Strom was happy in his simplicity, but you knew what I wanted. You knew how I chafed to be out on my own, to try my hand at so many things. I know that I am nearly Lorenz's equal in learning ability. Yet you kept drumming into me all those years that I would somehow be sinning against you and God if ever I aspired to anything more than the livery trade. You wouldn't even allow me to love as I wished to. Why?"

Garth clenched his fists before answering. "Because you are too much like me. I see in you the headstrong, ambitious young scalawag that I once was. When I saw how you wanted so many things *I* had wanted, I just didn't want you repeating my mistakes.

"I admit that I feared my hatred of what was done to me so deeply that I thought it might be kindled against Lorenz; so I . . . went too far . . . But I didn't love him more than you boys. You must believe that. I was selfish. I can see that now. Lorenz would outgrow us, outgrow his position in Vedun. He would leave, and the ledger would be clean. But you and Strom, you were all that I had to call my own. Maybe I feared that if I allowed you to grow, you would outgrow me, and I'd be left all alone. A broken old man.

"Wilfred, I ask you . . ." Garth swallowed hard, his whole being seeming to sink. ". . . and I ask Strom, if he be capable of knowing, to forgive me for all the ways you've found me wanting as a father."

Wilf seemed dumbstruck. A second later they were embracing and weeping, apologies and words of affection forming in the emotional maelstrom.

"Garth," Gonji said as he rose very deliberately, "I commend you above all other men I have known. There are times when you exhibit the finest qualities of both my land and yours. I am honored to call you friend." He bowed deeply.

Garth blushed and returned the bow self-consciously, though he seemed preoccupied by the joy of reconciliation to Wilf.

"Well, gentils, I'll drink to that," Monetto said, hefting a cask from the catacomb stores, "and I trust that our accusations and self-torment are spent."

They rested, ate, meditated and prayed, each man wrapped in his own thoughts, seeking his own sphere of peace.

And when dusk arrived and the night wind carried the stark sounds of merriment from the castle in the distance, Gonji rose beneath the flaring cresset and began to arm himself. He harnessed his swords and strapped a dirk inside a thick woollen sock, facing the exit tunnel.

"Mord," he lipped barely above a whisper. "I'm coming for you, Mord . . ." He moved to the firearms and selected two pistols, loaded and spanned them, stuffed them into his *obi,* feeling the twinge of pain in his side from the pressure, the sting of the cut along his lower back.

Wilfred was beside him now, charging a wheel-lock. "Everyone knows why I've got to go."

"I must ask Olga," Garth joined, belting on his baldric and heavy broadsword, "why she has done this. And Lorenz—"

"*Ja,*" Wilf took up, "my half-brother has a lot to answer for."

"Why aid the filthy sorcerer?" Gonji offered in example.

Wilf nodded. "And why kill the little guy? Poor Strom always looked up to him so."

"Wilfred, I must ask you," Garth said with concern, "to use sound judgment, should you encounter your brother. Temper your anger with mercy."

"God's will be done," Wilf said without rancor.

Arvin rose. "Amen to that." He fended off their curious looks with one of his own. "Well, I don't suppose you all mind if I . . . see this through? I need to know. To know myself."

Gonji smiled at him and tossed him a wheel-lock. They began stringing longbows. Then Eddings was standing before Gonji, staring somberly. He looked at Arvin, then spoke.

At length Arvin shook his head and raised an argument. But Eddings shouted him down and tilted his head at Gonji.

"He says he's going along because he wants to be there to see you die," Arvin translated. "There, I told him."

Gonji thought a moment. "Tell Eddings he'll have to stay alive to do that."

Eddings cast the samurai a fell grin to hear Arvin's

translation. Gonji handed him two pistols, and the Englishman spoke again.

"He says he promises he will. Blasted *Anglais* . . ."

"That one's mine," Monetto said when they had strung Gerhard's legendary longbow.

"So sorry, my friend, but you're not going along."

"Now wait a minute, Gonji—how are you going to do it? The tunnel to the dungeons? Who's going to dig your way through—Tumo? I assure you we did a thorough job of collapsing it. The main gate of Castle Lenska? Highly unlikely, unless the garrison dies of fright to see you still alive. So what's left? And who's the best climber here, eh?"

Gonji scratched his head. "Oh, Aldo, I don't know. We've enough good men to mourn."

"If Karl had lived, that bow of his would be with you. He'd want it to be. *Sylva* would want it to be. For one shot. And I won't give it up. Look—I'll get you up on the battlements, that's all. I promise. For Karl . . ."

At length they reluctantly assented. They moved out to the horses, where they sat awhile, armed to the teeth, listening.

"Let's go for it," Wilf said finally. And Gonji could not help remembering those same words coming from another Wilf. So long ago, it seemed.

## Chapter Twenty-five

There was celebration at Castle Lenska, but its tone depended on where one looked. And its opposite, mourning, was no less in evidence.

The drawbridge was down, the portcullis raised, and the gates were thrown open to the encamped remnant of the mercenary companies, those soldiers-of-fortune who hadn't already decided to grab their fortune where it lay and flee this forbidding territory. The free companions' carousal was wild and vulgar, watched over by grim Llorm sentries. Weary and bored, they manned the ramparts over the gatehouses to police the mercenaries' drunken revelry and make certain that no firearms passed inside the walls in defiance of King Klann's orders.

The free companions drank and cavorted in bleary triumph. They staged mock duels and feasted in the wards, still soaked from the long rain. The outer halls were filled with bawdy songs and ribald humor; no servant girl was safe outside her chamber.

Even Tumo was drunk. The cretin giant was an awful caricature of a battlefield casualty, with an eyepatch fashioned of a large pair of pantaloons and bedsheets bandaging half his naked body. Soldiers cracked open kegs of ale for him, with which he washed down the raw slabs of meat he masticated. He bawled and slobbered, tottering about the outer ward and slapping at mercenaries who prodded him with pikes. They wagered on feats of daring. Some paid dearly, when they struck him in tender areas.

Only the towers and gatehouses of the battlements were manned by Llorm sentries now, these from the portion of the garrison left back during the counterattack at the city. The rest were relieved of duty in order to recuperate, to recover from wounds in the overflow of human suffering in the hall sequestered for the sick and injured, or to comfort families of the many dead.

Private chambers were given over to mourning, to Akryllonian families huddled against the bleak promise of the future for the dwindling nomads, to concern for their king.

Klann sat brooding on his dais in the great hall, the restrained merriment about him a blur. He was heavy-lidded and sullen as his vision served up shattered hopes and dreams of futile keeping, the cruel light of events confirming the pessimism of the years. It was really coming to an end. All of it. The dream of Akryllon . . .

The Llorm and the survivors of the trusted 1st Free Company near him sensed his mood and drove themselves into hedonistic wastreling, the sensory glut that allowed brief, merciful forgetfulness. They slowly drifted farther from the dais when they heard the voices of the remaining personages, loosed by his heavy drinking.

The caustic, accusing counsel of the rational pair who suffered within. And, now and again—more often as he fell deeper into his cups—the mouth-gaping guttural noises of the Tainted One.

Hatred bloomed anew for the sorcerer he had so trusted. The magician had failed him. Then he saw Lady Olga Thorvald sidling through the crowd, her vain, persistent hope still in her eyes. When he saw her now he wondered at the mad folly of his dead brother's heart, he who had chosen her fleeting warmth over the vision of sweet return. For so he had marked the collapse of the dream of return to Akryllon; it had begun with the surrender to her seduction.

He thought then of Garth Iorgens, the mighty and faithful general she had brought low. And then of Iorgens' words . . . *Mord works against you.* He gazed about at the citizens in the hall with sudden clarity, saw their sickliness, their pallor. As if they'd been bled of life essence . . .

When she drew near the dais, he extracted his sword and leveled it at her serpent's heart, and she fled the hall in tears. Klann started to return the blade to its sheath, but then he stopped. He laid it across his lap and considered its gleaming edge.

Mord became desperate. His efforts at ordering the soldiers to round up the hostages Genya had freed proved futile. His confident sense of place in the cosmos had been dashed in a single night—the night when he had been told he would rise, resplendent in pure power.

The Dark Master had deceived and abandoned him. The soldiers had lost all fear and respect, refused to obey. Even the mercenaries in his private employ sneered and held out opened palms, trebling their price for their services. Klann was unapproachable. The Dark Lord turned a deaf ear to his pleas. He was alone.

*A weak conjurer of smoky serpents . . .*

He needed ritual human sacrifice to increase his mana. And even the anointed one had escaped, thanks to the madman's work. His attempts to sense her presence failed.

He found the traitor and his mother in the prison tower Mord had made his own.

"Did you find her yet?" Mord fumed.

"Mmm, *that* one," Lorenz chuckled, eyes shining. "She's a terror. You'd best tackle her yourself." He showed the bandage where Genya had cut him. "Then when you've done with her, tamed her a bit, pass her along to me, won't you?"

Mord glared at the madman balefully. And then Thorvald was badgering again.

"All my work for you—my son's work—gained me nothing, Mord. You promised you'd influence Klann, intercede for me with the king. *You've done nothing!* He won't even look at me! Liar!"

"None of us have gained what we bargained for in this business," Mord countered. "Klann is removed from my counsel as well now."

Lorenz chortled, gazing out a tower window at the mountains on the horizon. "Today Castle Lenska, tomorrow a palace on the Rhine," he rhapsodized. "Next year—perhaps the throne of England herself . . ."

"I know what you've done," Olga snarled at Mord. "You withheld all the intelligence Lorenz brought you for your own purposes. Told Klann only what was to your advantage. You wanted their destruction all along. Suppose I told the king how you manipulated behind his back?"

Mord moved toward her. "That would be . . . ill advised."

She held fast. "I don't fear you anymore. No one does. You're nothing without people's belief in what you can do. Isn't that so? You're nothing alone—*ahhh!*" He grabbed her wrist and twisted in his surprisingly strong, wiry grasp.

"Would you like to see what I can do?"

She grunted, a piercing whine escaping her throat. But she continued to struggle. "When have you ever had to resort to force before?" she screamed at him.

Mord stiffened. Lorenz clapped behind him. Olga broke free and bolted from the tower. Mord turned at the sound of Lorenz's clucking.

"Ah, women," the traitor reflected. "They don't understand about power, do they? I do. I know what you plan. You're holding it all back in reserve, aren't you? You've great plans up those ample sleeves. Plans of empire. I know. I know because I share them. We are of a kind in vision. I think we can help each other."

Mord regarded the madman's grandiose ranting a moment, then spoke patronizingly. "Yes, you do understand, don't you? I knew you were special, different from the others. Not bound by petty allegiances and provincial ambitions. You're right. Empire beckons. And it all begins with the . . . partaking of that girl you allowed to escape. Find her. Bring her here. And we shall begin to open the way . . ."

Lorenz jumped down from his perch on the sill. "*Ja,* I shall find the vixen, and we will cement our alliance with her soft flesh, eh?"

"Yes, our alliance . . ."

## Chapter Twenty-six

Wilf inhaled a shuddering breath of cold night air.

"Genya," he exhaled.

The night was clear and crisp, the moon a huge drooping disc, pale as if in sickly jaundice over what it had brought in its fullness.

They rode around half the perimeter of Castle Lenska, making their plans, chafing to use the weapons that festooned every man. They cursed in frustration to see the inviting channel opened through from drawbridge to inner gatehouse, knowing the impossibility of passing that gauntlet, despite the drunken aspects of the soldiers and the staggering giant.

They could wreak holy havoc and still never get close to Mord.

"Mord," Gonji kept reminding. "We work as a team until we get Mord. After that you're on your own. I don't care what you do or when you make your exit—except you," he added to a noncommittal Aldo Monetto.

They left the horses and approached the castle on foot. They had chosen the eastern rise of wall as their best bet. From a high vantage it had seemed only nominally manned. And the only Llorm sentries were atop the armorer's tower at the northeast corner. The prison tower, where the wyvern had late roosted, was shunned of men. Gonji made a weak joke in explanation of that fact in an effort to lighten their mood a tad. They would scale the wall near that southeast tower.

"There will be no guns within the walls but ours," Garth observed, "that is, if any semblance of Klann's order is still maintained."

They were all comforted to hear that, especially Arvin, who patted the four he carried, each in turn, to the others' fleeting amusement. "I was never very sharp with the sword, you'll recall."

Gonji removed his dented sallet and fingered the bullet crease for luck. He gazed up at the *ugetsu*—the pale and mysterious moon that always followed the rain.

"I've seen castles taken by means of sapper action," he noted. "Small parties of raiders—"

"Castles as big as this?" Wilf asked.

He cleared his throat. "Well, maybe not so big as Lenska."

"By so few raiders as we are?"

"Perhaps not so few," he allowed reluctantly, "but they didn't have you along, Wilf. You and your passionate love."

Wilf blushed. "Or you."

Gonji smiled. *"Hai*—or as many personal reasons . . . We have no idea what Mord may raise, but that's the least of our problems, at least at first. But I have a feeling there weren't many soldiers who had time to sing his chant last night. No supporters, no power. That's what Tralayn said."

"We've got to do what an army might not," Monetto told them. "Can you all climb that?" They all nodded in assent, even the boorish Eddings.

A booming from the walls startled them. A crash in the western foothills, followed by harsh laughter in the wind.

"They're playing with the bombards," the biller explained with a sudden enthusiasm. "That's good. Let them make all the noise they want—which reminds me—the largest mortar is set on the east wall. I used to be stationed here, you know. We all took our turn manning the big guns . . ."

"Forget it," Gonji said. "You get us up, that's all. Is it on the outer curtain?"

"No, I'm afraid. It sits on that tall middle bailey wall.

413

Climbing that is what bothers me most. Until we reach it, it's all killing ground. We're spotted once and fired on—" He made a throat-slitting gesture.

They made their plan and discussed the timing and signals they'd need for coordination.

"Let's do it," Gonji said. They shared a brief prayer led by Garth, ending with the petition composed by Gonji.

They jogged over the tors to the east, keeping low, and forded the river's shallow rapids. Then up the shale and scrub of the steep hill that supported the eastern wall. They reached the moat without compromise, panting but offering thanks that they'd made it that far.

Monetto whirled the grapple and missed engaging it the first time. It clinked and fell, and they flattened, motionless for three or four minutes. Either the noise in the wards had enveloped the sound or the outer bailey wall was unattended on this side.

They peered up. Still only one Llorm burgonet was to be seen, that atop the armorer's tower, a sentry who strolled the turret, whose walk they had timed. From his vantage he would not see them climb, but the outer wall allure was entirely within his view and illuminated by the moon for half its track.

Gonji hissed and drew a bead on the turret.

"That would be one helluva shot," Wilf surmised.

"Gerhard could do it," Monetto said. "Here—take his bow."

Gonji did so and handed his own to Arvin. He smiled to feel its heft. "I won't shoot unless I must. If he's not alone up there, we're finished."

Monetto swung the grapple again and flung it. This time it caught in an embrasure and held. They stilled their breathing, aiming pistols up to the walls. Nothing. The athletic biller skimmed across the moat and struck the narrow, packed-earth bank. Then he scampered up the wall with amazing speed and agility, gained the merlons, and hid in an embrasure until the guard had circled away again.

He disappeared from view, and just as the others became anxious, the second grapple rope dropped from the allure, farther down the wall. They ascended by twos, slowly and cautiously, Gonji waiting for last to cover their climb.

They found the outer curtain devoid of soldiers, but despair crumbled their sense of accomplishment as they crouched in shadow below the armorer's tower: They were trapped atop a twenty-foot thick wall of rock. Thirty feet below them was the outer ward, an empty killing ground bounded by sheer wall. The only thing that broke the dark enclosure was the impassable stone tunnel arch of an unattended postern gate. They had to breach the gap and scale a wall still thirty feet higher. On it could be heard the voices of many men, laughing and chattering. European voices. Should any of them glance down over the crenelled wall—

"Well, that's that," Arvin said almost hopefully, but he was ignored.

"Monetto—there'll be stairways in the towers?" Gonji inquired.

"*Si,* take your pick—the armory or the prison tower. Shall I knock?"

Gonji cursed in frustration. Iron-bound portals blocked their way. Wilf saw their looks and slammed a fist against rock.

"Well, dammit," he whispered, "don't sit there getting stiff. Gonji—you said there was always a way—"

They stared at him uncertainly.

He shook his head as if scolding them. "Remember—remember that time when you first came? How we brazened our way through them? At the gatehouse?" He licked his lips and scrambled out into the moonlight.

They all gasped. The pressure had driven him over the brink . . .

"Hey! Hey! You, up there!" he shouted at the turret sentry. "Open that God damn door! Do you think I'm

415

gonna stay out here all night?"

The others froze in the shadows and cursed in panic. Gonji craned his neck upward. The sentry peered down at Wilf and pointed his crossbow, calling out a challenge.

"Open that friggin' door!" Wilf pointed at the armorer's tower. The sentry jabbered back. "I don't speak Spanish— just open the damn door—they locked me out over here." Indicating the prison tower.

The sentry turned and called out.

"Holy Jesus!" Monetto swore. "Here comes the swarm."

Gonji pushed them all toward the tower door. "Hold your guns till last. *No noise.* Use the garrots."

They could hear the bootfalls clumping up the stairs. Their hearts pounded triple-time. A scraping and a hesitation—the sentry on the turret spotted the waiting *bushi* and yelled, but did not see Gonji, drawing back on his bow.

The door grated open as the samurai launched his shot. The two crossbowmen who pushed out first were garroted by Monetto and Garth. Gonji's shaft skimmed the wall and tore into the throat of the leaning sentry. He spun backward and fell out of sight.

They waited breathlessly for an alarm. None came. Arvin and Eddings held the incredulous Llorm squad at bay, long pistol barrels angled in deadly promise. The two garroted men slumped to the stone walk.

Gonji strode through the captives and into the tower as a bombard blasted another volley for the mercenaries' entertainment. Wilf followed quickly.

*"Un—deux—trois—quatre,"* Arvin told the four Llorm who stood with hands high. He showed them one pistol for each of them and laid a finger across his lips.

Monetto and Eddings dragged the two bodies into a garderobe and donned their uniforms and armor as the others covered them. A curious duty officer mounted the stairs. Wilf took him silently, strangling him with a

416

trembling, bulging arm.

Gonji mounted the spiral stairway to the door that led out onto the middle bailey wall, while Garth hurried down into the armory.

The samurai cracked open the door and espied the scene along the castle's tallest curtain. At least a dozen mercenaries lounged on the wall in the immediate area. Most sat gambling and guzzling near the mortar. Beyond—the main gatehouse was alive with Llorm, their security concentrated there due to the heavy traffic of free companions whom Klann didn't trust. What he could see of the inner bailey looked like a festival ground, and Tumo bellowed somewhere in the outer bailey. Torches and pennons fluttered in the night breeze all along the walls. Dogs and sheep, cattle and horses ran freely through the wards. And among them, their purpose concealed from his view by the long roof over the kitchens and bakehouse, a long line of mercenaries formed, angled toward the armorer's tower. He blew a breath and cursed. Then he saw the pair of adventurers ambling for his door.

Down at ground level, a black powder magazine was lifted by two grunting Llorm and carried out to the ward. The sentries slammed and barred the door. When they turned back to their posts, they saw the twin barrels aimed at them from the landing. They signaled to the officers at the counters and weapon vaults as they slowly unlimbered their arbalests.

"Hold it—stay your hands," the smith warned.

"Iorgens!" a surprised officer exclaimed, his face screwed up in disbelief. "These are powder magazines—are you mad?"

"If you fire those things in here—"

"*Ja,*" he replied, smiling thinly, "*quite* mad. Now leave your posts and come up with me. Slowly and carefully. Lay down those crossbows."

They began to comply nervously. A door opened on the

next level, and two Llorm emerged from a chamber, startled by the sight. Garth threatened them similarly and coaxed them into joining the somber procession upward.

"I don't know what you have in mind," the officer who knew Garth told him, "but you can't possibly succeed."

"That depends on what I have in mind."

Arvin joined him with the four from the outer bailey level, and they were all locked into a tight chamber with no window facing out. They hurled oaths and words of discouragement after the departing *bushi*.

"Holy stars above," Arvin intoned in amazement. "We've taken a whole tower without a shot—*mon Dieu!*"

The two mercenaries were admitted from the middle bailey curtain by the Llorm officer who closed the iron portal behind them. They emerged onto the landing to find the deadly blades of Wilf and Gonji awaiting them. Four lightning two-handed slashes—one man tipped over the balustrade and down to the magazine level.

The Llorm officer—Aldo Monetto—steeled himself and waved for Eddings to join him. They pulled their cloaks around them and strode casually out onto the allure, hands clasped behind them, buffes snapped shut. Their bows were slung over their backs.

"Gentlemen," Monetto spoke in an official tone, "get up and follow me, please." He had spoken Italian. A few translations were blurted.

"What for?"

"Without questions, please. We have an urgent duty."

"Who the hell you kiddin'? We're *off* duty." Grunts of support.

"No one is off duty now," he replied steadily, feeling Eddings waver at his side.

"Go screw yourself." Surly laughter as they warily resumed their gambling.

Monetto strode up calmly and kicked the speaker square in the face, knocking him off the wall and down onto the thatched roof of the kitchen and bakehouse building twenty feet below. He lay motionless in the depression his fall had made. The others were paralyzed by the immediacy of it, then they awkwardly went to their sword hilts.

Monetto and Eddings tossed their cloaks open and drew wheel-locks. The mercenary band fell back.

"We ain't allowed to wear no friggin' pistols here—how come you can?"

"I'm an officer of His Majesty. Now hear me well. We've just had word that werewolves are on their way to attack the castle. They're on the move. The gates are going to be shut, and we're preparing for a siege. Do you remember what it was like last night?" He didn't need an answer. "Then you'll please move to the mortar at once, charge it, and load it. Now. Quietly. And without panic." He pointed at the great-mouthed mortar barrel.

As they clumsily pursued the work, Monetto saw the urgency sweeping the ward below. The Llorm were reacting in confusion to the locked tower door. The lines of men refilling powder flasks there and at the far wall were beginning to disperse in bewilderment.

The mercenaries finished loading the mortar. The bombard on the far wall boomed again amid cheers and applause from its excited crew.

"All right, now angle that thing in on the wards," Monetto directed. "If those things get in here, we want to be ready."

The adventurers studied them narrowly, saw for the first time that their longbows were not the weapons of Llorm troops.

"*You're* no Llorm!" one of the mercenaries growled, moving away from the mortar. Eddings shot him.

"*Gracias* and good night," Aldo said, pushing two drunks off the allure at once, drawing and slashing his way through the stunned men with his axe. Eddings emptied another pistol. Two survivors broke away from them,

419

shouting for help.

Seizing a torch, Monetto cranked the ratchet that set the mortar's trajectory. Eddings helped him turn it. With the first reports of gunfire, chaos had broken out below, men sobering immediately. Llorm troopers tried to restore order, to make sense of the scene on the middle bailey wall. Panic gripped the ward when they saw the mortar angled to fire within the castle fastness.

Monetto touched it off.

Soldiers began streaming up the stairs at the tower corners. At the armory tower, Gonji and Wilf had emerged from one portal, Garth and Arvin from another. The mortar blasted with a thunderous explosion, the cast iron ball whistling high above Castle Lenska, its return spine-chilling to see.

Gonji and Wilf rained shafts into the mounting troops, pitching them backward into their fellows. Arvin's pistols barked from the roof of the great hall, to which he and Garth had dropped. The smith was a frightening apparition, axe and broadsword readied for a plunge into their midst.

On the middle bailey wall, Monetto and Eddings jumped for joy to see the great iron ball scatter a dozen troops and steeds with its shattering impact, fragments felling a few. Eddings' eyes gleamed with battle frenzy as he became caught up in it.

"Look out there!"

They picked off two men along the allure near the prison tower with shaft and pistol, but crossbow quarrels began to hiss by and shatter around them.

"Did you see how they did that? Do you think you can help me do it?" Monetto indicated the mortar, and Eddings bobbed his head readily, rose and squeezed off his last pistol shot. Using the mortar barrel for cover, they began clearing and reloading. Monetto pointed at the powder magazine abandoned in the ward below. "I used to be pretty good at aiming this thing . . ."

"Monetto—get out of here!" Gonji was shouting, halfway along the allure to them. "You're through."

"Not yet—just let me try something. Distract them for me, then get along before they pinpoint you—"

Gonji cast about, grabbed a torch. He glanced at the gatehouse. The Llorm had turned to direct their fire southward, clustering at the front of the battlements. He looked down at the gate as the great blast of wind ruffled his clothing and flared the torch. The mercenaries in the ward, running for their confiscated guns when they had come under fire, were turning back inside again, empty-handed. And out in the forest, something moved. Smoke. And sudden outbursts of flame—a flash fire. The drawbridge was being raised.

The samurai heard the howl of the werewolf, and Tumo tumbled into the middle ward with Simon on his back, the great axe buried between his shoulder blades. The giant shrieked and beat at the back of his head.

"Simon—it's Simon!" Wilf cried needlessly in glee. Gonji only nodded in awe.

The soldiers attempting to scale to the allure froze now, indecisive. Wilf resumed his arrow attack.

"Get out of here, Monetto," Gonji yelled over his shoulder, flinging the torch down the stairwell of the armorer's tower.

"You just get Mord!" The mortar boomed and sizzled the air to crash its ball into the southwest corner of the ward, nearer still to the powder kegs. The crazed mercenaries on the opposite wall took up the idea and angled their weaker bombards toward the *bushi,* filling them with stone shot.

Gonji's torch caught in the tower powder magazine. The resounding explosion cast heavy stone clear across the ward, felling men, shattering the kitchens and ripping the foundation from the tower. It sank ten feet and began to totter on its uneven mooring. Black smoke fumed for fifty yards across the open ward. Wilf was knocked flat on the allure, and the concussion dumped Arvin and Garth down from the roof and onto the veranda of the long hall. They shook it off, grinning at each other with streaked, sooty faces, and dropped to the street amongst their bedazzled enemies. Gonji and Wilf anchored their weapons and bolted the fulminating tower area.

"It was that damned Monetto's idea," Gonji called out, shaking a fist at the biller before he and Wilf sprang down to the still intact bakehouse roof. Flames spread rapidly to the crumbling kitchens, and servants ran everywhere, screaming.

Wilf and Gonji slashed their way through the fleeing soldiers who recognized them, quickly skittering toward the hall, where Arvin's pistol blared in the vestibule.

Out in the ward, unimpeded by the fire and thunder and pounding of feet and panicked steeds, Simon dug fore and hind talons into Tumo's pulpy flesh. He clung like some parasitic thing, and when he found space between the great flailing arms that beat at what Tumo could no longer see, he clamped powerful canine jaws down on the windpipe, and ripped.

All along the southern ramparts, wide-eyed sentries pointed.

Below—frantic mercenaries, fighting with gate guards over firearms and capstans. The drawbridge, portcullis, and gates were shut.

At the edge of the burning forest—the shapeless black mass that began to take form as it neared its quarry; the wailing and writhing of tormented shades out of perdition; the blackfire tracery, darker than the night, of unearthly claws and the gaping maw that seemed capable of swallowing sanity itself.

The Hell-Hound approached, scorching the earth with its touch from another world.

## Chapter Twenty-seven

"It's just the bombards, sire, that's all," the Llorm officer assured. "The adventurers are still—you know—frenzied from battle. They're undisciplined; it takes them days sometimes to—"

"I tell you I heard *pistols,*" Klann argued from where he stood on the dais, striving to listen, "here in the castle walls, where I've forbidden it."

General Gorkin hurried up to him, a questioning look on his face. He began to urge the soldiers in the hall to rouse themselves from their stupor; some had already fallen asleep and were kicked awake, murky-eyed and heads spinning.

Klann unsheathed his long blade and waved for his personal Llorm guards to accompany him out into the halls.

The explosion of the armorer's tower knocked them off their feet, the parquet floor splitting in places. Women screamed in the hall as they tumbled; some of the roisterers began to heave.

Bewildered by it all, King Klann shuffled out to see the scramble of men through the halls. A trio of Llorm spotted him and dashed toward him. "Your Majesty—*werewolves* without. They've killed Tumo. And we're under attack by bandits—"

"They've seen the samurai among them—"

"And something else," another man added breathlessly. "Some monstrous thing glowing in the forest—it's set the woods ablaze—*it's coming here.*"

"The drawbridge is raised," his commander growled. "Nothing can get in here now."

And then Mord was rushing up to them, panic-stricken, blaring something about a Hell-spawned beast and railing at them to take defensive measures. He darted past them, shouting all the while.

There were more gunshots—this time unmistakable—just outside the great hall's vaulted foyer.

"Get the king back inside the banquet hall!" Gorkin was ordering.

The Llorm produced their weapons now and were pressing unwilling mercenaries back toward the hall to defend the king. Officers began shouted arguments concerning chances of moving King Klann to the safety of the central keep. And then Klann allowed himself to be swept along by a tide of elite guards as horsemen clattered sharply over the stone floor of the corridors and steel clashed amid shouts and mortal cries.

Mord knew his peril. Before anyone had reported them, he sensed the approach of predator and prey—Wolverangue, the Hell-Spawn, whom he had invoked; and the bestial captive spirit that roamed in protection of the territory, the werewolf, that creature of conflicting forces Mord had never come to understand.

He swept through the middle bailey tunnels until he reached a narrow corridor to the great hall. Pushing past frightened, scurrying troops, he spotted Klann amidst a press of protective bodies.

"Milord! Milord king!" he bellowed in his thunderous voice. "Wolverangue has come—the Hell-Hound! It must not enter these walls, lest it destroy us all. They must stop it."

The sorcerer rushed on, sensing the girl's presence near the chapel at the northwest drum tower. His evil soul roiled in panic. There must be a way to control the Hell-Hound. He simply could not think of it in his weakened state. Perhaps if he had even a small influx of life energy, a single sacrifice—the girl he had anointed for the Dark Master. His Master must be angry with him that he had not completed the sacrifice. That was it, that was it . . .

He dragged her out from under the pew where she had been cringing, pulled her along by the hair. She fought like a wildcat, beating and clawing at him. He caught the hand that held the dagger and twisted the weapon out of her grasp. She kicked and snarled.

He slapped her soundly with the back of a gloved hand, knocking her senseless. Then he bore her along over a shoulder, taking the long way around the middle bailey hall, descending as soon as he could to the cellar level, then the subcellar. On toward the dungeons beneath his own tower.

There would be no one to stop him, and he would soon have the power he needed. When he neared the foundation of the central keep gatehouse, he narrowly missed being crushed by the collapse of a mountain of stone. A searing blast of heat flashed at his face. He would have to cut across a ward to reach the prison tower.

The Hell-Hound was at the gatehouse, burning its way through! Nothing could stop it. It would move over the earth, impervious to harm, until it destroyed the one it had come for.

For the first time he realized why the prey had led it here.

Garth and Arvin ran inside the great hall, which gave them access to Lenska's maze of inner corridors. They turned right, mingling with baffled mercenaries and Llorm alike, who stumbled to and fro, frantically inquiring into the nature and number of the enemy, reluctant to find out for themselves.

"Iorgens," a voice called ahead of them. Three Llorm charged them, swords and bucklers upraised in combative postures.

Arvin pulled free Gonji's bow and fumbled out a shaft. "Why don't you wear a damned close-helmet, *monsieur?*" The Frenchman grumbled. He dropped the arrow.

Garth tore into them with sword and axe, downing a man with the first pass and driving the other two back along the corridor.

"Why do you do this, Iorgens?" one Llorm cried. Arvin's shaft spun him down with a clatter. The last man was disarmed by the collapsing X-blow of Garth's twin arms. The smith leveled his broadsword, breathing hard. "Now . . . why don't you tell me . . . where I can find the blasted sorcerer . . ."

"If I knew that, I'd go after him myself," the man asserted.

Garth lowered his guard and turned. Arvin's shout came a second too late. The Llorm lunged for his blade and brought it up from the floor while on one knee. Their blade points plunged home simultaneously. Garth's lower left side began leaking blood through his pierced breastplate. But the Llorm yelled out a cry of mortal agony.

"Oh, Garth . . ." Arvin whined to see the blood.

"Never mind . . . let's move on . . ."

They turned a corner and ran head on into two mercenaries. Arvin clawed out his last pistol. The brigands halted and held up warding hands.

"The sorcerer—where is he?" Arvin snarled.

"Probably with the king. In the banquet hall." They backed away anxiously. One of them recognized Garth from the battle for Vedun. His eyes widened. "They're here!" They turned and sprinted off when they saw Arvin put up the weapon. He reached for a shaft, but Garth stayed his arm and called him back the way they had come.

Cutting through the helter-skelter dash of panicked troops, Wilf and Gonji used the fuming smoke and dust to conceal their run for the great hall. They gained two steeds and bounded for the portico steps. A press of Llorm blocked the archway.

Gonji nocked a cloth-yard shaft and drew back on Gerhard's mighty bow. Grunting with the searing pain in his ribs, he fired. The armor-piercer arrow tore clean through a hauberk of one man and entered the midsection of the soldier behind him.

Kicking the steed's flanks, he trampled through the falling bodies, catching a fleeting glimpse of Wilf's pained outcry. The hook of a pikeman's *ranseur* sliced open the young smith's side.

They charged through the vestibule corridor, slashing at the confused men who raised steel more in self-defense than attack. A well-aimed halberd, deflected by Gonji's *katana*, dug into his horse's shoulder. The shrieking steed tumbled, tossing Gonji to the stone floor. Rolling with the fall, he scurried after his lost weapons, retrieving the Sagami in time to parry a blow and slam down a saber-wielding mercenary.

Wilf clattered about, swinging and stamping astride his mount, clinging close to the withers. "Genya!" he roared. "Where is Genya?" His side leaked dark blood, though the wound had not been deep.

The samurai disarmed a mercenary and caught him up at the throat with a ridge hand. He held him against a wall, eyes glinting with savage determination.

"The sorcerer, brigand," he grated in Spanish. "Where is Mord?"

"I—I don't know—I *swear,*" the man choked out. Gonji increased the pressure.

"And Klann?"

"The hall—the banquet hall—" He pointed weakly.

Gonji kicked his downed blade far down the corridor, and the bandit ran off without it. Wilf stopped him, aiming a pistol. The free companion's face was a mask of terror.

"Do you know the servant Genya?" Wilf demanded.

"I don't know any servants," the man cried, slipping away, eyes intent on the wheel-lock.

"Come on, Wilf—" Gonji slung the longbow and quiver.

The young smith swung down from the horse and brought his bow, the pistol still at the ready. Two Llorm recognized them and came on. The first raised his arbalest, and Wilf's echoing pistol bowled him over. Gonji took the other man down with two efficient sword cuts.

Then they saw Arvin and Garth running toward them, and the four were reunited with cries of gleeful relief.

"The hall," Arvin shouted.

"We know." Gonji turned them down the corridor

toward the struggling band of Llorm and mercenaries outside the doors of the banquet hall.

Wilf saw his father's wounded state. "Look, Papa," he breathed, showing the blood. "Matching wounds, *nicht wahr?*" Garth shook his head in disapproval.

In the banquet hall, Klann took up a defensive posture behind an overturned table. Others were similarly upset. Llorm officers barked out orders of deployment, but the mercenaries had demurred, many of them attempting to quit the place, while faithful troops herded them back to defend the king. Several men were killed in the in-fighting. Bodies blocked the arched doors agape.

"Shut those damned doors!" Gorkin bellowed.

The werewolf howled in the vestibule of the great hall, and the fleeing mercenaries performed a swift about-face, dragging and pushing the dead and injured and jamming inside the doors.

Unnoticed in the shouting and din, the four *bushi* slipped into the hall, fanning out quickly. Wilf and Arvin ascended the stairs on two sides of the gallery; Gonji and Garth hunkered low, helms tipped away from the pitched defenders, pushing close behind stumbling mercenaries.

The doors were shut and barred.


The bombards on the far wall roared and tossed stone shot high into the air to sail over the walls at Monetto and Eddings' left. The mercenaries hooted and hastily reloaded; it had become a doomsday game to them as madness swept the walls.

Somewhere below, the werewolf snarled among screaming men and roiling smoke and dust.

Monetto touched off the mortar again, the cast iron shot lobbing among the stars. Another bombard on the west wall, overcharged by its crew, exploded, dislodging chunks of ashlar and strewing lifeless bodies.

The *bushi's* mortar round struck among the powder magazines. The ward went up in thunder and flash fire.

Aldo Monetto and William of Lancashire bellowed in

triumph. Then Eddings was slapped backward by the impact of a quarrel. He was killed instantly by the shot that penetrated his heart.

Monetto cried out in anguish, saw the soldiers mounting the stairs again, roaring vengefully at the prison tower. He grabbed a powder keg and poured out a thin line as bolts hissed by. Snapped up a torch and touched off the trail of black powder as he launched himself off the allure to the bakehouse roof below. As he regained his feet and scurried over the rooftop, the explosion tore the eastern middle curtain's allure to shreds, bowling him over. He rolled down the slope, caught the thatching at the edge, hung full length, and dropped behind the flaming kitchens.

Already the roofs were catching, the heat almost unbearable. He circled the long way, snapping shut his buffe. Then he was a Llorm officer again, racing among the panicked men and hurling conflicting orders at them.

He paused to feel the fervent heat that beat the ward in waves; saw the Llorm react to the great hissing column of steam from the moat. The barbican had collapsed, and the portcullis glowed red hot.

"You, there!" he called. "Stay out of the keep—the werewolves are everywhere! No, not the great hall, you idiots—the invaders have taken it!"

He made his way toward the hall into which his friends had disappeared. "Hey—follow me," he ordered three reluctant mercenaries in Spanish. They gained the hall and turned into the right corridor. He stopped in his tracks, whirled and tore into them with his axe, downing all three bewildered mercenaries.

But he'd been spotted. A soldier pointed. Heads turned to view him. Llorm. They charged him, shouting that he was a raider, an impostor.

Monetto's heart sank; he had lost his bow. No pistol. Only his biller's axe. He stood his ground.

Then they were skidding to a halt, their attention diverted. With a blood-curdling howl, the werewolf hurtled into the hall, lashing out with his huge broadaxe, scattering them. Monetto saw the burned fur, especially about the ruff; the many wounds, new and old.

And then the Beast was approaching him. Monetto tore off his helm.

"Hey—it's me, it's me! Ho-ho, am I glad to see you! Look—big axe, little axe—we can hold them, huh?"

Simon growled something he couldn't make out, and then they were under assault again. Monetto clapped on his helm as crossbows clacked, bolts striking the Beast. A swarm of desperate men, bent on gaining the exit, charged the bleeding Beast.

Furiously scything his axe through their numbers, Simon hewed a dozen men to pieces, Monetto concentrating on confused stragglers who stayed their hands an instant too long to see his Llorm uniform. Growling and frothing, Simon now and then stopped to rip bolts from his body. Monetto exclaimed in sympathetic pain to see it.

Then a spearing Llorm pierced Simon's back, causing the werewolf to shrill at the ceiling and drop his weapon as Monetto felled the attacker.

Aldo was knocked to the floor by a press of trampling bodies. When he regained his feet, Simon was gone, raging down another corridor. Monetto found himself surrounded by desperate soldiers. Alone.


## Chapter Twenty-eight


Gonji, Garth, Wilf, and Arvin quietly assumed strategic positions in the locked banquet hall. By the time alert troops had recognized any of them and commanded attention, they had drawn their beads.

*"Hold your fire, or the king dies,"* Gonji roared above the din, pulling back hard on Gerhard's powerful longbow.

Only three crossbows were present among the disorganized troops. All were behind the same banquet table that covered Klann from Gonji's fire. They came up to readiness, but the king halted them and stared. Gorkin and two elite guards raised themselves around the king, but they were caught in a crossfire: Arvin stood on one side of the gallery, his last pistol aimed into them; the musicians scuttled off to see Wilf's threatening posture on their side of the gallery, shaft nocked and bow drawn; Garth held back four footmen with his axe and broadsword; Gonji's eyes promised death from the sallet's slit visor.

"We've come for Mord, Klann," the samurai declared. Women and children could be heard whimpering under tables. "Deliver us the sorcerer, and we'll go without further trouble."

Klann looked furious, disbelief creasing his features to see the undying enemies who had invaded his sanctum. He seemed to be struggling in indecision. Quaking with an internal vibration, he raised his long blade when his eyes settled on Garth.

"Iorgens . . ." The name whistled out between gritted teeth. The primitive bellow of the Tainted One issued from his swelling throat as his head rolled toward the vaulted rafters.

The soldiers charged. Gorkin was the first to die, as Arvin's wheel-lock roared and belched black smoke. The banquet hall erupted in frenzied fighting.

Gonji's shaft tore through a faithful guard who leaped before his king. The samurai began running, a bolt sizzling the space he had occupied to chunker into a wall. He nocked and fired on the run, dropping the nearest threatening soldier.

Wilf poured his cloth-yard arrows down from behind a gallery column, studded quickly with quarrels. A crossbowman fell. Then another. The gaffle-time required to reload the weapons rendered them useless for long seconds while the raiders exacted their toll.

Arvin began unleashing Gonji's bow on the soldiers who scaled to the gallery after him. Garth, positioned on his side of the hall, took men down with bellows of battle fervor, slowing their advance.

His quiver at last emptied, Gonji flung away Gerhard's longbow and surged into their numbers with raging swords.

Women and children, voicing their terror, took to a rear door and streamed from the banquet hall, joined by free companions who had lost heart and could think only of escape.

Garth's propelling, razor steel began to waver as his wounds drained his strength. Klann cursed in his wrath, repeatedly calling out the smith's name, inching toward him behind his battery of protectors.

The samurai engaged in a running swordplay, leaping over tables to cross with Llorm swordsmen by ones and twos, stringing them out, his *katana* skewering the nearest attackers from unimaginable angles of thrust, while he mystically reacted in defense with the shorter *wakizashi* to turn the steel of their trailing fellows.

The oriental cut a blood swath toward the king, implacably, inexorably, though every twist of his body shocked his injured left side.

A scream from the gallery—Arvin pitched over the balustrade, still clutching Gonji's bow, dead before he struck the floor.

Gonji leapt over downed bodies of his foes as he made his way toward Klann. The elite guard split their number, half of them poising to take on the samurai, their eyes filled with apprehension. He slapped off his bobbing sallet and crossed his blades in deadly invitation, black eyes panning their sweating faces. Their leader cursed and lunged—

A twisting parry-slash—a turning undercut and a balletic turn to deflect a downward crashing blow—three silver-taloned gleaming edges raking through mortal screams—

Only debris and the dead lay between Gonji and the back of the enchanted king. But Klann had moved farther off, bearing down on Garth, who had been backed into a corner.

A door swung open off the hall. Lady Olga Thorvald appeared, calling out to Klann in desperate fear. Garth and Olga locked eyes for an instant. The smith lost his concentration. A plunging spear ripped through his shoulder, slamming him against the wall.

*"Garth!"* Gonji blared, surging to his aid.

Klann hesitated a long moment as Olga continued to appeal to him to flee. His remaining personal guards took the initiative and pushed their reluctant liege to the portal, though his face, tilted back toward his downed ex-comrade, had suddenly gone ashen, as if out of concern.

Wilf saw them rush the king toward safety and seized his last few shafts, sticking them in the floor. He notched and launched. His steel-headed arrow spindled a retainer, tearing through his back up to the stabilizing feathers. Another—

A Llorm gained the bannister at his feet, dangling with one arm and thrusting with the other.

—Wilf's shaft tore through the neck of the king as he passed the doorway—the door slammed shut in the faces of the guards.

*"I got him!"*

His roar of triumph was cut short by the stabbing pain in his inner thigh. The Llorm pulled back for another strike. Wilf cried out and drew Spine-cleaver, leaning over the balustrade to strike off the man's gripping arm, sending him plummeting in a crimson spray. He fell back against the wall and examined his leg. It bled freely and burned with a maddening intensity, but it would not debilitate him. The muscles seemed intact. He wincingly bound the gash with a shredded tunic sleeve. As he did so, he spotted his brother.

"Lorenz—*you bloody bastard,*" he cried in a long wail, scrabbling up in his pain to nock and launch his final arrow at the sneering man on the far side of the gallery.

Lorenz bowed like a courtier and casually pulled the door closed as the war arrow struck the lintel. Wilf slapped the balustrade and threw his bow down into the shambles, taking the stairs over downed bodies to rejoin Gonji, who bent over his fallen father.

Wilf's mouth funneled and he forgot his own pain when he saw Garth being helped aloft beneath the blood-smeared wall.

The remaining soldiers, seeing now the raiders' number and condition, regrouped and came on, swords and pole-arms extended for the kill. Wilf and Gonji set themselves, casting each other a doomed farewell . . .

The doors squealed on their hinges and flattened inward, battered by the werewolf's massive shoulder. The Beast tumbled in and rolled, sailed his axe along the floor, men leaping and falling to avoid its screeching slide.

The werewolf seized an overturned table and slammed it into a backpedaling party of six soldiers. The beaten Llorm began to disperse in terror, injury, and despair. Doors flew open in every wall.

"Let them go, Simon," Gonji ordered. "Garth's hurt—and we still haven't found Mord—Wilf, where the hell are you off to now?"

The young smith had begun to move up the gallery stair. *"Lorenz,"* he shouted back. "He's up here somewhere."

Garth was waving him off weakly.

Gonji railed at his tormented friend. "Get back here. Forget him. Who did you come here for? We get Mord, and you get your Genya. There isn't time for anything else."

Wilf bitterly abandoned his vengeance with a last look up to the walkway. They helped the badly injured Garth to his feet.

"Oh, Papa," Wilf fretted to see his father's wounds.

"Never mind that," Garth gasped. "You go on . . . all of you . . . I must seek Olga. I'll—I'll join you later, *ja?"*

"It's worse than any of you think," Simon rasped. "There's something tracking me—a demon out of Hell—"

*"What?"*

"Mord's work, I think," Simon clarified, pawing blood from his slashed muzzle. He squatted down low, shuddering. There were hideous rents in his blood-matted golden fur. "We must find Mord," he growled with pained determination. *"I* must find him—get out of here, all of you—"

He pushed off and loped through the smashed doors with

a terrifying howl, his axe forgotten.

"Simon!"

Garth struggled out of their grasp, letting his axe fall weakly. Hefting his broadsword, he moved off. "You must go," he said with effort. "Each of you has his quest. Fulfill it . . . and go from this place."

"Papa—" Wilf caught him in a swoon and embraced him. It lasted but briefly, and they parted, Wilf and Gonji watching the valiant smith shuffle off through a north corridor before turning right toward an area of living quarters.

The pair moved in the opposite direction, thinking to make their way back across the middle ward to the central keep, and from there through the inner maze of halls to the prison tower where Mord's wyvern once roosted.

The halls were filled with screams and blood, panicked people everywhere, fighting one another in their frenzied efforts at escape. Localized fires had broken out from torches flung at the werewolf and the raging of the ignited magazines. Only small pockets of troops now acted in defense of the castle. Most passers-by took little notice of the invaders. Gonji and Wilf began to wonder whether there wasn't more at work than the actions of the raiding party when they caught sight of the soul-chilling apparition without.

The unearthly thing that Simon had spoken of.

It moved through the ward in gathering chaos, something that belonged nowhere in the natural order. It looked like a gaping hole in the space above the ward, yet shaped like something reptilian. And its eyes, its horrible yellow eyes, seemed to see everywhere at once, to burn into the soul of the watcher with ghastly promise of lost eternity. In its wake it carried . . . dancing things, whirling and lashing about in tormented rhythm. Lost souls, grasping for a purchase in the world of men that always seemed close, yet ever out of their reach. The apparition stepped lightly in the ward, the whimpering and wailing of the spirits ever more piercing. Each step burned the paving stones of the courtyard until they were molten, dully glowing.

A suggestion of teeth and claws. The fathomless maw spreading . . .

Wilf and Gonji retreated from the vestibule hall, for the hellish thing was coming straight for them. The ward being out of the question now, the pair wished each other good fortune and split up to increase their odds of success.

### Chapter Twenty-nine

Wilfred was the first of them to find an object of his quest, though it was not the desire of his heart that was fulfilled but the passion of his angry spirit.

He made his way through a corridor past the banquet hall, out past the flaming ruin of the armorer's tower, reentering the corridor maze below the battlements of the mighty central keep.

He climbed to the second level, filled with desperate Akryllonian nationals—women and children, for the most part—who sought an exit to freedom. The gates were impassable, seared to molten rock and iron by the passing of Wolverangue.

Wilf avoided crossing paths with the many Llorm troops who tried to evacuate their families in the din and confusion. A servant had told Wilf that Genya had been seen in the keep earlier that day. All he could do was follow up the frightened girl's word.

That was when he found Lorenz.

His treacherous half-brother leaned casually against the door jamb of a bedchamber, smiling coyly. Wilf sucked in a hot breath and strove to dash the red lights that obscured his vision. He squeezed the *katana* in a cold, sweating fist and walked toward him slowly, scanning him. No pistol; rapier still in the sheath.

Screaming people dotted the hall, crossed between them

436

as they locked gazes. Wilf stopped, ten feet from him, mouth working at forming words.

"Well, Wilfred—late as usual." Lorenz consulted a Nuremberg egg watch, replaced it in the pocket of his waistcoat. He laughed complacently. "You wanted to get inside the castle all this time—all you had to do was ask. All this . . . violence wasn't necessary."

Wilf found his voice. "Why did you kill poor Strom? The little fellow *idolized* you."

"I had to get to the castle," he replied, shrugging. "So I gave him a choice. He refused, provincial little thinker that he was. I was forced to eliminate him, use him for a smokescreen, with the aid of Mord's black ram, of course. Perhaps I asked the wrong brother, eh? You're the one who wanted to breach the castle walls."

*"Why,* Lorenz? Why do all this . . . *outrage?* Why did our mother do this evil thing? What could Mord have offered you both?"

"She despised you and Strom, you know. For being sired by the brutish blacksmith. He forced himself on her, did you know that? Unthinkable treatment, for such a lady. That's why she loved only me all these years. Does that make you jealous, Wilfred?"

Wilf shook his head slowly, Lorenz's madness becoming clear. "Could such a mother love any of her issue?"

Lorenz's gaze lofted skyward as he went on rhapsodically, almost as if he'd forgotten Wilf's presence.

"I used to dream of a life in the great courts of Europe, those places I saw as an errand boy of a glorified Carpathian peasant village. Imagine my joy to discover the Akryllonian nomads during my last business venture abroad. To learn, quite by accident, that mother was among them. We recognized each other at once. It was . . . almost magick, of the sort the peasants shiver at before their fires. I remembered her—you were too young, but I remembered. She looks grand, Wilf. She's scarcely aged at all. And Wilf—she's told me who my father is. My *true* father . . ."

"The raving lunatic—I've heard."

Lorenz snorted. "You dare to speak that way, knowing that you are of the seed of that cuckolded bull who—"

Wilf raised Spine-cleaver and leveled it at Lorenz's face. "He raised you from a whelp, you dung-eating bastard. Gave you everything, and that's what made you crazy, because you don't know how to deal with that much unearned love—" He exhaled raggedly, trying to control his flaring temper.

"Draw your sword."

Lorenz sighed. "I supposed it had to come to that, knowing the quality of your mind. Well, come ahead, then, noble *bushi.*"

The traitor drew steel and danced backward into the sumptuous chamber in *en garde.* Before Wilf advanced, he heeded the warning that flashed in the back of his mind. Something Gonji had taught: *An enemy who regards you too casually probably has accomplices . . .*

Wilf lunged to the door and stopped. Lorenz flashed surprise. The young smith pulled a dirk from the back of his belt and cocked it to throw.

*"Nein*—that's not fair—" Lorenz dropped his guard and staggered back as Wilf dove through the portal and tumbled into the room, rolling to his feet in time to fire the knife at the nearer of the two ambushers. The blade dug into the brigand's chest. He flung his saber and gasped to look at himself.

Wilf caught the flailing steel of a *schiavona* in front of his eyes, saw Lorenz's telegraphed advance for his injured side and snapped down a sparking parry, twisting out of their reach. The accomplice lunged deeply and low. Wilf bound his blade, circled a two-handed parry that drove the point far out of engagement, and struck out with a right hand thrust that tore through the man's gut. The *katana* came free, its stained blade wetly red again. He turned to Lorenz.

Breathing huffily, Wilf clashed with his wild-eyed brother, blades singing off each other again and again. Cursing and spitting imprecations, they danced around the room, Lorenz's mad strength and well-rested body keeping

438

Wilf at bay.

"What's wrong, Wilfred?—*sensei* didn't teach you the *coup de grace?*—did you think I dawdled away those trips to France?—the finest fencers in Europe, Wilfred, the French—their teachers are the masters—did Gonji show you *this*—?"

Lorenz lunged and dropped his point to new engagement in mid-thrust. Wilf missed his parry and the slim rapier grazed his wounded side. Pain flared in hot white pinpoints. Wilf began to back away, falling into a defensive, *iai-jutsu* posture. But in his failing strength, his ripostes repeatedly fell short.

He was soon backed nearly to the wall. His rear foot brushed the hem of the heavy decorative drapery. He was cornered, the canopy bed blocking retreat.

Wilf batted Lorenz's blade and feinted a two-handed lunge. Then he leapt onto the bed and slashed the canopy, a long ragged edge trailing him as he bounded out on the other side.

"That's my bed, you uncultured swine!" Lorenz fumed.

*"Ja,"* Wilf taunted, remembering now a lifetime of needling Lorenz in his fastidiousness. "All your finery—"

He slashed through a bedpost, the canopy flapping down in ruin. "How do you like it?"

"Stop that! Wilfred—you son of a bitch!"

"The same bitch that mothered you!" Wilf swept his blade through the velvet drapery. A long swatch fell to the floor.

*"Stop it, I say—"*

Lorenz rushed around the corner of the bed as Wilf shattered a crystal chandelier in a rain of shards. The traitor stamped forward and lunged. Wilf deflected his rapier past. It dug into the wall and became bound up in the folds of the drapery. Spine-cleaver whirled up and over in a quick circle.

The rapier snapped in two. Lorenz glanced at his broken forte. Roaring out his refined indignance, he thrust with his half-blade. He plunged onto Wilf's point as the *katana*

439

returned to disciplined middle guard.

Wilf withdrew the blade with a short tug. For an instant Lorenz seemed unhurt despite the blood. Then he staggered away a few paces and fell, making no sound but the soft crumple of his form.

Wilf stood over his brother. "Genya, Lorenz—where is she?"

A small whining laugh. "You'll find her . . . with her new lover—Mord." Lorenz began to speak in a strange voice that prattled a dream of empire. Unable to bear it, Wilf mopped his face and, signing the cross, hurried from the room.

*"Olgaaaaa—"*

She stood with her back to him in a chamber doorway, four Llorm guards around her, in a corridor of the central keep that swarmed with rushing people. Servants' quarters were at the end of the hall; chambermaids had found refuge wherever they could when the madness had struck.

Some of them stopped in their tracks now and covered their mouths to see the state of the best-loved man in Vedun, now that Flavio was gone.

Lady Olga Thorvald turned slowly and faced her husband. The Llorm swordsmen brandished their blades in warning, but their officer, knowing him, stayed their hands.

Garth drew a shuddering breath, and a pained expression dawned when he saw her smile. To him, she was still his wife, still breathtakingly beautiful.

"Stand fast," he told the guards, "and let me speak with my wife. Then . . . then you may do with me as you will."

Olga kept smiling as she backed confidently into the chamber, eyeing the guards, past a woman in a traveling mantua who tripped backward lightly to give them space. Garth stalked his wife, his crushed spirit and broken heart plain in his eyes.

His left side was coated with blood from shoulder to boot as he spoke to her. "Why?" he asked, raising a pleading

440

hand. "Why all this horror, Olga? Wasn't it enough that you—"

"You looked just as I imagined, Garth," she broke in, "that day of the banquet. Of course Klann forbade me to attend, but I couldn't help myself—I sneaked a peek at you from the gallery."

*"Why?"*

"To win back the king's love, that's why," she answered. "I needed to regain the place I once held in his life. And Lorenz wished to be with me, to be with King Klann in his glorious return to Akryllon. We didn't know it would come to this. No one did."

Garth seemed astonished. "Akryllon is a lost dream," he said in a labored voice. "Surely even Klann accepts that by now. We knew it all those years ago. After that terrible voyage. Akryllon is something men may never again possess. How could you do this? Lead Lorenz into a hollow dream. *He murdered his brother*—have you no remorse?"

She held her head high. "I would do it again, if I thought my liege lord would benefit by it, as would Lorenz. Do you know, Garth—he reminds me of his father. So elegant, so cavalier. He wrote songs to me under the stars, while you boasted of your kills."

"And so God laid me low, for I wrote you songs with my sword, thinking—fool that I was—that that was what you wanted . . ."

"A woman such as I was could have no limits inscribed around her desires, Garth."

"Your collusion with the sorcerer has driven you mad, Olga," Garth said in amazement, pressing at his torn shoulder.

"What are you talking about?" she retorted acidly.

"Did you have no compassion even for your *sons?*"

"*Your* sons. Those cubs you forced on me by your brutish attentions. And now I understand you've become a Churchman, *nicht wahr?* For a long time Klann and I both feared what you might do if you found out about us. And now your faith won't permit you even a final victory, will it?"

441

Anger broiled in the smith's eyes. "There are many men dead in my wake back there, Olga."

"Ah, but fighting men," she qualified as he advanced at a shuffle. "You couldn't strike down a helpless woman, could you—unarmed, soft of flesh—*a woman you still love?*" She smiled in imperious triumph.

He took a heavy step and raised his broadsword. The Llorm guards tensed but remained in the corridor. "As God is my witness—I—" He lowered the blade heavily and fell to one knee, breath shivering out of him as he rubbed his eyes to clear his vision. "It is . . . not for me . . . to judge you . . ." He looked up at her serenely smiling countenance. The last thing he ever saw.

The war arrow tore into his back. He fell on his face, dead instantly from the well-aimed shot.

"Oh, Garth," the tall woman in the mantua said as she gazed down upon his silent form, "it is only by my hand that you should die, for it is by my foolish kin that you were slain, so long ago—*curse your intemperate heart, lost brother!*"

"A—a well-placed shot, milady," Olga said apprehensively.

Slowly, Klann looked up at the scheming woman. The new Queen Klann, the fifth personage of the royal seven-in-one, was a tall, statuesque, and powerful woman. Sure of herself, knowing in furious despair that she alone among the progeny of the House of Bel might have regained lost Akryllon.

"Look at him, my worthies," she said to the gathered guards, though her eyes were still on Thorvald. "Here lies the noblest of warriors. *A curse on you powers that be—why am I emerged so late?* . . . Too, too late . . . I could have loved him. I *did*. Helplessly. I would have taken him to husband, and together we would have taken back what was mine—ours—*gone forever!* And you, spiteful bitch, how I envied you . . ."

She began advancing on the wide-eyed Olga, stopping to look back at Garth again. "You gave him the sons we could *never* have because of our accursed birthing. And then you

442

*destroyed* them in your madwoman's passion!''

''Milady—I—'' Olga was terrified now, as she saw the queen reach down for Garth's broadsword.

Klann held the blood-stained steel before her eyes.

''Know ye the price for faithlessness and treachery,'' she said in a harsh whisper. She moved for Olga.

Lady Thorvald raised a fending hand, shrieking as the blade pierced her belly. She doubled over, and Queen Klann struck her head from her shoulders in a single fierce blow.

Klann exhaled, the spell of the moment broken. ''Get me armor,'' she ordered. She hastily donned the proffered Llorm outfit and, with a final look to Garth, hurried out into the chaos of Castle Lenska.

There were screams and explosions in the wards as the new queen assessed her situation. Her personal guard remained with her, but she found that she could command little additional support; few believed in the new Rising. The imposing dark-haired woman's commands brought only stares and epithets. She watched in bewilderment as curtain walls and outbuildings exploded, felt the singeing heat waves from the track of the Hell-Hound as it plodded after the werewolf, pulverizing the castle section by section.

She could not tell how many or even what nature her besiegers were now. Tears of rage began to flow. She could sense the end of it all. Centuries of quest, dashed forever. Mercenaries had begun pouring into the hills, carrying off what spoils they could. She and her Llorm retainers were forced to tilt with the mutinous free companions. She killed several by her own hand, outraged and indignant at this ironic turning. She lusted after the destruction of the invaders, man and demon alike, as she watched the broken families of her hereditary army scale the walls in frenzied flight, soon to be lost amongst the peoples of the continent, their heritage and blood mingled, diminished until Akryllon itself had become a legend, sneered at by the ignorant, recounted in sodden folklore.

The gods had abandoned her and her people. All that remained was vengeance. She watched her army scatter in dismay, and her hatred began to focus on Mord.

Gesturing to her three surviving elite guards, she made her way toward the dungeons.


### Chapter Thirty


Gonji and Wilf nearly collided—and almost engaged swords—at a corner of the castle keep's labyrinth. So disheveled and gore-streaked were they that it took them an instant to recognize each other.

Young Gundersen grabbed Gonji excitedly and, crying out in pain both physical and emotional, he recapped what he'd seen and done as they took a short breather.

Then Gonji led him to the chamber he'd found, where Garth and Olga lay dead, but the samurai's effort at preparing him for the grisly sight merely forestalled Wilf's anguished reaction.

He fell on his knees in the room and began to weep bitterly, choking out futile oaths. "It's the first time I ever remember seeing my parents together . . ." were his first words when he had collected himself.

Gonji found himself deeply grieved. He took Wilf by the shoulders and led him away with a gentle urging that there were yet things to do.

They leapt over many strewn corpses in the halls, Wilf identifying one as Chooch, the Steward of the Larders whom Lottie Kovacs had implicated for his perversity. Then, drawn by the clashing in another hall as they wended their way toward the prison tower, they spotted the woman who led the tiny Llorm detachment, and understood what must have transpired.

"Klann—" Gonji breathed. "She must be . . . Klann."

They followed her party down to a first-level prison tower door, accosting her as she gained the open portal.

"Klann!" Wilfred cried out, circling her in the corridor

nexus. The three Llorm bodyguards fanned out menacingly, blades flourished for engagement. "I am . . . I am Wilfred *Iorgens,*" he blared.

She gazed at him in surprise, her mouth widening and her dark eyes shimmering in a look almost of exultation. Then she tossed her head back and laughed loud and long at the bitter irony of it all. Gonji stood coiled for a strike, a spearlength from the nearest guards.

"So be it, then, young Iorgens," she declared. "I've struck down your noble father. You intend to avenge him? Fight well!" She pushed her guards toward Gonji and attacked Wilf with his father's broadsword.

Gonji was backed down the hallway, fighting defensively against the pinch of a halberd and two long blades. Wilf's last sight of him was a glimpse of the samurai ducking a stone-shattering blow in an archway and riposting with a low scything slash. Then he was through the portal after the queen, who alternately pressed a two-handed power assault and fell back toward the dungeon stair.

Their blades clashed and echoed in the dank chamber of the prison tower under murky torchlight. She spoke to him as she fought, though he understood little of it, most of it in the Kunan tongue his father had shared with her kin.

Ultimately they found themselves on the dungeon stairwell. A hard push would send one or both of them crashing to the stones. But they held their ground as they descended to the cellar level, filled with the echoing mewlings of the half-humans still farther below.

And Wilf began to marvel at the savagery of her attack; awkward and imprecise though it was as she learned the limits of her new form, she seemed fearless and cunning. He experienced natterings of doubt, his waning strength beginning to tell, though he employed every skill, every blade trick he had practiced so assiduously under Gonji and his father. Her confident chiding of him over his strange sword style ate at him; they cut each other once, twice. Fought down to the subcellar, the chaos above ground forgotten for the nonce.

445

He slammed her broadsword against the grimy wall with a mighty twist, saw the defiance in her regal eyes, and grimaced.

His blade flashed unbidden in the technique driven home by Gonji, though his eyes clamped tightly shut.

Mord held a gloved hand over Genya's mouth, the saber in his other fist pressing her soft throat with its gleaming edge. His serpent eyes brightened as he heard, and sensed, and understood . . .

They leaned behind the door of his chamber of spells, Genya's eyes wide with horror to see the altar stone, the stained manacles suspended above it by rusted chains.

"Do you hear, girl?" he said in sudden amusement. "Klann is dead—long live . . . *Klann!*" He broke into a booming laugh that might have issued from the keeper to the gate of Hell. "Would you like to see the king who so doted on you, clever girl?"

Genya seized the moment and broke from his grasp, running to his shelves of phials and retorts. He continued laughing as she hurled objects at him; the chamber filled with splashing explosions. Genya prayed that her lost dagger might be returned to her hand as the sorcerer pushed her to the door at swordpoint, grabbed her again and turned the key to force her out into the dark corridor.

She screamed: "Wilf!" The monster had seized the young *bushi* with a long, web-fingered arm and flung him against a wall. He cried out and slumped to lie helpless before it.

Genya ran forward, stopped, Mord's laughter filling the hall behind her.

A Llorm trooper crashed through the portal on the landing above to flatten at the monster's broad feet. Gonji staggered into the archway above and stared down at the sixth Klann personage.

The Tainted One. A hideous amphibian mutation. A mindless primitive introduced into Klann's lineage by unholy human-inhuman couplings in the dim ancestral past, when men dared to intermix with those things that called themselves gods.

Gonji saw Mord behind Genya and was momentarily indecisive. The sorcerer was shocked to see the samurai still alive, to catch the glint of hatred in his eyes. He caught Genya's shoulder, but she twisted out of his grasp and scrambled along the wall toward Gonji. Mord cursed and turned, running into the bleak corridor, past the cells of puling mutilations.

The Tainted One rushed Genya. Gonji leapt down the stair and sliced open its gray belly. A swipe of its misshapen arm, fortified by a raging bellow, knocked the samurai flat, breath *whoofing* out of him. Genya ran for Wilf. He was dazed and moaning; his left arm swelled, broken.

The monster closed an amphibian appendage around Gonji's leg and began to bounce him down the stair. He slashed and cut at it with the Sagami. It fell back, maddened and leaking dark fluid.

A flashing explosion above and the crumbling of masonry as a tower wall collapsed—smoke billowed into the dungeon—Wolverangue had circled through the castle, leveling wall after wall, still seeking Simon.

"Get Wilf—get out of here—free those people!" Gonji shouted at Genya as the monster came at him again.

Genya whimpered and dragged Wilf onto his feet, picking up his downed sword. They staggered into the corridor again. She fumbled with the cell locks, doors creaking open.

"We can't get out," Genya shrieked back at Gonji.

The samurai sliced open the monster's twisted mouth with a one-handed uppercut. "Mord must have, somehow," he roared. Then he took to the corridor after them, the Tainted One in raging pursuit.

The suffering half-humans crawled from the cells as the three survivors stumbled about in the darkness. Then Gonji saw the bar of moonlight, and watched it shuttered at once by the slamming of the iron hatch, high above.

"This way!" he yelled. The Tainted One half-loped,

half-hopped after them, its froglike bulk scraping the walls of the narrow corridor. It became entangled with the victims of Mord's spells, batting them out of its way.

Wilf moaned behind him as Gonji gained the portal, kicked it ajar—it led into the outer ward below the prison tower. And Simon was there, amidst a whirling vortex of wind, snowed under by a grim squad of Llorm. He was weaponless, save for his rendings fangs and talons, and the Llorm laid into him with pike and sword, charged to intrepid fury to see his weakness. He fought them on all fours now like a dying beast.

Gonji bellowed and cut a swath through the determined men as Genya supported Wilf across the ward toward the wrecked gatehouse. The Llorm fell back, disheartened at the terrible sight of the samurai, though his every *kiyai* was charged with the knifing pain in his ribs and his eye was swelling shut from a blow he scarcely remembered.

The Llorm fell away, some of them discarding their weapons and dropping in an emotional heap. For now, they too saw the thing that their noble king had become.

The mutant reeled into the ward. Simon mounted his last howling attack, meeting the Tainted One in a challenge to mutual extinction, grasping its pulpy flesh and digging in.

Amid the whipping wind and pulings of panicked stray animals, the raging heat wave preceded the molten hissing of stone a hundred feet away along the middle bailey wall.

The Hell-Hound pulverized the final barrier to its prey, a mountain of ashlar and masonry bursting into the ward.

Genya and Wilf were lost to Gonji's view. His heart sank as he cried out in surfeit to the *kami* of war.

Simon and the mutated Klann separated and took flight before the searing approach of the Hell-Hound. The tormented souls that whirled about it became animated to frenzy, knowing their time of viewing the world of the living to be at an end. The Tainted One hobbled off, savagely wounded; Simon crawled away in a spiraling path, maddened in his pain. Over the din he called out to Gonji, over and over, a single name: *Mord*.

Wolverangue glowed redly in anticipation.

Gonji fell back, gasping and throwing an arm over his face to stave the heat waves. He cast about in desperate helplessness. When his eyes scanned the rubble-strewn ward a second time, he caught sight of the foul enchanter. As the fragmented humans dragged themselves through the cellar door, Mord slunk away behind the supply drays and private coaches assembled under the outer curtain wall. Horses and domestic animals bolted and cried, trapped in the ward, lurching across Gonji's path as he ran toward the drays.

Mord spotted him, screaming and yammering in warning, motioning with conjurer's gesticulations that produced no effect. The samurai raised his *katana* high, a long growl burning his throat as he bore down.

"No!" Simon cried, giving him pause, a taloned arm staying his blow.

Gonji looked from the sorcerer to the werewolf, failing to understand. Mord took the opportunity to turn and run. Gonji cursed and put up the Sagami, sprinted after Mord and hit him from behind in a flying tackle. They tumbled to the paving stones, rolling and grasping. Mord's sword arm came up, and Gonji caught it, staving its edge from his uncovered skull. He struck the enchanter a hard but ineffectual punch in the midsection. Mord laughed in his face, his breath the breath of a carrion-eater.

They regained their feet, breaking their hold. Mord swung a low arcing blow that Gonji sprang over, drawing the Sagami again with a gurgle of pain.

"You can't destroy me, fool," Mord boasted. "I'm an immortal servant of the Dark Lord—"

"Your Dark Lord has lied," Gonji replied.

Simon bellowed behind them, crawling along, dragging a ruined leg, yelling for Gonji not to kill him. The samurai battled defensively. Their blades whanged off each other repeatedly, Gonji's fury stoked anew with every crossing.

Mord cut his leg with a pass, a superficial blow, but it enraged Gonji. He surged at him, pressing the attack now, oblivious to everything save his loathing for Mord.

449

Mord blared a cavernous laugh and lunged deeply. Gonji sidestepped the thrust and snapped his blade upward—

The sorcerer's sword arm was severed almost to the shoulder. Mord shrieked in an intensity of pain he hadn't known in centuries. Gonji's following sequence of slashes cut open his breast and belly, then another ground-to-sky cut that knocked loose his ominous golden mask—

Gonji retreated a pace and grimaced. The sorcerer was hideously deformed, his face a shriveled thing; the eyes, solid black marble chips; his skin, wrinkled and sere, mottled gray-green like a serpent's. And where he bled from Gonji's swordcuts—even at the stump of his right arm— there emerged only a trickle of pale blood. An ancient, withered, evil being who had no place outside the Pit . . .

Mord hissed at Gonji through a lipless mouth filled with tiny, pointed teeth. A long, leathery tongue darted at the samurai in threat as the sorcerer backed away. But Simon circled around the drays as Gonji felt the awesome heat at his back. The shambling chaos burned its footprints but fifty feet behind.

Simon seized the sorcerer and dragged him down, enfolded him in his long arms and dug his talons into the monstrous adept.

"The dray—tie him in the dray—"

And Gonji understood at last. He grabbed a harness and helped Simon wrestle the struggling sorcerer into the dray bed. They lashed him tightly to the small wagon and together wheeled it around by the hitch to face the oncoming horror. With a grunting push, they rumbled toward the gaping maw that spread wide to receive the offering.

Mord's long wail of despair and appeal to his Dark Master was engulfed, as if drowned in an endless fiery tunnel. There came a shocking concussion of dimensions disentangled from each other, a snapping withdrawal that slapped the pair of them onto their backs. And in a red flash of unholy flame whose heat flared and subsided in a second, both the Hell-Spawn and its invoker were gone from the world. Hell had reclaimed its own.

The Hell-Hound had found the offering satisfactory.


## Chapter Thirty-one


The end of their struggle clear, the remaining soldiers, crouched at the walls, put up their weapons.

Gonji peered over at the weakly pawing werewolf, a great sympathy overwhelming him. He had no idea what to do for his terribly wounded friend, who had secured the lives of so many.

His own wounds began to take their toll; he sat back, grunting with every movement, still clutching his sword, but his fighting spirit smothered.

He spotted the Tainted One, ravaged and moaning, trying vainly to scale the outer bailey wall. Some of the Llorm sat with their backs to it, weeping in their defeat and disorientation.

A shaft whistled from the low-slung dungeon hatch to pierce the mutant's back. It went down in a heap in the fuming dust and clouding black smoke. The fires raged on through the castle, as refugees streamed through the now cooled main gatehouse, only to find the rubble impassable. Others made their way through the miller's gate and postern, or over the walls by ropes.

The evacuation of Castle Lenska had begun.

Gonji blinked and wiped his eyes to get a clear look at the apparition that stepped through the smoke, bearing two longbows. A Llorm officer. It was Aldo Monetto.

"Follow the Devil, and you find a samurai," Monetto said, his begrimed face breaking into a smile. His teeth were the only recognizable part of him.

Gonji began to laugh, tossing his head back wearily, a sound of forlorn relief. "Oh, Aldo . . . it's all over . . ."

"I retrieved your bow, and Karl's," the biller said. "For a time there, I thought I'd never find any of you alive."

Gonji remembered. "Wilfred and Genya—they're over there somewhere. At least I think they're still alive. See if they need help. Wilf's hurt pretty badly."

Monetto saluted carelessly and, with a frown aimed at Simon, loped away.

Then Gonji saw the small figure of the naked woman, seated near the wall, smoke obscuring her, then parting to reveal her again. He pushed up with a mighty effort and strode toward her, scowling. He reached her as a single Llorm trooper draped his surcoat about her and knelt at her feet, weeping.

The seventh and final Klann personage, a frail blonde queen, wistful in defeat. Gonji found his heart going out to her. He fell to one knee. "Your . . . your Highness . . ." he found himself saying.

She rose and spoke to no one in particular.

"I'm sorry for the horror of it all," she said haltingly in Kunan. "But I cannot help being most sorry for myself . . ." She looked down at Gonji and continued in Italian. "I'm alone now, you see. So very alone. I once wondered what others meant when they spoke of . . . loneliness. Wondered whether it was not something to be desired, to have the peace of one's own quiet, distinct thoughts. It's not a good thing, this loneliness. It's so . . . cold and empty inside now . . ."

She wrapped her arms about her and shivered. Gonji's mouth twisted to see the discarded skin of the Tainted One. At length, Queen Klann went on.

"Tell them, please, won't you, that I'm very sorry for what's happened to them. To their city. Tell them—tell them Klann suffered for it, far more than they can ever understand. I alone have known the death of each child of the House of Bel. There is but one more scion left to die . . ."

She took a dirk from the belt of her retainer. Her remaining soldiers gathered around her. Gonji stood and backed away, at last believing, in part understanding, sympathizing with the centuries-old quest after a lost throne that had ended in such catastrophe.

He turned and moved away toward his fellows.

Monetto found Wilf and Genya alive and overcome with emotion to be at last together, locked in an awkward embrace. Wilf was in obvious pain. Aldo helped her fashion a splint for the young smith's broken arm, and a Llorm trooper came up on his way out of the demolished stronghold and offered them water and mead. They accepted it gratefully, and before the soldier departed, Aldo made a point of offering his hand in friendship, telling the man to spread the word to his fellows and their families that they would be welcome to join the Vedunian party.

"Oh God, Wilf, is it really over?" Genya asked as she bound his wounds and tried to relieve his discomfort.

"Done, Genya," he replied. "We'll never be apart again."

She began to cry softly. "I was so afraid. Will you . . . take me as I am?" she queried curiously.

"What the hell does that mean?"

She touched her forehead. But the oily red mark was gone. She began to laugh exultantly when Wilf assured her that there was nothing on her face that a good scrubbing wouldn't remove.

Then they saw Tomas emerge, battered and begrimed, from the burning keep. When he saw Genya's ugly stare, and Wilf with his *katana* still clutched in a bloody fist, with Aldo standing by, his axe over his shoulder, the Keeper of the miller's gate halted and gaped. His face drained of color. Genya rose and took one meaningful step toward him.

Tomas emitted a short, choked cry and stumbled backward. He returned the way he had come, back into the smoking ruins.

Gonji came up to them, and they shared the congratulations of the survived. Genya embraced and kissed him for having helped Wilf back to her, watched over him. He dismissed it all as karma, but inside he was warmed and comforted.

The night sky shrank before the darkest hour, the Hour

of the Tiger, but the flames of Castle Lenska blazed the environs alight.

The samurai fell to dry heaving, and they gave him water and a little bread, brought by assembling servants who were lost for guidance. Aldo tightly bound Gonji's staved-in ribs and laved his many cuts. The samurai's left eye had swollen completely shut, giving rise to a series of jibes by the again light-hearted biller.

When Genya unbound Wilf's leg wound to display the awful rent in his thigh, the flesh laid open raggedly to bleed anew, Wilf gasped and passed out.

Genya began to treat it, shushing Monetto's chuckling.

"That's a good sign, milady," Aldo assured. "It means he's still human after all this."

"I'm glad he waited until now to go faint-hearted on me," Gonji jested.

More servants and soldiers emerged from the smoking inner wards and halls, choking and wounded. They streamed from the burning keep, the drum towers, from every level of Castle Lenska the Unassailable, which had twice been assailed in scarcely more than a moon. Soldiers and servants aided one another, all weapons abandoned.

Monetto nudged Gonji. Richard the baker staggered out with a fresh band of escapees. Genya rushed past them.

"Richard! You're alive!" She ushered him over to Wilf to share in her joy over her love's survival.

"Shouldn't we tell him that Lottie's well?" Monetto asked when Gonji grabbed his arm to restrain him.

"*Iyé*. If it's their karma to find each other again, then it will be as it will be. Let them live with their loss for now. Perhaps they'll have gained the courage they needed to fortify their love by then."

Monetto frowned but shrugged it off and let it be.

There was one broad, still area in the outer ward, the place where the werewolf lay, comatose, breathing with a labored gargling sound that chilled them. Neither man nor beast would approach the supine form.

Gonji told Monetto what to do.

"All right, you people—you men there," Aldo said, "you've just been conscripted again. One more duty, and then you're free to go." He instructed them to build a litter with which to carry off Simon.

Regrettably forced to guide them under threat of the axe, Monetto saw them through the dismantling of a wagon which could not pass the rubble. But even under Aldo's threat, none would take up the burden of the now trembling and moaning Beast.

Gonji strode up to them and drew the Sagami. "This is a *man,*" he bellowed. "He's given his life, accursed though it is, to save your miserable asses. *Pick him up.*"

Quailing under the threat, they crossed themselves and hefted the litter, grunting as one under the weight.

Wilf had come to. He and Genya moved up behind Gonji to join the grim procession out of the destroyed castle.

"He really *was* the Deathwind," Wilf declared.

"Mmm." Gonji's lips twisted, and he became glumly taciturn as they made their way out and over the stone-filled moat, the litter bearers in awe of their rasping, bloody, and burned charge. They babbled in quaking voices that wondered:

Of what use could such a monster possibly be, especially in its present state?

## Chapter Thirty-two

They made their way into the hills, setting up a camp. Monetto retrieved their horses and a few animals for eating from among the straying flocks and herds. Servants were put to work tending fires and preparing food, but those sent off for any water or provisions invariably disappeared.

They set Simon apart in a glade, out of sight. They ate, tended their wounds, and slept under canopies in the clear light of a cool day. When they awoke, they found that most of the servants had fled.

Simon had indeed transformed back into a naked figure of a wretchedly crushed man. He remained comatose, and Monetto shook his head bleakly over Simon's chances for survival. Genya summoned her courage and treated his many and varied wounds as best she knew how, though she wept with frustration at the task and threw her hands up at last over the worst. The burns seemed untreatable, though she tried every provincial remedy any of them suggested. There seemed to be no hope. Just when she thought she had the bleeding stopped, night fell. She scurried away, gasping; the writhing agony of the transformation caused the wounds to bleed again.

Yet Gonji took hope. He noted that the werewolf seemed somehow stronger now than it had the night before. Simon's incredible recuperative powers were evinced in the swift receding of the burns; already most of the fur had grown back where the Hell-Hound had scorched it.

He remained feverish and unconscious for two days and nights, the sun and moon revealing to the astonished onlookers the unbelievable agony of the changes from man to wolf and back, each change again laying open the wounds. But each day he drew stronger and the wounds receded. And with each transmutation, the *kamikaze*—the divine wind—grew in force.

A light breeze ruffled the yellow blossoms of the furze in the cool evening shadows. Autumn approached swiftly on the heels of the rainy season.

Wilf came up behind Gonji, who sat cross-legged, quietly contemplating the edge of his *wakizashi*.

"Not still thinking about *seppuku*, are you?" the smith whispered at his ear. He knelt beside the oriental, an impish smile perking the corners of his mouth. "Between problems of faith, plus my not believing you deserve suicide, I don't think I can assist you. Then you might make the bad cut, and you'd be writhing around on the ground, and then Genya would get nauseous, and—"

*"All-recht,* smart ass," Gonji said, sheathing the short sword, "you've made your point. Quit now before your other arm gets broken. So *now* what do you have in mind?"

Before Wilf could respond, Genya and Monetto pounded up on horseback, returning from the encampment of the Llorm and the Akryllonian survivors, where they had been helping with the sick and injured and kindling hope for the future. The Akryllonians were in sorrow over their lost heritage and certain assimilation of their blood by the European culture they were left with. Gonji knew their woe, keenly appreciating the problem.

"Well, back among the lepers, we are," Monetto joked. "Say—I know you. Aren't you the Red Blade from the East?" Genya laughed, a high, merry tinkling sound that always brought them cheer.

Gonji sighed as they dismounted. *"Hai."* He waxed contemplative again. "Why do I only mark my passing with the sword? I can do other things. I'm an educated man. I can sing songs, compose poetry, yet—

"I need to know, Wilf. Why did all this happen? Why are so many dead? Am I to blame, as so many have said—Eddings, Verrico?"

"Maybe you think yourself too important," Wilf reflected. "People die eventually. All these people might have died anyway if you hadn't passed through. Maybe sooner, maybe more of them. It's probably just as the prophetess said."

"I just can't help feeling like a harbinger of Death. Or like Death itself . . ."

Monetto passed wineskins around. "Try this stuff—it's from the castle cellars—"

"You know," Gonji went on, "I used to have a real grasp of things, a system that made sense, a true set of beliefs a man could live by. Now I live by the headlong rush my needs push me into, *neh?"*

"Not true," Monetto said airily.

"Hmm?"

"You stopped here, didn't you? Helped us with

*our* needs.''

He chortled sadly.

"Genya and I will be leaving tomorrow," Wilf announced.

"Me, too, I suppose," Monetto added. "Sylva's going to be crazy with worry, if none of those servants spoke to her."

Gonji looked mildly disappointed when he addressed Wilf. "So we're not riding off in search of adventure, then? I entertained such glorious visions." He smiled at them.

Wilf cleared his throat, but Genya spoke first.

"We can go along with Gonji, Wilf. I don't care where we go, so long as we're together. I suppose I could learn to use the sword very well." They laughed and grunted approvingly when she drew Spine-cleaver at Wilf's side and executed a few passes.

But Wilf's melancholy shifted their mood. "I thought warfare was noble and glorious." He shook his head. "It . . . wasn't as I expected . . .''

"Such things are attendant on battles that yield a victor," Gonji explained. "There was no victor here."

Monetto *tsked* and tossed his head in disagreement.

*"Nein,* you're wrong," Wilf said. "Genya and I are together."

They embraced warmly, and some of Gonji's gloom dispersed.

"What will you do?" Wilf asked him.

Gonji scratched his stubbled jaw. "I'm not sure. I'll need time to think, to meditate. Perhaps I'll go back to the Land of the Gods. This past month has set my mind reeling; so much has happened . . . I'll need to sort through the experiences here. I hardly know who or what I am anymore." He blurted a laugh. "I wish Paille were here to read back to me the record of it all."

Monetto laughed heartily. "Then you'd know less than you do now! Anyway, you'd be old and gray before you finished!"

Their shared mirth cheered them considerably.

"We'll be moving on to find Genya's parents, then,"

Wilf said at length. "Join up with the Benedettos. Who knows? Maybe come back to Vedun and start all over."

Gonji became serious. "Then you'd best police your horizons. Fortified peace—that's what you must seek."

"I sure miss Papa," Wilf said wistfully. "And Strom. And, I guess, even Lorenz in his way. He *was* my brother, *neh?*"

"No less your brother than Tatsuya was mine. Yet no less an antagonist for being a brother."

A brooding settled over Wilf as he stood. "Genya," he said solemnly, "if you ever failed to love any of our children, I think I'd kill you." He snapped out of it to see their expressions. Sighed. "I hope that's the last violent statement I'll ever have to make."

"Then I know," Gonji replied softly, "that we'll not be off soldiering together . . ."

The night passed and morning dawned, cloudy and gray with the promise of rain. The leaves had begun to quit the trees.

Simon came down to their fire, clothed in a dead man's garb, sullen and laconic. He made brief farewells to Wilf, Genya, and Aldo as they mounted, then moved away to be alone.

"Come back here in a year or two," Wilf told Gonji, "and I think you'll find us all back in Vedun. Living our lives as Flavio would have wished. The Carpathians feel clean—smell the air! The evil is gone for good from these mountains."

Gonji smiled thinly. "For now. It must replenish itself."

"Why don't you come with us, Gonji?" Genya asked. "The people would love to have you."

"Sure," Monetto agreed, "in a year's time everyone will be wearing their hair like that!" He pointed at Gonji's topknot, a twinkle in his eye.

The samurai shook his head as he stood before them, thumbs hooked into his *obi*.

"I'd wager Helena will be waiting for you," Wilf added.

Gonji made a thoughtful sound. "I'll give that tempting

thought some consideration. But don't forget that it wouldn't be easy—I'm a barbarian, remember?" None of them had ever heard him refer to himself by the insult before. "At least . . . to *your* people," he qualified.

"Goodbye, Gunnar!"

They exchanged a hearty laugh and many farewells. Gonji watched them ride off until they were out of sight in the hills to the west, angling south for the Roman road.

He was left alone. Alone with Simon Sardonis.

## EPILOGUE

Now that he was strong enough to move about under his own power, Simon's first act was to remove himself farther from Gonji's camp. Thus to be alone at dusk and dawn during the bestial agonies of the embarrassing transformations.

"None may witness my torment," he explained, "save the God who has ordained it."

It seemed to Gonji that the shaky camaraderie they had effected had disintegrated with the completion of their objectives. He was as sulky and irascible as he had been on their first meeting, sharing Gonji's food and fire only grudgingly. His wounds were healing with amazing speed, scar tissue performing the saving closures Genya could not maintain. He began to wax resolute again, a far-off look in his eye. He waved aside all Gonji's suggestions of a joint course of action for them.

"I could help you find this 'demon-father' Grimmolech—"

"*Non,* I must go alone."

Gonji pondered. "What will you do on the Night of Chains—when there are no chains?"

"I'll manage," Simon replied in irritation. "I'll go off somewhere where no living thing moves."

"Not a bad idea," Gonji agreed. "I heard my mother speak once of a northern land where the sun shines for half the year. Of course, it's night for the other half, but maybe you'd find that without the moonlight—"

"I said *non!*"

Gonji scowled, weary of the ensorceled man's moodiness. "Does the taste of blood ever leave your mouth?" His endeavor was intended as a spiteful dig. It had sunk deep.

*"Never,"* Simon hissed, rushing off into the forest. Gonji felt remorse. He had heard the man choke back a sob.

At length they broke camp and prepared to part ways. Simon loaded satchels onto a skittish tethered steed.

Gonji moved up behind him quietly, hands behind his back. He studied the man, wondering if this parting was all his life had come to, the culmination of his quest.

"What a waste of good lives back there, *neh?*" he said.

*"Oui,"* Simon agreed without looking back.

"Garth . . . what a splendid samurai he would have made . . . Flavio, gentle, sincere, wise . . . Tralayn, with the fiery determination of a small volcano . . . Hildegarde . . ."

"Dobret," Simon added, patting the horse gently.

*"Hai*—all good people. Simon . . . are you the Deathwind they speak of?"

He stopped and turned. "That . . . may be what men call me in their distorted effort at understanding."

Gonji nodded. "That's all the answer I can ask for."

"What will you do now?"

Gonji shrugged. "I'm thinking about going back to *Dai Nihon*. My quest seems ended, though its worth escapes me. I'll go back, take what is rightly mine. There's a good life to be had there once I assume my heritage. Take a wife, consorts, produce heirs . . ." He paused to study the effect his words had on the other.

Simon cleared his throat. "That's good. Do it. *My* quest continues." He untied the horse and eased up into the saddle. When he had gained it, he smiled with his eyes at the samurai. "Look—I'm riding. Something to thank you for.

How does it feel to have stabbed in the dark and come up with a piece of truth?"

Gonji bowed to him.

Simon looked uneasy, embarrassed. "Look, I—I do appreciate your keeping me alive. You and the others. I might not have pulled through—"

"I only did it so that you could be killed properly."

Simon started. "Well . . . *merci*. And *bon jour.*"

"*Sayonara.* Away with you." Gonji turned and squared his shoulders as he strutted off toward his belongings.

"You're a brave warrior, *monsieur le samurai*—and a good friend."

Gonji turned slowly, but Simon had yanked the reins and clucked his steed off at a canter.

He stood for a time, the wind ruffling his hair and clothing, watching Simon ride away toward the mountain passes in the northwest. Then he loaded his things on a pack horse and climbed aboard Tora, patting the nickering stallion affectionately. He looked longingly to the East, the land of his birth; to the West, and the track of the caravan.

Then, his jaw clicking, he kicked off to the north at an easy gait, following in Simon's spoor.

# CHARACTER INDEX

**Kovacs**—a lorimer, father of Lottie
**Lady Gorkin**—wife of the castellan
**Lady Thorvald**—mistress of the king
**Lancaster**—an English merchant, companion of Goodwin
**Lorenz Gundersen**—son of Garth, Vedun's Chancellor
**Lottie Kovacs**—a servant, lover of Richard
**Luba**—a bald mercenary
**Lydia Benedetto**—wife of Michael
**Mark Benedetto**—brother of Michael
**Michael Benedetto**—Flavio's protegé in the city council
**Miklos Zarek**—a fisherman
**Milorad Vargo**—Flavio's friend and adviser, husband of Anna
**Mongols (Ling and Hu San)**—antagonists of Gonji with the 3rd Free Company
**Mord**—a sorcerer
**Nikolai Nagy**—a hostler, partner of Berenyi
**Old Gort**—gatekeeper in Vedun
**Paolo Sauvini**—a wagoner
**Peter Foristek**—a farmer
**Phlegor**—craft guild leader
**Radetzky**—a foster
**Richard**—a baker, lover of Lottie
**Riemann**—a German highwayman
**Roric Amsgard**—chief provisioner
**Salavar the Slayer**—a mercenary
**Simon Sardonis**—mystery man sojourning near Vedun
**Sophia**—mother of Helena
**Stanek**—a mercenary under Julian
**Stefan Berenyi**—a hostler, partner of Nagy
**Strom Gundersen**—son of Garth, a shepherd
**Sylva Monetto**—wife of Aldo
**Tadeusz**—a militiaman
**Tiva**—little girl in Eduardo's bunch
**Tralayn**—prophetess residing in Vedun
**Tumo**—a cretin giant
**Vaclav**—father of Tiva
**Verrico**—Vedun's surgeon
**Vlad Dobroczy**—a farmer
**Wilfred Gundersen**—son of Garth, a smith, lover of Genya
**William Eddings**—a sundrier
**Wolverangue**—demon invoked by Mord
**Wyvern**—a flying serpent, familiar of Mord
**Yuschak**—a farmer